The Best Supernatural
Stories of
JOHN BUCHAN

By the same Editor:

The Best Supernatural Stories of Wilkie Collins

The Best Supernatural Stories of JOHN BUCHAN

Selected & Introduced by
Peter Haining

ROBERT HALE · LONDON

© *Selection and Introduction Peter Haining 1991*
First published in Great Britain 1991

ISBN 0 7090 4293 0

Robert Hale Limited
Clerkenwell House
Clerkenwell Green
London EC1R 0HT

Photoset in Ehrhardt by
Derek Doyle & Associates, Mold, Clwyd.
Printed in Great Britain by
St Edmundsbury Press Ltd, Bury St Edmunds, Suffolk.
Bound by WBC Bookbinders Limited.

For
my father
– who introduced me to the
fantastic worlds of John Buchan
in the pages of *Greenmantle*

'Truth to tell, Buchan's own account of himself as a storyteller – one who would have been given the mammoth's bone at the conclusion of any cave-dweller's feast, as a reward for producing a good tale – is just. Nobody has ever told the tale better.'

Patrick Cosgrave
Daily Telegraph
21 February 1990

Contents

Editor's Note

AS the majority of John Buchan's short stories first appeared in British or American magazines, these original sources have been used for their republication in this book – except, of course, where the stories only appeared in volume form such as Buchan's *The Runagates Club* and *The Gap in the Curtain* and Cynthia Asquith's collections, *Sails of Gold* and *The Silver Ship*.

Introduction

IN a note prefacing what is undoubtedly his most famous novel, *The Thirty-Nine Steps*, John Buchan wrote that his aim as a story-teller was to create 'romance where the incidents defy the probabilities and march just inside the borders of the possible'. A number of critics and even one or two distinguished writers, including Raymond Chandler, have declared this to be the perfect formula for the thriller; others, myself included, see it as an equally true definition of the supernatural tale.

Buchan, who described his best-selling books of high adventure and espionage simply as 'Shockers' that should be put in the same category as the American 'Dime Novels', invariably spoke lightly of his own work though it is touched with a genius for atmosphere and authenticity and peopled with believable and exciting characters. This misnomer – for there is nothing to shock or revolt the reader in any of his tales – derived from the pleasure he got in the years preceding the First World War reading the cheap novels of murder and detection sold for one shilling (five pence) on bookstalls throughout the land which were widely referred to as 'Shilling Shockers'! It was the kind of understatement of his work of which Buchan was fond.

Readers, though, valued him much more highly. The Red Indians of Canada, for instance, made him an honorary Chief and named him 'Teller of Tales' when they added their acclaim to that of the rest of the world for his stories complete · with their 'atmosphere of expectancy, a sense of world-wide conspiracies and of old magics', to quote his biographer, Janet Adam Smith.

Though John Buchan's position as an outstanding author of supernatural fiction is overshadowed by his reputation as a thriller writer, the subject was one of his abiding interests – a hardly surprising fact, perhaps, for a Border Scot who had encountered the old legends and folklore of his native land while still in his infancy. All the more so for a man who read Charles Dickens' ghost stories as a child, declared that fellow Scot Robert Louis Stevenson was one of his literary idols, and greatly admired two of the most influential names in the supernatural genre – the French master of the *conte cruel*, Villiers de l'Isle Adam, and the founding father of modern horror fiction, Edgar Allan Poe. (Buchan, in fact, edited a collection of Poe's stories for the popular Nelson Library Series in 1911.)

David Daniell, the author of a critical assessment of Buchan's work, *The Interpreter's House* (1975), has described him as 'a Christian who had glimpsed the Devil', and certainly when studying the writer's life and work there is plenty of evidence that he had enough strange encounters with the forces of the unknown to give any writer the raw material for a lifetime of tales. And if it was not enough to grow up in an area filled with stories of ghosts, witches and all the little folk of fable, in June 1893 while cycling home on a dark, stormy night he suddenly fell from his bicycle and found himself lying next to a spread-eagled corpse at the roadside.

'I did not hold an inquest on the dead man,' Buchan wrote later in his posthumously published autobiography, *Memory Hold The Door* (1940), 'still less did I inform a policeman, since there wasn't one nearer than six miles, and that one was in bed. What I did was to bolt on as fast as the broken bicycle and a lame leg allowed me.'

There were other frightening experiences during his childhood, too – one of which, curiously, came when he read Lewis Carroll's classic, *Alice in Wonderland*. Though the youngster had already happily imbibed a diet of the fairy stories of the Brothers Grimm, Hans Christian Andersen and George Macdonald, the idea of going down a rabbit-hole and Alice's loss of identity 'haunted him like a nightmare' according to Janet Adam Smith. Small wonder, then, his first literary creations written in a school exercise book should have been a story (unfinished) entitled, 'The Tale of a Midsummer Night' and the first verses of a poem all about Hell!

Though John Buchan had a typical Scot's healthy respect for the Devil, he still saw him as a kind of Hallowe'en bogey, half humorous and half earthy. Again, he wrote in *Memory Hold The Door* of exploring his native Tweed, and being inexorably drawn to the spot 'where the river has its source and then, beyond the divide, was the mysterious green chasm called the "Devil's Beef Tub".'

When Buchan went up to Brasenose College, Oxford, he also had no compunction in occupying rooms where in 1830 – according to legend – a former President of the Brasenose Hellfire Club had carried out a blasphemous ceremony and been snatched up by his hair by the Devil and dragged away, never to be seen again. The pragmatic Buchan declared the room to be one of the best in the College (which it was) and an ideal setting in which stories of the supernatural might be created.

He also had a frightening experience when he took up mountaineering as a hobby. One day, while in a wood in the Bavarian Alps, something that he could not name or explain jangled his nerves.

'I ran,' he said later, 'some power not myself constraining me. Terror had seized me also, but I did not know what I dreaded.'

Buchan's third child, William, in an entertaining biography, *John Buchan: A Memoir* (1982), has told us that his father was always attracted to old legends and secret places, and tracked them down in places as far flung as the hills of the Scottish Borders, the Wood Bush in Africa and even the rolling Oxfordshire countryside where he finally settled.

'It would be a singularly unimaginative boy,' William Buchan wrote of his father's childhood, 'who would not respond to the contrast between the beauty of that countryside and the violent events of its human past, knowing its clear streams to have been many times coloured with blood, its secret places to have harboured desperate men, robbers and reivers or scholarly fanatics driven into the wild to starve or be murdered for a religious cause.'

Indeed, during his youth in Scotland John Buchan mixed with all manner of local folk, poachers and drovers particularly appealing to his fancy with their exciting and colourful tales of a life lived on the fringes of the rest of society. One of these drovers told Buchan a particularly hair-raising story which no doubt helped fire his interest in the macabre. He included it in an essay about droving published by *Macmillan's Magazine* in 1895, and I have extracted the relevant paragraphs for inclusion here as further evidence of Buchan's delight in the uncanny. Buchan wrote:

> I heard a story from one of the drovers which borders on the gruesome, but which, coming as it does from the times of Burke and Hare the bodysnatchers, may very well be true.
>
> A drover came from Edinburgh to an inn in Tweeddale, having much money in his breast-pocket, and a following of some half dozen town good-for-naughts at his heels. He slept the night in a bedroom on the ground floor, locking the door and taking every precaution.
>
> In the early morning, the innkeeper heard a noise from the place, which made him force the door, and to his horror he found the drover dead, stabbed to the heart. An open window pointed to the means by which death had visited him. The place was lonely. There were no men about save the ostlers, and they had drunk too deeply the night before to be of any use. The city was not twenty miles away, so thither the host set out to tell his tale.
>
> He had walked some seven miles of the road, so the story goes, when

a gig overtook him in which sat three men. It was one of the old-fashioned farmer's conveyances, wide enough to seat four abreast and ponderous as a cart. They stopped and offered him a lift which he gratefully accepted, and he sat down next to the middle man of the three. The other two talked gaily and laughed, but the man on his left uttered not one word.

They had gone maybe two miles when our friend said casually that 'his neebor on the left was verra quiet' and as he spoke looked into his face. With a sickening terror he recognised that it was none other than the man who had been murdered not two hours before in his own house, lashed to the gig and presenting a ghastly semblance of life.

With his brain on fire with sheer terror, he dealt the man on his right one tremendous blow, leaped over the wheels, fell headlong, was on his feet in a trice and running homeward for dear life. He reached the inn, and lo! the body of his guest was gone, and from that hour he heard no more of gig or drover …

———

JOHN Buchan was born on 26 August 1875 at 20, York Place in Perth, the eldest son of Reverend John Buchan, the minister of the local John Knox Free Church, and Helen Buchan, née Masterton, who was related to the great Scottish family of the Stewarts of Appin. The following year, Reverend Buchan was moved to Pathhead, Fife where he was to remain for the next twelve years and raise his four other children, Anna (born 1877), William (1880), Walter (1883) and Violet who was born in 1888, but died tragically in 1893.

As a baby, John Buchan suffered poor health – he was a 'miserable, headachy little boy' to quote his own words – but following what could well have been a fatal accident at the age of five when he fell from a carriage and the back wheel ran over his head, his health dramatically improved and he was scarcely sick for the next thirty years. The accident did, however, leave him with a scar for life across his left forehead, which Janet Adam Smith who met him says 'enhanced the lean Red Indian character of his face'.

During his convalescence from the accident, Buchan began to develop the love of books and story-telling which were to influence his life. From his father, a gentle and dreamy man, he heard stories of legend and magic about the Peebles area where he had grown up; while his mother, an energetic and organized woman, taught him to love books – reading him endless tales of fairies and fantasy – and it was from her that he inherited the ability to be an outstanding story-teller.

When not attending the Board School in Fife, John spent most of his holidays with his mother's family in the little community of Broughton amidst the fields, woods and high, bare hills of the Upper Tweed. These days of exploration and discovery went on happily even when the Reverend Buchan was moved on to the Knox Free Church in the notorious Glasgow slum area, the Gorbals. John Buchan's education was continued at Hutchesons' Grammar School on the outskirts of the Gorbals, and then in 1892, aged sixteen, he won an Open Scholarship to Glasgow University.

Though Buchan was by all accounts a conscientious and hard-working student, he later remembered spending what he called 'summers of pagan idleness' by the Tweed where he mostly fished or read, but occasionally let his sense of adventure get him into trouble. Such as the time when he joined a gang of salmon-poachers and, arrested, was hauled up before the local Magistrate. A horrified Mrs. Buchan later chastised her eldest son, 'Oh, John, John, where'll you end? There's nothing but the gallows if you're going on the way you do now!'

In fact, John already had thoughts about becoming a writer – putting some of his experiences and the tales he had heard into essays and stories. In June 1894 he began to keep a notebook of literary projects, which has fortunately survived, and which proves to be full of ideas for short stories and even novels. One of the first fruits of this ambition found publication in his own *Glasgow University Magazine* in October 1894. It was a grim little tale, 'The Keeper of Cademuir' and even at that stage clearly revealed Buchan's fascination with the macabre. The story naturally makes a most suitable opening item for this collection.

The contribution is doubly interesting because of its connection with the Upper Tweed, 'where the grace of old times seems to have long lingered' according to a prefatory note by its author, and because it is written very much in the style of Robert Louis Stevenson. Years later, in 1929, when addressing the Stevenson Club in Edinburgh, Buchan acknowledged his debt to his mentor.

'His expertness, even his preciousness, were salutory models for they meant hard and conscientious labour,' Buchan said. 'As a guide and a friend to the young Scotsmen of the Nineties, Stevenson filled the bill completely.'

David Daniell has made an interesting comparison between the two writers. 'Though never quite catching the music of Stevenson at his best in his prose line,' he says, 'Buchan equalled him in the special understanding of the Jekyll and Hyde-ness of the human situation, and managed to do what sometimes eluded R.L.S., catch it in a whole fictional vessel. So he can run his frontier between a surprising number of different territories, all somewhere under the surveillance of the Greatest Powers, divine and satanic.'

In truth, once John Buchan the writer had started exploring these 'different territories' he began to find his readership and never looked back.

IN October 1895 Buchan took up the scholarship he had won the previous December, travelled south, and entered Brasenose College, Oxford. A very significant period of the young Scotsman's life now began.

Buchan was to spend four years studying the 'Greats' (the Classics, plus Ancient History and Philosophy) but was anxious to be self-supporting and not have to ask for money from his father. With this in mind, he busied himself when not at his studies with journalism and writing short stories.

Soon his literary activity was interesting London publishers, in particular John Lane of The Bodley Head. And it was in Lane's famous quarterly publication, *The Yellow Book*, which had nurtured the talents of Aubrey Beardsley, Kenneth Grahame and Max Beerbohm among others, that Buchan next enjoyed publication with his first true supernatural story, 'A Journey of Little Profit' which appeared in the April 1896 issue.

This tale of an ungodly drover who carouses with the Devil was again drawn from Buchan's memories of his younger days. In particular a visit he had made to Stirling Fair where he had, to use his own words, 'associated with a lot of Highland drovers from whom I got splendid material for stories.' The tale, which appears in this collection, was well received both by the editor and readers, and Buchan made two other contributions to the magazine: 'At the Article of Death' about an old Scottish shepherd dying alone and disillusioned, and 'A Captain of Salvation' set in the slums of Limehouse which, though featuring an area he could scarcely have known well, was reminiscent of the Gorbals near his father's church.

That same autumn of 1896, John Lane published a collection of Buchan's essays entitled *Scholar Gipsies*, which was embellished with a striking cover featuring a goat-footed Pan piping to three nymphs. Lane also helped his young author's finances by employing him to report on manuscripts. At the same time Buchan worked away on what was to be his first full-length novel, *John Burnet of Barns*, a historical romance very much in the style of Stevenson about a young man driven by a desire for study and a passion for adventure who becomes embroiled in the battles of the Covenanters in the late 1600s. A young man in part like the author himself.

John Burnet of Barns was published in 1898, the same year that John Buchan wrote his next supernatural tale. 'The Outgoing of the Tide', although this short story was not offered for publication until four years later. The tale, considered by some critics to be among the very best of Buchan's shorter works, again features the Devil, plus a young couple in pre-modern Scotland who meet for a lovers' tryst on Sker Sands on Beltane Eve (30 April) with fatal results. The story demonstrates Buchan's knowledge of witchcraft and is quite clearly a forerunner of his outstanding novel, *Witch Wood* (1927), a book which he later numbered as one of his favourites. Set in his beloved Broughton three centuries earlier, *Witch Wood* recounts the adventures of David Sempill in his battle against a group of Satanists.

Buchan has himself written about this book which he considered, 'the most successful of my attempts at imaginative fiction.' In *Memory Hold The Door* he says:

> The best of my imaginative fiction is, I think, *Witch Wood*, in which I wrote of the Tweedside parish of my youth at the time when the old Wood of Caledon had not wholly disappeared, and when the rigours of the new Calvinism were contending with the ancient secret rites of Diana. I believe that my picture is historically true, and I could have documented almost every sentence from my researches on Montrose.

The author's affection for his book was shared by many of his readers, including C.S. Lewis who wrote, 'For *Witch Wood* specially I am always grateful; all that devilment spouting up out of a beginning like Galt's *Annals of the Parish*. That's the way to do it!'

At about this time, Buchan secured himself a literary agent, A.P. Watt, who naturally enough began looking for new outlets for his client's work, especially abroad where fees were usually higher – and 'The Outgoing of the Tide' was first published in America in the *Atlantic Monthly* in January 1902, just ahead of the British publication in *Blackwood's Magazine*.

Buchan had, in fact, begun sending stories and essays to *Blackwood's* in Edinburgh in 1899, making an auspicious debut in the January of that year with 'No-man's-land'. This story of an Oxford scholar who discovers that a group of Ancient Picts have survived underground to the present day in the Scottish hills has been described as 'an early example of Science Fiction' by the American authority, Everett F. Bleiler. Janet Adam Smith is another admirer of the tale and has said of it, 'the hairy Picts give off an authentic whiff of supernatural horror.'

It was also in 1899 that Buchan left Oxford rewarded with a First in 'Greats' and settled in London where he took up the study of Law as well as broadening his journalistic endeavours by producing regular columns for *The Spectator*. He worked on his first contemporary novel, *The Half-Hearted*, a story of a Russian plot to conquer India written in the style of Rider Haggard and a pointer to the direction his fiction was to take. He was busy writing short stories, too, and December 1900 saw the publication of another outstanding supernatural story of demonic possession, 'The Watcher By The Threshold' which appeared simultaneously in Britain and America in the Christmas issues of *Blackwood's* and the *Atlantic Magazine*.

'The Watcher By The Threshold' which was later to become the title story of a collection of Buchan's short tales published by Blackwood in 1902 has prompted considerable comment among students of Buchan's work because of its theme of a Scottish laird haunted by a spirit that manifests itself as neural agony. It has been suggested that it is of considerable autobiographical significance because Buchan was known to suffer from psychosomatic pains. Jack Sullivan in *The Encyclopedia of Horror and the Supernatural* (1986), for instance, has written, 'Although elements of the story are undoubtedly taken from Bulwer Lytton's 'Dweller of the Threshold' in his novel, *Zanoni* (1842), Buchan's story also has a personal reference because he suffered from neural disorders.'

Whether we accept this statement or not, Buchan himself described the piece as 'my "horrible" story' and said it was an attempt 'to fit a sort of gruesome comedy to a particular type of Scotch moor.' Interestingly, too, I have discovered that there are two quite different versions of this story: the version published in *Blackwood's Magazine* and later in the book of that title, and a second, shorter version which was use by the *Atlantic*. Because of the rarity of the American version (it has not been republished since 1900) and its undoubted interest to scholars, I have chosen it for these pages. It has every bit as much fascination and chill as the longer version.

AS the twentieth century dawned, Buchan looked upon himself as 'half barrister and half writer'. But a chance meeting with a journalist from *The Times* named L.S. Amery in March 1901 brought a dramatic change in his life. Amery had just returned from South Africa where he had been working on a history of the Boer War, now virtually over. The journalist had also become an intimate of Lord Milner, the British

High Commissioner for South Africa, who was then in the process of trying to find bright young men for his Secretariat.

Buchan and Amery met at a dinner and the young barrister/writer's achievements and thirst for new experiences so impressed the man from *The Times* that he put forward his name to Lord Milner. On the strength of Amery's recommendation Buchan was offered a two-year contract in South Africa and accepted it gleefully.

From 1901–3, John Buchan lived in Johannesburg, spending a lot of his time travelling around the country visiting the refugee camps and helping to administer the new colonies. Apart from the invaluable aid he was able to offer to the people, the journeys also provided him with numerous interesting and exciting experiences in the 'secret places' he so loved to visit. Soon his imagination was beginning to stir with ideas for new stories. But the demands of his work were such that writing fiction was all but impossible, though by the time he returned to England he had the plots for several short stories and a novel worked out in his head. In particular, two tales about the power of the supernatural in the great vastness of the African wilderness.

The first of these, 'The Grove of Ashtaroth' deals with ritual magic and the adventures of a young man who falls under the spell of an old temple in Zimbabwe dedicated to the worship of an ancient goddess. The man is partly Jewish and the stress Buchan laid on his ancestry was one of the planks that later critics of the author's work used to accuse him of anti-Semitism. In fact, although Buchan might be accused of having made the occasional tasteless remark about the Jews in his fiction – as did many other writers of the period – he numbered several among his friends and wrote strenuous defences of the 'Jewish Question' in *The Spectator* during the years of Hitler's rise to power when the German leader's increasing persecution of the race became evident.

Buchan published 'The Grove of Ashtaroth' in *Blackwood's Magazine* in June 1910, and two years later wrote another tale based on the supernatural in South Africa which he called 'The Green Wildebeest'. This story set in the Transvaal around the year 1900 deals with the violation of a shrine dedicated to a sacred creature – the green wildebeest – by a young Boer which brings down a terrible supernatural vengeance upon him.

The story is also of interest because it is told by Richard Hannay, the hero modelled on one of Buchan's military idols, Colonel Edmond 'Tiny' Ironside, and the central figure of four of his best known novels: *The Thirty-Nine Steps* (1915) *Greenmantle* (1916) *Mr. Standfast* (1919) and *The Three Hostages* (1924). Ironside, whom Buchan had met in South

Africa, was a towering man over six foot four inches tall, who could speak fourteen languages, had done intelligence work, was a master of disguise and had fought with distinction throughout the entire Boer War. He was a man born to adventure, and later became the first British officer in uniform to land in France in 1914, remaining on the Western Front until 1918. Then after being sent to quell uprisings in Turkey and Persia, 'Tiny' Ironside was made the youngest Major-General in the British Army. Small wonder Buchan held him in the highest regard and used him as the model for his intrepid Hannay.

In 'The Green Wildebeest', which was published in 1928, Hannay is an old man recounting an adventure from his younger days. And in both this story and 'The Grove of Ashtaroth' can be seen elements that Buchan incorporated into another of his famous books, *Prester John*, about the reincarnation of the great warrior in a modern man to lead a native rising against the whites. Interestingly, that novel was first written as a story for boys called 'The Black General' and published as a serial in *The Captain* from April to September 1910. Later in the year it appeared as a book with the familiar nomenclature – although in America it was also published under a different title, *The Great Diamond Pipe*. Some critics have pointed to a number of similarities between *Prester John* and Stevenson's *Treasure Island*, but both books undoubtedly deserve their stature as classics of high adventure.

When Buchan returned to England in August 1903, he again took up legal work for a while before following his inclination towards the written word by joining the publishing firm of Thomas Nelson with whom he was to enjoy a close relationship for the rest of his life. He also met and later married the beautiful Susan Grosvenor who was to bear him four children, Alice (born 1908), John (1911), William (1916) and Alastair (1918), upon all of whom he doted.

The taste for adventure which had been so stimulated in South Africa now prompted Buchan to take up mountaineering along with more foreign travel. He had done some mountain scrambling in South Africa, but now sought out more demanding climbs in his native Scotland and in Europe. In 1906 he went mountaineering in the Alps, especially around the Petits Charmoz, and there found the inspiration for another story, 'Space' which he wrote in 1910.

'Space' is the story of a mathematician named Hollond who discovers he can move about freely in space while he is asleep – but there encounters terrible 'presences'. It has two particular points of interest. Firstly, it introduces another of John Buchan's memorable characters, Edward Leithen, a lawyer, man of action and dedicated climber (almost Buchan to a tee) who is to reappear in other short stories and four novels, *The Power House* (1916) *John Macnab* (1925) *The Dancing Floor* (1926) and *Sick Heart River*, published in 1940, and in which, like Buchan at that time, he is facing death. And, secondly, Buchan the mountaineer showed considerable presentiment in the tale by referring to new routes up the Montanvert side of the Charmoz and to the Mer de Glace face of the Grepon which were not, in fact, climbed until the summer of 1911, some months *after* the publication of the story in *Blackwood's* in May 1911. (Despite the fact that Buchan made no great claims about his prowess as a mountaineer, as a result of his climbs in Scotland, South Africa and the Alps he was elected to the Alpine Club in 1906.)

John Buchan and his new wife began to travel widely, too, and in 1910 sailed through the Aegean on a yacht, stopping on one of the isolated Petali islands which provided the inspiration for another supernatural short story. Susan Buchan herself has described how 'Basilissa' came to be written.

After landing and being curiously ignored by a group of silent Greek peasants huddled around a fire, she says, the Buchan party found themselves confronted by something stranger still.

'Some way back from the shore, standing in what appeared to be walled gardens, stood a long low house with a mellow red roof. It was shuttered and impenetrable. We stared at it hoping that someone might emerge from it who would tell us who lived there, but no one came.'

Using the island and the house as his background, Buchan created the tale of a man who has a recurring dream about a strange house and one day finds himself in front of the self-same building which is occupied by a woman who the local people think is a witch. When the man and the woman come face to face the story of 'Basilissa' takes an even stranger turn. Although the origins of this story are well enough documented, the odd fact remains that though Buchan published it in *Blackwood's* in April 1914, it never appeared in any subsequent collection of his tales – its appearances here being the first time in volume form in Britain. Curious, indeed, for a story that Everett Bleiler has called 'among Buchan's best work'.

In the years immediately prior to the outbreak of the First World War, Buchan continued to work at Thomas Nelson as well as writing short stories, novels and pieces of journalism. On the prompting of some friends he also began to develop an interest in politics, and was adopted as Unionist candidate for Peebles and Selkirk. Then, in 1915, he produced two literary masterstrokes which did much for his own fortunes and those of Nelson's: he initiated *Nelson's History of the War* (soon becoming regarded as an authority on the progress of the war) and wrote his first, and still greatest, 'Shocker', *The Thirty-Nine Steps*, which he dedicated to Thomas Arthur Nelson. It is perhaps no surprise to learn that same year he was made a director of the company!

ALTHOUGH his health ruled out John Buchan serving as a soldier during the Great War, he was asked by *The Times* to visit the Front in France as a Special Correspondent and from there contributed a series of on-the-spot articles to the 'Thunderer' which undoubtedly helped increase the general public's awareness of what was taking place. Such, indeed, was his perception of the conflict that early in 1916 the Foreign Office began employing him on intelligence work, and then in February 1917 he was asked by the Government to become Director of Propaganda and handle the release of all official information.

Buchan's role brought him into contact with the highest authorities in the land and also gave him an intimate knowledge of the workings of Parliament. His success in the role unquestionably influenced public opinion and, in turn, the ultimate success of the Allied cause. But there was a personal cost to this success – John lost his youngest brother, Alastair, who died on 9 April as a result of gunshot wounds sustained during the Battle of Arras. Because Alastair was some twenty years younger, Buchan looked upon him more as an elder child than a brother and mourned his loss deeply. It has been suggested that the story '*Tendebant Manus*' was partially inspired by Alastair's death.

'*Tendebant Manus*' has been categorized as borderline supernatural in its telling of the story of two brothers, George a politician and Reggie a soldier, and how the strong personality of Reggie animates the largely ineffectual George after the Army man is killed in action during World War I. But the tale is rather more complex and thought-provoking than that – and certainly has a conclusion that is genuinely spine-chilling.

The tale further demonstrates Buchan's knowledge of both the war and politics – though he did not, in fact, become an MP until 1927 when he was elected as MP for the Scottish Universities. It is also interesting as being one of a series of stories which Buchan wrote under the collective title of *The Runagates Club*, each tale being related by the members of a London dining-club.

'The Wind in the Portico' which follows is another of the Runagates stories. The time period here is just after the end of the war and the story is told by Henry Nightingale, a versatile young man who is a Greek scholar and soldier, and has for a time been the captain of a tribe of Bedawins. In 'The Wind in the Portico', Nightingale recounts the strange and frightening events which follow the discovery of some buried paraphernalia dating from the worship of the old Celtic god of evil, Vaunus.

In 1919, while Buchan was still recovering from his exertions during the war and had become increasingly prone to duodenal attacks, he sought a country retreat for himself and his family. His 'Shockers' were selling extremely well and this plus his work for Nelsons and a recent appointment as a director of the Reuter's News Agency, made him comfortably well-off.

Buchan found precisely what he was looking for in the small village of Elsfield, four miles from Oxford. He wanted to be within travelling distance of London for his work – which Elsfield Manor was – and in a roomy property set among the sort of countryside in which he had grown up – the Manor faced forty miles of open land to the western Cotswolds. The house itself has been originally built in the seventeenth century and substantially added-to during the Victorian era: but possessed a charm and sense of history which immediately appealed to the countryman in Buchan. Elsfield Manor was to be his home for the rest of his life.

The influence of the Manor on the author was felt straightaway in 'Fullcircle', a story which Buchan wrote the following year and published in *Atlantic Magazine* in June 1920. It is a haunted house tale, but unlike any other of its kind – for reasons which I shall not disclose here. It also features the imperturbable Edward Leithen once again.

Buchan had the opportunity to spend many happy hours with his children in the grounds of the manor house, and all of the youngsters were to remember their childhood with great affection. In particular, the tales their father delighted in telling them – for he had inherited his mother's skill as an oral story-teller. Writing of this aspect of Buchan's life in her biography, Janet Adam Smith says:

> 'Everything at home sprang into cheerful new life the moment my father entered the front door,' said one of his children, but they also remembered how the sound of his stick or umbrella being put with a thump into the stand in the hall, 'caused a wave of energy to go through the house. Everything was quickly tidied up, and books were put back in their right places. He liked books to be read and immediately replaced on the library shelves.' Buchan enjoyed the company of his children, and liked entering into their lives and interests. When his sons were at school at Oxford he would sometimes go down on Sunday evenings and read to the Dragon boys after prayers or – with the lights out – tell them stories.

A number of the stories which Buchan told his offspring were later committed to paper and published in collections such as the evocatively titled *Book of Escapes and Hurried Journeys* (1922) and *The Last Secrets* (1923). Another, 'The Magic Walking Stick', Buchan wrote for an anthology, *Sails of Gold*, compiled in 1927 by Lady Cynthia Asquith, the secretary to J.M. Barrie, who was then also becoming known as a writer and anthologizer of ghost stories.

'The Magic Walking Stick' proved to be one of those ideas which kept insinuating itself into Buchan's thoughts, and several years later he turned the short story into a full-length juvenile novel for Hodder & Stoughton, who published it in 1932 complete with some excellent illustrations by Morton Sale. The rare original short version of the tale which has never been reprinted will be found in these pages.

Lady Asquith, who is today regarded as one of the macabre genre's most important early anthologists – *vide* her books, *The Ghost Book* (1927) *The Black Cap* (1928) and *When Churchyards Yawn* (1931) – and who could number among her friends such famous ghost story writers as Algernon Blackwood, Arthur Machen and Hugh Walpole, prevailed upon Buchan to contribute to another of her anthologies. *The Silver Ship*, published in 1932. This time he responded with 'The Strange Adventure of Mr. Andrew Hawthorn' a story of a mysterious disappearance which has also been unavailable since the book went out of print half a century ago.

The 1930s saw Buchan continue his political career, and he was awarded several honours for his contributions to public life including a Companion of Honour in 1932. As far as his writing was concerned, he now found greater satisfaction in biography than fiction, and produced splendid studies of a number of famous figures including *Sir Walter Scott* (1932), *Oliver Cromwell* (1934) and *Augustus* (1937).

He continued to travel, too, particularly enjoying visits to Canada and America, and when he was invited to become Governor-General of Canada in 1935 he was pleased to accept. That same year he was also created Baron Tweedsmuir, and though no one expressed surprise that Buchan should have chosen the countryside of his youth for his title, there were those who jokingly thought he might perhaps have thought of calling himself 'Lord Greenmantle'!

The success of Buchan's final years in Canada as diplomat and statesman need only the briefest mention here. He proved a skilful administrator who travelled widely throughout North America; an excellent host to President Roosevelt (1936) and King George VI and Queen Elizabeth (1939); and a Governor-General who did much to publicize and promote the nation he came to love. Sadly, the decline in his health and his death in Montreal on 11 February 1940 brought to an end both the plans he had for Canada and the books and stories he still wanted to write.

One final item closes this anthology, 'The Death Notice' from *The Gap in the Curtain* which John Buchan wrote in 1932. This book consists of a group of related tales about six people who are given a sudden glimpse of the future through the medium of a copy of *The Times* dated one year ahead. Each learns what fate holds in store for them – and the stories detail the course of events during their next twelve months. Buchan had been inspired to write these stories after reading J.W. Dunne's pioneer work on the nature of dreaming and the concept of time, *An Experiment With Time*, published in 1927. The story I have selected concerns the dashing young Captain Charles Ottery and the effect upon him of reading a death notice in the paper … his own.

The late master of the macabre, Dennis Wheatley, has said of this story, 'it would be difficult to find in any other book a finale that equals it in suspense'; while on the strength of the work as a whole a number of French critics have recently declared Buchan to be 'one of the fathers of science fiction'. David Daniell has awarded him a further laurel as a pioneer of 'mythical fiction'.

'The ability to create fiction which has the characteristics of myth is rare enough to be saluted as significant,' Daniell has written, 'especially when the fiction is not fanciful, as in C.S. Lewis or J.R.R. Tolkien, but deals with recognizable contemporary characters and events, as Buchan did supremely in *Greenmantle* and *Mr.Standfast*. It is ironic that when the group in Oxford which included Lewis and Tolkien and Charles Williams was so concerned about the vitality of myth in modern life, and seeking to create it (their fiction now having an enormous cult success in the United States) Buchan had not only successfully done a much harder thing, twenty years before, but was simultaneously reaching a huge audience in Britain and being ignored by the critics.'

These are claims that the modest author himself would probably have shrugged off as he did the accolades paid to his 'Shockers', but nevertheless they do demonstrate the importance which, rightly in my opinion, continues to be attached to his work and its influence upon later generations of writers in his fields. An importance and influence which I also believe deserves even wider recognition.

On the fiftieth anniversary of John Buchan's death in February 1990, *The Times* carried a lengthy feature on the man and his work, paying this tribute along the way, 'John Buchan's many novels – the most read of which are *The Thirty-Nine Steps, Greenmantle* and *Prester John* – lie along that straight line from Conan Doyle and Conrad to Ian Fleming and John Le Carré.' As I hope the stories in the pages which follow will prove, Buchan was also a master of the supernatural tale along the line of Poe and Stevenson by way of Bram Stoker and M.R. James to today's hugely successful exponents such as Ray Bradbury and Stephen King. He would surely be delighted that what so fascinated him about the mysterious, the uncanny and the inexplicable has continued to intrigue and entertain us, too.

PETER HAINING
Boxford, Suffolk
February 1991

The Keeper of Cademuir

THE gamekeeper of Cademuir strode in leisurely fashion over the green side of the hill. The bright chilly morning was past, and the heat had all but begun; but he had lain long a-bed, deeming that life was too short at the best, and there was little need to hurry it over. He was a man of a bold carriage, with the indescribable air of one whose life is connected with sport and rough moors. A steady grey eye and a clean chin were his best features; otherwise, he was of the ordinary make of a man, looking like one born for neither good nor evil in any high degree. The sunlight danced around him, and flickered among the brackens; and though it was an everyday sight with him, he was pleased, and felt cheerful, just like any wild animal on a bright day. If he had had his dog with him, he would have sworn at it to show his pleasure; as it was, he contented himself with whistling 'The Linton Ploughman', and setting his heels deep into the soft green moss.

The day was early and his way was long, for he purposed to go up Manor Water to the shepherd's house about a matter of some foxes. It might be ten miles, it might be more; and the keeper was in no great haste, for there was abundant time to get his dinner and a smoke with the herd, and then come back in the cool of the evening; for it was summer-time, when men of his class have their holiday. Two miles more, and he would strike the highway; he could see it even now coiling beneath the straight sides of the glen. There it was easy walking, and he would get on quickly; but now he might take his time. So he lit his pipe, and looked complacently around him.

At the turn of the hill, where a strip of wood runs up the slope, he stopped, and a dark shadow came over his face. This was the place where, not two weeks ago, he had chased a poacher, and but for the fellow's skill in doubling, would have caught him. He cursed the whole tribe in his heart. They were the bane of his easy life. They came at night, and took him out on the bleak hillside when he should have been in his bed. They might have a trap there even now. He would go and see, for it was not two hundred yards from his path.

So he climbed up the little howe in the hill beside the firwood, where the long thickets of rushes, and the rabbit-warrens made a happy hunting-ground for the enemies of the law. A snipe or two flew up as he approached, and a legion of rabbits scurried into their holes. He had all but given up the quest, when the gleam of something among the long grass caught his attention, and in a trice he had pulled back the herbage, and disclosed a neatly set and well-constructed trap.

It was a very admirable trap. He had never seenone like it; so in a sort of angry exultation, as he thought of how he would spoil this fine game, he knelt down to examine it. It was no mere running noose, but of strong steel, and firmly fixed to the trunk of an old tree. No unhappy pheasant would ever move it, were its feet once caught in its strong teeth. He felt the iron with his hand, feeling down the sides for the spring; when suddenly with a horrid snap the thing closed on him, pinning his hand below the mid-finger, and he was powerless.

The pain was terrible, agonising. His hand burned like white fire, and every nerve of his body tingled. With his left hand he attempted to loosen it, but the spring was so well concealed, that he could not find it. Perhaps, too, he may have lost his wits, for in any great suffering the brain is seldom clear. After a few minutes of feeble searching and tugging, every motion of which gave agony to his imprisoned hand, he gave it up, and in something very like panic, sought for his knife to try to cut the trap loose from the trunk. And now a fresh terror awaited him, for he found that he had no knife; he had left it in another coat, which was in his room at home. With a sigh of infinite pain, he stopped the search, and stared drearily before him.

He confusedly considered his position. He was fixed with no possibility of escape, some two miles from the track of any chance passer-by. They would not look for him at home until the evening, and the shepherd at Manor did not know of his coming. Someone might be on the hill, but then this howe was on a remote side where few ever came, unless their duty brought them. Below him in the valley was the road with some white cottages beside it. There were women in those houses, living and moving not far from him; they might see him if he were to wave something as a signal. But then, he reflected with a groan, that though he could see their dwellings, they could not see him, for he was hidden by the shoulder of the hill.

Once more he made one frantic effort to escape, but it was unsuccessful. Then he leant back upon the heather, gnawing his lips to help him to endure the agony of the wound. He was a strong man, broad and sinewy, and where a weaker might have swooned, he was left to endure the burden of a painful consciousness. Again he thought of escape. The man who had set the trap must come to see it, but it might not be that day, nor the next. He pictured his friends hunting up and down Manor Water, every pool and wood; passing and re-passing not two hundred yards from where he was lying dead, or worse than dead. His mind grew sick at the thought, and he had almost fainted in spite of his strength.

Then he fell into a panic, the terror of rough 'hard-handed men, which never laboured in their mind.' His brain whirled, his eyes were stelled, and a shiver shook him like a reed. He puzzled over his past life, feeling, in a dim way, that it had not been as it should be. He had been drunk often; he had not been over-careful of the name of the Almighty; was not this some sort of retribution? He strove to pray, but he could think of no words. He had been at church last Sunday, and he tried to think of what he had heard; but try as he would, nothing came to his mind, but the chorus of a drinking-song he had often heard sung in the public-house at Peebles:

> When the hoose is rinnin' round about,
>   It's time eneuch to flit;
> For we've lippened aye to Providence,
>   And sae will we yet.

The irony of the words did not strike him; but fervently, feverishly, he repeated them, as if for the price of his soul.

The fit passed, and a wild frenzy of rage took him. He cursed like a fiend, and yelled horrible menaces upon the still air. If he had the man who set this trap, he would strangle the life out of him here on this spot. No, that was too merciful. He would force his arm into the trap, and take him to some lonely place where never a human being came from one year's end to the other. Then he would let him die, and come to gloat over his suffering. With every turn of his body he wrenched his hand, and with every wrench, he yelled more madly, till he lay back exhausted, and the green hills were left again in peace.

Then he slept a sleep which was half a swoon, for maybe an hour, though to him it seemed like ages. He seemed to be dead, and in torment; and the place of his torment was this same hillside. On the brae face, a thousand evil spirits were mocking his anguish, and not only his hand, but his whole body was imprisoned in a remorseless trap. He felt the keen steel crush through his bones, like a spade through a frosted turnip. He woke screaming with nameless dread, looking on every side for the infernal faces of his dreams, but seeing nothing but a little chaffinch hopping across the turf.

Then came for him a long period of slow, despairing agony. The hot air glowed, and the fierce sun beat upon his face. A thousand insects hummed about him, bees and butterflies and little hillmoths. The wholesome smell of thyme and bent was all about him, and every now and then a little breeze broke the stillness, and sent a ripple over the grass. The genial warmth seemed stifling; his head ached, and his breath came in sudden gasps. An overpowering thirst came upon him, and his tongue was like a burnt stick in his mouth. Not ten feet off, a little burn danced over a minute cascade. He could see the dust of spray, which wet the cool green rushes. The pleasant tinkle sang in his ears, and mocked his fever. He tried to think of snow and ice and cold water, but his brain refused to do its part, and he could get nothing but an intolerable void.

Far across the valley, the great forehead of Dollar Law raised itself, austere and lofty. To his unquiet sight, it seemed as if it rolled over on Scrape, and the two played pranks among the lower hills beyond. The idea came to him, how singularly unpleasant it would be for the people there – among them a shepherd to whom he owed two pounds. He would be crushed to powder, and there would be no more of the debt at any rate. Then a text from the Scriptures came to haunt him, something, he could scarce tell exactly, about the hills and mountains leaping like rams. Here it was realised before his very eyes. Below him, in the peaceful valley, Manor Water seemed to be wrinkled across it, like a scrawl from the pen of a bad writer. When a bird flew past, or a hare started from its form, he screamed with terror, and all the wholesome sights of a summer day were wrought by his frenzied brain into terrible phantoms. So true is it that Natura Benigna and Natura Maligna may walk hand in hand upon the same hillside.

Then came the time when the strings of the reason are all but snapped, and a man becomes maudlin. He thought of his young wife, not six weeks married, and grieved over her approaching sorrow. He wept unnatural tears, which, if any one had been there to see him, would have been far more terrible than his frantic ravings. He pictured to himself in gruesome detail, the finding of his body, how his wife would sob, and his friends would shake their heads, and swear that he had been an honest fellow, and that it was a pity that he was away. The place would soon forget him; his wife would marry again; his dogs would get a new master, and he – ay, that was the question, where would he be? and a new dread took him, as he thought of the fate which might await him. The unlettered man, in his times of dire necessity, has nothing to go back upon but a mind full of vivid traditions, which are the most merciless of things.

It might be about three or four o'clock, but by the clock in his brain it was weeks later, that he suffered that last and awful pain, which any one who has met it once, would walk to the end of the earth to avoid. The world shrank away from him; his wits forsook him; and he cried out, till the lonely rocks rang, and the whaups mingled their startled cries with his. With a last effort, he crushed down his head with his unwounded hand upon the tree-trunk, till blessed unconsciousness took him into her merciful embrace.

AT nine o'clock that evening, a ragged, unshorn man, with the look of one not well at ease with the world, crept up the little plantation. He had a sack on his back for his ill-gotten plunder, and a mighty stick in case of a chance encounter. He visited his traps, hidden away in little nooks, where no man might find them, and it would have seemed as if trade were brisk, for his sack was heavy, and his air was cheerful. He looked out from behind the dyke at his last snare carefully, as behoved one in danger; and then with a start he crouched, for he saw the figure of a man.

There was no doubt about it; it was his bitterest enemy, the keeper of Cademuir. He made as if to crawl away, when by chance he looked again. The man lay very still. A minute later he had rushed forward with a white face, and was working as if for his life.

In half an hour two men might have been seen in that little glen. One, with a grey, sickened face, was gazing vacantly around him, with the look of some one awakened from a long sleep. By dint of much toil, and half a bottle of brandy, he had been brought back from what was like to have been the longest sleep he had ever taken. Beside him on the grass, with wild eyes, sat the poacher, shedding hysterical tears. 'Dae onything ye like wi' me,' he was saying, 'kick me or kill me, an' am ready. I'll gang to jail wi' ye, to Peebles or the Calton, an' no say a word. But oh –! ma God, I thocht ye were bye wi't.'

A Journey of Little Profit

The Devil he sang, the Devil he played
High and fast and free.
And this was ever the song he made,
As it was told to me.
Oh, I am the king of the air and the ground,
And lord of the seasons' roll,
And I will give you a hundred pound,
If you will give me your soul!
The Ballad of Grey Weather

THE cattle market of Inverforth is, as all men know north of the Tweed, the greatest market of the kind in the land. For days in the late Autumn there is the lowing of oxen and the bleating of sheep among its high wooden pens, and in the rickety sale-rings the loud clamour of auctioneers and the talk of farmers. In the open yard where are the drovers and the butchers, a race always ungodly and law-despising, there is such a Babel of cries and curses as might wake the Seven Sleepers. From twenty different adjacent eating-houses comes the clatter of knives, where the country folk eat their dinner of beef and potatoes, with beer for sauce, and the collies grovel on the ground for stray morsels. Hither come a hundred types of men from the Highland cateran with scarce a word of English, and the shentleman-farmer of Inverness and Ross, to lowland graziers and city tradesmen, not to speak of blackguards of many nationalities and more professions.

It was there I first met Duncan Stewart of Clachamharstan, in the Moor of Rannoch, and there I heard this story. He was an old man when I knew him, grizzled and wind-beaten; a prosperous man, too, with many herds like Jacob and much pasture. He had come down from the North with kyloes, and as he waited on the Englishmen with whom he had trysted, he sat with me through the long day and beguiled the time with many stories. He had been a drover in his youth, and had travelled on foot the length and breadth of Scotland; and his memory went back hale and vigorous to times which are now

30

all but historical. This tale I heard among many others as we sat on a pen amid the smell of beasts and the jabber of Gaelic:

'When I was just turned of twenty-five I was a wild young lad as ever was heard of. I had taken to the droving for the love of a wild life, and a wild life I led. My father's heart would be broken long syne with my doings, and well for my mother that she was in her grave since I was six years old. I paid no heed to the ministrations of godly Mr. Macdougall of the Isles, who bade me turn from the error of my ways, but went on my own evil course, making siller, for I was a brawl lad at the work and a trusted, and knowing the inside of every public from the pier of Cromarty to the streets of York. I was a wild drinker, caring in my cups for neither God nor man, a great hand with the cards, and fond of the lasses past all telling. It makes me shameful to this day to think on my evil life when I was twenty-five.

'Well, it chanced that in the back of the month of September I found myself in the city of Edinburgh with a flock of fifty sheep which I had bought as a venture from a drunken bonnet-laird and was thinking of selling somewhere wast the country. They were braw beasts, Leicester every one of them, well-fed and dirt-cheap at the price I gave. So it was with a light heart that I drove them out of the town by the Merchiston Road along by the face of the Pentlands. Two or three friends came with me, all like myself for folly, but maybe a little bit poorer. Indeed, I cared little for them, and they valued me only for the whisky which I gave them to drink my health in at the parting. They left me on the near side of Colinton, and I went on my way alone.

'Now, if you'll be remembering the road, you will mind that at the place called Kirk Newton, just afore the road begins to twine over the Big Muir and almost at the head of the Water o' Leith, there is a verra fine public. Indeed, it would be no lee to call it the best public between Embro' and Glesca. The good wife, Lucky Craik by name, was an old friend of mine, for many a good gill of her prandy have I bought; so what would I be doing but just turning aside for refreshment? She met me at the door, verra pleased-like to see me, and soon I had my legs aneath her table and a basin of toddy on the board before me. And whom did I find in the same place but my old comrade Toshie Maclean from the backside of Glen-Lyon. Toshie and I were acquaintances so old that it did not behoove us to be parting quick. Forbye the day was chill without; and within the fire was grand and the crack of the best.

'Then Toshie and I got on quarrelling about the price of Lachlan Farawa's beasts that he sold at Falkirk; and, the drink having aye a bad effect on my temper, I was for giving him the lie and coming off in a great rage. It was about six o'clock in the evening and an hour to nightfall, so Mistress Craik comes in to try and keep me. 'Losh, Duncan,' says she, 'ye'll never try and win ower the muir the nicht. It's mae than ten mile to Carnwath, and there's nocht atween it and this but whaups and heathery braes.' But when I am roused I will be more obstinate than ten mules, so I would be going, though I knew not under Heaven where I was going till. I was too full of good liquor and good meat to be much worth at thinking, so I got my sheep on the road an a big bottle in my pouch and set off into the heather. I knew not what my purpose was, whether I thought to reach the shieling of Carnwath, or whether I expected some house of entertainment to spring up by the wayside. But my fool's mind was set on my purpose of getting some miles further in my journey ere the coming of darkness.

'For some time I jogged happily on, with my sheep running well before me and my dogs trotting at my heels. We left the trees behind and struck out on the proad grassy path which bands the moor like the waist-strap of a sword. It was most dreary and lonesome with never a house in view, only bogs and grey hillsides and ill-looking waters. It was stony, too, and this more than aught else caused my Dutch courage to fail me, for I soon fell wearied, since much whisky is bad travelling fare, and began to curse my folly. Had my pride no kept me back, I would have returned to Lucky Craik's; but I was like the devil, for stiff-neckedness and thought of nothing but to push on.

'I own that I was verra well tired and quite spiritless when I first saw the House. I had scarce been an hour on the way, and the light was not quite gone; but still it was geyan dark, and the place sprang somewhat suddenly on my sight. For, looking a little to the left, I saw over a little strip of grass a big square dwelling with many outhouses, half farm and half pleasure-house. This, I thought, is the verra place I have been seeking and made sure of finding; so whistling a gay tune, I drove my flock toward it.

'When I came to the gate of the court, I saw better of what sort was the building I had arrived at. There was a square yard with monstrous high walls, at the left of which was the main block of the house, and on the right what I took to be the byres and stables. The place looked ancient, and the stone in many places was crumbling away; but the style was of yesterday and in no way differing from that of a hundred steadings in the land. There were some kind of arms above the gateway, and a bit of an iron stanchion; and when I had my sheep inside of it, I saw that the court was all grown up with green grass. And what seemed queer in that dusky half-light was the want of sound.

There was no neichering of horses, nor routing of kye, nor clack of hens, but all as still as the top of Ben Cruachan. It was warm and pleasant too, though the night was chill without.

'I had no sooner entered the place than a row of sheep-pens caught my eye, fixed against the wall in front. This I thought mighty convenient, so I made all haste to put my beasts into them; and finding that there was a good supply of hay within, I leff them easy in my mind, and turned about to look for the door of the house.

'To my wonder, when I found it, it was open wide to the wall; so, being confident with much whisky, I never took thought to knock, but walked boldly in. There's some careless folk here, thinks I to myself, and I much misdoubt if the man knows aught about farming. He'll maybe just be a town's body taking the air on the muirs.

'The place I entered upon was a hall, not like a muirland farmhouse, but more fine than I had ever seen. It was laid with a verra fine carpet, all red and blue and gay colours, and in the corner in a fireplace a great fire crackled. There were chairs, too, and a walth of old rusty arms on the walls, and all manner of whigmaleeries that folk think ornamental. But nobody was there, so I made for the staircase which was at the further side, and went up it stoutly. I made scarce any noise so thickly was it carpeted, and I will own it kind of terrified me to be walking in such a place. But when a man has drunk well he is troubled not overmuckle with modesty or fear, so I e'en stepped out and soon came to a landing where was a door.

'Now, thinks I, at last I have won to the habitable parts of the house; so laying my finger on the sneck I lifted it and entered. And there before me was the finest room in all the world; indeed I abate not a jot of the phrase, for I cannot think of anything finer. It was hung with braw pictures and lined with big bookcases of oak well-filled with books in fine bindings. The furnishing seemed carved by a skilled hand, and the cushions and curtains were soft velvet. But the best thing was the table, which was covered with a clean white cloth and set with all kind of good meat and drink. The dishes were of silver and as bright as Loch Awe water in an April sun. Eh, but it was a braw braw sight for a drover! And there at the far end, with a great pottle of wine before him, sat the master.

'He rose as I entered, and I saw him to be dressed in the pink of town fashion, a man of maybe fifty years, but hale and well-looking, with a peaked beard and trimmed moustache and thick eyebrows. His eyes were slanted a thought, which is a thing I hate in any man, but his whole appearance was pleasing.

' "Mr. Stewart?" says he courteously, looking at me. "Is it Mr. Duncan Stewart that I will be indebted to for the honour of this visit?"

'I stared at him blankly, for how did he ken my name?

' "That is my name," I said, "but who the tevil tell't you about it?"

' "Oh, my name is Stewart myself," says he, "and all Stewarts should be well acquaint."

' "True," said I, "though I don't mind your face before. But now I am here, I think you have a most gallant place, Mr. Stewart."

' "Well enough. But how have you come to't? We've few visitors."

'So I told him where I had come from, and where I was going, and why I was forwandered at this time of night among the muirs. He listened keenly, and when I had finished, he says verra friendly-like, "Then you'll bide all night and take supper with me. It would never be doing to let one of the clan go away without breaking bread. Sit ye down, Mr. Duncan."

'I sat down gladly enough, though I own that at first I did not half-like the whole business. There was something unchristian about the place, and for certain it was not seemly that the man's name should be the same as my own, and that he should be so well posted in my doings. But he seemed so well-disposed that my misgivings soon vanished.

'So I seated myself at the table opposite my entertainer. There was a place laid ready for me, and beside the knife and fork a long horn-handled spoon. I had never seen a spoon so long and queer, and I asked the man what it meant. "Oh," says he, "the broth in this house is very often hot, so we need a long spoon to sup it. It is a common enough thing, is it not?"

'I could answer nothing to this, though it did not seem to me sense, and I had an inkling of something I had heard about long spoons which I thought was not good; but my wits were not clear, as I have told you already. A serving man brought me a great bowl of soup and set it before me. I had hardly plunged spoon intil it, when Mr. Stewart cries out from the other end: "Now, Mr. Duncan, I call you to witness that you sit down to supper of your own accord. I've an ill name in these parts for compelling folk to take meat with me when they dinna want it. But you'll bear me witness that you're willing."

' "Yes, by God, I am that," I said, for the savoury smell of the broth was rising to my nostrils. The other smiled at this as if well-pleased.

'I have tasted many soups, but I swear there never was one like that. It was as if all the good things in the world were mixed thegether – whisky and kale and shortbread and cocky-leeky and honey and salmon. The taste of it was enough to make a body's heart loup with fair gratitude. The smell of it was like the spicy winds of Arabia, that you read about in the Bible, and when you had taken a spoonful you felt as happy as if you had sellt a hundred yowes at twice their reasonable worth. Oh, it was grand soup!

' "What Stewarts did you say you comed from," I asked my entertainer.

' "Oh," he says, "I'm connected with them all, Athole Stewarts, Appin Stewarts, Rannoch Stewarts; and a' I've a heap o' land thereaways."

' "Whereabouts?" says I, wondering. "Is't at the Blair o' Athole, or along by Tummel side, or wast the Loch o' Rannoch, or on the Muir, or in Mamore?"

' "In all the places you name," says he.

' "Got damn," says I, "then what for do you not bide there instead of in these stinking lawlands?"

'At this he laughed softly to himself. "Why, for maybe the same reason as yoursel, Mr. Duncan. You know the proverb, 'A' Stewarts are sib to the Deil.' "'

'I laughed loudly; "Oh, you've been a wild one, too, have you? Then you're not worse than mysel. I ken the inside of every public in the Cowgate and Cannongate, and there's no another drover on the road my match at fechting and drinking and dicing." And I started on a long shameless catalogue of my misdeeds. Mr. Stewart meantime listened with a satisfied smirk on his face.

' "Yes, I've heard tell of you, Mr. Duncan," he says. "But here's something more, and you'll doubtless be hungry."

'And now there was set on the table a round of beef garnished with pot-herbs, all most delicately fine to the taste. From a great cupboard were brought many bottles of wine, and in a massive silver bowl at the table's head were put whisky and lemons and sugar. I do not know well what I drank, but whatever it might be it was the best ever brewed. It made you scarce feel the earth round about you, and you were so happy you could scarce keep from singing. I wad give much siller to this day for the receipt.

'Now, the wine made me talk, and I began to boast of my own great qualities, the things I had done and the things I was going to do. I was a drover just now, but it was not long that I would be being a drover. I had bought a flock of my own, and would sell it for a hundred pounds, no less; with that I would buy a bigger one till I had made money enough to stock a farm; and then I would leave the road and spend my days in peace, seeing to my land and living in good company. Was not my father, I cried, own cousin, thrice removed, to the Macleans o' Duart, and my mother's uncle's wife a Rory of Balnacroy? And I am a scholar too, said I, for I was a matter of two years at Embro' College, and might have been roaring in the pulpit, if I hadna liked the drink and the lassies too well.

' "See," said I, "I will prove it to you;" and I rose from the table and went to one of the bookcases. There were all manner of books, Latin and Greek, poets and philosophers, but in the main, divinity. For there I saw Richard Baxter's 'Call to the Unconverted,' and Thomas Boston of Ettrick's 'Fourfold State,' not to speak of the *Sermons* of half a hundred auld ministers, and the 'Hind let Loose,' and many books of the covenanting folk.

' "Faith," I says, "you've a fine collection, Mr. What's-your-name," for the wine had made me free in my talk. "There is many a minister and professor in the Kirk, I'll warrant, who has a less godly library. I begin to suspect you of piety, sir."

' "Does it not behoove us," he answered in an unctuous voice, "to mind the words of Holy Writ that evil communications corrupt good manners, and have an eye to our company? These are all the company I have, except when some stranger such as you honours me – with a visit."

'I had meantime been opening a book of plays, I think by the famous William Shakespeare, and I here proke into a loud laugh. "Ha, ha, Mr. Stewart," I says, "here's a sentence I've lighted on which is hard on you. Listen! "The Devil can quote Scripture to advantage."

'The other laughed long. "He who wrote that was a shrewd man," he said, "but I'll warrant if you'll open another volume, you'll find some quip on yourself."

'I did as I was bidden, and picked up a white-backed book, and opening it at random, read: "There be many who spend their days in evil and wine-bibbing, in lusting and cheating, who think to mend while yet there is time; but the opportunity is to them for ever awanting, and they go down open-mouthed to the great fire."

' "Psa," I cried, "some wretched preaching book, I will have none of them. Good wine will be better than bad theology." So I sat down once more at the table.

' "You're a clever man, Mr. Duncan," he says, "and a well-read one. I commend your spirit in breaking away from the bands of the kirk and the college, though your father was so thrawn against you."

' "Enough of that," I said, "though I don't know who telled you;" I was angry to hear my father spoken of, as though the grieving him was a thing to be proud of.

' "Oh, as you please," he says; "I was just going to say that I commended your spirit in sticking the knife into the man in the Pleasaunce, the time you had to hide for a month about the backs o' Leith."

' "How do you ken that," I asked hotly, "you've heard more about me than ought to be repeated, let me tell you."

' "Don't be angry," he said sweetly; "I like you well for these things, and you mind the lassie in Athole that was so fond of you. You treated her well, did you not?"

'I made no answer, being too much surprised at his knowledge of things which I thought none knew but myself.

' "Oh yes, Mr. Duncan. I could tell you what you were doing to-day, how you cheated Jock Gallowa out of six pounds, and sold a horse to the farmer of Haypath that was scarce fit to carry him home. And I know what you are meaning to do the morn at Glesca, and I wish you well of it."

' "I think you must be the Devil," I said blankly.

' "The same, at your service," said he, still smiling.

'I looked at him in terror, and even as I looked I kenned by something in his eyes and the twitch of his lips that he was speaking the truth.

' "And what place is this, you ..." I stammered.

' "Call me Mr. S.," he says gently, "and enjoy your stay while you are here and don't concern yourself about the lawing."

' "The lawing!" I cried in astonishment, "and is this a house of public entertainment?"

' "To be sure, else how is a poor man to live?"

' "Name it," said I, "and I will pay and be gone."

' "Well," said he, "I make it a habit to give a man his choice. In your case it will be your wealth or your chances hereafter, in plain English your flock or your –"

' "My immortal soul," I gasped.

' "Your soul," said Mr. S., bowing, "though I think you call it by too flattering an adjective."

' "You damned thief," I roared, "you would entice a man into your accursed house and then strip him bare."

' "Hold hard," said he, "don't let us spoil our good fellowship by incivilities. And, mind you, I took you to witness to begin with that you sat down of your own accord."

' "So you did," said I, and could say no more.

' "Come, come," he says, "don't take it so bad. You may keep all your gear and yet part from here in safety. You've but to sign your name, which is no hard task to a college-bred man, and go on living as you live just now to the end. And let me tell you, Mr. Duncan Stewart, that you should take it as a great obligement that I am willing to take your bit soul instead of fifty sheep. There's no many would value it so high."

' "Maybe no, maybe no," I said sadly, "but it's all I have. D'ye no see that if I gave it up, there would be no chance left of mending? And I'm sure I do not want your company to all eternity."

' "Faith, that's uncivil," he says; "I was just about to say that we had had a very pleasant evening."

'I sat back in my chair very down-hearted. I must leave this place as poor as a kirk-mouse, and begin again with little but the clothes on my back. I was strongly tempted to sign the bit paper thing and have done with it all, but somehow I could not bring myself to do it. So at last I says to him: "Well, I've made up my mind. I'll give you my sheep, sorry though I be to lose them, and I hope I may never come near this place again as long as I live."

' "On the contrary," he said, "I hope often to have the pleasure of your company. And seeing that you've paid well for your lodging, I hope you'll make the best of it. Don't be sparing on the drink."

'I looked hard at him for a second. "You've an ill name, and an ill trade, but you're no a bad sort yoursel, and, do you ken, I like you."

' "I'm much obliged to you for the character," says he, "and I'll take your hand on't."

'So I filled up my glass and we set to, and such an evening I never mind of. We never got fou, but just in a fine good temper and very entertaining. The stories we told and the jokes we cracked are still a kind of memory with me, though I could not come over one of them. And then, when I got sleepy, I was shown to the brawest bedroom, all hung with pictures and looking-glasses, and with bed-clothes of the finest linen and a coverlet of silk. I bade Mr. S. good-night, and my head was scarce on the pillow ere I was sound asleep.

'When I awoke the sun was just newly risen, and the frost of a September morning was on my clothes. I was lying among green braes with nothing near me but crying whaups and heathery hills, and my two dogs running round about and howling as they were mad.'

The Outgoing of the Tide*

'Between the hours of twelve and one, even at the turning of the tide.'

MEN come from distant parts to admire the tides of Solway, which race in at flood and retreat at ebb with a greater speed than a horse can follow. But nowhere are there queerer waters than in our own parish of Caulds, at the place called the Sker Bay, where between two horns of land a shallow estuary receives the stream of the Sker. I never daunder by its shores and see the waters hurrying like messengers from the great deep without solemn thoughts, and a memory of Scripture words on the terror of the sea. The vast Atlantic may be fearful in its wrath, but with us it is no clean open rage, but the deceit of the creature, the unholy ways of quicksands when the waters are gone, and their stealthy return like a thief in the night watches. But in times of which I write there were more awful fears than any from the violence of nature. It was before the day of my ministry in Caulds, for then I was a tot callant in short clothes in my native parish of Lesmahagow; but the worthy Dr. Chrystal, who had charge of spiritual things, has told me often of the power of Satan and his emissaries in that lonely place. It was the day of warlocks and apparitions, now happily driven out by the zeal of the General Assembly. Witches pursued their wanchancy calling, bairns were spirited away, young lassies selled their souls to the Evil One, and the Accuser of the Brethren, in the shape of a black tyke, was seen about cottage doors in the gloaming. Many and earnest were the prayers of good Dr. Chrystal, but the evil thing, in spite of his wrestling, grew and flourished in his midst. The parish stank of idolatry, abominable rites were practiced in secret, and in all the bounds there was no one had a more evil name for the black traffic than one Alison Sempill, who bode at the Skerburnfoot.

The cottage stood nigh the burn, in a little garden, with lilyoaks and

---

* From the unpublished Remains of the Reverend John Dennistoun. Sometime Minister of the Gospel in the Parish of Caulds, and Author of Satan's Artifices against the Elect.

grosart bushes lining the pathway. The Sker ran by in a line among rowand trees, and the noise of its waters was ever about the place. The highroad on the other side was frequented by few, for a nearer-hand way to the west had been made through the lower Moss. Sometimes a herd from the hills would pass by with sheep, sometimes a tinkler or a wandering merchant, and once in a long while the laird of Heriotside on his grey horse riding to Gledsmuir. And they who passed would see Alion trupling in her garden, speaking to herself like the ill wife she was, or sitting on a cutty-stool by the doorside, with her eyes on other than mortal sights. Where she came from no man could tell. There were some said she was no woman, but a ghost haunting some mortal tenement. Others would threep she was gentrice, come of a persecuting family in the west, who had been ruined in the Revolution wars. She never seemed to want for siller; the house was as bright as a new preen, the yaird better delved than the manse garden; and there was routh of fowls and doos about the small steading, forbye a whee sheep and milk-kye in the fields. No man ever saw Alison at any market in the countryside, and yet the Skerburnfoot was plenished yearly in all proper order. One man only worked on the place, a doited lad who had long been a charge to the parish, and who had not the sense to fear danger or the wit to understand it. Upon all others the sight of Alison, were it but for a moment, cast a cold grue, not to be remembered without terror. It seems she was not ordinarily ill-famed, as men use the word. She was maybe sixty years in age, small and trig, with her grey hair folded neatly under her mutch. But the sight of her eyes was not a thing to forget. John Dodds said they were the een of a deer with the Devil ahint them; and indeed, they would so appal an onlooker that a sudden unreasoning terror came into his heart, while his feet would impel him to flight. Once John, being overtaken in drink on the roadside by the cottage, and dreaming that he was burning in hell, awoke and saw the old wife hobbling toward him. Thereupon he fled soberly to the hills, and from that day became a quiet-living, humble-minded Christian. She moved about the country like a ghost, gathering herbs in dark loanings, lingering in kirkyairds, and casting a blight on innocent bairns. Once Robert Smellie found her in a ruinous kirk on the Lang Muir, where of old the idolatrous rites of Rome were practiced. It was a hot day, and in the quiet place the flies buzzed in clouds, and he noted that she sat clothed in them as with a garment, yet suffering no discomfort. Then he, having mind of Beelzebub, the god of flies, fled without a halt homewards; but, falling in the coo's loan, broke two ribs and a collar bone, the whilk misfortune was much blessed to his soul. And there were darker tales in the countryside, of weans stolen, of lassies misguided, of innocent beasts cruelly tortured, and in one and all there came in the name of the wife of the Skerburnfoot. It was noted by them that kenned best that her cantrips were at their worst when the tides in the Sker Bay ebbed between the hours of twelve and one. At this season of the night the tides of mortality run lowest, and when the outgoing of these unco waters fell in with the setting of the current of life, then indeed was the hour for unholy revels. While honest men slept in their beds, the auld rudas carlines took their pleasure. That there is a delight in sin no man denies, but to most it is but a broken glint in the pauses of their conscience. But what must be the hellish joy of those lost beings who have forsworn God, and trysted with the Prince of Darkness, it is not for a Christian to say. Certain it is that it must be great, though their master waits at the end of the road to claim the wizened things they call their souls. Serious men – notably Gidden Scott in the Bach of the Hill, and Simon Wanch in the Sheilin of Chasehope – have seen Alison wandering on the wet sands, dancing to no earthy musick, while the heavens, they said, were full of lights and sounds which betokened the presence of the Prince of the Powers of the Air. It was a season of heart-searching for God's saints in Caulds, and the dispensation was blessed to not a few.

It will seem strange that in all this time the Presbytery was idle, and no effort was made to rid the place of so fell an influence. But there was a reason, and the reason, as in most like cases, was a lassie. Forbye Alison there lived at the Skerburnfoot a young maid, Ailie Sempill, who by all accounts was as good and bonnie as the other was evil. She passed for a daughter of Alison's – whether born in wedlock or not I cannot tell; but there were some said she was no kin to the auld witch wife, but some bairn spirited away from honest parents. She was young and blithe, with a face like an April morning, and a voice in her that put the laverocks to shame. When she sang in the kirk, folk have told me that they had a foretaste of the musick of the New Jerusalem, and when she came in by the village of Caulds old men stottered to their doors to look at her. Moreover, from her earliest days the bairn had some glimmerings of grace. Though no minister would visit the Skerburnfoot, or, if he went, departed quicker than he came, the girl Ailie attended regular at the catechising at the mains of Sker. It may be that Alison thought she would be a better offering for the Devil if she were given the chance of forswearing God, or it may be that she was so occupied in her own dark business that she had no care of the bairn. Meanwhile, the lass grew up in the nurture and admonition of the Lord. I have heard Dr. Chrystal say that he never had a communicant more full of the things of the Spirit. From the day when she first declared her wish to come forward to the hour when she broke bread at the table, she walked like one in a dream. The lads of the parish might cast admiring eyes on her bright cheeks and yellow hair, as she sat in her white gown in the kirk, but well they knew she was not for them. To be the bride of Christ was the thought that filled her heart; and when, at the fencing of the table, Dr. Chrystal preached from Matthew nine and fifteen, 'Can the children of the bridechamber mourn as long as the bridegroom is with them?' it was remarked by sundry that Ailie's face was liker the countenance of an angel than of a mortal lass.

It is with the day of her first communion that this narrative of mine begins. As she walked home, after the morning table, she communed in secret, and her heart sang within her. She had mind of God's mercies in the past; how he had kept her feet from the snares of evil doers which had been spread around her youth. She had been told unholy charms like the Seven South Streams and the Nine Rowand Berries, and it was noted, when she went first to the catechising, that she prayed, 'Our Father which wert in heaven,' the prayer which the ill wife Alison had taught her; meaning by it Lucifer, who had been in heaven, and had been cast out therefrom. But when she had come to years of discretion, she had freely chosen the better part, and evil had ever been repelled from her soul like gled water from the stones of Gled brig. Now she was in a rapture of holy content. The Druchen Bell – for the ungodly fashion lingered in Caulds – was ringing in her ears as she left the village, but to her it was but a kirk bell and a goodly sound. As she went through the woods where the primroses and the whitethorn were blossoming, the place seemed as the land of Elim, wherein there were twelve wells and threescore and ten palm trees. And then, as it might be, another thought came into her head, for it is ordained that frail mortality cannot long continue in holy joy. In the kirk she had been only the bride of Christ, but as she came through the wood, with the birds lilting and the winds of the world blowing, she had mind of another lover; for this lass, though so cold to men, had not escaped the common fate. It seems that the young Heriotside, riding by one day, stopped to speir something or other, and got a glisk of Ailie's face which caught his fancy. He passed the road again many times, and then he would meet her in the gloaming, or of a morning in the field as she went to fetch the kye. 'Blue are the hills that are far away,' is an owercome in the countryside, and while at first on his side it may have been but a young man's fancy, to her he was like the god Apollo descending from the skies. He was good to look on, brawly dressed, and with a tongue in his head that would have wiled the bird from the tree. Moreover, he was of gentle kin, and she was a poor lass biding in a cot house with an ill-reputed mother. It seems that in time the young man, who had begun the affair with no good intentions, fell honestly in love, while she went singing about the doors as innocent as a bairn, thinking of him when her thoughts were not on higher things. So it came about that long ere Ailie reached home it was on young Heriotside that her mind dwelled, and it was the love of him that made her eyes glow and her cheeks redden.

Now it chanced that at that very hour her master had been with Alison, and the pair of them were preparing a deadly pit. Let no man say that the Devil is not a cruel tyrant. He may give his folk some scrapings of unhallowed pleasure, but he will exact tithes, yea, of anise and cummin, in return, and there is aye the reckoning to pay at the hinder end. It seems that now he was driving Alison hard. She had been remiss of late – fewer souls sent to hell, less zeal in quenching the Spirit, and, above all, the crowning offense that her bairn had communicated in Christ's kirk. She had waited overlong, and now it was like that Ailie would escape her toils. I have no skill of fancy to tell of that dark collogue, but the upshot was that Alison swore by her lost soul and the pride of sin to bring the lass into thrall to her master. The fiend had bare departed when Ailie came over the threshold to find the auld carline glunching over the fire.

It was plain she was in the worst of tempers. She flyted on the lass till the poor thing's cheek paled. 'There you gang,' she cries, 'broking wi' thae wearifu' Pharisees o' Caulds, whae daurna darken your mither's door! A bonnie dutiful child, quotha! Wumman, hae ye nae pride, or even the excuse o' a tinkler-lass?' And then she changed her voice and would be as saft as honey: 'My puir wee Ailie, was I thrawn till ye? Never mind, my bonnie. You and me are a' that's left, and we maunna be ill to ither.' And then the two had their dinner, and all the while the auld wife was crooning over the lass. 'We maun 'gree weel,' she says, 'for we 're like to be our lee-lane for the rest o' our days. They tell me Heriotside is seeking Joan o' the Croft, and they're sune to be cried in Gledsmuir's kirk.'

It was the first the lass had heard of it, and you may fancy she was struck dumb. And so with one thing and other the auld witch raised the fiends of jealousy in that innocent heart. She would cry out that Heriotside was an ill-doing wastrel, and had no business to come and flatter honest lassies. And then she would speak of his gentle birth and his leddy mother, and say it was indeed presumption to hope that so great a gentleman could mean all that he said. Before long Ailie was silent and white, while her mother rimed on about men and their ways. And then she could thole it no longer, but must go out and walk by the burn to cool her hot brow and calm her thoughts, while the witch indoors laughed to herself at her devices.

For days Ailie had an absent eye and a sad face, and it so fell out that in all that time young Heriotside, who had scarce missed a day, was laid up with a broken arm and never came near her. So in a week's time she was beginning to hearken to her mother when she spoke of incantations and charms for restoring love. She kenned it was sin, but though not seven days syne she had sat at the Lord's table, so strong is love in a young heart that she was on the very brink of it. But the grace of God was stronger than her weak will. She would have none of her mother's runes and philters, though her soul cried out for them. Always when she was most disposed to listen some merciful power stayed her consent. Alison grew thrawner as the hours passed. She kenned of Heriotside's broken arm, and she feared that any day he might recover and put her stratagems to shame. And then it seems that she collogued with her master and heard word of a subtler device. For it was approaching that uncanny time of year, the festival of Beltane, when the auld pagans were wont to sacrifice to their god Baal. In this season warlocks and carlines have a special dispensation to do evil, and Alison waited on its coming with graceless joy. As it happened, the tides in the Sker Bay ebbed at this time between the hours of twelve and one, and, as I have said, this was the hour above all others when the Powers of Darkness were most potent. Would the lass but consent to go abroad in the unhallowed place at this awful season and hour of the night, she was as firmly handfasted to the Devil as if she had signed a bond with her own blood; for then, it seemed, the forces of good fled far away, the world for one hour was given over to its ancient prince, and the man or woman who willingly sought the spot was his bondservant forever. There are deadly sins from which God's people may recover. A man may even communicate unworthily, and yet, so be it he sin not against the Holy Ghost, he may find forgiveness. But it seems that for the Beltane sin there could be no pardon, and I can testify from my own knowledge that they who once committed it became lost souls from that day. James Denchar, once a promising professor, fell thus out of sinful bravery and died blaspheming; and of Kate Mallison, who went the same road, no man can tell. Here indeed was the witch wife's chance; and she was the more keen, for her master had warned her that this was her last chance. Either Ailie's soul would be his, or her auld wrunkled body and black heart would be flung from this pleasant world to their apportioned place.

Some days later it happened that young Heriotside was stepping home over the Lang Muir about ten at night, it being his first jaunt from home since his arm had mended. He had been to the supper of the Forest Club at the Cross Keys in Gledsmuir, a clamjamphry of wild young blades who passed the wine and played at cartes once a fortnight. It seems he had drunk well, so that the world ran round about and he was in the best of tempers. The moon came down and bowed to him, and he took off his hat to it. For every step he traveled miles, so that in a little he was beyond Scotland altogether and pacing the Arabian desert. He thought he was the Pope of Rome, so he held out his foot to be kissed, and rolled twenty yards to the bottom of a small brae. Syne he was the king of France, and fought hard with a whin bush till he had banged it to pieces. After that nothing would content him but he must be a bogle, for he found his head dunting on the stars and his legs were knocking the hills together. He thought of the mischief he was doing to the auld earth, and sat down and cried at his wickedness. Then he went on, and maybe the steep road to the Moss Rig helped him, for he began to get soberer and ken his whereabouts.

On a sudden he was aware of a man linking along at his side. He cried a fine night, and the man replied. Syne, being merry from his cups, he tried to slap him on the back. The next he kenned he was rolling on the grass, for his hand had gone clean through the body and found nothing but air.

His head was so thick with wine that he found nothing droll in this. 'Faith, friend,' he says, 'that was a nasty fall for a fellow that has supped weel. Where might your road be gaun to?'

'To the World's End,' said the man, 'but I stop at the Skerburnfoot.'

'Bide the night at Heriotside,' says he. 'It's a thought out of your way, but it's a comfortable bit.'

'There's mair comfort at the Skerburnfoot,' said the dark man.

Now the mention of the Skerburnfoot brought back to him only the thought of Ailie, and not of the witch wife, her mother. So he jaloused no ill, for at the best he was slow in the uptake.

The two of them went on together for a while, Heriotside's fool head filled with the thought of the lass. Then the dark man broke silence. 'Ye 're thinkin' o' the maid Ailie Sempill,' says he.

'How ken ye that?' asked Heriotside.

'It is my business to read the hearts o' men,' said the other.

'And who may ye be?' said Heriotside, growing eerie.

'Just an auld packman,' says he, 'nae name ye wad ken, but kin to mony gentle houses.'

'And what about Ailie, you that ken sae muckle?' asked the young man.

'Naething,' was the answer, – 'naething that concerns you, for ye'll never get the lass.'

'By God and I will!' says Heriotside, for he was a profane swearer.

'That's the wrong name to seek her in, ony way,' said the man.

At this the young laird struck a great blow at him with his stick, but found nothing to resist him but the hill wind.

When they had gone on a bit the dark man spoke again. 'The lassie is thirled to holy things,' says he; 'she has nae care for flesh and blood, – only for devout contemplation.'

'She loves me,' says Heriotside.

'Not you,' says the other, 'but a shadow in your stead.'

At this the young man's heart began to tremble, for it seemed that there was truth in what his companion said, and he was owerdrunk to think gravely.

'I kenna whatna man ye are,' he says, 'but ye have the skill of lassies' hearts. Tell me truly, is there no way to win her to common love?'

'One way there is,' said the man, 'and for our friendship's sake I will tell you it. If ye can ever tryst wi' her on Beltane's E'en on the Sker sands, at the green link o' the burn where the sands begin, on the ebb o' the tide when the midnight is by, but afore cockcrow, she'll be yours, body and soul, for this world and forever.'

And then it appeared to the young man that he was walking his love up the grass walk of Heriotside, with the house close by him. He thought no more of the stranger he had met, but the word stuck in his heart.

It seems that about this very time Alison was telling the same tale to poor Ailie. She cast up to her every idle gossip she could think of. 'It's Joan o' the Croft,' was aye her owercome, and she would threep that they were to be cried in kirk on the first Sabbath of May. And then she would rime on about the black cruelty of it, and cry down curses on the lover, so that her daughter's heart grew cauld with fear. It is terrible to think of the power of the world even in a redeemed soul. Here was a maid who had drunk of the well of grace and tasted of God's mercies, and yet there were moments when she was ready to renounce her hope. At those awful seasons God seemed far off and the world very nigh, and to sell her soul for love looked a fair bargain; at other times she would resist the Devil and comfort herself with prayer; but aye when she awoke there was the sore heart, and when she went to sleep there were the weary eyes. There was no comfort in the goodliness of spring or the bright sunshine weather, and she who had been wont to go about the doors lightfoot and blithe was now as dowie as a widow woman.

And then one afternoon in the hinder end of April came young Heriotside riding to the Skerburnfoot. His arm was healed, he had got him a fine new suit of green, and his horse was a mettle beast that well set off his figure. Ailie was standing by the doorstep as he came down the road, and her heart stood still with joy. But a second thought gave her anguish. This man, so gallant and braw, would never be for her; doubtless the fine suit and the capering horse were for Joan o' the Croft's pleasure. And he, in turn, when he remarked her wan cheeks and dowie eyes, had mind to what the dark man said on the muir, and saw in her a maid sworn to no mortal love. Yet his passion for her had grown fiercer than ever, and he swore to himself that he would win her back from her phantasies. She, one may believe, was ready enough to listen. As she walked with him by the Sker water his words were like musick to her ears, and Alison within doors laughed to herself and saw her devices prosper.

He spoke to her of love and his own heart, and the girl hearkened gladly. Syne he rebuked her coldness and cast scorn upon her piety, and so far was she beguiled that she had no answer. Then from one thing and another he spoke of some true token of their love. He said he was jealous, and craved something to ease his care. 'It's but a small thing I ask,' says he, 'but it will make me a happy man, and nothing ever shall come atween us. Tryst wi' me for Beltane's E'en on the Sker sands, at the green link o' the burn where the sands begin, on the ebb o' the tide when midnight is by, but afore cockcrow. For,' said he, 'that was our forbears' tryst for true lovers, and wherefore no for you and me?'

The lassie had grace given her to refuse, but with a woeful heart, and Heriotside rode off in black discontent, leaving poor Ailie to sigh her love. He came back the next day and the next, but aye he got the same answer. A season of great doubt fell upon her soul. She had no clearness in her hope, nor any sense of God's promises. The Scriptures were an idle tale to her, prayer brought her no refreshment, and she was convicted in her conscience of the unpardonable sin. Had she been less full of pride, she would have taken her troubles to good Dr. Chrystal and got comfort; but her grief made her silent and timorous, and she found no help anywhere. Her mother was ever at her side, seeking with coaxings and evil advice to drive her to the irrevocable step. And all the while there was her love for the man riving in her bosom, and giving her no ease by night or day. She believed she had driven him away, and repented her denial. Only her pride held her back from going to Heriotside and seeking him herself. She watched the road hourly for a sight of his face, and when the darkness came she would sit in a corner brooding over her sorrows.

At last he came, speiring the old question. He sought the same tryst, but now he had a further tale. It seemed he was eager to get her away from the Skerburnside and auld Alison. His aunt, Lady Balerynie, would receive her gladly at his request till the day of their marriage; let her but tryst with him at the hour and place he named, and he would carry her straight to Balerynie, where she would be safe and happy. He named that hour, he said, to escape men's observation, for the sake of her own good name. He named that place, for it was near her dwelling, and on the road between Balerynie and Heriotside, which fords the Sker Burn. The temptation was more than mortal heart could resist. She gave him the promise he sought, stifling the voice of conscience; and as she clung to his neck it seemed to her that heaven was a poor thing compared with a man's love.

Three days remained till Beltane's E'en, and throughout this time it was noted that Heriotside behaved like one possessed. It may be that his conscience pricked him, or that he had a glimpse of his sin and its coming punishment. Certain it is that if he had been daft before, he now ran wild in his pranks, and an evil report of him was in every mouth. He drank deep at the Cross Keys, and fought two battles with young lads that had angered him. One he let off with a touch on the shoulder; the other goes lame to this day from a wound he got in the groin. There was word of the procurator fiscal taking note of his doings, and troth, if they had continued long he must have fled the country. For a wager he rode his horse down the Dow Craig, wherefore the name of the place has been the Horseman's Craig ever since. He laid a hundred guineas with the laird of Slofferfield that he would drive four horses through the Slofferfield loch, and in the prank he had his bit chariot dung to pieces and a good mare killed. And all men observed that his eyes were wild and the face grey and thin, and that his hand would twitch, as he held the glass, like one with the palsy.

The Eve of Beltane was lower and hot in the low country, with fire hanging in the clouds and thunder grumbling about the heavens. It seems that up in the hills it had been an awesome deluge of rain, but on the coast it was still dry and lowering. It is a long road from Heriotside to the Skerburnfoot. First you go down the Heriot water, and syne over the Lang Muir to the edge of Mucklewhan. When you pass the steadings of Mirehope and Cockmalane, you turn to the right and ford the Mire Burn. That brings you on to the turnpike road, which you will ride till it bends inland, while you keep on straight over the Whinny Knowes to the Sker Bay. There, if you are in luck, you will find the tide out and the place fordable dryshod for a man on a horse. But if the tide runs, you will do well to sit down on the sands and content yourself till it turn, or it will be the solans and scarts of the Solway that will be seeing the next of you. On this Beltane's E'en, the young man, after supping with some wild young blades, bade his horse be saddled about ten o'clock. The company were eager to ken his errand, but he waved them back. 'Bide here,' he says, 'and boil the wine till I return. This is a ploy of my own on which no man follows me.' And there was that in his face, as he spoke, which chilled the wildest, and left them well content to keep to the good claret and the saft seat, and let the daft laird go his own ways.

Well and on he rode down the bridle path in the wood, along the top of the Heriot glen, and as he rode he was aware of a great noise beneath him. It was not wind, for there was none, and it was not the sound of thunder; and aye as he speired at himself what it was it grew the louder, till he came to a break in the trees. And then he saw the cause, for Heriot was coming down in a furious flood, sixty yards wide, tearing at the roots of the aiks and flinging red waves against the drystone dykes. It was a sight and sound to solemnise a man's mind, deep calling unto deep, the great waters of the hills running to meet with the great waters of the sea. But Heriotside recked nothing of it, for his heart had but one thought and the eye of his fancy one figure. Never had he been so filled with love of the lass; and yet it was not happiness, but a deadly, secret fear.

As he came to the Lang Muir it was gey and dark, though there was a moon somewhere behind the clouds. It was little he could see of the road, and ere long he had tried many moss pools and sloughs, as his braw new coat bare witness. Aye in front of him was the great hill of Mucklewhan, where the road turned down by the Mire. The noise of the Heriot had not long fallen behind him ere another began, the same eerie sound of burns crying to ither in the darkness. It seemed that the whole earth was overrun with waters. Every little runnel in the bay was astir, and yet the land around him was as dry as flax, and no drop of rain had fallen. As he rode on the din grew louder, and as he came over the top of Mirehope he kenned by the mighty rushing noise that something uncommon was happening with the Mire Burn. The light from Mirehope Sheilin twinkled on his left, and had the man not been dozened with his fancies he might have observed that the steading was deserted and men were crying below in the fields. But he rode on, thinking of but one thing, till he came to the cot house of Cockmalane, which is nigh the fords of the Mire.

John Dodds, the herd who bode in the place, was standing at the door, and he looked to see who was on the road so late.

'Stop!' says he, – 'stop, Laird Heriotside! I kenna what your errand is, but it is to no holy purpose that ye're out on Beltane E'en. D' ye no hear the warring o' the waters?'

And then in the still night came the sound of Mire like the clash of armies.

'I must win over the ford,' says the laird quickly, thinking of another thing.

'Ford!' cried John, in scorn. 'There'll be nae ford for you the nicht unless it was the ford o' the river Jordan. The burns are up and bigger than man ever saw them. It'll be a Beltane's E'en that a' folk will remember. They tell me that Gled valley is like a loch, and that there's an awesome heap o' folk drouned in the hills. Gin ye were ower the Mire, what about crossin' the Caulds and the Sker?' says he, for he jaloused he was going to Gledsmuir.

And then it seemed that that word brought the laird to his senses. He looked the airt the rain was coming from, and he saw it was the airt the Sker flowed. In a second, he has told me, the works of the Devil were revealed to him. He saw himself a tool in Satan's hands; he saw his tryst a device for the destruction of the body as it was assuredly meant for the destruction of the soul; and there came black on his mind the picture of an innocent lass borne down by the waters, with no place for repentance. His heart grew cold in his breast. He had but one thought, – a sinful and reckless one: to get to her side, that the two might go together to their account. He heard the roar of the Mire as in a dream, and when John Dodds laid hands on his bridle he felled him to the earth. And the next seen of it was the laird riding the floods like a man possessed.

The horse was the grey stallion he aye rode, the very beast he had ridden for many a wager with the wild lads of the Cross Keys. No man but himself durst back it, and it had lamed many a hostler lad and broke two necks in its day. But it seems it had the mettle for any flood, and took the Mire with little spurring. The herds on the hillside looked to see man and steed swept into eternity; but though the red waves were breaking about his shoulders, and he was swept far down, he aye held on for the shore. The next thing the watchers saw was the laird struggling up the far bank and casting his coat from him, so that he rode in his sark. And then he set off like a wildfire across the muir toward the turnpike road. Two men saw him on the road, and have recorded their experience. One was a gangrel, by name McNab, who was travelling from Gledsmuir to Allerkirk with a heavy pack on his back and a bowed head. He heard a sound like wind afore him, and, looking up, saw coming down the road a grey horse stretched out to a wild gallop, and a man on its back with a face like a soul in torment. He kenned not whether it was devil or mortal, but flung himself on the roadside and lay like a corp for an hour or more, till the rain aroused him. The other was one Sim Doolittle, the fish hawker from Allerfoot, jogging home in his fish cart from Gledsmuir fair. He had drunk more than was fit for him, and he was singing some light song, when he saw approaching, as he said, the pale horse mentioned in the Revelation, with Death seated as the rider. Thought of his sins came on him like a thunderclap; fear loosened his knees. He leaped from the cart to the road, and from the road to the back of a dyke; thence he flew to the hills, and was found the next morning far up among the Mire Craigs, while his horse and cart were gotten on the Aller sands, the horse lamed and the cart without the wheels.

At the tollhouse the road turns inland to Gledsmuir, and he who goes to the Sker Bay must leave it and cross the wild land called the Whinny Knowes, a place rough with bracken and foxes' holes and old stone cairns. The toll-man, John Gilzean, was opening the window to get a breath of air in the lower night, when he heard or saw the approaching horse. He kenned the beast for Heriotside's, and, being a friend of the laird's, he ran down in all haste to open the yett, wondering to himself about the laird's errand on this night. A voice came down the road to him bidding him hurry; but John's old fingers were slow with the keys, and so it happened that the horse had to stop, and John had time to look up at the gast and woeful face.

'Where away the nicht sae late, laird?' says John.

'I go to save a soul from hell,' was the answer.

And then it seems that through the open door there came the chapping of a clock.

'Whatna hour is that?' asks Heriotside.

'Midnicht,' says John, trembling, for he did not like the look of things.

There was no answer but a groan, and horse and man went racing down the dark hollows of the Whinny Knowes.

How he escaped a broken neck in that dreadful place no human being will ever ken. The sweat, he has told me, stood in cold drops upon his forehead; he scarcely was aware of the saddle in which he sat, and his eyes were stelled in his head so that he saw nothing but the sky ayont him. The night was growing colder, and there was a small sharp wind stirring from the east. But hot or cold, it was all one to him, who was already cold as death. He heard not the sound of the sea nor the peeseweeps startled by his horse, for the sound that ran in his ears was the roaring Sker water and a girl's cry. The thought kept goading him, and he spurred the grey horse till the creature was madder than himself. It leaped the hole which they call the Devil's Mull as I would step over a thristle, and the next he kenned he was on the edge of the Sker Bay.

It lay before him white and ghaistly, with mist blowing in wafts across it and a slow swaying of the tides. It was the better part of a mile wide, but save for some fathoms in the middle, where the Sker current ran, it was no deeper even at flood than a horse's fetlocks. It looks eerie at bright midday, when the sun is shining and whaups are crying among the seaweeds; but think what it was on that awesome night, with the Powers of Darkness brooding over it like a cloud! The rider's heart quailed for a moment in natural fear. He stepped his beast a few feet in, still staring afore him like a daft man. And then something in the sound or the feel of the waters made him look down, and he perceived that the ebb had begun and the tide was flowing out to sea.

He kenned that all was lost, and the knowledge drove him to stark despair. His sins came in his face like birds of night, and his heart shrunk like a pea. He knew himself for a lost soul, and all that he loved in the world was out in the tides. There, at any rate, he could go, too, and give back that gift of life he had so blackly misused. He cried small and saft like a bairn, and drove the grey out into the water. And aye as he spurred it the foam should have been flying as high as his head, but in that uncanny hour there was no foam; only the waves running sleek like oil. It was not long ere he had come to the Sker channel, where the red moss waters were roaring to the sea, – an ill place to ford in midsummer heat, and certain death, as folk reputed it, at the smallest spate. The grey was swimming; but it seemed the Lord had other purposes for him than death, for neither man nor horse could droun. He tried to leave the saddle, but he could not; he flung the bridle from him, but the grey held on as if some strong hand were guiding. He cried out upon the Devil to help his own; he renounced his Maker and his God: but whatever his punishment, he was not to be drouned. And then he was silent, for something was coming down the tide.

It came down as quiet as a sleeping bairn, straight for him as he sat with his horse breasting the waters; and as it came the moon crept out of a cloud, and he saw a glint of yellow hair. And then his madness died away, and he was himself again, a weary and stricken man. He hung down over the tide and caught the body in his arms, and then let the grey make for the shallows. He cared no more for the Devil and all his myrmidons, for he kenned brawly he was damned. It seemed to him that his soul had gone from him, and he was as toom as a hazel shell. His breath rattled in his throat, the tears were dried up in his head, his body had lost its strength, and yet he clung to the drouned maid as to a hope of salvation. And then he noted something at which he marvelled dumbly. Her hair was drookit back from her clay-cold brow, her eyes were shut, but in her face there was the peace of a child; it seemed even that her lips were smiling. Here, certes, was no lost soul, but one who had gone joyfully to meet her Lord. It may be in that dark hour at the burn-foot, before the spate caught her, she had been given grace to resist her adversary and fling herself upon God's mercy. And it would seem that it had been granted; for when he came to the Skerburnfoot, there in the corner sat the weird wife Alison, dead as a stone.

For days Heriotside wandered the country, or sat in his own house with vacant eye and trembling hands. Conviction of sin held him like a vice: he saw the lassie's death laid at his door; her face haunted him by day and night, and the word of the Lord dirled in his ears, telling of wrath and punishment. The greatness of his anguish wore him to a shadow, and at last he was stretched on his bed and like to perish. In his extremity worthy Dr. Chrystal went to him unasked, and strove to comfort him. Long, long the good man wrestled, but it seemed as if his ministrations were to be of no avail. The fever left his body, and he rose to stotter about the doors; but he was still in his torments, and the mercy-seat was far from him. At last in the back end of the year came Mungo Muirhead to Caulds to the autumn communion, and nothing would serve him but he must try his hand at the storm-tossed soul. He spoke with power and unction, and a blessing came with his words: the black cloud lifted and showed a glimpse of grace, and in a little the man had some assurance of salvation. He became a pillar of Christ's kirk, prompt to check abominations, notably the sin of witchcraft; foremost in good works, but with it all a humble man who walked contritely till his death. When I came first to Caulds I sought to prevail upon him to accept the eldership, but he aye put me by, and when I heard his tale I saw that he had done wisely. I mind him well as he sat in his chair or daundered through Caulds, a kind word for every one and sage counsel in time of distress, but withal a severe man to himself and a crucifier of the body. It seems that this severity weakened his frame, for three years syne come Martinmas he was taken ill with a fever of the bowels, and after a week's sickness he went to his account, where I trust he is accepted.

No-man's-land

I   The Shieling of Farawa

IT was with a light heart and a pleasing consciousness of holiday that I set out from the inn at Allermuir to tramp my fifteen miles into the unknown. I walked slowly, for I carried my equipment on my back – my basket, fly-books and rods, my plaid of Grant tartan (for I boast myself a distant kinsman of that house), and my great staff, which had tried ere then the front of the steeper Alps. A small valise with books and some changes of linen clothing had been sent on ahead in the shepherd's own hands. It was yet early April, and before me lay four weeks of freedom – twenty-eight blessed days in which to take fish and smoke the pipe of idleness. The Lent term had pulled me down, a week of modest enjoyment thereafter in town had finished the work; and I drank in the sharp moorish air like a thirsty man who has been forwandered among deserts.

I am a man of varied tastes and a score of interests. As an undergraduate I had been filled with the old mania for the complete life. I distinguished myself in the Schools, rowed in my college eight, and reached the distinction of practising for three weeks in the Trials. I had dabbled in a score of learned activities, and when the time came that I won the inevitable St. Chad's fellowship on my chaotic acquirements, and I found myself compelled to select if I would pursue a scholar's life, I had some toil in finding my vocation. In the end I resolved that the ancient life of the North, of the Celts and the Northmen and the unknown Pictish tribes, held for me the chief fascination. I had acquired a smattering of Gaelic, having been brought up as a boy in Lochaber, and now I set myself to increase my store of languages. I mastered Erse and Icelandic, and my first book – a monograph on the probable Celtic elements in the Eddic songs – brought me the praise of scholars and the deputy-professor's chair of Northern Antiquities. So much for Oxford. My vacations had been spent mainly in the North – in Ireland, Scotland, and the Isles, in Scandinavia and Iceland, once even in the far limits of Finland. I was a keen sportsman of a sort, an old-experienced fisher, a fair shot with gun and rifle, and in my hillcraft I might well stand comparison with most men. April has ever seemed to me the finest season of the year even in our cold northern altitudes, and the memory of many bright Aprils had brought me up from the South on the night before to Allerfoot, whence a dogcart had taken me up Glen Aller to the inn at Allermuir; and now the same desire had set me on the heather with my face to the cold brown hills.

You are to picture a sort of plateau, benty and rock-strewn, running ridge-wise above a chain of little peaty lochs and a vast tract of inexorable bog. In a mile the ridge ceased in a shoulder of hill, and over this lay the head of another glen, with the same doleful accompaniment of sunless lochs, mosses, and a shining and resolute water. East and west and north, in every direction save the south, rose walls of gashed and serrated hills. It was a grey day with blinks of sun, and when a ray chanced to fall on one of the great dark faces, lines of light and colour sprang into being which told of mica and granite. I was in high spirits, as on the eve of holiday; I had breakfasted excellently on eggs and salmon-steaks; I had no cares to speak of, and my prospects were not uninviting. But in spite of myself the landscape began to take me in thrall and crush me. The silent vanished peoples of the hills seemed to be stirring; dark primeval faces seemed to stare at me from behind boulders and jags of rock. The place was so still, so free from the cheerful clamour of nesting birds, that it seemed a *temenos* sacred to some old-world god. At my feet the lochs lapped ceaselessly; but the waters were so dark that one could not see bottom a foot from the edge. On my right the links of green told of snakelike mires waiting to crush the unwary wanderer. It seemed to me for the moment a land of death, where the tongues of the dead cried aloud for recognition.

My whole morning's walk was full of such fancies. I lit a pipe to cheer me, but the things would not be got rid of. I thought of the Gaels who had held those fastnesses; I thought of the Britons before them, who yielded to their advent. They were all strong peoples in their day, and now they had gone the way of the earth. They had left their mark on the levels of the glens and on the more habitable uplands, both in names and in actual forts, and graves where men might still dig curios. But the hills – that black stony amphitheatre before me – it seemed strange that the hills bore no traces of them. And then with some uneasiness I reflected on that older and stranger race who were said to have held the hill-tops. The Picts, the Picti – what in the name of goodness were they? They had troubled me in all my studies, a sort of blank wall to put an end to speculation. We knew nothing of them save certain strange names which men called Pictish, the names of those hills in front of me – the Muneraw, the Yirnie, the Calmarton. They were the *corpus vile* for learned experiment; but Heaven alone knew what dark abyss of savagery once yawned in the midst of the desert.

And then I remembered the crazy theories of a pupil of mine at St. Chad's, the son of a small landowner on the Aller, a young gentleman who had spent his substance too freely at Oxford, and was now dreeing his weird in the Backwoods. He had been no scholar; but a certain imagination marked all his doings, and of a Sunday night he would come and talk to me of the North. The Picts were his special subject, and his ideas were mad. 'Listen to me,' he would say, when I had mixed him toddy and given him one of my cigars; 'I believe there are traces – ay, and more than traces – of an old culture lurking in those hills and waiting to be discovered. We never hear of the Picts being driven from the hills. The Britons drove them from the lowlands, the Gaels from Ireland did the same for the Britons; but the hills were left unmolested. We hear of no one going near them except outlaws and tinklers. And in that very place you have the strangest mythology. Take the story of the Brownie. What is that but the story of a little swart man of uncommon strength and cleverness, who does good and ill indiscriminately, and then disappears. There are many scholars, as you yourself confess, who think that the origin of the Brownie was in some mad belief in the old race of the Picts, which still survived somewhere in the hills. And do we not hear of the Brownie in authentic records right down to the year 1756? After that, when people grew more incredulous, it is natural that the belief should have begun to die out; but I do not see why stray traces should not have survived till late.'

'Do you not see what that means?' I had said in mock gravity. 'Those same hills are, if anything, less known now than they were a hundred years ago. Why should not your Picts or Brownies be living to this day?'

'Why not, indeed?' he had rejoined, in all seriousness.

I laughed, and he went to his rooms and returned with a large leather-bound book. It was lettered, in the rococo style of a young man's taste, 'Glimpses of the Unknown,' and some of the said glimpses he proceeded to impart to me. It was not pleasant reading; indeed, I had rarely heard anything so well fitted to shatter sensitive nerves. The early part consisted of folk-tales and folk-sayings, some of them wholly obscure, some of them with a glint of meaning, but all of them with some hint of a mystery in the hills. I heard the Brownie story in countless versions. Now the thing was a friendly little man, who wore grey breeches and lived on brose; now he was a twisted being, the sight of which made the ewes miscarry in the lambing-time. But the second part was the stranger, for it was made up of actual tales, most of them with date and place appended. It was a most Bedlamite catalogue of horrors, which, if true, made the wholesome moors a place instinct with tragedy. Some told of children carried away from villages, even from towns, on the verge of the uplands. In almost every case they were girls, and the strange fact was their utter disappearance. Two little girls would be coming home from school, would be seen last by a neighbour just where the road crossed a patch of heath or entered a wood, and then – no human eye ever saw them again. Children's cries had startled outlying shepherds in the night, and when they had rushed to the door they could hear nothing but the night wind. The instances of such disappearances were not very common – perhaps once in twenty years – but they were confined to this one tract of country, and came in a sort of fixed progression from the middle of last century, when the record began. But this was only one side of the history. The latter part was all devoted to a chronicle of crimes which had gone unpunished, seeing that no hand had ever been traced. The list was fuller in last century; in the earlier years of the present it had dwindled; then came a revival about the 'fifties; and now again in our own time it had sunk low. At the little cottage of Auchterbrean, on the roadside in Glen Aller, a labourer's wife had been found pierced to the heart. It was thought to be a case of a woman's jealousy, and her neighbour was accused, convicted, and hanged. The woman, to be sure, denied the charge with her last breath; but circumstantial evidence seemed sufficiently strong against her. Yet some people in the glen believed her guiltless. In particular, the carrier who had found the dead woman declared that the way in which her neighbour received the news was a sufficient proof of innocence; and the doctor who was first summoned professed himself unable to tell with what instrument the wound had been given. But this was all before the days of expert evidence, so the woman had been hanged without scruple. Then there had been another story of peculiar horror, telling of the death of an old man at some little lonely shieling called Carrickfey. But at this point I had risen in protest, and made to drive the young idiot from my room.

'It was my grandfather who collected most of them,' he said. 'He had theories,* but people called him mad, so he was wise enough to hold his tongue. My father declares the whole thing mania; but I rescued the book had it bound, and added to the collection. It is a queer hobby; but,

---

* In the light of subsequent events I have jotted down the materials to which I refer. The last authentic record of the Brownie is in the narrative of the shepherd of Clachlands, taken down towards the close of last century by the Reverend Mr. Gillespie, minister of Allerkirk, and included by him in his 'Songs and Legends of Glen Aller'.

as I say, I have theories, and there are more things in heaven and earth –'

But at this he heard a friend's voice in the Quad., and dived out, leaving the *banal* quotation unfinished.

Strange though it may seem, this madness kept coming back to me as I crossed the last few miles of moor. I was now on a rough tableland, the watershed between two lochs, and beyond and above me rose the stony backs of the hills. The burns fell down in a chaos of granite boulders, and huge slabs of grey stone lay flat and tumbled in the heather. The full waters looked prosperously for my fishing, and I began to forget all fancies in anticipation of sport.

Then suddenly in a hollow of land I came on a ruined cottage. It had been a very small place, but the walls were still half-erect, and the little moorland garden was outlined on the turf. A lonely apple-tree, twisted and gnarled with winds, stood in the midst.

From higher up on the hill I heard a loud roar, and I knew my excellent friend the shepherd of Farawa, who had come thus far to meet me. He greeted me with the boisterous embarrassment which was his way of prefacing hospitality. A grave reserved man at other times, on such occasions he thought it proper to relapse into hilarity. I fell into step with him, and we set off for his dwelling. But first I had the curiosity to look back to the tumble-down cottage and ask him its name.

A queer look came into his eyes. 'They ca' the place Carrickfey,' he said. 'Naebody has daured to bide there this twenty year sin' – but I see ye ken the story.' And, as if glad to leave the subject, he hastened to discourse on fishing.

II   Tells of an Evening's Talk

THE shepherd was a masterful man; tall, save for the stoop which belongs to all moorland folk, and active as a wild goat. He was not a new importation, nor did he belong to the place; for his people had

---

The authorities on the strange carrying-away of children are to be found in a series of articles in a local paper, the 'Allerfoot Advertiser', September and October 1878, and a curious book published anonymously at Edinburgh in 1848, entitled 'The Weathergaw'. The records of the unexplained murders in the same neighbourhood are all contained in Mr. Fordoun's 'Theory of Expert Evidence', and an attack on the book in the 'Law Review' for June 1881. The Carrickfey case has a pamphlet to itself—now extremely rare—a copy of which was recently obtained in a bookseller's shop in Dumfries by a well-known antiquary, and presented to the library of the Supreme Court in Edinburgh.

lived in the remote Borders, and he had come as a boy to this shieling of Farawa. He was unmarried, but an elderly sister lived with him and cooked his meals. He was reputed to be extraordinarily skilful in his trade; I know for a fact that he was in his way a keen sportsman; and his few neighbours gave him credit for a sincere piety. Doubtless this last report was due in part to his silence, for after his first greeting he was wont to relapse into a singular taciturnity. As we strode across the heather he gave me a short outline of his year's lambing. 'Five pair o' twins yestreen, twae this morn; that makes thirty-five yowes that hae lambed since the Sabbath. I'll dae weel if God's willin'.' Then, as I looked towards the hill-tops whence the thin mist of morn was trailing, he followed my gaze. 'See,' he said with uplifted crook – 'see that sicht. Is that no what is written of in the Bible when it says, "The mountains do smoke".' And with this piece of apologeties he finished his talk, and in a little we were at the cottage.

It was a small enough dwelling in truth, and yet large for a moorland house, for it had a garret below the thatch, which was given up to my sole enjoyment. Below was the wide kitchen with box-beds, and next to it the inevitable second room, also with its cupboard sleeping-places. The interior was very clean, and yet I remember to have been struck with the faint musty smell which is inseparable from moorland dwellings. The kitchen pleased me best, for there the great rafters were black with peat-reek, and the uncovered stone floor, on which the fire gleamed dully, gave an air of primeval simplicity. But the walls spoiled all, for tawdry things of to-day had penetrated even there. Some grocers' almanacs – years old – hung in places of honour, and an extraordinary lithograph of the Royal Family in its youth. And this, mind you, between crooks and fishing-rods and old guns, and horns of sheep and deer.

The life for the first day or two was regular and placid. I was up early, breakfasted on porridge (a dish which I detest), and then off to the lochs and streams. At first my sport prospered mightily. With a drake-wing I killed a salmon of seventeen pounds, and the next day had a fine basket of trout from a hill-burn. Then for no earthly reason the weather changed. A bitter wind came out of the north-east, bringing showers of snow and stinging hail, and lashing the waters into storm. It was now farewell to fly-fishing. For a day or two I tried trolling with the minnow on the lochs, but it was poor sport, for I had no boat, and the edges were soft and mossy. Then in disgust I gave up the attempt, went back to the cottage, lit my biggest pipe, and sat down with a book to await the turn of the weather.

The shepherd was out from morning till night at his work, and when he came in at last, dog-tired, his face would be set and hard, and his eyes heavy with sleep. The strangeness of the man grew upon me. He had a shrewd brain beneath his thatch of hair, for I had tried him once or twice, and found him abundantly intelligent. He had some smattering of an education, like all Scottish peasants, and, as I have said, he was deeply religious. I set him down as a fine type of his class, sober, serious, keenly critical, free from the bondage of superstition. But I rarely saw him, and our talk was chiefly in monosyllables – short interjected accounts of the number of lambs dead or alive on the hill. Then he would produce a pencil and notebook, and be immersed in some calculation; and finally he would be revealed sleeping heavily in his chair, till his sister wakened him, and he stumbled off to bed.

So much for the ordinary course of life; but one day – the second I think of the bad weather – the extraordinary happened. The storm had passed in the afternoon into a resolute and blinding snow, and the shepherd, finding it hopeless on the hill, came home about three o'clock. I could make out from his way of entering that he was in a great temper. He kicked his feet savagely against the door-post. Then he swore at his dogs, a thing I had never heard him do before. 'Hell!' he cried, 'can ye no keep out o' my road, ye britts?' Then he came sullenly into the kitchen, thawed his numbed hands at the fire, and sat down to his meal.

I made some aimless remark about the weather.

'Death to man and beast,' he grunted. 'I hae got the sheep doun frae the hill, but the lambs will never thole this. We maun pray that it will no last.'

His sister came in with some dish. 'Margit,' he cried, 'three lambs away this morning, and three deid wi' the hole in the throat.'

The woman's face visibly paled. 'Guid help us, Adam; that hasna happened this three year.'

'It has happened noo,' he said, surlily. 'But, by God! if it happens again I'll gang mysel' to the Scarts o' the Muneraw.'

'O Adam!' the woman cried shrilly, 'haud your tongue. Ye kenna wha hears ye.' And with a frightened glance at me she left the room.

I asked no questions, but waited till the shepherd's anger should cool. But the cloud did not pass so lightly. When he had finished his dinner he pulled his chair to the fire and sat staring moodily. He made some sort of apology to me for his conduct. 'I'm sore troubled, sir; but I'm vexed ye should see me like this. Maybe things will be better the morn.' And then, lighting his short black pipe, he resigned himself to his meditations.

But he could not keep quiet. Some nervous unrest seemed to have possessed the man. He got up with a start and went to the window, where the snow was drifting, unsteadily past. As he stared out into the storm I heard him mutter to himself, 'Three away, God help me, and three wi' the hole in the throat.'

Then he turned round to me abruptly. I was jotting down notes for an article I contemplated in the 'Revue Celtique,' so my thoughts were far away from the present. The man recalled me by demanding fiercely. 'Do ye believe in God?'

I gave him some sort of answer in the affirmative.

'Then do ye believe in the Devil?' he asked.

The reply must have been less satisfactory, for he came forward, and flung himself violently into the chair before me.

'What do ye ken about it?' he cried. 'You that bides in a southern toun, what can ye ken o' the God that works in thae hills and the Devil – ay, the manifold devils – that He suffers to bide here? I tell ye, man, that if ye had seen what I have seen ye wad be on your knees at this moment praying to God to pardon your unbelief. There are devils at the back o' every stane and hidin' in every cleuch, and it's by the grace o' God alone that a man is alive upon the earth.' His voice had risen high and shrill, and then suddenly he cast a frightened glance towards the window and was silent.

I began to think that the man's wits were unhinged, and the thought did not give me satisfaction. I had no relish for the prospect of being left alone in this moorland dwelling with the cheerful company of a maniac. But his next movements reassured me. He was clearly only dead-tired, for he fell sound asleep in his chair, and by the time his sister brought tea and wakened him, he seemed to have got the better of his excitement.

When the window was shuttered and the lamp lit, I set myself again to the completion of my notes. The shepherd had got out his Bible, and was solemnly reading with one great finger travelling down the lines. He was smoking, and whenever some text came home to him with power he would make pretence to underline it with the end of the stem. Soon I had finished the work I desired, and, my mind being full of my pet hobby, I fell into an inquisitive frame of mind, and began to question the solemn man opposite on the antiquities of the place.

He stared stupidly at me when I asked him concerning monuments or ancient weapons.

'I kenna,' said he. 'There's a heap o' queer things in the hills.'

'This place should be a centre for such relics. You know that the name of the hill behind the house, as far as I can make it out, means the "Place of the Little Men." It is a good Gaelic word, though there is some doubt about its exact interpretation. But clearly the Gaelic peoples did not speak of themselves when they gave the name; they must have referred to some older and stranger population.'

The shepherd looked at me dully, as not understanding.

'It is partly this fact – besides the fishing, of course – which interests me in this countryside,' said I, gaily.

Again he cast the same queer frightened glance towards the window. 'If ye'll tak the advice of an aulder man,' he said, slowly, 'ye'll let well alane and no meddle wi' uncanny things.'

I laughed pleasantly, for at last I had found out my hard-headed host in a piece of childishness. 'Why, I thought that you of all men would be free from superstition.'

'What do ye call supersteetion?' he asked.

'A belief in old wives' tales,' said I, 'a trust in the crude supernatural and the patently impossible.'

He looked at me beneath his shaggy brows. 'How do ye ken what is impossible? Mind ye, sir, ye're no in the toun just now, but in the thick of the wild hills.'

'But, hang it all, man,' I cried, 'you don't mean to say that you believe in that sort of thing? I am prepared for many things up here, but not for the Brownie, – though, to be sure, if one could meet him in the flesh, it would be rather pleasant than otherwise, for he was a companionable sort of fellow.'

'When a thing pits the fear o' death on a man he aye speaks well of it.'

It was true – the Eumenides and the Good Folk over again; and I awoke with interest to the fact that the conversation was getting into strange channels.

The shepherd moved uneasily in his chair. 'I am a man that fears God, and has nae time for daft stories; but I havena traivelled the hills for twenty years wi' my een shut. If I say that I could tell ye stories o' faces seen in the mist, and queer things that have knocked against me in the snaw, wad ye believe me? I wager ye wadna. Ye wad say I had been drunk, and yet I am a God-fearing temperate man.'

He rose and went to a cupboard, unlocked it, and brought out something in his hand, which he held out to me. I took it with some curiosity, and found that it was a flint arrow-head.

Clearly a flint arrow-head, and yet like none that I had ever seen in any collection. For one thing it was larger, and the barb less clumsily thick. More, the chipping was new, or comparatively so; this thing had not stood the wear of fifteen hundred years among the stones of the hillside. Now there are, I regret to say, institutions which manufacture primitive relics; but it is not hard for a practised eye to see the difference. The chipping has either a regularity and a balance which is unknown in the real thing, or the rudeness has been overdone, and the result is an implement incapable of harming a mortal creature. But this was the real thing if it ever existed; and yet – I was prepared to swear on my reputation that it was not half a century old.

'Where did you get this?' I asked with some nervousness.

'I hae a story about that,' said the shepherd. 'Outside the door there ye can see a muckle flat stane aside the buchts. One simmer nicht I was sitting there smoking till the dark, and I wager there was naething on the stane then. But that same nicht I awoke wi' a queer thocht, as if there were folk moving around the hoose – folk that didna mak' muckle noise. I mind o' lookin' out o' the windy, and I could hae sworn I saw something black movin' amang the heather and intil the buchts. Now I had maybe threescore o' lambs there that nicht, for I had to tak' them many miles off in the early morning. Weel, when I gets up about four o'clock and gangs out, as I am passing the muckle stane I finds this bit errow. "That's come here in the nicht," says I, and I wunnered a wee and put it in my pouch. But when I came to my faulds what did I see? Five o' my best hoggs were away, and three mair were lying deid wi' a hole in their throat.'

'Who in the world –?' I began.

'Dinna ask,' said he. 'If I aince sterted to speir about thae maitters, I wadna keep my reason.'

'Then that was what happened on the hill this morning?'

'Even sae, and it has happened mair than aince sin' that time. It's the most uncanny slaughter, for sheep-stealing I can understand, but no this pricking o' the puir beasts' wizands. I kenna how they dae't either, for it's no wi' a knife or ony common tool.'

'Have you never tried to follow the thieves?'

'Have I no?' he asked, grimly. 'If it had been common sheep-stealers I wad hae had them by the heels, though I had followed them a hundred miles. But this is no common. I've tracked them, and it's ill they are to track; but I never got beyond ae place, and that was the Scarts o' the Muneraw that ye've heard me speak o'.'

'But who in Heaven's name are the people? Tinklers or poachers or what?'

'Ay,' said he, drily. 'Even so. Tinklers and poachers whae wark wi' stane errows and kill sheep by a hole in their throat. Lord, I kenna what they are, unless the Muckle Deil himsel'.'

The conversation had passed beyond my comprehension. In this prosaic hard-headed man I had come on the dead-rock of superstition and blind fear.

'That is only the story of the Brownie over again, and he is an exploded myth,' I said, laughing.

'Are ye the man that exploded it?' said the shepherd, rudely. 'I trow no, neither you nor ony ither. My bonny man, if ye lived a twalmonth in thae hills, ye wad sing safter about exploded myths, as ye call them.'

'I tell you what I would do,' said I. 'If I lost sheep as you lose them, I would go up the Scarts of the Muneraw and never rest till I had settled the question once and for all.' I spoke hotly, for I was vexed by the man's childish fear.

'I daresay ye wad,' he said, slowly. 'But then I am no you, and maybe I ken mair o' what is in the Scarts o' the Muneraw. Maybe I ken that whilk, if ye kenned it, wad send ye back to the South Country wi' your hert in your mouth. But, as I say, I am no sae brave as you, for I saw something in the first year o' my herding here which put the terror o' God on me, and makes me a fearfu' man to this day. Ye ken the story o' the gudeman o' Carrickfey?'

I nodded.

'Weel, I was the man that fand him. I had seen the deid afore and I've seen them since. But never have I seen aucht like the look in that man's een. What he saw at his death I may see the morn, so I walk before the Lord in fear.'

Then he rose and stretched himself. 'It's bedding-time, for I maun be up at three,' and with a short good night he left the room.

III The Scarts of the Muneraw

THE next morning was fine, for the snow had been intermittent, and had soon melted except in the high corries. True, it was deceptive weather, for the wind had gone to the rainy south-west, and the masses of cloud on that horizon boded ill for the afternoon. But some days' inaction had made me keen for a chance of sport, so I rose with the shepherd and set out for the day.

He asked me where I proposed to begin.

I told him the tarn called the Loch o' the Threshes, which lies over the back of the Muneraw on another watershed. It is on the ground of the Rhynns Forest, and I had fished it of old from the Forest House. I knew the merits of the trout, and I knew its virtues in a south-west wind, so I had resolved to go thus far afield.

The shepherd heard the name in silence. 'Your best road will be ower that rig, and syne on to the water o' Caulds. Keep abune the moss till ye come to the place they ca' the Nick o' the Threshes. That will take ye to the very lochside, but it's a lang road and a sair.'

The morning was breaking over the bleak hills. Little clouds drifted athwart the corries, and wisps of haze fluttered from the peaks. A great rosy flush lay over one side of the glen, which caught the edge of the sluggish bog-pools and turned them to fire. Never before had I seen the mountain-land so clear, for far back into the east and west I saw mountain-tops set as close as flowers in a border, black crags seamed with silver lines which I knew for mighty waterfalls, and below at my feet the lower slopes fresh with the dewy green of spring. A name stuck in my memory from the last night's talk.

'Where are the Scarts of the Muneraw?' I asked.

The shepherd pointed to the great hill which bears the name, and which lies, a huge mass, above the watershed.

'D'ye see yon corrie at the east that runs straucht up the side? It looks a bit scart, but it's sae deep that it's aye derk at the bottom o't. Weel, at the tap o' the rig it meets anither corrie that runs doun the ither side, and that one they ca' the Scarts. There is a sort o' burn in it that flows intil the Dule and sae intil the Aller, and, indeed, if ye were gaun there it wad be from Aller Glen that your best road wad lie. But it's an ill bit, and ye'll be sair guidit if ye try't.'

There he left me and went across the glen, while I struck upwards over the ridge. At the top I halted and looked down on the wide glen of the Caulds, which there is little better than a bog, but lower down grows into a green pastoral valley. The great Muneraw still dominated the landscape, and the black scaur on its side seemed blacker than before. The place fascinated me, for in that fresh morning air the shepherd's fears seemed monstrous. 'Some day,' said I to myself, 'I will go and explore the whole of that mighty hill.' Then I descended and struggled over the moss, found the Nick, and in two hours' time was on the loch's edge.

I have little in the way of good to report of the fishing. For perhaps one hour the trout took well; after that they sulked steadily for the day. The promise, too, of fine weather had been deceptive. By midday the rain was falling in that soft soaking fashion which gives no hope of clearing. The mist was down to the edge of the water, and I cast my flies into a blind sea of white. It was hopeless work, and yet from a sort of ill-temper I stuck to it long after my better judgment had warned me of its folly. At last, about three in the afternoon, I struck my camp, and prepared myself for a long and toilsome retreat.

And long and toilsome it was beyond anything I had ever encountered. Had I had a vestige of sense I would have followed the burn from the loch down to the Forest House. The place was shut up, but the keeper would gladly have given me shelter for the night. But foolish pride was too strong in me. I had found my road in mist before, and could do it again.

Before I got to the top of the hill I had repented my decision; when I got there I repented it more. For below me was a dizzy chaos of grey; there was no landmark visible; and before me I knew was the bog through which the Caulds Water twined. I had crossed it with some trouble in the morning, but then I had light to pick my steps. Now I could only stumble on, and in five minutes I might be in a bog-hole, and in five more in a better world.

But there was no help to be got from hesitation, so with a rueful courage I set off. The place was if possible worse than I had feared. Wading up to the knees with nothing before you but a blank wall of mist and the cheerful consciousness that your next step may be your last – such was my state for one weary mile. The stream itself was high, and rose to my armpits, and once and again I only saved myself by a violent leap backwards from a pitiless green slough. But at last it was past, and I was once more on the solid ground of the hillside.

Now, in the thick weather I had crossed the glen much lower down than in the morning, and the result was that the hill on which I stood was one of the giants which, with the Muneraw for centre, guard the watershed. Had I taken the proper way, the Nick o' the Threshes would have led me to the Caulds, and then once over the bog a little ridge was all that stood between me and the glen of Farawa. But instead I had come a wild cross-country road, and was now, though I did not know it, nearly as far from my destination as at the start.

Well for me that I did not know, for I was wet and dispirited, and had I not fancied myself all but home, I should scarcely have had the energy to make this last ascent. But soon I found it was not the little ridge I had expected. I looked at my watch and saw that it was five o'clock. When, after the weariest climb, I lay on a piece of level ground which seemed the top, I was not surprised to find that it was now seven. The darkening must be at hand, and sure enough the mist seemed to be deepening into a greyish black. I began to grow desperate. Here was I on the summit of some infernal mountain, without any certainty where my road lay. I was lost with a vengeance, and at the thought I began to be acutely afraid.

I took what seemed to me the way I had come, and began to descend steeply. Then something made me halt, and the next instant I was lying on my face trying painfully to retrace my steps. For I had found myself slipping, and before I could stop, my feet were dangling over a precipice with Heaven alone knows how many yards of sheer mist between me and the bottom. Then I tried keeping the ridge, and took that to the right, which I thought would bring me nearer home. It was no good trying to think out a direction, for in the fog my brain was running round, and I seemed to stand on a pin-point of space where the laws of the compass had ceased to hold.

It was the roughest sort of walking, now stepping warily over acres of loose stones, now crawling down the face of some battered rock, and now wading in the long dripping heather. The soft rain had begun to fall again, which completed my discomfort. I was now seriously tired, and, like all men who in their day have bent too much over books, I began to feel it in my back. My spine ached, and my breath came in short broken pants. It was a pitiable state of affairs for an honest man who had never encountered much grave discomfort. To ease myself I was compelled to leave my basket behind me, trusting to return and find it, if I should ever reach safety and discover on what pathless hill I had been strayed. My rod I used as a staff, but it was of little use, for my fingers were getting too numb to hold it.

Suddenly from the blankness I heard a sound as of human speech. At first I thought it mere craziness – the cry of a weasel or a hill-bird distorted by my ears. But again it came, thick and faint, as through acres of mist, and yet clearly the sound of 'articulate-speaking men.' In a moment I lost my despair and cried out in answer. This was some forwandered traveller like myself, and between us we could surely find some road to safety. So I yelled back at the pitch of my voice and waited intently.

But the sound ceased, and there was utter silence again. Still I waited, and then from some place much nearer came the same soft mumbling speech. I could make nothing of it. Heard in that drear place it made the nerves tense and the heart timorous. It was the strangest jumble of vowels and consonants I had ever met.

A dozen solutions flashed through my brain. It was some maniac talking Jabberwock to himself. It was some belated traveller whose wits had given out in fear. Perhaps it was only some shepherd who was amusing himself thus, and whiling the way with nonsense. Once again I cried out and waited.

Then suddenly in the hollow trough of mist before me, where things could still be half discerned, there appeared a figure. It was little and squat and dark; naked, apparently, but so rough with hair that it wore the appearance of a skin-covered being. It crossed my line of vision, not staying for a moment, but in its face and eyes there seemed to lurk an elder world of mystery and barbarism, a troll-like life which was too horrible for words.

The shepherd's fear came back on me like a thunderclap. For one awful instant my legs failed me, and I had almost fallen. The next I had turned and ran shrieking up the hill.

If he who may read this narrative has never felt the force of an overmastering terror, then let him thank his Maker and pray that he never may. I am no weak child, but a strong grown man, accredited in general with sound sense and little suspected of hysterics. And yet I went up that brae-face with my heart fluttering like a bird and my throat aching with fear. I screamed in short dry gasps; involuntarily, for my mind was beyond any purpose. I felt that beast-like clutch at my throat; those red eyes seemed to be staring at me from the mist; I heard ever behind and before and on all sides the patter of those inhuman feet.

Before I knew I was down, slipping over a rock and falling some dozen feet into a soft marshy hollow. I was conscious of lying still for a second and whimpering like a child. But as I lay there I awoke to the silence of the place. There was no sound of pursuit; perhaps they had lost my track and given up. My courage began to return, and from this it was an easy step to hope. Perhaps after all it had been merely an illusion, for folk do not see clearly in the mist, and I was already done with weariness.

But even as I lay in the green moss and began to hope, the faces of my pursuers grew up through the mist. I stumbled madly to my feet; but I was hemmed in, the rock behind and my enemies before. With a cry I rushed forward, and struck wildly with my rod at the first dark body. It was as if I had struck an animal, and the next second the thing was wrenched from my grasp. But still they came no nearer. I stood trembling there in the centre of those malignant devils, my brain a mere weathercock, and my heart crushed shapeless with horror. At last the end came, for with the vigour of madness I flung myself on the nearest, and we rolled on the ground. Then the monstrous things seemed to close over me, and with a choking cry I passed into unconsciousness.

IV   The Darkness that is Under the Earth

THERE is an unconsciousness that is not wholly dead, where a man feels numbly and the body lives without the brain. I was beyond speech or thought, and yet I felt the upward or downward motion as the way lay in hill or glen, and I most assuredly knew when the open air was changed for the close underground. I could feel dimly that lights were flared in my face, and that I was laid in some bed on the earth. Then with the stopping of movement the real sleep of weakness seized me, and for long I knew nothing of this mad world.

Morning came over the moors with bird-song and the glory of fine weather. The streams were still rolling in spate, but the hill-pastures were alight with dawn, and the little seams of snow glistened like white fire. A ray from the sunrise cleft its path somehow into the abyss, and danced on the wall above my couch. It caught my eye as I wakened, and for long I lay crazily wondering what it meant. My head was splitting with pain, and in my heart was the same fluttering nameless fear. I did not wake to full consciousness; not till the twinkle of sun from the clean bright out-of-doors caught my senses did I realise that I lay in a great dark place with a glow of dull firelight in the middle.

In time things rose and moved around me, a few ragged shapes of men, without clothing, shambling with their huge feet and looking towards me with curved beast-like glances. I tried to marshal my thoughts, and slowly, bit by bit, I built up the present. There was no question to my mind of dreaming; the past hours had scored reality upon my brain. Yet I cannot say that fear was my chief feeling. The first crazy terror had subsided, and now I felt mainly a sickened disgust with just a tinge of curiosity. I found that my knife, watch, flask, and money had gone, but they had left me a map of the countryside. It seemed strange to look at the calico, with the name of a London printer stamped on the back, and lines of railway and highroad running through every shire. Decent and comfortable civilisation! And here was I a prisoner in this den of nameless folk, and in the midst of a life which history knew not.

Courage is a virtue which grows with reflection and the absence of the immediate peril. I thought myself into some sort of resolution, and lo! when the Folk approached me and bound my feet I was back at once in the most miserable terror. They tied me all but my hands with some strong cord, and carried me to the centre, where the fire was glowing. Their soft touch was the acutest torture to my nerves, but I stifled my cries lest some one should lay his hand on my mouth. Had that happened, I am convinced my reason would have failed me.

So there I lay in the shine of the fire, with the circle of unknown things around me. There seemed but three or four, but I took no note of number. They talked huskily among themselves in a tongue which sounded all gutturals. Slowly my fear became less an emotion than a habit, and I had room for the smallest shade of curiosity. I strained my ear to catch a word, but it was a mere chaos of sound. The thing ran and thundered in my brain as I stared dumbly into the vacant air. Then I thought that unless I spoke I should certainly go crazy, for my head was beginning to swim at the strange cooing noise.

I spoke a word or two in my best Gaelic, and they closed round me inquiringly. Then I was sorry I had spoken, for my words had brought them nearer, and I shrank at the thought. But as the faint echoes of my speech hummed in the rock-chamber, I was struck by a curious kinship of sound. Mine was sharper, more distinct, and staccato; theirs was blurred, formless, but still with a certain root-resemblance.

Then from the back there came an older being, who seemed to have heard my words. He was like some foul grey badger, his red eyes sightless, and his hands trembling on a stump of bog-oak. The others made way for him with such deference as they were capable of, and the thing squatted down by me and spoke.

To my amazement his words were familiar. It was some manner of speech akin to the Gaelic, but broadened, lengthened, coarsened. I remembered an old book-tongue, commonly supposed to be an impure dialect once used in Brittany, which I had met in the course of my researches. The words recalled it, and as far as I could remember the thing, I asked him who he was and where the place might be.

He answered me in the same speech – still more broadened, lengthened, coarsened. I lay back with sheer amazement. I had found the key to this unearthly life.

For a little an insatiable curiosity, the ardour of the scholar, prevailed. I forgot the horror of the place, and thought only of the fact that here before me was the greatest find that scholarship had ever made. I was precipitated into the heart of the past. Here must be the fountainhead of all legends, the chrysalis of all beliefs. I actually grew light-hearted. This strange folk around me were now no more shapeless things of terror, but objects of research and experiment. I almost came to think them not unfriendly.

For an hour I enjoyed the highest of earthly pleasures. In that strange conversation I heard – in fragments and suggestions – the history of the craziest survival the world has ever seen. I heard of the struggles with invaders, preserved as it were in a sort of shapeless poetry. There were bitter words against the Gaelic oppressor, bitterer words against the Saxon stranger, and for a moment ancient hatreds flared into life. Then there came the tale of the hill-refuge, the morbid hideous existence preserved for centuries amid a changing world. I heard fragments of old religions, primeval names of god and goddess, half-understood by the Folk, but to me the key to a hundred puzzles. Tales which survive to us in broken disjointed riddles were intact here in living form. I lay on my elbow and questioned feverishly. At any moment they might become morose and refuse to speak. Clearly it was my duty to make the most of a brief good fortune.

And then the tale they told me grew more hideous. I heard of the circumstances of the life itself and their daily shifts for existence. It was a murderous chronicle – a history of lust and rapine and unmentionable deeds in the darkness. One thing they had early recognised – that the race could not be maintained within itself; so that ghoulish carrying away of little girls from the lowlands began, which I had heard of but never credited. Shut up in those dismal holes, the girls soon died, and when the new race had grown up the plunder had been repeated. Then there were bestial murders in lonely cottages, done for God knows what purpose. Sometimes the occupant had seen more than was safe, sometimes the deed was the mere exuberance of a lust of slaying. As they gabbled their tales my heart's blood froze, and I lay back in the agonies of fear. If they had used the others thus, what way of escape was open for myself? I had been brought to this place, and not murdered on the spot. Clearly there was torture before death in store for me, and I confess I quailed at the thought.

But none molested me. The elders continued to jabber out their stories, while I lay tense and deaf. Then to my amazement food was brought and placed beside me – almost with respect. Clearly my murder was not a thing of the immediate future. The meal was some form of mutton – perhaps the shepherd's lost ewes – and a little smoking was all the cooking it had got. I strove to eat, but the tasteless morsels choked me. Then they set drink before me in a curious cup, which I seized on eagerly, for my mouth was dry with thirst. The vessel was of gold, rudely formed, but of the pure metal, and a coarse design in circles ran round the middle. This surprised me enough, but a greater wonder awaited me. The liquor was not water, as I had guessed, but a sort of sweet ale, a miracle of flavour. The taste was curious, but somehow familiar; it was like no wine I had ever drunk, and yet I had known that flavour all my life. I sniffed at the brim, and there rose a faint fragrance of thyme and heather honey and the sweet things of the moorland. I almost dropped the thing in my surprise; for here in this rude place I had stumbled upon that lost delicacy of the North, the heather ale.

For a second I was entranced with my discovery, and then the wonder of the cup claimed my attention. Was it a mere relic of pillage, or had this folk some hidden mine of the precious metal? Gold had once been common in these hills. There were the traces of mines on Cairnsmore; shepherds had found it in the gravel of the Gled Water;

and the name of a house at the head of the Clachlands meant the 'Home of Gold.'

Once more I began my questions, and they answered them willingly. There and then I heard that secret for which many had died in old time, the secret of the heather ale. They told of the gold in the hills, of corries where the sand gleamed and abysses where the rocks were veined. All this they told me, freely, without a scruple. And then, like a clap, came the awful thought that this, too, spelled death. These were secrets which this race aforetime had guarded with their lives; they told them generously to me because there was no fear of betrayal. I should go no more out from this place.

The thought put me into a new sweat of terror – not at death, mind you, but at the unknown horrors which might precede the final suffering. I lay silent, and after binding my hands they began to leave me and go off to other parts of the cave. I dozed in the horrible half-swoon of fear, conscious only of my shaking limbs, and the great dull glow of the fire in the centre. Then I became calmer. After all, they had treated me with tolerable kindness: I had spoken their language, which few of their victims could have done for many a century; it might be that I found favour in their eyes. For a little I comforted myself with this delusion, till I caught sight of a wooden box in a corner. It was of modern make, one such as grocers use to pack provisions in. It had some address nailed on it, and an aimless curiosity compelled me to creep thither and read it. A torn and weather-stained scrap of paper, with the nails at the corner rusty with age; but something of the address might still be made out. Amid the stains my feverish eyes read, 'To Mr. M – Carrickfey, by Allerfoot Station.'

The ruined cottage in the hollow of the waste with the single gnarled apple-tree was before me in a twinkling. I remembered the shepherd's shrinking from the place and the name, and his wild eyes when he told me of the thing that had happened there. I seemed to see the old man in his moorland cottage, thinking no evil; the sudden entry of the nameless things; and then the eyes glazed in unspeakable terror. I felt my lips dry and burning. Above me was the vault of rock; in the distance I saw the fire-glow and the shadows of shapes moving around it. My fright was too great for inaction, so I crept from the couch, and silently, stealthily, with tottering steps and bursting heart, I began to reconnoitre.

But I was still bound, my arms tightly, my legs more loosely, but yet firm enough to hinder flight. I could not get my hands at my leg-straps, still less could I undo the manacles. I rolled on the floor, seeking some sharp edge of rock, but all had been worn smooth by the use of centuries. Then suddenly an idea came upon me like an inspiration. The sounds from the fire seemed to have ceased, and I could hear them repeated from another and more distant part of the cave. The Folk had left their orgy round the blaze, and at the end of the long tunnel I saw its glow fall unimpeded upon the floor. Once there, I might burn off my fetters and be free to turn my thoughts to escape.

I crawled a little way with much labour. Then suddenly I came abreast an opening in the wall, through which a path went. It was a long straight rock-cutting, and at the end I saw a gleam of pale light. It must be the open air; the way of escape was prepared for me; and with a prayer I made what speed I could towards the fire.

I rolled on the verge, but the fuel was peat, and the warm ashes would not burn the cords. In desperation I went farther, and my clothes began to singe, while my face ached beyond endurance. But yet I got no nearer my object. The strips of hide warped and cracked, but did not burn. Then in a last effort I thrust my wrists bodily into the glow and held them there. In an instant I drew them out with a groan of pain, scarred and sore, but to my joy with the band snapped in one place. Weak as I was, it was now easy to free myself, and then came the untying of my legs. My hands trembled, my eyes were dazed with hurry, and I was longer over the job than need have been. But at length I had loosed my cramped knees and stood on my feet, a free man once more.

I kicked off my boots, and fled noiselessly down the passage to the tunnel mouth. Apparently it was close on evening, for the white light had faded to a pale yellow. But it was daylight, and that was all I sought, and I ran for it as eagerly as ever runner ran to a goal. I came out on a rock-shelf, beneath which a moraine of boulders fell away in a chasm to a dark loch. It was all but night, but I could see the gnarled and fortressed rocks rise in ramparts above, and below the unknown screes and cliffs which make the side of the Muneraw a place only for foxes and the fowls of the air.

The first taste of liberty is an intoxication, and assuredly I was mad when I leaped down among the boulders. Happily at the top of the gully the stones were large and stable, else the noise would certainly have discovered me. Down I went, slipping, praying, my charred wrists aching, and my stockinged feet wet with blood. Soon I was in the jaws of the cleft, and a pale star rose before me. I have always been timid in the face of great rocks, and now, had not an awful terror been dogging my footsteps, no power on earth could have driven me to that descent. Soon I left the boulders behind, and came to long spouts of little stones, which moved with me till the hillside seemed sinking under my feet. Sometimes I was face downwards, once and again I must have fallen for yards. Had there been a cliff at the foot, I should have gone over it without resistance; but by the providence of God the spout ended in a long curve into the heather of the bog.

When I found my feet once more on soft boggy earth, my strength was renewed within me. A great hope of escape sprang up in my heart. For a second I looked back. There was a great line of shingle with the cliffs beyond, and above all the unknown blackness of the cleft. There lay my terror, and I set off running across the bog for dear life. My mind was clear enough to know my road. If I held round the loch in front I should come to a burn which fed the Farawa stream, on whose banks stood the shepherd's cottage. The loch could not be far; once at the Farawa I would have the light of the shieling clear before me.

Suddenly I heard behind me, as if coming from the hillside, the patter of feet. It was the sound which white hares make in the winter-time on a noiseless frosty day as they patter over the snow. I have heard the same soft noise from a herd of deer when they changed their pastures. Strange that so kindly a sound should put the very fear of death in my heart. I ran madly, blindly, yet thinking shrewdly. The loch was before me. Somewhere I had read or heard, I do not know where, that the brutish aboriginal races of the North could not swim. I myself swam powerfully; could I but cross the loch I should save two miles of a desperate country.

There was no time to lose, for the patter was coming nearer, and I was almost at the loch's edge. I tore off my coat and rushed in. The bottom was mossy, and I had to struggle far before I found any depth. Something plashed in the water before me, and then something else a little behind. The thought that I was a mark for unknown missiles made me crazy with fright, and I struck fiercely out for the other shore. A gleam of moonlight was on the water at the burn's exit, and thither I guided myself. I found the thing difficult enough in itself, for my hands ached, and I was numb with my bonds. But my fancy raised a thousand phantoms to vex me. Swimming in that black bog water, pursued by those nameless things, I seemed to be in a world of horror far removed from the kindly world of men. My strength seemed inexhaustible from my terror. Monsters at the bottom of the water seemed to bite at my feet, and the pain of my wrists made me believe that the loch was boiling hot, and that I was in some hellish place of torment.

I came out on a spit of gravel above the burn mouth, and set off down the ravine of the burn. It was a strait place, strewn with rocks; but now and then the hill turf came in stretches, and eased my wounded feet. Soon the fall became more abrupt, and I was slipping down a hillside, with the water on my left making great cascades in the granite. And then I was out in the wider vale where the Farawa water flowed among links of moss.

Far in front, a speck in the blue darkness shone the light of the cottage. I panted forward, my breath coming in gasps and my back shot with fiery pains. Happily the land was easier for the feet as long as I kept on the skirts of the bog. My ears were sharp as a wild beast's with fear, as I listened for the noise of pursuit. Nothing came but the rustle of the gentlest hill-wind and the chatter of the falling streams.

Then suddenly the light began to waver and move athwart the window. I knew what it meant. In a minute or two the household at the cottage would retire to rest, and the lamp would be put out. True, I might find the place in the dark, for there was a moon of sorts and the road was not desperate. But somehow in that hour the lamplight gave a promise of safety which I clung to despairingly.

And then the last straw was added to my misery. Behind me came the pad of feet, the pat-patter, soft, eerie, incredibly swift. I choked with fear, and flung myself forward in a last effort. I give my word it was sheer mechanical shrinking that drove me on. God knows I would have lain down to die in the heather, had the things behind me been a common terror of life.

I ran as man never ran before, leaping hags, scrambling through green well-heads, straining towards the fast-dying light. A quarter of a mile and the patter sounded nearer. Soon I was not two hundred yards off, and the noise seemed almost at my elbow. The light went out, and the black mass of the cottage loomed in the dark.

Then, before I knew, I was at the door, battering it wearily and yelling for help. I heard steps within and a hand on the bolt. Then something shot past me with lightning force and buried itself in the wood. The dreadful hands were almost at my throat, when the door was opened and I stumbled in, hearing with a gulp of joy the key turn and the bar fall behind me.

―――――――――――――

V   The Troubles of a Conscience

MY body and senses slept, for I was utterly tired, but my brain all the night was on fire with horrid fancies. Again I was in that accursed cave; I was torturing my hands in the fire; I was slipping barefoot among jagged boulders; and then with bursting heart I was toiling the last mile with the cottage light – now grown to a great fire in the heavens –

blazing before me.

It was broad daylight when I awoke, and I thanked God for the comfortable rays of the sun. I had been laid in a box-bed off the inner room, and my first sight was the shepherd sitting with folded arms in a chair regarding me solemnly. I rose and began to dress, feeling my legs and arms still tremble with weariness. The shepherd's sister bound up my scarred wrists and put an ointment on my burns; and limping like an old man, I went into the kitchen.

I could eat little breakfast, for my throat seemed dry and narrow; but they gave me some brandy-and-milk, which put strength into my body. All the time the brother and sister sat in silence, regarding me with covert glances.

'Ye have been delivered from the jaws o' the Pit,' said the man at length. 'See that,' and he held out to me a thin shaft of flint. 'I fand that in the door this morning.'

I took it, let it drop, and stared vacantly at the window. My nerves had been too much tried to be roused by any new terror. Out of doors it was fair weather, flying gleams of April sunlight and the soft colours of spring. I felt dazed, isolated, cut off from my easy past and pleasing future, a companion of horrors and the sport of nameless things. Then suddenly my eye fell on my books heaped on a table, and the old distant civilisation seemed for the moment inexpressibly dear.

'I must go – at once. And you must come too. You cannot stay here. I tell you it is death. If you knew what I know you would be crying out with fear. How far is it to Allermuir? Eight, fifteen miles; and then ten down Glen Aller to Allerfoot, and then the railway. We must go together while it is daylight, and perhaps we may be untouched. But quick, there is not a moment to lose.' And I was on my shaky feet, and bustling among my possessions.

'I'll gang wi' ye to the station,' said the shepherd, 'for ye're clearly no fit to look after yourself. My sister will bide and keep the house. If naething has touched us this ten year, naething will touch us the day.'

'But you cannot stay. You are mad,' I began; but he cut me short with the words, 'I trust in God.'

'In any case let your sister come with us. I dare not think of a woman alone in this place.'

'I'll bide,' said she. 'I'm no feared as lang as I'm indoors and there's steeks on the windies.'

So I packed my few belongings as best I could, tumbled my books into a haversack, and, gripping the shepherd's arm nervously, crossed the threshold. The glen was full of sunlight. There lay the long shining links of the Farawa burn, the rough hills tumbled beyond, and far over all the scarred and distant forehead of the Muneraw. I had always looked on moorland country as the freshest on earth – clean, wholesome, and homely. But now the fresh uplands seemed like a horrible pit. When I looked to the hills my breath choked in my throat, and the feel of soft heather below my feet set my heart trembling.

It was a slow journey to the inn at Allermuir. For one thing, no power on earth would draw me within sight of the shieling of Carrickfey, so we had to cross a shoulder of hill and make our way down a difficult glen, and then over a treacherous moss. The lochs were now gleaming like fretted silver, but to me, in my dreadful knowledge, they seemed more eerie than on that grey day when I came. At last my eyes were cheered by the sight of a meadow and a fence; then we were on a little byroad; and soon the fir-woods and cornlands of Allercleuch were plain before us.

The shepherd came no farther, but with brief good-bye turned his solemn face hillwards. I hired a trap and a man to drive, and down the ten miles of Glen Aller I struggled to keep my thoughts from the past. I thought of the kindly South Country, of Oxford, of anything comfortable and civilised. My driver pointed out the objects of interest as in duty bound, but his words fell on unheeding ears. At last he said something which roused me indeed to interest – the interest of the man who hears the word he fears most in the world. On the left side of the river there suddenly sprang into view a long gloomy cleft in the hills, with a vista of dark mountains behind, down which a stream of considerable size poured its waters.

'That is the Water o' Dule,' said the man in a reverent voice. 'A graund water to fish, but dangerous to life, for it's a' linns. Awa' at the heid they say there's a terrible wild place called the Scarts o' Muneraw, – that's a shouther o' the muckle hill itsel' that ye see, – but I've never been there, and I never kent ony man that had either.'

At the station, which is a mile from the village of Allerfoot, I found I had some hours to wait on my train for the south. I dared not trust myself for one moment alone, so I hung about the goods-shed, talked vacantly to the porters, and when one went to the village for tea I accompanied him, and to his wonder entertained him at the inn. When I returned I found on the platform a stray bagman who was that evening going to London. If there is one class of men in the world which I heartily detest it is this; but such was my state that I hailed him as a brother, and besought his company. I paid the difference for a first-class fare, and had him in the carriage with me. He must have thought me an amiable maniac, for I talked in fits and starts, and when he fell asleep I would wake him up and beseech him to speak to me. At wayside stations I would pull down the blinds in case of recognition, for to my unquiet mind the world seemed full of spies sent by that terrible Folk of the Hills. When the train crossed a stretch of moor I would lie down on the seat in case of shafts fired from the heather. And then at last with utter weariness I fell asleep, and woke screaming about midnight to find myself well down in the cheerful English midlands, and red blast-furnaces blinking by the railway-side.

In the morning I breakfasted in my rooms at St. Chad's with a dawning sense of safety. I was in a different and calmer world. The lawn-like quadrangles, the great trees, the cawing of rooks, and the homely twitter of sparrows – all seemed decent and settled and pleasing. Indoors the oak-panelled walls, the shelves of books, the pictures, the faint fragrance of tobacco, were very different from the gimcrack adornments and the accursed smell of peat and heather in that deplorable cottage. It was still vacation-time, so most of my friends were down; but I spent the day hunting out the few cheerful pedants to whom term and vacation were the same. It delighted me to hear again their precise talk, to hear them make a boast of their work, and narrate the childish little accidents of their life. I yearned for the childish once more; I craved for women's drawing-rooms, and women's chatter, and everything which makes life an elegant game. God knows I had had enough of the other thing for a lifetime!

That night I shut myself in my rooms, barred my windows, drew my curtains, and made a great destruction. All books or pictures which recalled to me the moorlands were ruthlessly doomed. Novels, poems, treatises I flung into an old box, for sale to the second-hand bookseller. Some prints and water-colour sketches I tore to pieces with my own hands. I ransacked my fishing-book, and condemned all tackle for moorland waters to the flames. I wrote a letter to my solicitors, bidding them to go no further in the purchase of a place in Lorne I had long been thinking of. Then, and not till then, did I feel the bondage of the past a little loosed from my shoulders. I made myself a night-cap of rum-punch instead of my usual whisky-toddy, that all associations with that dismal land might be forgotten, and to complete the renunciation I returned to cigars and flung my pipe into a drawer.

But when I woke in the morning I found that it is hard to get rid of memories. My feet were still sore and wounded, and when I felt my arms cramped and reflected on the causes, there was that black memory always near to vex me.

In a little, term began, and my duties – as deputy-professor of Northern Antiquities – were once more clamorous. I can well believe that my hearers found my lectures strange, for instead of dealing with my favourite subjects and matters, which I might modestly say I had made my own, I confined myself to recondite and distant themes, treating even these cursorily and dully. For the truth is, my heart was no more in my subject. I hated – or I thought that I hated – all things Northern with the virulence of utter fear. My reading was confined to science of the most recent kind, to abstruse philosophy, and to foreign classics. Anything which savoured of romance or mystery was abhorrent; I pined for sharp outlines and the tangibility of a high civilisation.

All the term I threw myself into the most frivolous life of the place. My Harrow schooldays seemed to have come back to me. I had once been a fair cricketer, so I played again for my college, and made decent scores. I coached an indifferent crew on the river. I fell into the slang of the place, which I had hitherto detested. My former friends looked on me askance, as if some freakish changeling had possessed me. Formerly I had been ready for pedantic discussion, I had been absorbed in my work, men had spoken of me as a rising scholar. Now I fled the very mention of things I had once delighted in. The Professor of Northern Antiquities, a scholar of European reputation, meeting me once in the parks, embarked on an account of certain novel rings recently found in Scotland, and to his horror found that, when he had got well under weigh, I had slipped off unnoticed. I heard afterwards that the good old man was found by a friend walking disconsolately with bowed head in the middle of the High Street. Being rescued from among the horses' feet, he could only murmur, 'I am thinking of Graves, poor man! And a year ago he was as sane as I am!'

But a man may not long deceive himself. I kept up the illusion valiantly for the term; but I felt instinctively that the fresh schoolboy life, which seemed to me the extreme opposite to the ghoulish North, and as such the most desirable of things, was eternally cut off from me. No cunning affectation could ever dispel my real nature or efface the memory of a week. I realised miserably that sooner or later I must fight it out with my conscience. I began to call myself a coward. The chief thoughts of my mind began to centre themselves more and more round that unknown life waiting to be explored among the unfathomable wilds.

One day I met a friend – an official in the British Museum – who was full of some new theory about primitive habitations. To me it seemed inconceivably absurd; but he was strong in his confidence, and without flaw in his evidence. The man irritated me, and I burned to prove him wrong, but I could think of no argument which was final against his. Then it flashed upon me that my own experience held the disproof; and without more words I left him, hot, angry with myself, and tantalised by the unattainable.

I might relate my *bona-fide* experience, but would men believe me? I must bring proofs, I must complete my researches, so as to make them incapable of disbelief. And there in those deserts was waiting the key. There lay the greatest discovery of the century – nay, of the millennium. There, too, lay the road to wealth such as I had never dreamed of. Could I succeed, I should be famous for ever. I would revolutionise history and anthropology; I would systematise folk-lore; I would show the world of men the pit whence they were digged and the rock whence they were hewn.

And then began a game of battledore between myself and my conscience.

'You are a coward,' said my conscience.

'I am sufficiently brave,' I would answer. 'I have seen things and yet lived. The terror is more than mortal, and I cannot face it.'

'You are a coward,' said my conscience.

'I am not bound to go there again. It would be purely for my own aggrandisement if I went, and not for any matter of duty.'

'Nevertheless you are a coward,' said my conscience.

'In any case the matter can wait.'

'You are a coward.'

Then came one awful midsummer night, when I lay sleepless and fought the thing out with myself. I knew that the strife was hopeless, that I should have no peace in this world again unless I made the attempt. The dawn was breaking when I came to the final resolution; and when I rose and looked at my face in a mirror, lo! it was white and lined and drawn like a man of sixty.

VI   Summer on the Moors

THE next morning I packed a bag with some changes of clothing and a collection of notebooks, and went up to town. The first thing I did was to pay a visit to my solicitors. 'I am about to travel,' said I, 'and I wish to have all things settled in case any accident should happen to me.' So I arranged for the disposal of my property in case of death, and added a codicil which puzzled the lawyers. If I did not return within six months, communications were to be entered into with the shepherd at the shieling of Farawa – post-town Allerfoot. If he could produce any papers, they were to be put into the hands of certain friends, published, and the cost charged to my estate. From my solicitors, I went to a gunmaker's in Regent Street and bought an ordinary six-chambered revolver, feeling much as a man must feel who proposed to cross the Atlantic in a skiff and purchased a small life-belt as a precaution.

I took the night express to the North, and, for a marvel, I slept. When I woke about four we were on the verge of Westmoreland, and stony hills blocked the horizon. At first I hailed the mountain-land gladly; sleep for the moment had caused forgetfulness of my terrors. But soon a turn of the line brought me in full view of a heathery moor, running far to a confusion of distant peaks. I remembered my mission and my fate, and if ever condemned criminal felt a more bitter regret I pity his case. Why should I alone among the millions of this happy isle be singled out as the repository of a ghastly secret, and be cursed by a conscience which would not let it rest?

I came to Allerfoot early in the forenoon, and got a trap to drive me up the valley. It was a lowering grey day, hot and yet sunless. A sort of heathaze cloaked the hills, and every now and then a smurr of rain would meet us on the road, and in a minute be over. I felt wretchedly dispirited; and when at last the whitewashed kirk of Allermuir came into sight and the broken-backed bridge of Aller, man's eyes seemed to have looked on no drearier scene since time began.

I ate what meal I could get, for, fears or no, I was voraciously hungry. Then I asked the landlord to find me some man who would show me the road to Farawa. I demanded company, not for protection – for what could two men do against such brutish strength? – but to keep my mind from its own thoughts.

The man looked at me anxiously.

'Are ye acquaint wi' the folks, then?' he asked.

I said I was, that I had often stayed in the cottage.

'Ye ken that they've a name for being queer. The man never comes here forbye once or twice a-year, and he has few dealings wi' other herds. He's got an ill name, too, for losing sheep. I dinna like the country ava. Up by yon Muneraw – no that I've ever been there, but I've seen it afar off – is enough to put a man daft for the rest o' his days. What's taking ye thereaways? It's no the time for the fishing?'

I told him that I was a botanist going to explore certain hill-crevices for rare ferns. He shook his head, and then after some delay found me an ostler who would accompany me to the cottage.

The man was a shock-headed, long-limbed fellow, with fierce red hair and a humorous eye. He talked sociably about his life, answered my hasty questions with deftness, and beguiled me for the moment out of myself. I passed the melancholy lochs, and came in sight of the great stony hills without the trepidation I had expected. Here at my side was one who found some humour even in those uplands. But one thing I noted which brought back the old uneasiness. He took the road which led us farthest from Carrickfey, and when to try him I proposed the other, he vetoed it with emphasis.

After this his good spirits departed, and he grew distrustful.

'What mak's ye a freend o' the herd at Farawa?' he demanded a dozen times.

Finally, I asked him if he knew the man, and had seen him lately.

'I dinna ken him, and I hadna seen him for years till a fortnicht syne, when a' Allermuir saw him. He cam doun one afternoon to the public-hoose, and begood to drink. He had aye been kenned for a terrible godly kind o' a man, so ye may believe folk wondered at this. But when he had stuck to the drink for twae days, and filled himsel' blind-fou half-a-dozen o' times, he took a fit o' repentance, and raved and blethered about siccan a life as he led in the muirs. There was some said he was speakin' serious, but maist thocht it was juist daftness.'

'And what did he speak about?' I asked sharply.

'I canna verra weel tell ye. It was about some kind o' bogle that lived in the Muneraw – that's the shouthers o't ye see yonder – and it seems that the bogle killed his sheep and frichted himsel'. He was aye bletherin', too, about something or somebody ca'd Grave; but oh! The man wasna wise.' And my companion shook a contemptuous head.

And then below us in the valley we saw the shieling, with a thin shaft of smoke rising into the rainy grey weather. The man left me, sturdily refusing any fee. 'I wantit my legs stretched as weel as you. A walk in the hills is neither here nor there to a stoot man. When will ye be back, sir?'

The question was well-timed. 'To-morrow fortnight,' I said, 'and I want somebody from Allermuir to come out here in the morning and carry some baggage. Will you see to that?'

He said 'Ay,' and went off, while I scrambled down the hill to the cottage. Nervousness possessed me, and though it was broad daylight and the whole place lay plain before me, I ran pell-mell, and did not stop till I reached the door.

The place was utterly empty. Unmade beds, unwashed dishes, a hearth strewn with the ashes of peat, and dust thick on everything, proclaimed the absence of inmates. I began to be horribly frightened. Had the shepherd and his sister, also, disappeared? Was I left alone in the bleak place, with a dozen lonely miles between me and human dwellings? I could not return alone; better this horrible place than the unknown perils of the out-of-doors. Hastily I barricaded the door, and to the best of my power shuttered the windows; and then with dreary forebodings I sat down to wait on fortune.

In a little I heard a long swinging step outside and the sound of dogs. Joyfully I opened the latch, and there was the shepherd's grim face waiting stolidly on what might appear.

At the sight of me he stepped back. 'What in the Lord's name are ye daein' here?' he asked. 'Didna ye get enough afore?'

'Come in,' I said, sharply. 'I want to talk.'

In he came with those blessed dogs, – what a comfort it was to look on their great honest faces! He sat down on the untidy bed and waited.

'I came because I could not stay away. I saw too much to give me any peace elsewhere. I must go back, even though I risk my life for it. The cause of scholarship demands it as well as the cause of humanity.'

'Is that a' the news ye hae?' he said. 'Weel, I've mair to tell ye. Three weeks syne my sister Margit was lost, and I've never seen her mair.'

My jaw fell, and I could only stare at him.

'I cam hame from the hill at nightfa' and she was gone. I lookit for her up hill and doun, but I couldna find her. Syne I think I went daft. I went to the Scarts and huntit them up and doun, but no sign could I see. The folk can bide quiet enough when they want. Syne I went to Allermuir and drank mysel' blind, – me, that's a God-fearing man and a saved soul; but the Lord help me, I didna ken what I was at. That's my news, and day and nicht I wander thae hills, seekin' for what I canna find.'

'But, man, are you mad?' I cried. 'Surely there are neighbours to help you. There is a law in the land, and you had only to find the nearest police-office and compel them to assist you.'

'What guid can man dae?' he asked. 'An army o' sodgers couldna find that hidy-hole. Forby, when I went into Allermuir wi' my story the folk thocht me daft. It was that set me drinking for – the Lord forgive me! – I wasna my ain maister. I threepit till I was hairse, but the bodies just lauch'd.' And he lay back on the bed like a man mortally tired.

Grim though the tidings were, I can only say that my chief feeling was of comfort. Pity for the new tragedy had swallowed up my fear. I had now a purpose, and a purpose, too, not of curiosity but of mercy.

'I go to-morrow morning to the Muneraw. But first I want to give you something to do.' And I drew roughly a chart of the place on the back of a letter. 'Go into Allermuir to-morrow, and give this paper to the landlord at the inn. The letter will tell him what to do. He is to raise at once all the men he can get, and come to the place on the chart marked with a cross. Tell him life depends on his hurry.'

The shepherd nodded. 'D'ye ken the Folk are watching for you? They let me pass without trouble, for they've nae use for me, but I see fine they're seeking you. Ye'll no gang half a mile the morn afore they grip ye.'

'So much the better,' I said. 'That will take me quicker to the place I want to be at.'

'And I'm to gang to Allemuir the morn,' he repeated, with the air of a child conning a lesson. 'But what if they'll no believe me?'

'They'll believe the letter.'

'Maybe,' he said, and relapsed into a doze.

I set myself to put that house in order, to rouse the fire, and prepare some food. It was dismal work; and meantime outside the night darkened, and a great wind rose, which howled round the walls and lashed the rain on the windows.

VII   In tuas manus, Domine!

I had not got twenty yards from the cottage door ere I knew I was watched. I had left the shepherd still dozing, in the half-conscious state of a dazed and broken man. All night the wind had wakened me at intervals, and now in the half-light of morn the weather seemed more vicious than ever. The wind cut my ears, the whole firmament was full of the rendings and thunders of the storm. Rain fell in blinding sheets, the heath was a marsh, and it was the most I could do to struggle against the hurricane which stopped my breath. And all the while I knew I was not alone in the desert.

All men know – in imagination or in experience – the sensation of being spied on. The nerves tingle, the skin grows hot and prickly, and there is a queer sinking of the heart. Intensify this common feeling a hundredfold, and you get a tenth part of what I suffered. I am telling a plain tale, and record bare physical facts. My lips stood out from my teeth as I heard, or felt, a rustle in the heather, a scraping among stones. Some subtle magnetic link seemed established between my body and the mysterious world around. I became sick – acutely sick – with the ceaseless apprehension.

My fright became so complete that when I turned a corner of rock, or stepped in deep heather, I seemed to feel a body rub against me. This continued all the way up the Farawa water, and then up its feeder to the little lonely loch. It kept me from looking forward; but it likewise kept me in such a sweat of fright that I was ready to faint. Then the notion came upon me to test this fancy of mine. If I was tracked thus closely, clearly the trackers would bar my way if I turned back. So I wheeled round and walked a dozen paces down the glen.

Nothing stopped me. I was about to turn again, when something made me take six more paces. At the fourth something rustled in the heather, and my neck was gripped as in a vice. I had already made up my mind on what I would do. I would be perfectly still, I would conquer my fear, and let them do as they pleased with me so long as they took me to their dwelling. But at the touch of the hands my resolutions fled. I struggled and screamed. Then something was clapped on my mouth, speech and strength went from me, and once more I was back in the maudlin childhood of terror.

In the cave it was always a dusky twilight. I seemed to be lying in the same place, with the same dull glare of firelight far off, and the same close stupefying smell. One of the creatures was standing silently at my side, and I asked him some trivial question. He turned and shambled down the passage, leaving me alone.

Then he returned with another, and they talked their guttural talk to me. I scarcely listened till I remembered that in a sense I was here of my own accord, and on a definite mission. The purport of their speech seemed to be that, now I had returned, I must beware of a second flight. Once I had been spared; a second time I should be killed without mercy.

I assented gladly. The Folk, then, had some use for me. I felt my errand prospering.

Then the old creature which I had seen before crept out of some corner and squatted beside me. He put a claw on my shoulder, a horrible, corrugated, skeleton thing, hairy to the finger-tips and nailless. He grinned, too, with toothless gums, and his hideous old voice was like a file on sandstone.

I asked questions, but he would only grin and jabber, looking now and then furtively over his shoulder towards the fire.

I coaxed and humoured him, till he launched into a narrative of which I could make nothing. It seemed a mere string of names, with certain words repeated at fixed intervals. Then it flashed on me that this might be a religious incantation. I had discovered remnants of a ritual and a mythology among them. It was possible that these were sacred days, and that I had stumbled upon some rude celebration.

I caught a word or two and repeated them. He looked at me curiously. Then I asked him some leading question, and he replied with clearness. My guess was right. The midsummer week was the holy season of the year, when sacrifices were offered to the gods.

The notion of sacrifices disquieted me, and I would fain have asked
further. But the creature would speak no more. He hobbled off, and
left me alone in the rock-chamber to listen to a strange sound which
hung ceaselessly about me. It must be the storm without, like a pack of
artillery rattling among the crags. A storm of storms surely, for the
place echoed and hummed, and to my unquiet eye the very rock of the
roof seemed to shake!

Apparently my existence was forgotten, for I lay long before any one
returned. Then it was merely one who brought food, the same strange
meal as before, and left hastily. When I had eaten I rose and stretched
myself. My hands and knees still quivered nervously; but I was strong
and perfectly well in body. The empty, desolate, tomb-like place was
eerie enough to scare any one; but its emptiness was comfort when I
thought of its inmates. Then I wandered down the passage towards the
fire which was burning in loneliness. Where had the Folk gone? I
puzzled over their disappearance.

Suddenly sounds began to break on my ear, coming from some
inner chamber at the end of that in which the fire burned. I could
scarcely see for the smoke; but I began to make my way towards the
noise, feeling along the sides of rock. Then a second gleam of light
seemed to rise before me, and I came to an aperture in the wall which
gave entrance to another room.

This in turn was full of smoke and glow – a murky orange glow, as if
from some strange flame of roots. There were the squat moving
figures, running in wild antics round the fire. I crouched in the
entrance, terrified and yet curious, till I saw something beyond the
blaze which held me dumb. Apart from the others and tied to some
stake in the wall was a woman's figure, and the face was the face of the
shepherd's sister.

My first impulse was flight. I must get away and think, – plan,
achieve some desperate way of escape. I sped back to the silent
chamber as if the gang were at my heels. It was still empty, and I stood
helplessly in the centre, looking at the impassable walls of rock as a
wearied beast may look at the walls of its cage. I bethought me of the
way I had escaped before and rushed thither, only to find it blocked by
a huge contrivance of stone. Yards and yards of solid rock were
between me and the upper air, and yet through it all came the crash
and whistle of the storm. If I were at my wits' end in this inner
darkness, there was also high commotion among the powers of the air
in that upper world.

As I stood I heard the soft steps of my tormentors. They seemed to
think I was meditating escape, for they flung themselves on me and

bore me to the ground. I did not struggle, and when they saw me quiet, they squatted round and began to speak. They told me of the holy season and its sacrifices. At first I could not follow them; then when I caught familiar words I found some clue, and they became intelligible. They spoke of a woman, and I asked, 'What woman?' With all frankness they told me of the custom which prevailed – how every twentieth summer a woman was sacrificed to some devilish god, and by the hand of one of the stranger race. I said nothing, but my whitening face must have told them a tale, though I strove hard to keep my composure. I asked if they had found the victims. 'She is in this place,' they said; 'and as for the man, thou art he.' And with this they left me.

I had still some hours; so much I gathered from their talk, for the sacrifice was at sunset. Escape was cut off for ever. I have always been something of a fatalist, and at the prospect of the irrevocable end my cheerfulness returned. I had my pistol, for they had taken nothing from me. I took out the little weapon and fingered it lovingly. Hope of the lost, refuge of the vanquished, ease to the coward – blessed be he who first conceived it!

The time dragged on, the minutes grew to hours, and still I was left solitary. Only the mad violence of the storm broke the quiet. It had increased in violence, for the stones at the mouth of the exit by which I had formerly escaped seemed to rock with some external pressure, and cutting shafts of wind slipped past and cleft the heat of the passage. What a sight the ravine outside must be, I thought, set in the forehead of a great hill, and swept clean by every breeze! Then came a crashing, and the long hollow echo of a fall. The rocks are splitting, said I; the road down the corrie will be impassable now and for evermore.

I began to grow weak with the nervousness of the waiting, and by-and-by I lay down and fell into a sort of doze. When I next knew consciousness I was being roused by two of the Folk, and bidden get ready. I stumbled to my feet, felt for the pistol in the hollow of my sleeve, and prepared to follow.

When we came out into the wider chamber the noise of the storm was deafening. The roof rang like a shield which has been struck. I noticed, perturbed as I was, that my guards cast anxious eyes around them, alarmed, like myself, at the murderous din. Nor was the world quieter when we entered the last chamber, where the fire burned and the remnant of the Folk waited. Wind had found an entrance from somewhere or other, and the flames blew here and there, and the smoke gyrated in odd circles. At the back, and apart from the rest, I saw the dazed eyes and the white old drawn face of the woman.

They led me up beside her to a place where there was a rude flat stone, hollowed in the centre, and on it a rusty iron knife, which seemed once to have formed part of a scythe-blade. Then I saw the ceremonial which was marked out for me. It was the very rite which I had dimly figured as current among a rude people, and even in that moment I had something of the scholar's satisfaction.

The oldest of the Folk, who seemed to be a sort of priest, came to my side and mumbled a form of words. His fetid breath sickened me; his dull eyes, glassy like a brute's with age, brought my knees together. He put the knife in my hands, dragged the terror-stricken woman forward to the altar, and bade me begin.

I began by sawing her bonds through. When she felt herself free she would have fled back, but stopped when I bade her. At that moment there came a noise of rending and crashing as if the hills were falling, and for one second the eyes of the Folk were averted from the frustrated sacrifice.

Only for a moment. The next they saw what I had done, and with one impulse rushed towards me. Then began the last scene in the play. I sent a bullet through the right eye of the first thing that came on. The second shot went wide; but the third shattered the hand of an elderly ruffian with a cruel club. Never for an instant did they stop, and now they were clutching at me. I pushed the woman behind, and fired three rapid shots in blind panic, and then, clutching the scythe, I struck right and left like a madman.

Suddenly I saw the foreground sink before my eyes. The roof sloped down, and with a sickening hiss a mountain of rock and earth seemed to precipitate itself on my assailants. One, nipped in the middle by a rock, caught my eye by his hideous writhings. Two only remained in what was now a little suffocating chamber, with embers from the fire still smoking on the floor.

The woman caught me by the hand and drew me with her, while the two seemed mute with fear. 'There's a road at the back,' she screamed. 'I ken it. I fand it out.' And she pulled me up a narrow hole in the rock.

How long we climbed I do not know. We were both fighting for air, with the tightness of throat and chest, and the craziness of limb which mean suffocation. I cannot tell when we first came to the surface, but I remember the woman, who seemed to have the strength of extreme terror, pulling me from the edge of a crevasse and laying me on a flat rock. It seemed to be the depth of winter, with sheer-falling rain and a wind that shook the hills.

Then I was once more myself and could look about me. From my feet yawned a sheer abyss, where once had been a hill-shoulder. Some great mass of rock on the brow of the mountain had been loosened by the storm, and in its fall had caught the lips of the ravine and swept the nest of dwellings into a yawning pit. Beneath a mountain of rubble lay buried that life on which I had thought to build my fame.

My feeling – Heaven help me! – was not thankfulness for God's mercy and my escape, but a bitter mad regret. I rushed frantically to the edge, and when I saw only the blackness of darkness I wept weak tears. All the time the storm was tearing at my body, and I had to grip hard by hand and foot to keep my place.

Suddenly on the brink of the ravine I saw a third figure. We two were not the only fugitives. One of the Folk had escaped.

The thought put new life into me, for I had lost the first fresh consciousness of terror. There still remained a relic of the vanished life. Could I but make the thing my prisoner, there would be proof in my hands to overcome a sceptical world.

I ran to it, and to my surprise the thing as soon as it saw me rushed to meet me. At first I thought it was with some instinct of self-preservation, but when I saw its eyes I knew the purpose of fight. Clearly one or other should go no more from the place.

We were some ten yards from the brink when I grappled with it. Dimly I heard the woman scream with fright, and saw her scramble across the hillside. Then we were tugging in a death-throe, the hideous smell of the thing in my face, its red eyes burning into mine, and its hoarse voice muttering. Its strength seemed incredible; but I, too, am no weakling. We tugged and strained, its nails biting into my flesh, while I choked its throat unsparingly. Every second I dreaded lest we should plunge together over the ledge, for it was thither my adversary tried to draw me. I caught my heel in a nick of rock, and pulled madly against it.

And then, while I was beginning to glory with the pride of conquest, my hope was dashed in pieces. The thing seemed to break from my arms, and, as if in despair, cast itself headlong into the impenetrable darkness. I stumbled blindly after it, saved myself on the brink, and fell back, sick and ill, into a merciful swoon.

VIII   Note in conclusion by the Editor

AT this point the narrative of my unfortunate friend, Mr. Graves of St Chad's, breaks off abruptly. He wrote it shortly before his death, and was prevented from completing it by the shock of apoplexy which carried him off. In accordance with the instructions in his will, I have prepared it for publication, and now in much fear and hesitation give it to the world. First, however, I must supplement it by such facts as fall within my knowledge.

The shepherd seems to have gone to Allermuir and by the help of the letter convinced the inhabitants. A body of men was collected under the landlord, and during the afternoon set out for the hills. But unfortunately the great midsummer storm – the most terrible of recent climatic disturbances – had filled the mosses and streams, and they found themselves unable to proceed by any direct road. Ultimately late in the evening they arrived at the cottage of Farawa, only to find there a raving woman, the shepherd's sister, who seemed crazy with brain-fever. She told some rambling story about her escape, but her narrative said nothing of Mr. Graves. So they treated her with what skill they possessed, and sheltered for the night in and around the cottage. Next morning the storm had abated a little, and the woman had recovered something of her wits. From her they learned that Mr. Graves was lying in a ravine on the side of the Muneraw in imminent danger of his life. A body set out to find him; but so immense was the landslip, and so dangerous the whole mountain, that it was nearly evening when they recovered him from the ledge of rock. He was alive, but unconscious, and on bringing him back to the cottage it was clear that he was, indeed, very ill. There he lay for three months, while the best skill that could be got was procured for him. By dint of an uncommon toughness of constitution he survived; but it was an old and feeble man who returned to Oxford in the early winter.

The shepherd and his sister immediately left the countryside, and were never more heard of, unless they are the pair of unfortunates who are at present in a Scottish pauper asylum, incapable of remembering even their names. The people who last spoke with them declared that their minds seemed weakened by a great shock, and that it was hopeless to try to get any connected or rational statement.

The career of my poor friend from that hour was little short of a tragedy. He awoke from his illness to find the world incredulous; even the countryfolk of Allermuir set down the story to the shepherd's craziness and my friend's credulity. In Oxford his argument was received with polite scorn. An account of his experiences which he drew up for the 'Times' was refused by the editor; and an article on 'Primitive Peoples of the North,' embodying what he believed to be the result of his discoveries, was unanimously rejected by every responsible journal in Europe. Whether he was soured by such treatment, or whether his brain had already been weakened, he became a morose silent man, and for the two years before his death had few friends and no society. From the obituary notice in the 'Times' I take the following paragraph, which shows in what light the world had come to look upon him:

'At the outset of his career he was regarded as a rising scholar in one department of archaeology, and his Taffert lectures were a real contribution to an obscure subject. But in after-life he was led into fantastic speculations; and when he found himself unable to convince his colleagues, he gradually retired into himself, and lived practically a hermit's life till his death. His career, thus broken short, is a sad instance of the fascination which the recondite and the quack can exercise even on men of approved ability.'

And now his own narrative is published, and the world can judge as it pleases about the amazing romance. The view which will doubtless find general acceptance is that the whole is a figment of the brain, begotten of some harmless moorland adventure and the company of such religious maniacs as the shepherd and his sister. But some who knew the former sobriety and calmness of my friend's mind may be disposed timorously and with deep hesitation to another verdict. They may accept the narrative, and believe that somewhere in those moorlands he met with a horrible primitive survival, passed through the strangest adventure, and had his finger on an epoch-making discovery. In this case they will be inclined to sympathise with the loneliness and misunderstanding of his latter days. It is not for me to decide the question. That which alone could bring proof is buried beneath a thousand tons of rock in the midst of an untrodden desert.

The Watcher by the Threshold

A chill evening in the early October of the year 189 – found me driving
in a dogcart through the belts of antique woodland which form the
lowland limits of the hilly parish of More. The Highland express,
which brought me from the north, took me no farther than Perth.
Thence it had been a slow journey in a disjointed local train, till I
emerged on the platform at Morefoot, with a bleak prospect of pot
stalks, coal heaps, certain sour corn lands, and far to the west a line of
moor where the sun was setting. A neat groom and a respectable trap
took the edge off my discomfort, and soon I had forgotten my sacrifice
and found eyes for the darkening landscape. We were driving through
a land of thick woods, cut at rare intervals by old long-frequented
highways. The More, which at Morefoot is an open sewer, became a
sullen woodland stream, where the brown leaves of the season drifted.
At times we would pass an ancient lodge, and through a gap in the
trees would come a glimpse of chipped crowstep gable. The names of
such houses, as told me by my companion, were all famous. This one
had been the home of a drunken Jacobite laird, and a king of north
country Medmenham. Unholy revels had waked the old halls, and the
devil had been toasted at many a hell-fire dinner. The next was the
property of a great Scots law family, and there the old Lord of Session,
who built the place, in his frouzy wig and carpet slippers, had laid
down the canons of Taste for his day and society. The whole country
had the air of faded and bygone gentility. The mossy roadside walls
had stood for two hundred years; the few wayside houses were toll bars
or defunct hostelries. The names, too, were great: Scots baronial with
a smack of France, – Chatelray and Riverslaw, Black Holm and
Fountainblue. The place had a cunning charm, mystery dwelt in every,
cranny, and yet it did not please me. The earth smelt heavy and raw;
the roads were red underfoot; all was old, sorrowful, and uncanny.
Compared with the fresh Highland glen I had left, where wind and sun
and flying showers were never absent, all was chilly and dull and dead.
Even when the sun sent a shiver of crimson over the crests of certain

92

firs, I felt no delight in the prospect. I admitted shamefacedly to myself that I was in a very bad temper.

I had been staying at Glenaicill with the Clanroydens, and for a week had found the proper pleasure in life. You know the house with its old rooms and gardens, and the miles of heather which defend it from the world. The shooting had been extraordinary for a wild place late in the season; for there are few partridges, and the woodcock are notoriously late. I had done respectably in my stalking, more than respectably on the river, and creditably on the moors. Moreover, there were pleasant people in the house – and there were the Clanroydens. I had had a hard year's work, sustained to the last moment of term, and a fortnight in Norway had been disastrous. It was therefore with real comfort that I had settled myself down for another ten days in Glenaicill, when all my plans were shattered by Sibyl's letter. Sibyl is my cousin and my very good friend, and in old days when I was briefless I had fallen in love with her many times. But she very sensibly chose otherwise, and married a man Ladlaw – Robert John Ladlaw, who had been at school with me. He was a cheery, good-humoured fellow, a great sportsman, a justice of the peace, and deputy lieutenant for his county, and something of an antiquary in a mild way. He had a box in Leicestershire to which he went in the hunting season, but from February till October he lived in his moorland home. The place was called the House of More, and I had shot at it once or twice in recent years. I remembered its loneliness and its comfort, the charming diffident Sibyl, and Ladlaw's genial welcome. And my recollections set me puzzling again over the letter which that morning had broken into my comfort. 'You promised us a visit this autumn,' Sibyl had written, 'and I wish you would come as soon as you can.' So far common politeness. But she had gone on to reveal the fact that Ladlaw was ill; she did not know how, exactly, but something, she thought, about his heart. Then she had signed herself my affectionate cousin, and then had come a short, violent postscript, in which, as it were, the fences of convention had been laid low. 'For Heaven's sake, come and see us,' she scrawled below. 'Bob is terribly ill, and I am crazy. Come at once.' To cap it she finished with an afterthought: 'Don't bother about bringing doctors. It is not their business.'

She had assumed that I would come, and dutifully I set out. I could not regret my decision, but I took leave to upbraid my luck. The thought of Glenaicill, with the woodcock beginning to arrive and the Clanroydens imploring me to stay, saddened my journey in the morning, and the murky, coaly, midland country of the afternoon completed my depression. The drive through the woodlands of More failed to raise my spirits. I was anxious about Sibyl and Ladlaw, and this accursed country had always given me a certain eeriness on my first approaching it. You may call it silly, but I have no nerves and am little susceptible to vague sentiment. It was sheer physical dislike of the rich deep soil, the woody and antique smells, the melancholy roads and trees, and the flavor of old mystery. I am aggressively healthy and wholly Philistine. I love clear outlines and strong colors, and More with its half tints and hazy distances depressed me miserably. Even when the road crept uphill and the trees ended, I found nothing to hearten me in the moorland which succeeded. It was genuine moorland, close on eight hundred feet above the sea, and through it ran this old grass-grown coach road. Low hills rose to the left, and to the right, after some miles of peat, flared the chimneys of pits and oil works. Straight in front the moor ran out into the horizon, and there in the centre was the last dying spark of the sun. The place was as still as the grave save for the crunch of our wheels on the grassy road, but the flaring lights to the north seemed to endow it with life. I have rarely had so keenly the feeling of movement in the inanimate world. It was an unquiet place, and I shivered nervously. Little gleams of loch came from the hollows, the burns were brown with peat, and every now and then there rose in the moor jags of sickening red stone. I remembered that Ladlaw had talked about the place as the old Manann, the holy land of the ancient races. I had paid little attention at the time, but now it struck me that the old peoples had been wise in their choice. There was something uncanny in this soil and air. Framed in dank mysterious woods and a country of coal and ironstone, at no great distance from the capital city, it was a sullen relic of a lost barbarism. Over the low hills lay a green pastoral country with bright streams and valleys, but here, in this peaty desert, there were few sheep and little cultivation. The House of More was the only dwelling, and, save for the ragged village, the wilderness was given over to the wild things of the hills. The shooting was good, but the best shooting on earth would not persuade me to make my abode in such a place. Ladlaw was ill; well, I did not wonder. You can have uplands without air, moors that are not health-giving, and a country life which is more arduous than a townsman's. I shivered again, for I seemed to have passed in a few hours from the open noon to a kind of dank twilight.

We passed the village and entered the lodge gates. Here there were trees again – little innocent new-planted firs, which flourished ill. Some large plane trees grew near the house, and there were thickets upon thickets of the ugly elderberry. Even in the half darkness I could see that the lawns were trim and the flower beds respectable for the season; doubtless Sibyl looked after the gardeners. The oblong whitewashed house, more like a barrack than ever, opened suddenly on my sight, and I experienced my first sense of comfort since I left Glenaicill. Here I should find warmth and company; and sure enough, the hall door was wide open, and in the great flood of light which poured from it Sibyl stood to welcome me.

She ran down the steps as I dismounted, and, with a word to the groom, caught my arm and drew me into the shadow. 'Oh, Henry, it was so good of you to come. You mustn't let Bob think that you know he is ill. We don't talk about it. I'll tell you afterwards. I want you to cheer him up. Now we must go in, for he is in the hall expecting you.'

While I stood blinking in the light, Ladlaw came forward with outstretched hand and his usual cheery greeting. I looked at him and saw nothing unusual in his appearance; a little drawn at the lips, perhaps, and heavy below the eyes, but still fresh-colored and healthy. It was Sibyl who showed change. She was very pale, her pretty eyes were deplorably mournful, and in place of her delightful shyness there were the self-confidence and composure of pain. I was honestly shocked, and as I dressed my heart was full of hard thoughts about Ladlaw. What could his illness mean? He seemed well and cheerful, while Sibyl was pale; and yet it was Sibyl who had written the postscript. As I warmed myself by the fire, I resolved that this particular family difficulty was my proper business.

———

THE Ladlaws were waiting for me in the drawing-room. I noticed something new and strange in Sibyl's demeanor. She looked to her husband with a motherly, protective air, while Ladlaw, who had been the extreme of masculine independence, seemed to cling to his wife with a curious appealing fidelity. In conversation he did little more than echo her words. Till dinner was announced he spoke of the weather, the shooting, and Mabel Clanroyden. Then he did a queer thing; for when I was about to offer my arm to Sibyl he forestalled me, and clutching her right arm with his left hand led the way to the dining room, leaving me to follow in some bewilderment.

I have rarely taken part in a more dismal meal. The House of More has a pretty Georgian paneling through most of the rooms, but in the dining room the walls are level and painted a dull stone color. Abraham offered up Isaac in a ghastly picture in front of me. Some photographs of the Quorn hung over the mantelpiece, and five or six drab ancestors filled up the remaining space. But one thing was new and startling. A great marble bust, a genuine antique, frowned on me from a pedestal. The head was in the late Roman style, clearly of some emperor, and in its commonplace environment the great brows, the massive neck, and the mysterious solemn lips had a surprising effect. I nodded toward the thing, and asked what it represented.

Ladlaw grunted something which I took for 'Justinian,' but he never raised his eyes from his plate. By accident I caught Sibyl's glance. She looked toward the bust, and laid a finger on her lips.

The meal grew more doleful as it advanced. Sibyl scarcely touched a dish, but her husband ate ravenously of everything. He was a strong, thickset man, with a square kindly face burned brown by the sun. Now he seemed to have suddenly coarsened. He gobbled with undignified haste, and his eye was extraordinarily vacant. A question made him start, and he would turn on me a face so strange and inert that I repented the interruption.

I asked him about the autumn's sport. He collected his wits with difficulty. He thought it had been good, on the whole, but he had shot badly. He had not been quite so fit as usual. No, he had had nobody staying with him. Sibyl had wanted to be alone. He was afraid the moor might have been undershot, but he would make a big day with keepers and farmers before the winter.

'Bob has done pretty well,' Sibyl said. 'He hasn't been out often, for the weather has been very bad here. You can have no idea, Henry, how horrible this moorland place of ours can be when it tries. It is one great sponge sometimes, with ugly red burns and mud to the ankles.'

'I don't think it's healthy,' said I.

Ladlaw lifted his face. 'Nor do I. I think it's intolerable, but I am so busy I can't get away.'

Once again I caught Sibyl's warning eye as I was about to question him on his business.

Clearly the man's brain had received a shock, and he was beginning to suffer from hallucinations. This could be the only explanation, for he had always led a temperate life. The distrait, wandering manner was the only sign of his malady, for otherwise he seemed normal and mediocre as ever. My heart grieved for Sibyl, alone with him in this wilderness.

Then he broke the silence. He lifted his head and looked nervously around till his eye fell on the Roman bust.

'Do you know that this countryside is the old Manann?' he said.

It was an odd turn to the conversation, but I was glad of a sign of intelligence. I answered that I had heard so.

'It's a queer name,' he said oracularly, 'but the thing it stood for was queerer, Manann, Manaw,' he repeated, rolling the words on his tongue. As he spoke, he glanced sharply, and, as it seemed to me, fearfully, at his left side.

The movement of his body made his napkin slip from his left knee and fall on the floor. It leaned against his leg, and he started from its touch as if he had been bitten by a snake. I have never seen a more sheer and transparent terror on a man's face. He got to his feet, his strong frame shaking like a rush. Sibyl ran round to his side, picked up the napkin and flung it on a sideboard. Then she stroked his hair as one would stroke a frightened horse. She called him by his old boy's name of Robin, and at her touch and voice he became quiet. But the particular course then in progress was removed, untasted.

In a few minutes he seemed to have forgotten his behavior, for he took up the former conversation. For a time he spoke well and briskly. 'You lawyers,' he said, 'understand only the dry framework of the past. You cannot conceive the rapture, which only the antiquary can feel, of constructing in every detail an old culture. Take this Manann. If I could explore the secret of these moors, I would write the world's greatest book. I would write of that prehistoric life when man was knit close to nature. I would describe the people who were brothers of the red earth and the red rock and the red streams of the hills. Oh, it would be horrible, but superb, tremendous! It would be more than a piece of history; it would be a new gospel, a new theory of life. It would kill materialism once and for all. Why, man, all the poets who have deified and personified nature would not do an eighth part of my work. I would show you the unknown, the hideous, shrieking mystery at the back of this simple nature. Men would see the profundity of the old crude faiths which they affect to despise. I would make a picture of our shaggy, sombre-eyed forefather, who heard strange things in the hill silences. I would show him brutal and terror-stricken, but wise, wise, God alone knows how wise! The Romans knew it, and they learned what they could from him, though he did not tell them much. But we have some of his blood in us, and we may go deeper. Manann! A queer land nowadays! I sometimes love it and sometimes hate it, but I always fear it. It is like that statue, inscrutable.'

I would have told him that he was talking mystical nonsense, but I had looked toward the bust, and my rudeness was checked on my lips. The moor might be a common piece of ugly waste land, but the statue was inscrutable, – of that there was no doubt. I hate your cruel heavy-mouthed Roman busts; to me they have none of the beauty of life, and little of the interest of art. But my eyes were fastened on this as they had never before looked on marble. The oppression of the heavy woodlands, the mystery of the silent moor, seemed to be caught and held in this face. It was the intangible mystery of culture on the verge of savagery – a cruel, lustful wisdom, and yet a kind of bitter austerity which laughed at the game of life and stood aloof. There was no weakness in the heavy-veined brow and slumbrous eyelids. It was the face of one who had conquered the world, and found it dust and ashes; one who had eaten of the tree of the knowledge of good and evil, and scorned human wisdom. And at the same time, it was the face of one who knew uncanny things, a man who was the intimate of the half-world and the dim background of life. Why on earth I should connect the Roman grandee* with the moorland parish of More I cannot say, but the fact remains that there was that in the face which I knew had haunted me through the woodlands and bogs of the place – a sleepless, dismal, incoherent melancholy.

'I bought that at Colenzo's,' Ladlaw said, 'because it took my fancy. It matches well with this place?'

I thought it matched very ill with his drab walls and Quorn photographs, but I held my peace.

'Do you know who it is?' he asked. 'It is the head of the greatest man the world has ever seen. You are a lawyer and know your Justinian.'

The Pandects are scarcely part of the daily work of a common-law barrister. I had not looked into them since I left college.

'I know that he married an actress,' I said, 'and was a sort of all-round genius. He made law, and fought battles, and had rows with the Church. A curious man! And wasn't there some story about his selling his soul to the devil, and getting law in exchange? Rather a poor bargain!'

I chattered away, sillily enough, to dispel the gloom of that dinner table. The result of my words was unhappy. Ladlaw gasped and caught at his left side, as if in pain. Sibyl, with tragic eyes, had been making signs to me to hold my peace. Now she ran round to her husband's side and comforted him like a child. As she passed me, she managed to whisper in my ear to talk to her only, and let her husband alone.

For the rest of dinner I obeyed my orders to the letter. Ladlaw ate his food in gloomy silence, while I spoke to Sibyl of our relatives and friends, of London, Glenaicill, and any random subject. The poor girl was dismally forgetful, and her eye would wander to her husband with

---

* I have identified the bust, which, when seen under other circumstances, had little power to affect me. It was a copy of the head of Justinian in the Tesci Museum at Venice, and several duplicates exist, dating apparently from the seventh century, and showing traces of Byzantine decadence in the scroll work on the hair. It is engraved in M. Delacroix's Byzantium, and, I think, in Windscheid's Pandektenlehrbuch.

wifely anxiety. I remember being suddenly overcome by the comic aspect of it all. Here were we three fools alone in the dank upland: one of us sick and nervous, talking out-of-the-way nonsense about Manann and Justinian, gobbling his food and getting scared at his napkin; another gravely anxious; and myself at my wits' end for a solution. It was a Mad Tea-Party with a vengeance: Sibyl the melancholy little Dormouse, and Ladlaw the incomprehensible Hatter. I laughed aloud, but checked myself when I caught my cousin's eye. It was really no case for finding humor. Ladlaw was very ill, and Sibyl's face was getting deplorably thin.

I welcomed the end of that meal with unmannerly joy, for I wanted to speak seriously with my host. Sibyl told the butler to have the lamps lighted in the library. Then she leaned over toward me and spoke low and rapidly: 'I want you to talk with Bob. I'm sure you can do him good. You'll have to be very patient with him, and very gentle. Oh, please try to find out what is wrong with him. He won't tell me, and I can only guess.'

The butler returned with word that the library was ready to receive us, and Sibyl rose to go. Ladlaw half rose, protesting, making the most curious feeble clutches to his side. His wife quieted him. 'Henry will look after you, dear,' she said. 'You are going into the library to smoke.' Then she slipped from the room, and we were left alone.

He caught my arm fiercely with his left hand, and his grip nearly made me cry out. As we walked down the hall, I could feel his arm twitching from the elbow to the shoulder. Clearly he was in pain, and I set it down to some form of cardiac affection, which might possibly issue in paralysis.

I settled him in the biggest armchair, and took one of his cigars. The library is the pleasantest room in the house, and at night, when a peat fire burned on the old hearth and the great red curtains were drawn, it used to be the place for comfort and good talk. Now I noticed changes. Ladlaw's bookshelves had been filled with the Proceedings of antiquarian societies and many light-hearted works on sport. But now the Badminton library had been cleared out of a shelf where it stood most convenient to the hand, and its place taken by an old Leyden reprint of Justinian. There were books on Byzantine subjects of which I never dreamed he had heard the names; there were volumes of history and speculation, all of a slightly bizarre kind; and to crown everything, there were several bulky medical works with gaudily colored plates. The old atmosphere of sport and travel had gone from the room with the medley of rods, whips, and gun cases which used to cumber the tables. Now the place was moderately tidy and somewhat learned, and I did not like it.

Ladlaw refused to smoke, and sat for a little while in silence. Then of his own accord he broke the tension.

'It was devilish good of you to come, Harry. This is a lonely place for a man who is a bit seedy.'

'I thought you might be alone,' I said, 'so I looked you up on my way down from Glenaicill. I'm sorry to find you feeling ill.'

'Do you notice it?' he asked sharply.

'It's tolerably patent,' I said. 'Have you seen a doctor?'

He said something uncomplimentary about doctors, and kept looking at me with his curious dull eyes.

I remarked the strange posture in which he sat, his head screwed round to his right shoulder, and his whole body a protest against something at his left hand.

'It looks like a heart,' I said. 'You seem to have pains in your left side.'

Again a spasm of fear. I went over to him and stood at the back of his chair.

'Now for goodness' sake, my dear fellow, tell me what is wrong. You're scaring Sibyl to death. It's lonely work for the poor girl, and I wish you would let me help you.'

He was lying back in his chair now, with his eyes half shut, and shivering like a frightened colt. The extraordinary change in one who had been the strongest of the strong kept me from realizing his gravity. I put a hand on his shoulder, but he flung it off.

'For God's sake, sit down!' he said hoarsely. 'I'm going to tell you, but I'll never make you understand.'

I sat down promptly opposite him.

'It's the devil,' he said very solemnly.

I am afraid that I was rude enough to laugh. He took no notice, but sat, with the same tense, miserable air, staring over my head.

'Right,' said I. 'Then it is the devil. It's a new complaint, so it's as well I did not bring a doctor. How does it affect you?'

He made the old impotent clutch at the air with his left hand. I had the sense to become grave at once. Clearly this was some serious mental affection, some hallucination born of physical pain.

Then he began to talk in a low voice, very rapidly, with his head bent forward like a hunted animal's. I am not going to set down what he told me in his own words, for they were incoherent often, and there was much repetition. But I am going to write the gist of the odd story which took my sleep away on that autumn night, with such explanations and additions I think needful. The fire died down, the wind arose, the hour grew late, and still he went on in his mumbling recitative. I forgot to smoke, forgot my comfort – everything but the odd figure of my friend and his inconceivable romance. And the night before I had been in cheerful Glenaicill!

He had returned to the House of More, he said, in the latter part of May, and shortly after he fell ill. It was a trifling sickness, – influenza or something, – but he had never quite recovered. The rainy weather of June depressed him, and the extreme heat of July made him listless and weary. A kind of insistent sleepiness hung over him, and he suffered much from nightmare. Toward the end of July his former health returned, but he was haunted with a curious oppression. He seemed to himself to have lost the art of being alone. There was a perpetual sound in his left ear, a kind of moving and rustling at his left side, which never left him by night or day. In addition, he had become the prey of nerves and an insensate dread of the unknown.

Ladlaw, as I have explained, was a commonplace man, with fair talents, a mediocre culture, honest instincts, and the beliefs and incredulities of his class. On abstract grounds, I should have declared him an unlikely man to be the victim of an hallucination. He had a kind of dull bourgeois rationalism, which used to find reasons for all things in heaven and earth. At first he controlled his dread with proverbs. He told himself it was the sequel of his illness or the light-headedness of summer heat on the moors. But it soon outgrew his comfort. It became a living second presence, an *alter ego* which dogged his footsteps. He grew acutely afraid of it. He dared not be alone for a moment, and clung to Sibyl's company despairingly. She went off for a week's visit in the beginning of August, and he endured for seven days the tortures of the lost. The malady advanced upon him with swift steps. The presence became more real daily. In the early dawning, in the twilight, and in the first hour of the morning it seemed at times to take a visible bodily form. A kind of amorphous featureless shadow would run from his side into the darkness, and he would sit palsied with terror. Sometimes, in lonely places, his footsteps sounded double, and something would brush elbows with him. Human society alone exorcised it. With Sibyl at his side he was happy; but as soon as she left him, the thing came slinking back from the unknown to watch by him. Company might have saved him, but joined to his affliction was a crazy dread of his fellows. He would not leave his moorland home, but must bear his burden alone among the wild streams and mosses of that dismal place.

The 12th came, and he shot wretchedly, for his nerve had gone to pieces. He stood exhaustion badly, and became a dweller about the doors. But with this bodily inertness came an extraordinary intellectual revival. He read widely in a blundering way, and he speculated unceasingly. It was characteristic of the man that as soon as he left the paths of the prosaic he should seek his supernatural in a very concrete form. He assumed that he was haunted by the devil – the visible personal devil in whom our fathers believed. He waited hourly for the shape at his side to speak, but no words came. The Accuser of the Brethren in all but tangible form was his ever present companion. He felt, he declared, the spirit of old evil entering subtly into his blood. He sold his soul many times over, and yet there was no possibility of resistance. It was a Visitation more undeserved than Job's, and a thousandfold more awful.

For a week or more he was tortured with a kind of religious mania. When a man of a healthy secular mind finds himself adrift on the terrible ocean of religious troubles he is peculiarly helpless, for he has not the most rudimentary knowledge of the winds and tides. It was useless to call up his old carelessness; he had suddenly dropped into a new world where old proverbs did not apply. And all the while, mind you, there was the shrinking terror of it – an intellect all alive to the torture and the most unceasing physical fear. For a little he was on the far edge of idiocy.

Then by accident it took a new form. While sitting with Sibyl one day in the library, he began listlessly to turn over the leaves of an old book. He read a few pages, and found the hint to a story like his own. It was some French Life of Justinian, one of the unscholarly productions of last century, made up of stories from Procopius and tags of Roman law. Here was his own case written down in black and white; and the man had been a king of kings. This was a new comfort, and for a little – strange though it may seem – he took a sort of pride in his affliction. He worshiped the great Emperor, and read every scrap he could find on him, not excepting the Pandects and the Digest. He sent for the bust in the dining room, paying a fabulous price. Then he settled himself to study his imperial prototype, and the study became an idolatry. As I have said, Ladlaw was a man of ordinary talents, and certainly of meagre imaginative power. And yet from the lies of the Secret History and the crudities of German legalists he had constructed a marvelous portrait of a man. Sitting there in the half-lighted room, he drew the picture: the quiet cold man with his inheritance of Dacian mysticism, holding the great world in fee, giving it law and religion, fighting its wars, building its churches, and yet all the while intent upon his own private work of making his peace with his soul – the churchman and warrior whom all the world worshiped, and yet one going through life with his lip quivering. He Watched by the Threshold ever at the left side. Sometimes at night, in the great Brazen Palace, warders heard the Emperor walking in the dark corridors, alone, and yet not alone; for once, when a servant entered with a lamp, he saw his master with a face as of another world, and something beside him which had no face or shape, but which he knew to be that hoary Evil which is older than the stars.

Crazy nonsense! I had to rub my eyes to assure myself that I was not sleeping. No! There was my friend with his suffering face, and it was the library of More.

And then he spoke of Theodora, – actress, harlot, *dévote*, empress. For him the lady was but another part of the uttermost horror, a form of the shapeless thing at his side. I felt myself falling under the fascination. I have no nerves and little imagination, but in a flash I seemed to realize something of that awful featureless face, crouching ever at a man's hand, till darkness and loneliness come, and it rises to its mastery. I shivered as I looked at the man in the chair before me. These dull eyes of his were looking upon things I could not see, and I saw their terror. I realized that it was grim earnest for him. Nonsense or no, some devilish fancy had usurped the place of his sanity, and he was being slowly broken upon the wheel. And then, when his left hand twitched, I almost cried out. I had thought it comic before; now it seemed the last proof of tragedy.

He stopped, and I got up with loose knees and went to the window. Better the black night than the intangible horror within. I flung up the sash and looked out across the moor. There was no light; nothing but an inky darkness and the uncanny rustle of elder bushes. The sound chilled me, and I closed the window.

'The land is the old Manann,' Ladlaw was saying. 'We are beyond the pale here. Do you hear the wind?'

I forced myself back into sanity and looked at my watch. It was nearly one o'clock.

'What ghastly idiots we are!' I said. 'I am off to bed.'

Ladlaw looked at me helplessly. 'For God's sake, don't leave me alone!' he moaned. 'Get Sibyl.'

We went together back to the hall, while he kept the same feverish grasp on my arm. Some one was sleeping in a chair by the hall fire, and to my distress I recognized my hostess. The poor child must have been sadly wearied. She came forward with her anxious face.

'I'm afraid Bob has kept you very late, Henry,' she said. 'I hope you will sleep well. Breakfast at nine, you know.' And then I left them.

OVER my bed there was a little picture, a reproduction of some Italian work, of Christ and the Demoniac. Some impulse made me hold my candle up to it. The madman's face was torn with passion and suffering, and his eye had the pained furtive expression which I had come to know. And by his left side there was a dim shape crouching.

I got into bed hastily, but not to sleep. I felt that my reason must be going. I had been pitchforked from our clear and cheerful modern life into the mists of old superstition. Old tragic stories of my Calvinist upbringing returned to haunt me. The man dwelt in by a devil was no new fancy, but I believed that science had docketed and analyzed and explained the devil out of the world. I remembered my dabblings in the occult before I settled down to law – the story of Donisarius, the monk of Padua, the unholy legend of the Face of Proserpine, the tales of *succubi* and *incubi*, the Leannain Sith and the Hidden Presence. But here was something stranger still. I had stumbled upon that very possession which fifteen hundred years ago had made the monks of New Rome tremble and cross themselves. Some devilish occult force, lingering through the ages, had come to life after a long sleep. God knows what earthly connection there was between the splendid Emperor of the World and my prosaic friend, or between the glittering shores of the Bosporus and this moorland parish! But the land was the old Manann! The spirit may have lingered in the earth and air, a deadly legacy from Pict and Roman. I had felt the uncanniness of the place; I had augured ill of it from the first. And then in sheer disgust I rose and splashed my face with cold water.

I lay down again, laughing miserably at my credulity. That I, the sober and rational, should believe in this crazy fable was too palpably absurd. I would steel my mind resolutely against such harebrained theories. It was a mere bodily ailment – liver out of order, weak heart, bad circulation, or something of that sort. At the worst it might be some affection of the brain, to be treated by a specialist. I vowed to myself that next morning the best doctor in Edinburgh should be brought to More.

The worst of it was that my duty compelled me to stand my ground. I foresaw the few remaining weeks of my holiday blighted. I should be tied to this moorland prison, a sort of keeper and nurse in one, tormented by silly fancies. It was a charming prospect, and the thought of Glenaicill and the woodcock made me bitter against Ladlaw. But there was no way out of it. I might do Ladlaw good, and I could not have Sibyl worn to death by his vagaries.

My ill nature comforted me, and I forgot the horror of the thing in its vexation. After that I think I fell asleep and dozed uneasily till morning. When I woke I was in a better frame of mind. The early sun had worked wonders with the moorland. The low hills stood out fresh-colored and clear against a pale October sky; the elders sparkled with frost; the raw film of morn was rising from the little loch in tiny clouds. It was a cold, rousing day, and I dressed in good spirits and went down to breakfast.

I found Ladlaw looking ruddy and well; very different from the broken man I remembered of the night before. We were alone, for Sibyl was breakfasting in bed. I remarked on his ravenous appetite, and he smiled cheerily. He made two jokes during the meal; he laughed often, and I began to forget the events of the previous day. It seemed to me that I might still flee from More with a clear conscience. He had forgotten about his illness. When I touched distantly upon the matter he showed a blank face.

It might be that the affection had passed; on the other hand, it might return to him at the darkening. I had no means to decide. His manner was still a trifle distrait and peculiar, and I did not like the dullness in his eye. At any rate, I should spend the day in his company, and the evening would decide the question.

I proposed shooting, which he promptly vetoed. He was no good at walking, he said, and the birds were wild. This seriously limited the possible occupations. Fishing there was none, and hill-climbing was out of the question. He proposed a game at billiards, and I pointed to the glory of the morning. It would have been sacrilege to waste such sunshine in knocking balls about. Finally we agreed to drive somewhere and have lunch, and he ordered the dogcart.

In spite of all forebodings I enjoyed the day. We drove in the opposite direction from the woodland parts, right away across the moor to the coal country beyond. We lunched at the little mining town of Borrowmuir, in a small and noisy public house. The roads made bad going, the country was far from pretty, and yet the drive did not bore me. Ladlaw talked incessantly – talked as I had never heard man talk before. There was something indescribable in all he said, a different point of view, a lost groove of thought, a kind of innocence and archaic shrewdness in one. I can only give you a hint of it, by saying that it was like the mind of an early ancestor placed suddenly among modern surroundings. It was wise with a remote wisdom, and silly (now and then) with a quite antique and distant silliness.

I will give instances of both. He provided me with a theory of certain early fortifications, which must be true, which commends itself to the mind with overwhelming conviction, and yet which is so out of the way of common speculation that no man could have guessed it. I do not propose to set down the details, for I am working at it on my own account. Again, he told me the story of an old marriage custom, which till recently survived in this district – told it with full circumstantial detail and constant allusions to other customs which he could not possibly have known of. Now for the other side. He explained why well water is in winter warmer than a running stream, and this was his explanation: at the antipodes our winter is summer, consequently, the water of a well which comes through from the other side of the earth must be warm in winter and cold in summer, since in our summer it is winter there. You perceive what this is. It is no mere silliness, but a genuine effort of an early mind, which had just grasped the fact of the antipodes, to use it in explanation.

Gradually I was forced to the belief that it was not Ladlaw who was talking to me, but something speaking through him, something at once wiser and simpler. My old fear of the devil began to depart. This spirit, the exhalation, whatever it was, was ingenuous in its way, at least in its daylight aspect. For a moment I had an idea that it was a real reflex of Byzantine thought, and that by cross-examining I might make marvelous discoveries. The ardor of the scholar began to rise in me, and I asked a question about that much-debated point, the legal status of the *apocrisiarii*. To my vexation he gave no response. Clearly the intelligence of this familiar had its limits.

It was about three in the afternoon, and we had gone half of our homeward journey, when signs of the old terror began to appear. I was driving, and Ladlaw sat on my left. I noticed him growing nervous and silent, shivering at the flick of the whip, and turning halfway round toward me. Then he asked me to change places, and I had the unpleasant work of driving from the wrong side. After that I do not think he spoke once till we arrived at More, but sat huddled together, with the driving rug almost up to his chin – an eccentric figure of a man.

I foresaw another such night as the last, and I confess my heart sank. I had no stomach for more mysteries, and somehow with the approach of twilight the confidence of the day departed. The thing appeared in darker colors, and I found it in my mind to turn coward. Sibyl alone deterred me. I could not bear to think of her alone with this demented being. I remembered her shy timidity, her innocence. It was monstrous that the poor thing should be called on thus to fight alone with phantoms.

When we came to the House it was almost sunset. Ladlaw got out very carefully on the right side, and for a second stood by the horse. The sun was making our shadows long, and as I stood beyond him it seemed for a moment that his shadow was double. It may have been mere fancy, for I had not time to look twice. He was standing, as I have said, with his left side next the horse. Suddenly the harmless elderly cob fell into a very panic of fright, reared upright, and all but succeeded in killing its master. I was in time to pluck Ladlaw from under its feet, but the beast had become perfectly unmanageable, and we left a groom struggling to quiet it.

In the hall the butler gave me a telegram. It was from my clerk, summoning me back at once to an important consultation.

───────────

HERE was a prompt removal of my scruples. There could be no question of my remaining, for the case was one of the first importance, which I had feared might break off my holiday. The consultation fell in vacation time to meet the convenience of certain people who were going abroad, and there was the most instant demand for my presence. I must go, and at once; and, as I hunted in the time-table, I found that in three hours' time a night train for the south would pass Borrowmuir which might be stopped by special wire.

But I had no pleasure in my freedom. I was in despair about Sibyl, and I hated myself for my cowardly relief. The dreary dining room, the sinister bust, and Ladlaw crouching and quivering – the recollection, now that escape was before me, came back on my mind with the terror of a nightmare. My first thought was to persuade the Ladlaws to come away with me. I found them both in the drawing-room – Sibyl very fragile and pale, and her husband sitting as usual like a frightened child in the shadow of her skirts. A sight of him was enough to dispel my hope. The man was fatally ill, mentally, bodily; and who was I to attempt to minister to a mind diseased?

But Sibyl – she might be saved from the martyrdom. The servants would take care of him, and, if need be, a doctor might be got from Edinburgh to live in the house. So while he sat with vacant eyes staring into the twilight, I tried to persuade Sibyl to think of herself. I am frankly a sun worshiper. I have no taste for arduous duty, and the quixotic is my abhorrence. I labored to bring my cousin to this frame of mind. I told her that her first duty was to herself, and that this vigil of hers was beyond human endurance. But she had no ears for my arguments.

'While Bob is ill I must stay with him,' she said always in answer, and then she thanked me for my visit, till I felt a brute and a coward. I strove to quiet my conscience, but it told me always that I was fleeing from my duty; and then, when I was on the brink of a nobler resolution, a sudden overmastering terror would take hold of me, and I would listen hysterically for the sound of the dogcart on the gravel.

At last it came, and in a sort of fever I tried to say the conventional farewells. I shook hands with Ladlaw, and when I dropped his hand it fell numbly on his knee. Then I took my leave, muttering hoarse nonsense about having had a 'charming visit,' and 'hoping soon to see them both in town.' As I backed to the door, I knocked over a lamp on a small table. It crashed on the floor and went out, and at the sound Ladlaw gave a curious childish cry. I turned like a coward, and ran across the hall to the front door, and scrambled into the dogcart.

The groom would have driven me sedately through the park, but I must have speed or go mad. I took the reins from him and put the horse into a canter. We swung through the gates and out into the moor road, for I could have no peace till the ghoulish elder world was exchanged for the homely ugliness of civilization. Once only I looked back, and there against the sky line, with a solitary lit window, the House of More stood lonely in the red desert.

The Grove of Ashtaroth

WE were sitting around the camp fire, some thirty miles north of a place called Taqui, when Lawson announced his intention of finding a home. He had spoken little the last day or two, and I had guessed that he had struck a vein of private reflection. I thought it might be a new mine or irrigation scheme, and I was surprised to find that it was a country house.

'I don't think I shall go back to England,' he said, kicking a sputtering log into place. 'I don't see why I should. For business purposes I am far more useful to the firm in South Africa than in Throgmorton Street. I have no relations left except a third cousin, and I have never cared a rush for living in town. That beastly house of mine in Hill Street will fetch what I gave for it, – Isaacson cabled about it the other day, offering for furniture and all. I don't want to go into Parliament, and I hate shooting little birds and tame deer. I am one of those fellows who are born Colonial at heart, and I don't see why I shouldn't arrange my life as I please. Besides, for ten years I have been falling in love with this country, and now I am up to the neck.'

He flung himself back in the camp-chair till the canvas creaked, and looked at me below his eyelids. I remember glancing at the lines of him, and thinking what a fine make of a man he was. In his untanned, field-boots, breeches, and grey shirt he looked the born wilderness-hunter, though less than two months before he had been driving down to the City every morning in the sombre regimentals of his class. Being a fair man, he was gloriously tanned, and there was a clear line at his shirt-collar to mark the limits of his sunburn. I had first known him years ago, when he was a broker's clerk working on half commission. Then he had gone to South Africa, and soon I heard he was a partner in a mining house which was doing wonders with some gold areas in the North. The next step was his return to London as the new millionaire – young, good-looking, wholesome in mind and body, and much sought after by the mothers of marriageable girls. We played polo together, and hunted a little in the season, but there were signs

109

that he did not propose to become the conventional English gentleman. He refused to buy a place in the country, though half the Homes of England were at his disposal. He was a very busy man, he declared, and had not time to be a squire. Besides, every few months he used to rush out to South Africa. I saw that he was restless, for he was always badgering me to go big-game hunting with him in some remote part of the earth. There was that in his eyes, too, which marked him out from the ordinary blonde type of our countrymen. They were large and brown and mysterious, and the light of another race was in their odd depths.

To hint such a thing would have meant a breach of friendship, for Lawson was very proud of his birth. When he first made his fortune he had gone to the Heralds to discover his family, and those obliging gentlemen had provided a pedigree. It appeared that he was a scion of the house of Lowson or Lowieson, an ancient and rather disreputable clan on the Scottish side of the Border. He took a shooting in Teviotdale on the strength of it, and used to commit lengthy Border ballads to memory. But I had known his father, a financial journalist who never quite succeeded, and I had heard of a grandfather who sold antiques in a back street at Brighton. The latter, I think, had not changed his name, and still frequented the synagogue. The father was a progressive Christian, and the mother had been a blonde Saxon from the Midlands. In my mind there was no doubt, as I caught Lawson's heavy-lidded eyes fixed on me. My friend was of a more ancient race than the Lowsons of the Border.

'Where are you thinking of looking for your house?' I asked. 'In Natal or in the Cape Peninsula? You might get the Fishers' place if you paid a price.'

'The Fishers' place be hanged!' he said crossly. 'I don't want any stuccoed overgrown Dutch farm. I might as well be at Roehampton as in the Cape.'

He got up and walked to the far side of the fire, where a lane ran down through thornscrub to a gully of the hills The moon was silvering the bush of the plains, forty miles off and three thousand feet below us.

'I am going to live somewhere hereabouts,' he answered at last.

I whistled. 'Then you've got to put your hand in your pocket, old man. You'll have to make everything, including a map of the countryside.'

'I know,' he said; 'that's where the fun comes in. Hang it all, why shouldn't I indulge my fancy? I'm uncommonly well off, and I haven't chick or child to leave it to. Supposing I'm a hundred miles from a railhead, what about it? I'll make a motor-road and fix up a telephone. I'll grow most of my supplies, and start a colony to provide labour. When you come and stay with me, you'll get the best food and drink on earth, and sport that will make your mouth water. I'll put Lochleven trout in these streams – at 6000 feet you can do anything. We'll have a pack of hounds, too, and we can drive pig in the woods, and if we want big game there are the Mangwe flats at our feet. I tell you I'll make such a country-house as nobody ever dreamed of. A man will come plumb out of stark savagery into lawns and rose-gardens.' Lawson flung himself into his chair again and smiled dreamily at the fire.

'But why here, of all places?' I persisted. I was not feeling very well and did not care for the country.

'I can't quite explain. I think it's the sort of land I have always been looking for. I always fancied a house on a green plateau in a decent climate looking down on the tropics. I like heat and colour, you know, but I like hills too, and greenery, and the things that bring back Scotland. Give me a cross between Teviotdale and the Orinoco, and, by Gad! I think I've got it here.'

I watched my friend curiously, as with bright eyes and eager voice he talked of his new fad. The two races were very clear in him – the one desiring gorgeousness, the other athirst for the soothing spaces of the North. He began to plan out the house. He would get Adamson to design it, and it was to grow out of the landscape like a stone on the hillside. There would be wide verandahs and cool halls, but great fireplaces against winter time. It would all be very simple and fresh – 'clean as morning' was his odd phrase; but then another idea supervened, and he talked of bringing the Tintorets from Hill Street. 'I want it to be a civilised house, you know. No silly luxury, but the best pictures and china and books … I'll have all the furniture made after the old plain English models out of native woods. I don't want second-hand sticks in a new country. Yes, by Jove, the Tintorets are a great idea, and all those Ming pots I bought. I had meant to sell them, but I'll have them out here.'

He talked for a good hour of what he would do, and his dream grew richer as he talked, till by the time we went to bed he had sketched something liker a palace than a country-house. Lawson was by no means a luxurious man. At present he was well content with a Wolseley valise, and shaved cheerfully out of a tin mug. It struck me as odd that a man so simple in his habits should have so sumptuous a taste in bric-à-brac. I told myself, as I turned in, that the Saxon mother from the Midlands had done little to dilute the strong wine of the East.

It drizzled next morning when we inspanned, and I mounted my horse in a bad temper. I had some fever on me, I think, and I hated this lush yet frigid table-land, where all the winds on earth lay in wait for one's marrow. Lawson was, as usual, in great spirits. We were not hunting, but shifting our hunting-ground, so all morning we travelled fast to the north along the rim of the uplands.

At midday it cleared, and the afternoon was a pageant of pure colour. The wind sank to a low breeze; the sun lit the infinite green spaces, and kindled the wet forest to a jewelled coronal. Lawson gaspingly admired it all, as he cantered bareheaded up a bracken-clad slope. 'God's country,' he said twenty times. 'I've found it.' Take a piece of Saxon downland; put a stream in every hollow and a patch of wood; and at the edge, where the cliffs at home would fall to the sea, put a cloak of forest muffling the scarp and dropping thousands of feet to the blue plains. Take the diamond air of the Görnergrat, and the riot of colour which you get by a West Highland lochside in late September. Put flowers everywhere, the things we grow in hothouses, geraniums like sun-shades and arums like trumpets. That will give you a notion of the countryside we were in. I began to see that after all it was out of the common.

And just before sunset we came over a ridge and found something better. It was a shallow glen, half a mile wide, down which ran a blue-grey stream in linns like the Spean, till at the edge of the plateau it leaped into the dim forest in a snowy cascade. The opposite side ran up in gentle slopes to a rocky knoll, from which the eye had a noble prospect of the plains. All down the glen were little copses, half moons of green edging some silvery shore of the burn, or delicate clusters of tall trees nodding on the hill brow. The place so satisfied the eye that for the sheer wonder of its perfection we stopped and stared in silence for many minutes.

Then 'The House,' I said, and Lawson replied softly, 'The House!'

We rode slowly into the glen in the mulberry gloaming. Our transport waggons were half an hour behind, so we had time to explore. Lawson dismounted and plucked handfuls of flowers from the water-meadows. He was singing to himself all the time – an old French catch about *Cadet Rousselle* and his *trois maisons*.

'Who owns it?' I asked.

'My firm, as like as not. We have miles of land about here. But whoever the man is, he has got to sell. Here I build my tabernacle, old man. Here, and nowhere else!'

In the very centre of the glen, in a loop of the stream, was one copse which even in that half light struck me as different from the others. It was of tall, slim, fairy-like trees, the kind of wood the monks painted in old missals. No, I rejected the thought. It was no Christian wood. It was not a copse, but a 'grove,' – one such as Diana may have flitted through in the moonlight. It was small, forty or fifty yards in diameter, and there was a dark something at the heart of it which for a second I thought was a house.

We turned between the slender trees, and – was it fancy? – an odd tremor went through me. I felt as if I were penetrating the *temenos* of some strange and lovely divinity, the goddess of this pleasant vale. There was a spell in the air, it seemed, and an odd dead silence.

Suddenly my horse started at a flutter of light wings. A flock of doves rose from the branches, and I saw the burnished green of their plumes against the opal sky. Lawson did not seem to notice them. I saw his keen eyes staring at the centre of the grove and what stood there.

It was a little conical tower, ancient and lichened, but, so far as I could judge, quite flawless. You know the famous, Conical Temple at Zimbabwe, of which prints are in every guide-book. This was of the same type, but a thousand-fold more perfect. It stood about thirty feet high, of solid masonry, without door or window or cranny, as shapely as when it first came from the hands of the old builders. Again I had the sense of breaking in on a sanctuary. What right had I, a common vulgar modern, to be looking at this fair thing, among these delicate trees, which some white goddess had once taken for her shrine?

Lawson broke in on my absorption. 'Let's get out of this,' he said hoarsely, and he took my horse's bridle (he had left his own beast at the edge) and led him back to the open. But I noticed that his eyes were always turning back, and that his hand trembled.

'That settles it,' I said after supper. 'What do you want with your mediaeval Venetians and your Chinese pots now? You will have the finest antique in the world in your garden – a temple as old as time, and in a land which they say has no history. You had the right inspiration this time.'

I think I have said that Lawson had hungry eyes. In his enthusiasm they used to glow and brighten; but now, as he sat looking down at the olive shades of the glen, they seemed ravenous in their fire. He had hardly spoken a word since we left the wood.

'Where can I read about those things?' he asked, and I gave him the names of books.

Then, an hour later, he asked me who were the builders. I told him the little I knew about Phoenician and Sabaean wanderings, and the ritual of Sidon and Tyre. He repeated some names to himself and went soon to bed.

As I turned in, I had one last look over the glen, which lay ivory and black in the moon. I seemed to hear a faint echo of wings, and to see over the little grove a cloud of light visitants. 'The Doves of Ashtaroth have come back,' I said to myself. 'It is a good omen. They accept the new tenant.' But as I fell asleep I had a sudden thought that I was saying something rather terrible.

THREE years later, pretty nearly to a day, I came back to see what Lawson had made of his hobby. He had bidden me often to Welgevonden, as he chose to call it – though I do not know why he should have fixed a Dutch name to a countryside where Boer never trod. At the last there had been some confusion about dates, and I wired the time of my arrival, and set off without an answer. A motor met me at the queer little wayside station of Taqui, and after many miles on a doubtful highway I came to the gates of the park, and a road on which it was a delight to move. Three years had wrought little difference in the landscape. Lawson had done some planting, – conifers and flowering shrubs and such-like – but wisely he had resolved that Nature had for the most part forestalled him. All the same, he must have spent a mint of money. The drive could not have been beaten in England, and fringes of mown turf on either hand had been pared out of the lush meadows. When we came over the edge of the hill and looked down on the secret glen, I could not repress a cry of pleasure. The house stood on the farther ridge, the view-point of the whole neighbourhood; and its brown timbers and white rough-cast walls melted into the hillside as if it had been there from the beginning of things. The vale below was ordered in lawns and gardens. A blue lake received the rapids of the stream, and its banks were a maze of green shades and glorious masses of blossom. I noticed, too, that the little grove we had explored on our first visit stood alone in a big stretch of lawn, so that its perfection might be clearly seen. Lawson had excellent taste, or he had had the best advice.

The butler told me that his master was expected home shortly, and took me into the library for tea. Lawson had left his Tintorets and Ming pots at home after all. It was a long, low room, panelled in teak half-way up the walls, and the shelves held a multitude of fine bindings. There were good rugs on the parquet floor, but no ornaments anywhere, save three. On the carved mantelpiece stood two of the old soapstone birds which they used to find at Zimbabwe, and between, on an ebony stand, a half moon of alabaster, curiously carved with zodiacal figures. My host had altered his scheme of furnishing, but I approved the change.

He came in about half-past six, after I had consumed two cigars and all but fallen asleep. Three years make a difference in most men, but I was not prepared for the change in Lawson. For one thing, he had grown fat. In place of the lean young man I had known, I saw a heavy, flaccid being, who shuffled in his gait, and seemed tired and listless. His sunburn had gone, and his face was as pasty as a city clerk's. He had been walking, and wore shapeless flannel clothes, which hung loose even on his enlarged figure. And the worst of it was, that he did not seem over-pleased to see me. He murmured something about my journey, and then flung himself into an arm-chair and looked out of the window.

I asked him if he had been ill.

'Ill! No!' he said crossly. 'Nothing of the kind. I'm perfectly well.'

'You don't look as fit as this place should make you. What do you do with yourself? Is the shooting as good as you hoped?'

He did not answer, but I thought of heard him mutter something like 'shooting be damned.'

Then I tried the subject of the house. I praised it extravagantly, but with conviction. 'There can be no place like it in the world,' I said.

He turned his eyes on me at last, and I saw that they were as deep and restless as ever. With his pallid face they made him look curiously Semitic. I had been right in my theory about his ancestry.

'Yes,' he said slowly, 'there is no place like it – in the world.'

Then he pulled himself to his feet. 'I'm going to change,' he said. 'Dinner is at eight. Ring for Travers, and he'll show you your room.'

I dressed in a noble bedroom, with an outlook over the garden-vale and the escarpment to the far line of the plains, now blue and saffron in the sunset. I dressed in an ill temper, for I was seriously offended with Lawson, and also seriously alarmed. He was either very unwell or going out of his mind, and it was clear, too, that he would resent any anxiety on his account. I ransacked my memory for rumours, but found none. I had heard nothing of him except that he had been extraordinarily successful in his speculations, and that from his hill-top he directed his firm's operations with uncommon skill. If Lawson was sick or mad, nobody knew of it.

Dinner was a trying ceremony. Lawson, who used to be rather particular in his dress, appeared in a kind of smoking suit with a flannel collar. He spoke scarcely a word to me, but cursed the servants with a brutality which left me aghast. A wretched footman in his nervousness spilt some sauce over his sleeve. Lawson dashed the dish from his hand, and volleyed abuse with a sort of epileptic fury. Also he, who had been the most abstemious of men, swallowed disgusting quantities of champagne and old brandy.

He had given up smoking, and half an hour after we left the dining-room he announced his intention of going to bed. I watched him as he waddled upstairs with a feeling of angry bewilderment. Then I went to the library and lit a pipe. I would leave first thing in the morning – on that I was determined. But as I sat gazing at the moon of alabaster and the soapstone birds my anger evaporated, and concern took its place. I remembered what a fine fellow Lawson had been, what good times we had had together. I remembered especially that evening when we had found this valley and given rein to our fancies. What horrid alchemy in the place had turned a gentleman into a brute? I thought of drink and drugs and madness and insomnia, but I could fit none of them into my conception of my friend. I did not consciously rescind my resolve to depart, but I had a notion that I would not act on it.

The sleepy butler met me as I went to bed. 'Mr. Lawson's room is at the end of your corridor, sir,' he said. 'He don't sleep over well, so you may hear him stirring in the night. At what hour would you like breakfast, sir? Mr. Lawson mostly has his in bed.'

My room opened from the great corridor, which ran the full length of the front of the house. So far as I could make out, Lawson was three rooms off, a vacant bedroom and his servant's room being between us. I felt tired and cross, and tumbled into bed as fast as possible. Usually I sleep well, but now I was soon conscious that my drowsiness was wearing off and that I was in for a restless night. I got up and laved my face, turned the pillows, thought of sheep coming over a hill and clouds crossing the sky; but none of the old devices were any use. After about an hour of make-believe I surrendered myself to facts, and, lying on my back, stared at the white ceiling and the patches of moonshine on the walls.

It certainly was an amazing night. I got up, put on a dressing-gown, and drew a chair to the window. The moon was almost at its full, and the whole plateau swam in a radiance of ivory and silver. The banks of the stream were black, but the lake had a great belt of light athwart it, which made it seem like a horizon, and the rim of land beyond it like a contorted cloud. Far to the right I saw the delicate outlines of the little wood which I had come to think of as the Grove of Ashtaroth. I listened. There was not a sound in the air. The land seemed to sleep peacefully beneath the moon, and yet I had a sense that the peace was an illusion. The place was feverishly restless.

I could have given no reason for my impression, but there it was. Something was stirring in the wide moonlit landscape under its deep mask of silence. I felt as I had felt on the evening three years ago when I had ridden into the grove. I did not think that the influence, whatever it was, was maleficent. I only knew that it was very strange, and kept me wakeful.

By-and-by I bethought me of a book. There was no lamp in the corridor save the moon, but the whole house was bright as I slipped down the great staircase and over the hall to the library. I switched on the lights and then switched them off. They seemed a profanation, and I did not need them.

I found a French novel, but the place held me and I stayed. I sat down in an arm-chair before the fireplace and the stone birds. Very odd those gawky things, like prehistoric Great Auks, looked in the moonlight. I remember that the alabaster moon shimmered like translucent pearl, and I fell to wondering about its history. Had the old Sabaeans used such a jewel in their rites in the Grove of Ashtaroth?

Then I heard footsteps pass the window. A great house like this would have a watchman, but these quick shuffling footsteps were surely not the dull plod of a servant. They passed on to the grass and died away. I began to think of getting back to my room.

In the corridor I noticed that Lawson's door was ajar, and that a light had been left burning. I had the unpardonable curiosity to peep in. The room was empty, and the bed had not been slept in. Now I knew whose were the footsteps outside the library window.

I lit a reading-lamp and tried to interest myself in 'La Cruelle Enigme.' But my wits were restless, and I could not keep my eyes on the page. I flung the book aside and sat down again by the window. The feeling came over me that I was sitting in a box at some play. The glen was a huge stage, and at any moment the players might appear on it. My attention was strung as high as if I had been waiting for the advent of some world-famous actress. But nothing came. Only the shadows shifted and lengthened as the moon moved across the sky.

Then quite suddenly the restlessness left me, and at the same moment the silence was broken by the crow of a cock and the rustling of trees in a light wind. I felt very sleepy, and was turning to bed when again I heard footsteps without. From the window I could see a figure moving across the garden towards the house. It was Lawson, got up in the sort of towel dressing-gown that one wears on board ship. He was walking slowly and painfully, as if very weary. I did not see his face, but the man's whole air was that of extreme fatigue and dejection.

I tumbled into bed and slept profoundly till long after daylight.

THE man who valeted me was Lawson's own servant. As he was laying out my clothes I asked after the health of his master, and was told that he had slept ill and would not rise till late. Then the man, an anxious-faced Englishman, gave me some information on his own account. Mr. Lawson was having one of his bad turns. It would pass away in a day or two, but till it had gone he was fit for nothing. He advised me to see Mr. Jobson, the factor, who would look to my entertainment in his master's absence.

Jobson arrived before luncheon, and the sight of him was the first satisfactory thing about Welgevonden. He was a big, gruff Scot from Roxburghshire, engaged, no doubt, by Lawson as a duty to his Border ancestry. He had short grizzled whiskers, a weatherworn face, and a shrewd, calm blue eye. I knew now why the place was in such perfect order.

We began with sport, and Jobson explained what I could have in the way of fishing and shooting. His exposition was brief and business-like, and all the while I could see his eye searching me. It was clear that he had much to say on other matters than sport.

I told him that I had come here with Lawson three years before, when he chose the site. Jobson continued to regard me curiously. 'I've heard tell of ye from Mr. Lawson. Ye're an old friend of his, I understand.'

'The oldest,' I said. 'And I am sorry to find that the place does not agree with him. Why it doesn't I cannot imagine, for you look fit enough. Has he been seedy for long?'

'It comes and goes,' said Mr. Jobson. 'Maybe once a month he has a bad turn. But on the whole it agrees with him badly. He's no' the man he was when I first came here.'

Jobson was looking at me very seriously and frankly. I risked a question.

'What do you suppose is the matter?'

He did not reply at once, but leaned forward and tapped my knee.

'I think it's something that doctors canna cure. Look at me, sir. I've always been counted a sensible man, but if I told you what was in my head you would think me daft. But I have one word for you. Bide till to-night is past and then speir your question. Maybe you and me will be agreed.'

The factor rose to go. As he left the room he flung me back a remark over his shoulder – 'Read the eleventh chapter of the First Book of Kings.'

After luncheon I went for a walk. First I mounted to the crown of the hill and feasted my eyes on the unequalled loveliness of the view. I saw the far hills in Portuguese territory, a hundred miles away, lifting up thin blue fingers into the sky. The wind blew light and fresh, and the place was fragrant with a thousand delicate scents. Then I descended to the vale, and followed the stream up through the garden. Poinsettias and oleanders were blazing in coverts, and there was a paradise of tinted water-lilies in the slacker reaches. I saw good trout rise at the fly, but I did not think about fishing. I was searching my memory for a recollection which would not come. By-and-by I found myself beyond the garden, where the lawns ran to the fringe of Ashtaroth's Grove.

It was like something I remembered in an old Italian picture. Only, as my memory drew it, it should have been peopled with strange figures – nymphs dancing on the sward, and a prick-eared faun peeping from the covert. In the warm afternoon sunlight it stood, ineffably gracious and beautiful, tantalising with a sense of some deep hidden loveliness. Very reverently I walked between the slim trees, to where the little conical tower stood half in sun and half in shadow. Then I noticed something new. Round the tower ran a narrow path, worn in the grass by human feet. There had been no such path on my first visit, for I remembered the grass growing tall to the edge of the stone. Had the Kaffirs made a shrine of it, or were there other and stranger votaries?

When I returned to the house I found Travers with a message for me. Mr. Lawson was still in bed, but he would like me to go to him. I found my friend sitting up and drinking strong tea – a bad thing, I should have thought, for a man in his condition. I remember that I looked over the room for some sign of the pernicious habit of which I believed him a victim. But the place was fresh and clean, with the windows wide open, and, though I could not have given my reasons, I was convinced that drugs or drink had nothing to do with the sickness.

He received me more civilly, but I was shocked by his looks. There were great bags below his eyes, and his skin had the wrinkled puffy appearance of a man in dropsy. His voice, too, was reedy and thin. Only his great eyes burned with some feverish life.

'I am a shocking bad host,' he said, 'but I'm going to be still more inhospitable. I want you to go away. I hate anybody here when I'm off colour.'

'Nonsense,' I said; 'you want looking after. I want to know about this sickness. Have you had a doctor?'

He smiled wearily. 'Doctors are no earthly use to me. There's nothing much the matter, I tell you. I'll be all right in a day or two, and then you can come back. I want you to go off with Jobson and hunt in the plains till the end of the week. It will be better fun for you, and I'll feel less guilty.'

Of course I pooh-poohed the idea, and Lawson got angry. 'Damn it, man,' he cried, 'why do you force yourself on me when I don't want you? I tell you your presence here makes me worse. In a week I'll be as right as the mail, and then I'll be thankful for you. But get away now; get away, I tell you.'

I saw that he was fretting himself into a passion. 'All right,' I said soothingly; 'Jobson and I will go off hunting. But I am horribly anxious about you, old man.'

He lay back on his pillows. 'You needn't trouble. I only want a little rest. Jobson will make all arrangements, and Travers will get you anything you want. Good-bye.'

I saw it was useless to stay longer, so I left the room. Outside I found the anxious-faced servant. 'Look here,' I said, 'Mr. Lawson thinks I ought to go, but I mean to stay. Tell him I'm gone if he asks you. And for Heaven's sake keep him in bed.'

The man promised, and I thought I saw some relief in his face.

I went to the library, and on the way remembered Jobson's remark about 1st Kings. With some searching I found a Bible and turned up the passage. It was a long screed about the misdeeds of Solomon, and I read it through without enlightenment. I began to re-read it, and a word suddenly caught my attention –

'*For Solomon went after Ashtaroth, the goddess of the Zidonians.*'

That was all, but it was like a key to a cipher. Instantly there flashed over my mind all that I had heard or read of that strange ritual which seduced Israel to sin. I saw a sunburnt land and a people vowed to the stern service of Jehovah. But I saw, too, eyes turning from the austere sacrifice to lonely hill-top groves and towers and images, where dwelt some subtle and evil mystery. I saw the fierce prophets, scourging the votaries with rods, and a nation penitent before the Lord; but always the backsliding again, and the hankering after forbidden joys. Ashtaroth was the old goddess of the East. Was it not possible that in all Semitic blood there remained, transmitted through the dim generations, some craving for her spell? I thought of the grandfather in the back street at Brighton and of those burning eyes upstairs.

As I sat and mused my glance fell on the inscrutable stone birds. They knew all those old secrets of joy and terror. And that moon of alabaster! Some dark priest had worn it on his forehead when he worshipped, like Ahab, 'all the host of Heaven.' And then I honestly began to be afraid. I a prosaic, modern Christian gentleman, a half-believer in casual faiths, was in the presence of some hoary mystery of sin far older than creeds or Christendom. There was fear in my heart, – a kind of uneasy disgust, and above all a nervous eerie disquiet. Now I wanted to go away, and yet I was ashamed of the cowardly thought. I pictured Ashtaroth's Grove with sheer horror. What tragedy was in the air? what secret awaited twilight? For the night was coming, the night of the Full Moon, the season of ecstasy and sacrifice.

I do not know how I got through that evening. I was disinclined for dinner, so I had a cutlet in the library and sat smoking till my tongue ached. But as the hours passed a more manly resolution grew up in my mind. I owed it to old friendship to stand by Lawson in this extremity. I could not interfere, – God knows, his reason seemed already rocking, – but I could be at hand in case my chance came. I determined not to undress, but to watch through the night. I had a bath, and changed into light flannels and slippers. Then I took up my position in a corner of the library close to the window, so that I could not fail to hear Lawson's footsteps if he passed.

Fortunately I left the lights unlit, for as I waited I grew drowsy, and fell asleep. When I woke the moon had risen, and I knew from the feel of the air that the hour was late. I sat very still, straining my ears, and as I listened I caught the sound of steps. They were crossing the hall stealthily, and nearing the library door. I huddled into my corner as Lawson entered.

He wore the same towel dressing-gown, and he moved swiftly and silently as if in a trance. I watched him take the alabaster moon from the mantelpiece and drop it in his pocket. A glimpse of white skin showed that the gown was his only clothing. Then he moved past me to the window, opened it, and went out.

Without any conscious purpose I rose and followed, kicking off my slippers that I might go quietly. He was running, running fast, across the lawns in the direction of the grove – an odd shapeless antic in the moonlight. I stopped, for there was no cover, and I feared for his reason if he saw me. When I looked again he had disappeared among the trees.

I saw nothing for it but to crawl, so on my belly I wormed my way over the dripping sward. There was a ridiculous suggestion of deer-stalking about the game which tickled me and dispelled my uneasiness. Almost I persuaded myself I was tracking an ordinary

sleep-walker. The lawns were broader than I imagined, and it seemed
an age before I reached the edge of the grove. The world was so still
that I appeared to be making a most ghastly amount of noise. I
remember that once I heard a rustling in the air, and looked up to see
the green doves circling about the treetops.

There was no sign of Lawson. On the edge of the grove I think that
all my assurance vanished. I could see between the trunks to the little
tower, but it was quiet as the grave, save for the wings above. Once
more there came over me the unbearable sense of anticipation I had
felt the night before. My nerves tingled with mingled expectation and
dread. I did not think that any harm would come to me, for the powers
of the air seemed not malignant. But I knew them for powers, and felt
awed and abased. I was in the presence of the 'host of Heaven,' and I
was no stern Israelitish prophet to prevail against them.

I must have lain for hours waiting in that spectral place, my eyes
riveted on the tower and its golden cap of moonshine. I remember that
my head felt void and light, as if my spirit were becoming disembodied
and leaving its dew-drenched sheath far below. But the most curious
sensation was of something drawing me to the tower, something mild
and kindly and rather feeble, for there was some other and stronger
force keeping me back. I yearned to move nearer, but I could not drag
my limbs an inch. There was a spell somewhere which I could not
break. I do not think I was in any way frightened now. The starry
influence was playing tricks with me, but my mind was half asleep.
Only I never took my eyes from the little tower. I think I could not, if I
had wanted to.

Then suddenly from the shadows came Lawson. He was
stark-naked, and he wore, bound across his brow, the half moon of
alabaster. He had something, too, in his hand – something which
glittered.

He ran round the tower, crooning to himself, and flinging wild arms
to the skies. Sometimes the crooning changed to a shrill cry of passion,
such as a maenad may have uttered in the train of Bacchus. I could
make out no words, but the sound told its own tale. He was absorbed
in some infernal ecstasy. And as he ran, he drew his right hand across
his breast and arms, and I saw that it held a knife.

I grew sick with disgust – not terror, but honest physical loathing.
Lawson, gashing his fat body, affected me with an overpowering
repugnance. I wanted to go forward and stop him, and I wanted, too, to
be a hundred miles away. And the result was that I stayed still. I believe
my own will held me there, but I doubt if in any case I could have
moved my legs.

The dance grew swifter and fiercer. I saw the blood dripping from Lawson's body, and his face ghastly white above his scarred breast. And then suddenly the horror left me; my head swam; and for one second – one brief second – I seemed to peer into a new world. A strange passion surged up in my heart. I seemed to see the earth peopled with forms – not human, scarcely divine, but more desirable than man or god. The calm face of Nature broke up for me into wrinkles of wild knowledge. I saw the things which brush against the soul in dreams, and found them lovely. There seemed no cruelty in the knife or the blood. It was a delicate mystery of worship, as wholesome as the morning song of birds. I do not know how the Semites found Ashtaroth's ritual; to them it may well have been more rapt and passionate than it seemed to me. For I saw in it only the sweet simplicity of Nature, and all riddles of lust and terror soothed away as a child's nightmares are calmed by a mother. I found my legs able to move, and I think I took two steps through the dusk towards the tower.

And then it all ended. A cock crew, and the homely noises of earth were renewed. While I stood dazed and shivering, Lawson plunged through the Grove towards me. The impetus carried him to the edge, and he fell fainting just outside the shade.

My wits and common-sense came back to me with my bodily strength. I got my friend on my back, and staggered with him towards the house. I was afraid in real earnest now, and what frightened me most was the thought that I had not been afraid sooner. I had come very near the 'abomination of the Zidonians.'

At the door I found the scared valet waiting. He had apparently done this sort of thing before.

'Your master has been sleep-walking, and has had a fall,' I said. 'We must get him to bed at once.'

We bathed the wounds as he lay in a deep stupor, and I dressed them as well as I could. The only danger lay in his utter exhaustion, for happily the gashes were not serious, and no artery had been touched. Sleep and rest would make him well, for he had the constitution of a strong man. I was leaving the room when he opened his eyes and spoke. He did not recognise me, but I noticed that his face had lost its strangeness, and was once more that of the friend I had known. Then I suddenly bethought me of an old hunting remedy which he and I always carried on our expeditions. It is a pill made up from an ancient Portuguese prescription. One is an excellent specific for fever. Two are invaluable if you are lost in the bush, for they send a man for many hours into a deep sleep, which prevents suffering and madness, till help comes. Three give a painless death. I went to my room and found

the little box in my jewel-case. Lawson swallowed two, and turned
wearily on his side. I bade his man let him sleep till he woke, and went
off in search of food.

———

I had business on hand which would not wait. By seven, Jobson, who
had been sent for, was waiting for me in the library. I knew by his grim
face that here I had a very good substitute for a prophet of the Lord.

'You were right,' I said. 'I have read the 11th chapter of 1st Kings,
and I have spent such a night as I pray God I shall never spend again.'

'I thought you would,' he replied. 'I've had the same experience
myself.'

'The Grove?' I said.

'Ay, the wud,' was the answer in broad Scots.

I wanted to see how much he understood.

'Mr. Lawson's family is from the Scotch Border?'

'Ay. I understand they come off Borthwick Water side,' he replied,
but I saw by his eyes that he knew what I meant.

'Mr. Lawson is my oldest friend,' I went on, 'and I am going to take
measures to cure him. For what I am going to do I take the sole
responsibility. I will make that plain to your master. But if I am to
succeed I want your help. Will you give it to me? It sounds like
madness, and you are a sensible man and may like to keep out of it. I
leave it to your discretion.'

Jobson looked me straight in the face. 'Have no fear for me,' he said;
'there is an unholy thing in that place, and if I have the strength in me I
will destroy it. He has been a good master to me, and forbye, I am a
believing Christian. So say on, sir.'

There was no mistaking the air. I had found my Tishbite.

'I want men,' I said, – 'as many as we can get.'

Jobson mused. 'The Kaffirs will no' gang near the place, but there's
some thirty white men on the tobacco farm. They'll do your will, if you
give them an indemnity in writing.'

'Good,' said I. 'Then we will take our instructions from the only
authority which meets the case. We will follow the example of King
Josiah.' I turned up the 23rd Chapter of 2nd Kings, and read;

And the high places that were before Jerusalem, which were on the right
hand of the Mount of Corruption, which Solomon the king of Israel had
builded for Ashtaroth the abomination of the Zidonians ... did the king
defile.

And he brake in pieces the images, and cut down the groves, and filled their places with the bones of men.

Moreover the altar that was at Beth-el, and the high place which Jeroboam the son of Nebat, who made Israel to sin, had made, both that altar and the high place he brake down, and burned the high place, and stamped it small to powder, and burned the grove.

Jobson nodded. 'It'll need dinnymite. But I've plenty of yon down at the workshops. I'll be off to collect the lads.'

Before nine the men had assembled at Jobson's house. They were a hardy lot of young farmers from home, who took their instructions docilely from the masterful factor. On my orders they had brought their shot-guns. We armed them with spades and woodmen's axes, and one man wheeled some coils of rope in a hand-cart.

In the clear, windless air of morning the Grove, set amid its lawns, looked too innocent and exquisite for ill. I had a pang of regret that a thing so fair should suffer; nay, if I had come alone, I think I might have repented. But the men were there, and the grim-faced Jobson was waiting for orders. I placed the guns, and sent beaters to the far side. I told them that every dove must be shot.

It was only a small flock, and we killed fifteen at the first drive. The poor birds flew over the glen to another spinney, but we brought them back over the guns and seven fell. Four more were got in the trees, and the last I killed myself with a long shot. In half an hour there was a pile of little green bodies on the sward.

Then we went to work to cut down the trees. The slim stems were an easy task to a good woodman, and one after another they toppled to the ground. And meantime, as I watched, I became conscious of a strange emotion.

It was as if someone were pleading with me. A gentle voice, not threatening, but pleading – something too fine for the sensual ear, but touching inner chords of the spirit. So tenuous it was and distant that I could think of no personality behind it. Rather it was the viewless, bodiless grace of this delectable vale, some old exquisite divinity of the groves. There was the heart of all sorrow in it, and the soul of all loveliness. It seemed a woman's voice, some lost lady who had brought nothing but goodness unrepaid to the world. And what the voice told me was that I was destroying her last shelter.

That was the pathos of it – the voice was homeless. As the axes flashed in the sunlight and the wood grew thin, that gentle spirit was pleading with me for mercy and a brief respite. It seemed to be telling of a world for centuries grown coarse and pitiless, of long sad wanderings, of hardly won shelter, and a peace which was the little all she sought from men. There was nothing terrible in it, no thought of wrongdoing. The spell which to Semitic blood held the mystery of evil, was to me, of the Northern race, only delicate and rare and beautiful. Jobson and the rest did not feel it, I with my finer senses caught nothing but the hopeless sadness of it. That which had stirred the passion in Lawson was only wringing my heart. It was almost too pitiful to bear. As the trees crashed down and the men wiped the sweat from their brows, I seemed to myself like the murderer of fair women and innocent children. I remember that the tears were running over my cheeks. More than once I opened my mouth to countermand the work, but the face of Jobson, that grim Tishbite, held me back. I knew now what gave the Prophets of the Lord their mastery, and I knew also why the people sometimes stoned them.

The last tree fell, and the little tower stood like a ravished shrine, stripped of all defence against the world. I heard Jobson's voice speaking. 'We'd better blast that stane thing now. We'll trench on four sides and lay the dinnymite. Ye're no' looking weel, sir. Ye'd better go and sit down on the brae-face.'

I went up the hillside and lay down. Below me, in the waste of shorn trunks, men were running about, and I saw the mining begin. It all seemed like an aimless dream in which I had no part. The voice of that homeless goddess was still pleading. It was the innocence of it that tortured me. Even so must a merciful Inquisitor have suffered from the plea of some fair girl with the aureole of death on her hair. I knew I was killing rare and unrecoverable beauty. As I sat dazed and heartsick, the whole loveliness of Nature seemed to plead for its divinity. The sun in the heavens, the mellow lines of upland, the blue mystery of the far plains, were all part of that soft voice. I felt bitter scorn for myself. I was guilty of blood; nay, I was guilty of the sin against light which knows no forgiveness. I was murdering innocent gentleness, and there would be no peace on earth for me. Yet I sat helpless. The power of a sterner will constrained me. And all the while the voice was growing fainter and dying away into unutterable sorrow.

Suddenly a great flame sprang to heaven, and a pall of smoke. I heard men crying out, and fragments of stone fell around the ruins of the grove. When the air cleared, the little tower had gone out of sight.

The voice had ceased and there seemed to me to be a bereaved silence in the world. The shock moved me to my feet, and I ran down the slope to where Jobson stood rubbing his eyes.

'That's done the job. Now we maun get up the tree-roots. We've no time to howk. We'll just dinnymite the feck o' them.'

The work of destruction went on, but I was coming back to my senses. I forced myself to be practical and reasonable. I thought of the night's experience and Lawson's haggard eyes, and I screwed myself into a determination to see the thing through. I had done the deed; it was my business to make it complete. A text in Jeremiah came into my head: '*Their children remember their altars and their groves by the green trees upon the high hills.*' I would see to it that this grove should be utterly forgotten.

We blasted the tree roots, and, yoking oxen, dragged the *débris* into a great heap. Then the men set to work with their spades, and roughly levelled the ground. I was getting back to my old self, and Jobson's spirit was becoming mine.

'There is one thing more,' I told him. 'Get ready a couple of ploughs. We will improve upon King Josiah.' My brain was a medley of Scripture precedents, and I was determined that no safeguard should be wanting.

We yoked the oxen again and drove the ploughs over the site of the grove. It was rough ploughing, for the place was thick with bits of stone from the tower, but the slow Afrikander oxen plodded on, and sometime in the afternoon the work was finished. Then I sent down to the farm for bags of rock-salt, such as they use for cattle. Jobson and I took a sack apiece, and walked up and down the furrows, sowing them with salt.

The last act was to set fire to the pile of tree-trunks. They burned well, and on the top we flung the bodies of the green doves. The birds of Ashtaroth had an honourable pyre.

Then I dismissed the much-perplexed men, and gravely shook hands with Jobson. Black with dust and smoke I went back to the house, where I bade Travers pack my bags and order the motor. I found Lawson's servant, and heard from him that his master was sleeping peacefully. I gave some directions, and then went to wash and change.

Before I left I wrote a line to Lawson. I began by transcribing the verses from the 23rd Chapter of 2nd Kings. I told him what I had done, and my reason. 'I take the whole responsibility upon myself,' I wrote. 'No man in the place had anything to do with it but me. I acted as I did for the sake of our old friendship, and you will believe it was no easy task for me. I hope you will understand. Whenever you are able to see me send me word, and I will come back and settle with you. But I think you will realise that I have saved your soul.'

The afternoon was merging into twilight as I left the house on the road to Taqui. The great fire, where the grove had been, was still blazing fiercely, and the smoke made a cloud over the upper glen, and filled all the air with a soft violet haze. I knew that I had done well for my friend, and that he would come to his senses and be grateful. My mind was at ease on that score, and in something like comfort I faced the future. But as the car reached the ridge I looked back to the vale I had outraged. The moon was rising and silvering the smoke, and through the gaps I could see the tongues of fire. Somehow, I know not why, the lake, the stream, the garden-coverts, even the green slopes of hill, wore an air of loneliness and desecration.

And then my heartache returned, and I knew that I had driven something lovely and adorable from its last refuge on earth.

The Green Wildebeest

JUST after the Boer War I was on a prospecting job in the north-eastern Transvaal. I was a mining engineer, with copper as my speciality, and I had always a notion that copper might be found in big quantities in the Zoutpansberg foothills. There was of course Messina at the west end, but my thoughts turned rather to the north-east corner, where the berg breaks down to the crook of the Limpopo. I was a young man then, fresh from two years' campaigning with the Imperial Light Horse, and I was thirsty for better jobs than trying to drive elusive burghers up against barbed wire and blockhouses. When I started out with my mules from Pietersburg on the dusty road to the hills, I think I felt happier than ever before in my life.

I had only one white companion, a boy of twenty-two called Andrew Du Preez. Andrew, not Andries, for he was named after the Reverend Andrew Murray, who had been a great Pope among the devout Afrikanders. He came of a rich Free State farming family, but his particular branch had been settled for two generations in the Wakkerstroom region along the upper Pongola. The father was a splendid old fellow with a head like Moses, and he and all the uncles had been on commando, and most of them had had a spell in Bermuda or Ceylon. The boy was a bit of a freak in that stock. He had been precociously intelligent, and had gone to a good school in the Cape and afterwards to a technical college in Johannesburg. He was as modern a product as the others were survivals, with none of the family religion or family politics, very keen on science, determined to push his way on the Rand – which was the Mecca of all enterprising Afrikanders – and not very sorry that the War should have found him in a place from which it was manifestly impossible to join the family banner. In October '99 he was on his first job in a new mining area in Rhodesia, and as he hadn't much health he was wise enough to stick there till peace came.

I had known him before, and when I ran across him on the Rand I asked him to come with me, and he jumped at the offer. He had just returned from the Wakkerstroom farm, to which the rest of his clan had been repatriated, and didn't relish the prospect of living in a tin-roofed shanty with a father who read the Bible most of the day to find out why exactly he had merited such misfortunes. Andrew was a hard young sceptic, in whom the family piety produced acute exasperation ... He was a good-looking boy, always rather smartly dressed, and at first sight you would have taken him for a young American, because of his heavy hairless chin, his dull complexion, and the way he peppered his ordinary speech with technical and business phrases. There was a touch of the Mongol in his face, which was broad, with high cheek bones, eyes slightly slanted, short thick nose and rather full lips. I remembered that I had seen the same thing before in young Boers, and I thought I knew the reason. The Du Preez family had lived for generations close up to the Kaffir borders, and somewhere had got a dash of the tar-brush.

We had a light wagon with a team of eight mules, and a Cape-cart drawn by four others; five boys went with us, two of them Shangaans, and three Basutos from Malietsie's location north of Pietersburg. Our road was over the Wood Bush, and then north-east across the two Letabas to the Pufuri river. The countryside was amazingly empty. Beyer's commandos had skirmished among the hills, but the war had never reached the plains; at the same time it had put a stop to all hunting and prospecting and had scattered most of the native tribes. The place had become in effect a sanctuary, and I saw more varieties of game than I had ever seen before south of the Zambesi, so that I wished I were on a hunting trip instead of on a business job. Lions were plentiful, and every night we had to build a *scherm* for our mules and light great fires, beside which we listened to their eerie serenades.

It was early December, and in the Wood Bush it was the weather of an English June. Even in the foothills, among the wormwood and wild bananas, it was pleasant enough, but when we got out into the plains it was as hot as Tophet. As far as the eye could reach the bushveld rolled its scrub like the scrawled foliage a child draws on a slate, with here and there a baobab swimming unsteadily in the glare. For long stretches we were away from water, and ceased to see big game – only Kaffir queens and tick-birds, and now and then a wild ostrich. Then on the sixth day out from Pietersburg we raised a blue line of mountains on the north, which I knew to be the eastern extension of the Zoutpansberg. I had never travelled this country before, and had never met a man who had, so we steered by compass, and by one of the old bad maps of the Transvaal Government. That night we crossed the Pufuri, and next day the landscape began to change. The ground rose, so that we had a sight of the distant Lebombo hills to the east, and mopani bushes began to appear – a sure sign of a healthier country.

That afternoon we were only a mile or two from the hills. They were the usual type of berg which you find everywhere from Natal to the Zambesi – cut sheer, with an overhang in many places, but much broken up by kloofs and fissures. What puzzled me was the absence of streams. The ground was as baked as the plains, all covered with aloe and cactus and thorn, with never a sign of water. But for my purpose the place looked promising. There was that unpleasant metallic green that you find in a copper country, so that everything seemed to have been steeped in a mineral dye – even the brace of doves which I shot for luncheon.

We turned east along the foot of the cliffs, and presently saw a curious feature. A promontory ran out from the berg, connected by a narrow isthmus with the main *massif*. I suppose the superficial area of the top might have been a square mile or so; the little peninsula was deeply cut into by ravines, and in the ravines tall timber was growing. Also we came to well-grassed slopes, dotted with mimosa and syringa bushes. This must mean water at last, for I had never found yellowwoods and stinkwoods growing far from a stream. Here was our outspan for the night, and when presently we rounded a corner and looked down into a green cup I thought I had rarely seen a more habitable place. The sight of fresh green herbage always intoxicated me, after the dust and heat and the ugly greys and umbers of the bushveld. There was a biggish kraal in the bottom, and a lot of goats and leggy Kaffir sheep on the slopes. Children were bringing in the cows for the milking, smoke was going up from the cooking fires, and there was a cheerful evening hum in the air. I expected a stream, but could see no sign of one: the cup seemed to be as dry as a hollow of the Sussex Downs. Also, though there were patches of mealies and Kaffir corn, I could see no irrigated land. But water must be there, and after we had fixed a spot for our outspan beside a clump of olivewoods, I took Andrew and one of our boys and strolled down to make inquiries.

I daresay many of the inhabitants of that kraal had never seen a white man before, for our arrival made a bit of a sensation. I noticed that there were very few young men about the place, but an inordinate number of old women. The first sight of us scattered them like plovers, and we had to wait for half an hour, smoking patiently in the evening sun, before we could get into talk with them. Once the ice was broken, however, things went well. They were a decent peaceable folk, very shy and scared and hesitating, but with no guile in them. Our presents of brass and copper wire and a few tins of preserved meat made a tremendous impression. We bought a sheep from them at a ridiculously small price, and they threw in a basket of green mealies. But when we raised the water question we struck a snag.

There was water, good water, they said, but it was not in any pan or stream. They got it morning and evening from up there – and they pointed to the fringe of a wood under the cliffs where I thought I saw the roof of a biggish *rondavel*. They got it from their Father; they were Shangaans, and the word they used was not the ordinary word for chief, but the name for a great priest and medicine-man.

I wanted my dinner, so I forbore to inquire further. I produced some more Kaffir track, and begged them to present it with my compliments to their Father, and to ask for water for two white strangers, five of their own race, and twelve mules. They seemed to welcome the proposition, and a string of them promptly set off uphill with their big calabashes. As we walked back I said something foolish to Andrew about having struck a Kaffir Moses who could draw water from the rock. The lad was in a bad temper. 'We have struck an infernal rascal who has made a corner in the water supply and bleeds these poor devils. He's the kind of grafter I would like to interview with a sjambok.'

In an hour we had all the water we wanted. It stood in a row of calabashes, and beside it the presents I had sent to the provider. The villagers had deposited it and then vanished, and our boys who had helped them to carry it were curiously quiet and solemnised. I was informed that the Father sent the water as a gift to the strangers without payment. I tried to cross-examine one of our Shangaans, but he would tell me nothing except that the water had come from a sacred place into which no man could penetrate. He also muttered something about a wildebeest which I couldn't understand. Now the Kaffir is the most superstitious of God's creatures. All the way from Pietersburg we had been troubled by the vivid imaginations of our outfit. They wouldn't sleep in one place because of a woman without a head who haunted it; they dared not go a yard along a particular road after dark because of a spook that travelled it in the shape of a rolling ball of fire. Usually their memories were as short as their fancies were quick, and five minutes after their protest they would be laughing like baboons. But that night they seemed to have been really impressed by something. They did not chatter or sing over their supper, but gossiped in undertones, and slept as near Andrew and myself as they dared.

Next morning the same array of gourds stood before our outspan, and there was enough water for me to have a tub in my collapsible bath. I don't think I ever felt anything colder.

I had decided to take a holiday and go shooting. Andrew would stay in camp and tinker up one of the wheels of the mule-wagon which had suffered from the bush roads. He announced his intention of taking a walk later and interviewing the water-merchant.

'For Heaven's sake, be careful,' I said. 'Most likely he's a priest of sorts, and if you're not civil to him we'll have to quit this country. I make a point of respecting the gods of the heathen.'

'All you English do,' he replied tartly. 'That's why you make such a damned mess of handling Kaffirs ... But this fellow is a business man with a pretty notion of cornering public utilities. I'm going to make his acquaintance.'

I had a pleasant day in that hot scented wilderness. First I tried the low ground, but found nothing there but some old spoor of kudu, and a paauw which I shot. Then I tried the skirts of the berg to the east of the village, and found that the kloofs, which from below looked climbable, had all somewhere a confounded overhang which checked me. I saw no way of getting to the top of the plateau, so I spent the afternoon in exploring the tumbled glacis. There was no trace of copper here, for the rock was a reddish granite, but it was a jolly flowery place, with green dells among the crags, and an amazing variety of birds. But I was glad that I had brought a water-bottle, for I found no water; it was there all right, but it was underground. I stalked a bushbuck ram and missed him, but I got one of the little buck like chamois which the Dutch call *klipspringer*. With it and the paauw strung round my neck I sauntered back leisurely to supper.

As soon as I came in sight of the village I saw that something had played the deuce with it. There was a great hubbub going on, and all the folk were collected at the end farthest away from our camp. The camp itself looked very silent. I could see the hobbled mules, but I could see nothing of any of our outfit. I thought it best in these circumstances to make an inconspicuous arrival, so I bore away to my left, crossed the hollow lower down where it was thick with scrub, and came in on the outspan from the south. It was very silent. The cooking fires had been allowed to go out, though the boys should have been getting ready the evening meal, and there seemed to be not a single black face on the premises. Very uneasy, I made for our sleeping tent, and found Andrew lying on his bed, smoking.

'What on earth has happened?' I demanded. 'Where are Coos and Klemboy and ...'

'Quit,' he said shortly. 'They've all quit.'

He looked sulky and tired and rather white in the face, and there seemed to be more the matter with him than ill temper. He would lay down his pipe, and press his hand on his forehead like a man with a bad headache. Also he never lifted his eyes to mine. I daresay I was a bit harsh, for I was hungry, and there were moments when I thought he was going to cry. However at last I got a sort of story out of him.

He had finished his job on the wagon wheel in the morning, and after luncheon had gone for a walk to the wood above the village at the foot of the cliffs. He wanted to see where the water came from and to have a word with the man who controlled it. Andrew, as I have told you, was a hard young realist and, by way of reaction from his family, a determined foe of superstition, and he disliked the notion of this priest and his mumbo-jumbo. Well, it seemed that he reached the priest's headquarters – it was the big *rondavel* we had seen from below, and there was a kind of stockade stretching on both sides, very strongly fenced, so that the only entrance was through the *rondavel*. He had found the priest at home, and had, according to his account, spoken to him civilly and had tried to investigate the water problem. But the old man would have nothing to say to him and peremptorily refused his request to be allowed to enter the enclosure. By and by Andrew lost his temper, and forced his way in. The priest resisted and there was a scuffle; I daresay Andrew used his sjambok, for a backveld Dutchman can never keep his hands off a Kaffir.

I didn't like the story, but it was no use being angry with a lad who looked like a sick dog.

'What is inside? Did you find the water?' I asked.

'I hadn't time. It's a thick wood and full of beasts. I tell you I was scared out of my senses and had to run for my life.'

'Leopards?' I asked. I had heard of native chiefs keeping tame leopards.

'Leopards be damned. I'd have faced leopards. I saw a wildebeest as big as a house – an old brute, grey in the nozzle and the rest of it green – green, I tell you. I took a pot shot at it and ran ... When I came out the whole blasted kraal was howling. The old devil must have roused them. I legged it for home ... No, they didn't follow, but in half an hour all our outfit had cut their stick ... didn't wait to pick up their duds ... Oh, hell, I can't talk. Leave me alone.'

I had laughed in spite of myself. A wildebeest is not ornamental at the best, but a green one must be a good recipe for the horrors. All the same I felt very little like laughing. Andrew had offended the village and its priest, played havoc with the brittle nerves of our own boys, and generally made the place too hot to hold us. He had struck some kind of native magic, which had frightened him to the bone for all his scepticism. The best thing I could do seemed to be to try and patch up a peace with the water merchant. So I made a fire and put on a kettle to boil, stayed my hunger with a handful of biscuits, and started out for the *rondavel*. But first I saw that my revolver was loaded, for I fancied that there might be trouble. It was a calm bright evening, but up from the hollow where the kraal lay there rose a buzz like angry wasps.

No one interfered with me; indeed, I met no one till I presented myself at the *rondavel* door. It was a big empty place, joined to the stockades on both sides, and opposite the door was another which opened on to a dull green shade. I never saw a *scherm* so stoutly built. There was a palisade of tall pointed poles, and between them a thick wall of wait-a-bit thorns interlaced with a scarlet-flowered creeper. It would have taken a man with an axe half a day to cut a road through. The only feasible entrance was by the *rondavel*.

An old man was squatted on an earthen floor, which had been so pounded and beaten that it looked like dark polished stone. His age might have been anything above seventy from the whiteness of his beard, but there seemed a good deal of bodily strength left in him, for the long arms which rested on his knees were muscular. His face was not the squat face of the ordinary Kaffir, both high-boned and regular, like some types of well-bred Zulu. Now that I think of it, there was probably Arab blood in him. He lifted his head at the sound of my steps, and by the way he looked at me I knew that he was blind.

There he sat without a word, every line of his body full of dejection and tragedy. I had suddenly a horrible feeling of sacrilege. That that young fool Andrew should have lifted his hand upon an old man and a blind man and outraged some harmless *tabu* seemed to me an abominable thing. I felt that some holiness had been violated, something ancient and innocent cruelly insulted. At that moment there was nothing in the world I wanted so much as to make restitution.

I spoke to him, using the Shangaan word which means both priest and king. I told him that I had been away hunting and had returned to find that my companion had made bad mischief. I said that Andrew was very young, and that his error had been only the foolishness and hotheadedness of youth. I said – and my voice must have shown him that I meant it – that I was cut to the heart by what had happened, that I bowed my head in the dust in contrition, and that I asked nothing better than to be allowed to make atonement … Of course I didn't offer money. I would as soon have thought of offering a tip to the Pope.

He never lifted his head, so I said it all over again, and the second time it was genuine pleading. I had never spoken like that to a Kaffir before, but I could not think of that old figure as a Kaffir, but as the keeper of some ancient mystery which a rude hand had outraged.

He spoke at last. 'There can be no atonement,' he said. 'Wrong has been done, and on the wrong-doer must fall the penalty.'

The words were wholly without menace; rather he spoke as if he were an unwilling prophet of evil. He was there to declare the law, which he could not alter if he wanted.

I apologised, I protested, I pled, I fairly grovelled; I implored him to tell me if there was no way in which the trouble could be mended; but if I had offered him a million pounds I don't believe that that old fellow would have changed his tone. He seemed to feel, and he made me feel it too, that a crime had been committed against the law of nature, and that it was nature, not man, that would avenge it. He wasn't in the least unfriendly; indeed, I think he rather liked the serious way I took the business and realised how sorry I was; his slow sentences came out without a trace of bitterness. It was this that impressed me so horribly – he was like an old stone oracle repeating the commands of the God he served.

I could make nothing of him, though I kept at it till the shadows had lengthened outside, and it was almost dark within the *rondavel*. I wanted to ask him at least to help me to get back my boys, and to make our peace with the village, but I simply could not get the words out. The atmosphere was too solemn to put a practical question like that …

I was turning to go away, when I looked at the door on the far side. Owing to the curious formation of the cliffs the sinking sun had only now caught the high tree-tops, and some ricochet of light made the enclosure brighter than when I first arrived. I felt suddenly an overwhelming desire to go inside.

'Is it permitted, Father,' I said, 'to pass through that door?'

To my surprise he waved me on. 'It is permitted,' he said, 'for you have a clean heart.' Then he added a curious thing. 'What was there is there no more. It has gone to the fulfilling of the law.'

It was with a good deal of trepidation that I entered that uncanny *enceinte*. I remembered Andrew's terror, and I kept my hand on my revolver, for I had a notion that there might be some queer fauna inside. There was light in the upper air, but below it was a kind of olive-green dusk. I was afraid of snakes, also of tiger-cats, and there was Andrew's green wildebeest!

The place was only a couple of acres in extent, and though I walked very cautiously I soon had made the circuit of it. The *scherm* continued in a half-moon on each side till it met the sheer wall of the cliffs. The undergrowth was not very thick, and out of it grew tall straight trees, so that the wood seemed like some old pagan grove. When one looked up the mulberrry sunset sky showed in patches between the feathery tops, but where I walked it was very dark.

There was not a sign of life in it, not a bird or beast, not the crack of a twig or a stir in the bushes; all was as quiet and dead as a crypt. Having made the circuit I struck diagonally across, and presently came on what I had been looking for – a pool of water. The spring was nearly circular, with a diameter of perhaps six yards, and what amazed me was that it was surrounded by a parapet of hewn stone. In the centre of the grove there was a little more light, and I could see that that stonework had never been made by Kaffir hands. Evening is the time when water comes to its own; it sleeps in the day but it has its own strange life in the darkness. I dipped my hand in it and it was as cold as ice. There was no bubbling in it, but there seemed to be a slow rhythmical movement, as if fresh currents were always welling out of the deeps and always returning. I have no doubt that it would have been crystal clear if there had been any light, but, as I saw it, it was a surface of darkest jade, opaque, impenetrable, swaying to some magic impulse from the heart of the earth.

It is difficult to explain just the effect it had on me. I had been solemnised before, but this grove and fountain gave me the abject shapeless fear of a child. I felt that somehow I had strayed beyond the reasonable world. The place was clean against nature. It was early summer, so these dark aisles should have been alive with moths and flying ants and all the thousand noises of night. Instead it was utterly silent and lifeless, dead as a stone except for the secret pulsing of the cold waters.

I had had quite enough. It is an absurd thing to confess, but I bolted – shuffled through the undergrowth and back into the *rondavel*, where the old man still sat like Buddha on the floor.

'You have seen?' he asked.

'I have seen,' I said – 'but I do not know what I have seen. Father, be merciful to foolish youth.'

He repeated again the words, that had chilled me before. 'What was there has gone to fulfil the law.'

I ran all the way back to our outspan, and took some unholy tosses on the road, for I had got it into my head that Andrew was in danger. I don't think I ever believed in his green wildebeest, but he had been positive that the place was full of animals, and I knew for a fact that it was empty. Had some fearsome brute been unloosed on the world?

I found Andrew in our tent, and the kettle I had put on to boil empty and the fire out. The boy was sleeping heavily with a flushed face, and I saw what had happened. He was practically a teetotaller, but he had chosen to swallow a good third of one of our four bottles of whisky. The compulsion must have been pretty strong which drove him to drink.

AFTER that our expedition went from bad to worse. In the morning there was no water to be had, and I didn't see myself shouldering a calabash and going back to the grove. Also our boys did not return, and not a soul in the kraal would come near us. Indeed, all night they had kept up a most distressing racket, wailing and beating little drums. It was no use staying on, and, for myself, I had a strong desire to get out of the neighbourhood. The experience of the night before had left an aftertaste of disquiet in my mind, and I wanted to flee from I knew not what. Andrew was obviously a sick man. We did not carry clinical thermometers in those days, but he certainly had fever on him.

So we inspanned after breakfast, and a heavy job trekking is when you have to do all the work yourself. I drove the wagon and Andrew the Cape-cart, and I wondered how long he would be able to sit on his seat. My notion was that by going east we might be able to hire fresh boys, and start prospecting in the hill-country above the bend of the Limpopo.

But the word had gone out against us. You know the way in which Kaffirs send news for a hundred miles as quick as the telegraph – by drum-taps or telepathy – explain it any way you like. Well, we struck a big kraal that afternoon, but not a word would they say to us. Indeed, they were actually threatening, and I had to show my revolver and speak pretty stiffly before we got off. It was the same next day, and I grew nervous about our provisions, for we couldn't buy anything – not a chicken or an egg or a mealie-cob. Andrew was a jolly companion. He had relapsed into the primeval lout, and his manners were those of a cave-man. If he had not been patently suffering, I would have found it hard to keep my temper.

Altogether it was a bright look-out, and to crown all on the third morning Andrew went down like a log with the worst bout of malaria I have ever seen. That fairly put the lid on it. I thought it was going to be black-water, and all my irritation at the boy vanished in my anxiety. There was nothing for it but to give up the expedition and make the best speed possible to the coast. I made for Portuguese territory, and that evening got to the Limpopo. Happily we struck a more civil brand of native, who had not heard of our performances, and I was able to make a bargain with the headman of the village, who undertook to take charge of our outfit till it was sent for, and sold us a big native boat. I hired four lusty fellows as rowers and next morning we started down the river.

We spent a giddy five days before I planted Andrew in hospital at Lourenço Marques. The sickness was not black-water, thank God, but it was a good deal more than ordinary malaria; indeed, I think there was a touch of brain fever in it. Curiously enough I was rather relieved when it came. I had been scared by the boy's behaviour the first two days. I thought that the old priest had actually laid some curse on him; I remembered how the glade and the well had solemnised even me, and I considered that Andrew, with a Kaffir strain somewhere in his ancestry, was probably susceptible to something which left me cold. I had knocked too much about Africa to be a dogmatic sceptic about the mysteries of the heathen. But this fever seemed to explain it. He had been sickening for it; that was why he had behaved so badly to the old man, and had come back babbling about a green wildebeest. I knew that the beginnings of fever often make a man light-headed so that he loses all self-control and gets odd fancies ... All the same I didn't quite convince myself. I couldn't get out of my head the picture of the old man and his ominous words, or that empty grove under the sunset.

I did my best for the boy, and before we reached the coast the worst had passed. A bed was made for him in the stern, and I had to watch him by night and day to prevent him going overboard among the crocodiles. He was apt to be violent, for in his madness he thought he was being chased, and sometimes I had all I could do to keep him in the boat. He would scream like a thing demented, and plead, and curse, and I noticed as a queer thing that his ravings were never in Dutch but always in Kaffir – mostly the Sesutu which he had learnt in his childhood. I expected to hear him mention the green wildebeest, but to my comfort he never uttered the name. He gave no clue to what frightened him, but it must have been a full-sized terror, for every nerve in his body seemed to be quivering, and I didn't care to look at his eyes.

The upshot was that I left him in bed in hospital, as weak as a kitten, but with the fever gone and restored to his right mind. He was again the good fellow I had known, very apologetic and grateful. So with an easy conscience I arranged for the retrieving of my outfit and returned to the Rand.

———

WELL, for six months I lost sight of Andrew. I had to go to Namaqualand, and then up to the copper country of Barotseland, which wasn't as easy a trek as it is to-day. I had one letter from him, written from Johannesburg – not a very satisfactory epistle, for I gathered that the boy was very unsettled. He had quarrelled with his family, and he didn't seem to be contented with the job he had got in the goldfields. As I had known him he had been a sort of school-book industrious apprentice, determined to get on in the world, and not in the least afraid of a dull job and uncongenial company. But this letter was full of small grouses. He wanted badly to have a talk with me – thought of chucking his work and making a trip north to see me; and he ended with an underlined request that I should telegraph when I was coming down-country. As it happened I had no chance just then of sending a telegram, and later I forgot about it.

By and by I finished my tour and was at the Falls, where I got a local Rhodesian paper. From it I had news of Andrew with a vengeance. There were columns about a murder in the bushveld – two men had gone out to look for Kruger's treasure and one had shot the other, and to my horror I found that the one who was now lying in Pretoria gaol under sentence of death was my unhappy friend.

You remember the wild yarns after the Boer War about a treasure of gold which Kruger in his flight to the coast had buried somewhere in the Selati country. That, of course, was all nonsense: the wily ex-President had long before seen the main funds safe in a European bank. But I daresay some of the officials had got away with Treasury balances, and there may have been bullion cached in the bushveld. Anyhow every scallywag south of the Zambesi was agog about the business, and there were no end of expeditions which never found a single Transvaal sovereign. Well, it seemed that two months before Andrew and a Dutchman called Smit had started out to try their luck, and somewhere on the Olifants the two had gone out one evening and only one had returned. Smit was found by the native boys with a hole in his head, and it was proved that the bullet came from Andrew's rifle, which he had been carrying when the two set out. After that the story became obscure. Andrew had been very excited when he returned and declared that he had 'done it at last,' but when Smit's body was found he denied that he had shot him. But it was clear that Smit had been killed by Andrew's sporting .303, and the natives swore that the men had been constantly quarrelling and that Andrew had always shown a very odd temper. The Crown prosecutor argued that the two believed they had found treasure, and that Andrew had murdered Smit in cold blood to prevent his sharing. The defence seemed to be chiefly the impossibilty of a guilty man behaving as Andrew had behaved, and the likelihood of his having fired at a beast in the dark and killed his companion. It sounded to me very thin, and the jury did not believe it, for their verdict was wilful murder.

I knew that it was simply incredible that Andrew could have committed the crime. Men are queer cattle, and I wouldn't have put even murder past certain fairly decent fellows I knew, but this boy was emphatically not one of them. Unless he had gone stark mad I was positive that he could never have taken human life. I knew him intimately, in the way you know a fellow you have lived alone with for months, and that was one of the things I could bank on. All the same it seemed clear that he had shot Smit ... I sent the longest telegram I ever sent in my life to a Scotch lawyer in Johannesburg called Dalgleish whom I believed in, telling him to move heaven and earth to get a reprieve. He was to see Andrew and wire me details about his state of mind. I thought then that temporary madness was probably our best line, and I believed myself that that was the explanation. I longed to take the train forthwith to Pretoria, but I was tied by the heels till the rest of my outfit came in. I was tortured by the thought that the hanging might have already taken place, for that wretched newspaper was a week old.

In two days I got Dalgleish's reply. He had seen the condemned man, and had told him that he came from me. He reported that Andrew was curiously peaceful and apathetic, and not very willing to talk about the business except to declare his innocence. Dalgleish thought him not quite right in his mind, but he had been already examined, and the court had rejected the plea of insanity. He sent his love to me and told me not to worry.

I stirred up Dalgleish again, and got a further reply. Andrew admitted that he had fired the rifle, but not at Smit. He had killed something, but what it was he would not say. He did not seem to be in the least keen to save his neck.

When I reached Bulawayo, on my way south, I had a brain-wave, but the thing seemed so preposterous that I could hardly take it seriously. Still I daren't neglect any chance, so I wired again to Dalgleish to try to have the execution postponed, until he got hold of the priest who lived in the berg above the Pufuri. I gave him full directions how to find him. I said that the old man had laid some curse on Andrew, and that that might explain his state of mind. After all demoniacal possession must be equivalent in law to insanity. But by this time I had become rather hopeless. It seemed a futile thing to be wiring this rigmarole when every hour was bringing the gallows nearer.

I left the railroad at Mafeking, for I thought I could save the long circuit by De Aar by trekking across country. I would have done better to stick to the train, for everything went wrong with me. I had a breakdown at the drift of the Selous river and had to wait a day in

Rustenburg, and I had trouble again at Commando Nek, so that it was the evening of the third day before I reached Pretoria ... As I feared, it was all over. They told me in the hotel that Andrew had been hanged that morning.

I went back to Johannesburg to see Dalgleish with a cold horror at my heart and complete mystification in my head. The Devil had taken an active hand in things and caused a hideous miscarriage of justice. If there had been anybody I could blame I would have felt better, but the fault seemed to lie only with the crookedness of fate. Dalgleish could tell me little. Smit had been the ordinary scallywag, not much of a fellow and no great loss to the world; the puzzle was why Andrew wanted to go with him. The boy in his last days had been utterly apathetic – bore no grudge against anybody – appeared at peace with the world, but didn't seem to want to live. The predikant who visited him daily could make nothing of him. He appeared to be sane enough, but, beyond declaring his innocence, was not inclined to talk, and gave no assistance to those who were trying to get a reprieve ... scarcely took any interest in it ... He had asked repeatedly for me, and had occupied his last days in writing me a long letter, which was to be delivered unopened into my hand. Dalgleish gave me the thing, seven pages in Andrew's neat caligraphy, and in the evening on his stoep I read it.

It was like a voice speaking to me out of the grave, but it was not the voice I knew. Gone was the enlightened commercially-minded young man, who had shed all superstition, and had a dapper explanation for everything in heaven and earth. It was a crude boy who had written those pages, a boy in whose soul old Calvinistic terrors had been awakened, and terrors older still out of primordial African shadows.

He had committed a great sin – that was the point he insisted upon, and by this sin he had set free something awful to prey on the world. ... At first it seemed sheer raving mania to me, but as I mused on it I remembered my own feelings in that empty grove. I had been solemnised, and this boy, with that in his blood which was not in mine, had suffered a cataclysmic spiritual experience. He did not dwell on it, but his few sentences were eloquent in their harsh intensity. He had struggled, he had tried to make light of it, to forget it, to despise it; but it rode him like a nightmare. He thought he was going mad. I had been right about that touch of brain fever.

As far as I could make it out, he believed that from that outraged sanctuary something real and living had gone forth, something at any rate of flesh and blood. But this idea may not have come to him till later, when his mind had been for several months in torture, and he had lost the power of sleep. At first, I think, his trouble was only an indefinite haunting, a sense of sin and impending retribution. But in Johannesburg the *malaise* had taken concrete form. He believed that through his act something awful was at large, with infinite power for evil – evil not only against the wrongdoer himself but against the world. And he believed that it might still be stopped, that it was still in the eastern bush. So crude a fancy showed how his normal intelligence had gone to bits. He had tumbled again into the blackveld world of his childhood.

He decided to go and look for it. That was where the tough white strain in him came out. He might have a Kaffir's blind terrors, but he had the frontier Boer's cast-iron courage. If you think of it, it needed a pretty stout heart to set out to find a thing the thought of which set every nerve quivering. I confess I didn't like to contemplate that lonely, white-faced, tormented boy. I think he knew that tragedy must be the end of it, but he had to face up to that and take the consequences.

He heard of Smit's expedition, and took a half share in it. Perhaps the fact that Smit had a baddish reputation was part of the attraction. He didn't want as companion a man with whom he had anything in common, for he had to think his own thoughts and follow his own course.

Well, you know the end of it. In his letter he said nothing about the journey, except that he had found what he sought. I can readily believe that the two did not agree very well – the one hungry for mythical treasure, the other with a problem which all the gold in Africa could not solve … Somewhere, somehow, down in the Selati bushveld his incubus took bodily form, and he met – or thought he met – the thing which his impiety had released. I suppose we must call it madness. He shot his comrade, and thought he had killed an animal. 'If they had looked next morning they would have found the spoor,' he wrote. Smit's death didn't seem to trouble him at all – I don't think he quite realised it. The thing that mattered for him was that he had put an end to a terror and in some way made atonement. 'Good-bye, and don't worry about me,' were the last words, 'I am quite content.'

I sat a long time thinking, while the sun went down over the Magaliesberg. A gramophone was grinding away on an adjacent stoep, and the noise of the stamps on the Rand came like far-away drums. People at that time used to quote some Latin phrase about a new thing always coming out of Africa. I thought that it was not the new things in Africa that mattered so much as the old things.

I proposed to revisit that berg above the Pufuri and have a word with the priest, but I did not get a chance till the following summer, when I trekked down the Limpopo from Main Drift. I didn't like the job, but I felt bound to have it out with that old man for Andrew's sake. You see, I wanted something more to convince the Wakkerstroom household that the boy had not been guilty, as his father thought, of the sin of Cain.

I came round the corner of the berg one January evening after a day of blistering heat, and looked down on the cup of green pasture. One glance showed me that there was not going to be any explanation with the priest ... A bit of the cliff had broken away, and the rock fall had simply blotted out the grove and the *rondavel*. A huge mass of debris sloped down from half-way up the hill, and buried under it were the tall trees through which I had peered up at the sky. Already it was feathered with thorn-bush and grasses. There were no patches of crops on the sides of the cup, and crumbling mud walls were all that remained of the kraal. The jungle had flowed over the village, and, when I entered it, great moon flowers sprawled on the rubble, looking in the dusk like ghosts of a vanished race.

There was one new feature in the place. The landslip must have released the underground water, for a stream now flowed down the hollow. Beside it, in a meadow full of agapanthus and arum lilies, I found two Australian prospectors. One of them – he had been a Melbourne bank-clerk – had a poetic soul. 'Nice little place,' he said. 'Not littered up with black fellows. If I were on a homesteading job, I reckon I'd squat here.'

Space

'*Est impossibile? Certum est.*'
Tertullian

LEITHEN told me this story one evening in early September as we sat beside the pony track which gropes its way from Glenavelin up the Correi na Sidhe. I had arrived that afternoon from the south, while he had been taking an off-day from a week's stalking, so we had walked up the glen together after tea to get the news of the forest. A rifle was out on the Correi na Sidhe beat, and a thin spire of smoke had risen from the top of Sgurr Dearg to show that a stag had been killed at the burn-head. The lumpish hill pony with its deer-saddle had gone up the Correi in a gillie's charge, while we followed at leisure, picking our way among the loose granite rocks and the patches of wet bogland. The track climbed high on one of the ridges of Sgurr Dearg, till it hung over a caldron of green glen with the Alt-na-Sidhe churning in its linn a thousand feet below. It was a breathless evening, I remember, with a pale-blue sky just clearing from the haze of the day. West-wind weather may make the North, even in September, no bad imitation of the Tropics, and I sincerely pitied the man who all these stifling hours had been toiling on the screes of Sgurr Dearg. By-and-by we sat down on a bank of heather, and idly watched the trough swimming at our feet. The clatter of the pony's hoofs grew fainter, the drone of bees had gone, even the midges seemed to have forgotten their calling. No place on earth can be so deathly still as a deer forest early in the season before the stags have begun roaring, for there are no sheep with their homely noises, and only the rare croak of a raven breaks the silence. The hillside was far from sheer – one could have walked down with a little care – but something in the shape of the hollow and the remote gleam of white water gave it an air of extraordinary depth and space. There was a shimmer left from the day's heat, which invested bracken and rock and scree with a curious airy unreality. One could almost have believed that the eye had tricked the mind, that all was mirage,

145

that five yards from the path the solid earth fell away into nothingness. I have a bad head, and instinctively I drew further back into the heather. Leithen's eyes were looking vacantly before him.

'Did you ever know Hollond?' he asked.

Then he laughed shortly. 'I don't know why I asked that, but somehow this place reminded me of Hollond. That glimmering hollow looks as if it were the beginning of eternity. It must be eerie to live with the feeling always on one.'

Leithen seemed disinclined for further exercise. He lit a pipe and smoked quietly for a little. 'Odd that you didn't know Hollond. You must have heard his name. I thought you amused yourself with metaphysics.'

Then I remembered. There had been an erratic genius who had written some articles in *Mind* on that dreary subject, the mathematical conception of infinity. Men had praised them to me, but I confess I never quite understood their argument. 'Wasn't he some sort of mathematical professor?' I asked.

'He was, and, in his own way, a tremendous swell. He wrote a book on Number which has translations in every European language. He is dead now, and the Royal Society founded a medal in his honour. But I wasn't thinking of that side of him.'

It was the time and place for a story, for the pony would not be back for an hour. So I asked Leithen about the other side of Hollond which was recalled to him by Correi na Sidhe. He seemed a little unwilling to speak ...

'I wonder if you will understand it. You ought to, of course, better than me, for you know something of philosophy. But it took me a long time to get the hang of it, and I can't give you any kind of explanation. He was my fag at Eton, and when I began to get at the Bar I was able to advise him on one or two private matters, so that he rather fancied my legal ability. He came to me with his story because he had to tell someone, and he wouldn't trust a colleague. He said he didn't want a scientist to know, for scientists were either pledged to their own theories and wouldn't understand, or, if they understood, would get ahead of him in his researches. He wanted a lawyer, he said, who was accustomed to weighing evidence. That was good sense, for evidence must always be judged by the same laws, and I suppose in the long-run the most abstruse business comes down to a fairly simple deduction from certain data. Anyhow, that was the way he used to talk, and I listened to him, for I liked the man, and had an enormous respect for his brains. At Eton he sluiced down all the mathematics they could give him, and he was an astonishing swell at Cambridge. He was a simple fellow, too, and talked no more jargon than he could help. I used to climb with him in the Alps now and then, and you would never have guessed that he had any thoughts beyond getting up steep rocks.

'It was at Chamonix, I remember, that I first got a hint of the matter that was filling his mind. We had been taking an off-day, and were sitting in the hotel garden, watching the Aiguilles getting purple in the twilight. Chamonix always makes me choke a little – it is so crushed in by those great snow masses. I said something about it – said I liked open spaces like the Gornergrat or the Bel Alp better. He asked me why: if it was the difference of the air, or merely the wider horizon? I said it was the sense of not being crowded, of living in an empty world. He repeated the word "empty" and laughed.

' "By 'empty' you mean," he said, "where things don't knock up against you?" '

'I told him No. I meant just empty, void, nothing but blank aether.

' "You don't knock up against things here, and the air is as good as you want. It can't be the lack of ordinary emptiness you feel."

'I agreed that the word needed explaining. "I suppose it is mental restlessness," I said. "I like to feel that for a tremendous distance there is nothing round me. Why, I don't know. Some men are built the other way and have a terror of space.

'He said that that was better. "It is a personal fancy, and depends on your *knowing* that there is nothing between you and the top of the Dent Blanche. And you know because your eyes tell you there is nothing. Even if you were blind, you might have a sort of sense about adjacent matter. Blind men often have it. But in any case, whether got from instinct or sight, the *knowledge* is what matters."

'Hollond was embarking on a Socratic dialogue in which I could see little point. I told him so, and he laughed.

' "I am not sure that I am very clear myself. But yes – there *is* a point. Supposing you knew – not by sight or by instinct, but by sheer intellectual knowledge, as I know the truth of a mathematical proposition – that what we call empty space was full, crammed. Not with lumps of what we call matter like hills and houses, but with things as real – as real to the mind. Would you still feel crowded?"

' "No," I said, "I don't think so. It is only what we call matter that signifies. It would be just as well not to feel crowded by the other thing, for there would be no escape from it. But what are you getting at? Do you mean molecules or electric currents or what?"

'He said he wasn't thinking about that sort of thing, and began to talk of another subject.

'Next night, when we were pigging it at the Géant *cabane*, he started again on the same tack. He asked me how I accounted for the fact that animals could find their way back over great tracts of unknown country. I said I supposed it was the homing instinct.

' "Rubbish, man," he said. "That's only another name for the puzzle, not an explanation. There must be some reason for it. They must *know* something that we cannot understand. Tie a cat in a bag and take it fifty miles by train and it will make its way home. That cat has some clue that we haven't."

'I was tired and sleepy, and told him that I did not care a rush about the psychology of cats. But he was not to be snubbed, and went on talking.

' "How if Space is really full of things we cannot see and as yet do not know? How if all animals and some savages have a cell in their brain or a nerve which responds to the invisible world? How if all Space be full of these landmarks, not material in our sense, but quite real? A dog barks at nothing, a wild beast makes an aimless circuit. Why? Perhaps because Space is made up of corridors and alleys, ways to travel and things to shun? For all we know, to a greater intelligence than ours the top of Mont Blanc may be as crowded as Piccadilly Circus."

'But at that point I fell asleep and left Hollond to repeat his questions to a guide who knew no English and a snoring porter.

'Six months later, one foggy January afternoon, Hollond rang me up at the Temple and proposed to come to see me that night after dinner. I thought he wanted to talk Alpine shop, but he turned up in Duke Street about nine with a kit-bag full of papers. He was an odd fellow to look at – a yellowish face with the skin stretched tight on the cheek-bones, clean-shaven, a sharp chin which he kept poking forward, and deep-set, greyish eyes. He was a hard fellow, too, always in a pretty good condition, which was remarkable considering how he slaved for nine months out of the twelve. He had a quiet, slow-spoken manner, but that night I saw that he was considerably excited.

'He said that he had come to me because we were old friends. He proposed to tell me a tremendous secret. "I must get another mind to work on it or I'll go crazy. I don't want a scientist. I want a plain man."

'Then he fixed me with a look like a tragic actor's. "Do you remember that talk we had in August at Chamonix – about Space? I daresay you thought I was playing the fool. So I was in a sense, but I was feeling my way towards something which has been in my mind for ten years. Now I have got it, and you must hear about it. You may take my word that it's a pretty startling discovery."

'I lit a pipe and told him to go ahead, warning him that I knew about as much science as the dustman.

'I am bound to say that it took me a long time to understand what he meant. He began by saying that everybody thought of Space as an "empty homogeneous medium." "Never mind at present what the ultimate constituents of that medium are. We take it as a finished product, and we think of it as mere extension, something without any quality at all. That is the view of civilised man. You will find all the philosophers taking it for granted. Yes, but every living thing does not take that view. An animal, for instance. It feels a kind of quality in Space. It can find its way over new country, because it perceives certain landmarks, not necessarily material, but perceptible, or if you like intelligible. Take an Australian savage. He has the same power, and I believe, for the same reason. He is conscious of intelligible landmarks."

' "You mean what people call a sense of direction," I put in.

' "Yes, but what in Heaven's name is a sense of direction? The phrase explains nothing. However incoherent the mind of the animal or the savage may be, it is there somewhere, working on some data. I've been all through the psychological and anthropological side of the business, and after you eliminate clues from sight and hearing and smell and half-conscious memory there remains a solid lump of the inexplicable."

'Hollond's eye had kindled, and he sat doubled up in his chair, dominating me with a finger.

' "Here, then, is a power which man is civilising himself out of. Call it anything you like, but you must admit that it is a power. Don't you see that it is a perception of another kind of reality that we are leaving behind us? ... Well, you know the way nature works. The wheel comes full circle, and what we think we have lost we regain in a higher form. So for a long time I have been wondering whether the civilised mind could not recreate for itself this lost gift, the gift of seeing the quality of Space. I mean that I wondered whether the scientific modern brain could not get to the stage of realising that Space is not an empty homogeneous medium, but full of intricate differences, intelligible and real, though not with our common reality."

'I found all this very puzzling, and he had to repeat it several times before I got a glimpse of what he was talking about.

' "I've wondered for a long time," he went on, "but now, quite suddenly, I have begun to know.' He stopped and asked me abruptly if I knew much about mathematics.

' "It's a pity," he said, "but the main point is not technical, though I wish you could appreciate the beauty of some of my proofs." Then he began to tell me about his last six months' work. I should have mentioned that he was a brilliant physicist besides other things. All Hollond's tastes were on the borderlands of sciences, where mathematics fades into metaphysics and physics merges in the abstrusest kind of mathematics. Well, it seems he had been working for years at the ultimate problem of matter, and especially of that rarefied matter we call aether or space. I forget what his view was – atoms or molecules or electric waves. If he ever told me I have forgotten, but I'm not certain that I ever knew. However, the point was that these ultimate constituents were dynamic and mobile, not a mere passive medium but a medium in constant movement and change. He claimed to have discovered – by ordinary inductive experiment – that the constituents of aether possessed certain functions, and moved in certain figures obedient to certain mathematical laws. Space, I gathered, was perpetually "forming fours" in some fancy way.

'Here he left his physics and became the mathematician. Among his mathematical discoveries had been certain curves or figures or something whose behaviour involved a new dimension. I gathered that this wasn't the ordinary Fourth Dimension that people talk of but that fourth-dimensional inwardness or involution was part of it. The explanation lay in the pile of manuscripts he left with me, but though I tried honestly I couldn't get the hang of it. My mathematics stopped with desperate finality just as he got into his subject.

'His point was that the constituents of Space moved according to these new mathematical figures of his. They were always changing, but the principles of their change were as fixed as the law of gravitation. Therefore, if you once grasped these principles you knew the contents of the void. What do you make of that?'

I said that it seemed to me a reasonable enough argument, but that it got one very little way forward. 'A man,' I said, 'might know the contents of Space and the laws of their arrangement and yet be unable to see anything more than his fellows. It is a purely academic knowledge. His mind knows it as the result of many deductions, but his senses perceive nothing.'

Leithen laughed. 'Just what I said to Hollond. He asked the opinion of my legal mind. I said I could not pronounce on his argument, but that I could point out that he had established no *trait d'union* between the intellect which understood and the senses which perceived. It was like a blind man with immense knowledge but no eyes, and therefore no peg to hang his knowledge on and make it useful. He had not explained his savage or his cat. "Hang it, man," I said, "before you can appreciate the existence of your Spacial forms you have to go through elaborate experiments and deductions. You can't be doing that every minute. Therefore you don't get any nearer to the *use* of the sense you say that man once possessed, though you can explain it a bit." '

'What did he say?' I asked.

'The funny thing was that he never seemed to see my difficulty. When I kept bringing him back to it he shied off with a new wild theory of perception. He argued that the mind can live in a world of realities without any sensuous stimulus to connect them with the world of our ordinary life. Of course that wasn't my point, I supposed that this world of Space was real enough to him, but I wanted to know how he got there. He never answered me. He was the typical Cambridge man, you know – dogmatic about uncertainties, but curiously diffident about the obvious. He laboured to get me to understand the notion of his mathematical forms, which I was quite willing to take on trust from him. Some queer things he said, too. He took our feeling about Left and Right as an example of our instinct for the quality of Space. But when I objected that Left and Right varied with each object, and only existed in connection with some definite material thing, he said that that was exactly what he meant. It was an example of the mobility of the Spacial forms. Do you see any sense in that?'

I shook my head. It seemed to me pure craziness.

'And then he tried to show me what he called the "involution of Space," by taking two points on a piece of paper. The points were a foot away when the paper was flat, but they coincided when it was doubled up. He said that there were no gaps between the figures, for the medium was continuous, and he took as an illustration the loops on a cord. You are to think of a cord always looping and unlooping itself according to certain mathematical laws. Oh, I tell you, I gave up trying to follow him. And he was so desperately in earnest all the time. By his account Space was a sort of mathematical pandemonium.'

LEITHEN stopped to refill his pipe, and I mused upon the ironic fate which had compelled a mathematical genius to make his sole confidant of a philistine lawyer, and induced that lawyer to repeat it confusedly to an ignoramus at twilight on a Scotch hill. As told by Leithen it was a very halting tale.

'But there was one thing I could see very clearly,' Leithen went on, 'and that was Hollond's own case. This crowded world of Space was perfectly real to him. How he had got to it I do not know. Perhaps his mind, dwelling constantly on the problem, had unsealed some atrophied cell and restored the old instinct. Anyhow, he was living his daily life with a foot in each world.

'He often came to see me, and after the first hectic discussions he didn't talk much. There was no noticeable change in him – a little more abstracted perhaps. He would walk in the street or come into a room with a quick look round him, and sometimes for no earthly reason he would swerve. Did you ever watch a cat crossing a room? It sidles along by the furniture and walks over an open space of carpet as if it were picking its way among obstacles. Well, Hollond behaved like that, but he had always been counted a little odd, and nobody noticed it but me.

'I knew better than to chaff him, and we had stopped argument, so there wasn't much to be said. But sometimes he would give me news about his experiences. The whole thing was perfectly clear and scientific and above-board, and nothing creepy about it. You know how I hate the washy supernatural stuff they give us nowadays. Hollond was well and fit, with an appetite like a hunter. But as he talked, sometimes – well, you know I haven't much in the way of nerves or imagination – but I used to get a little eerie. Used to feel the solid earth dissolving round me. It was the opposite of vertigo, if you understand me – a sense of airy realities crowding in on you – crowding the mind, that is, not the body.

'I gathered from Hollond that he was always conscious of corridors and halls and alleys in Space, shifting, but shifting according to inexorable laws. I never could get quite clear as to what this consciousness was like. When I asked he used to look puzzled and worried and helpless. I made out from him that one landmark involved a sequence, and once given a bearing from an object you could keep the direction without a mistake. He told me he could easily, if he wanted, go in a dirigible from the top of Mont Blanc to the top of Snowdon in the thickest fog and without a compass, if he were given the proper angle to start from. I confess I didn't follow that myself. Material objects had nothing to do with the Spacial forms, for a table or a bed in our world might be placed across a corridor of Space. The forms played their game independent of our kind of reality. But the worst of it was, that if you kept your mind too much in one world you were apt to forget about the other, and Hollond was always barking his shins on stones and chairs and things.

'He told me all this quite simply and frankly. Remember his mind and no other part of him lived in his new world. He said it gave him an odd sense of detachment to sit in a room among people, and to know that nothing there but himself had any relation at all to the infinite strange world of Space that flowed around them. He would listen, he said, to a great man talking, with one eye on the cat on the rug, thinking to himself how much more the cat knew than the man.'

'How long was it before he went mad?' I asked.

It was a foolish question, and made Leithen cross. 'He never went mad in your sense. My dear fellow, you're very much wrong if you think there was anything pathological about him – then. The man was brilliantly sane. His mind was as keen as a keen sword. I couldn't understand him, but I could judge of his sanity right enough.'

I asked if it made him happy or miserable.

'At first I think it made him uncomfortable. He was restless because he knew too much and too little. The unknown pressed in on his mind, as bad air weighs on the lungs. Then it lightened, and he accepted the new world in the same sober practical way that he took other things. I think that the free exercise of his mind in a pure medium gave him a feeling of extraordinary power and ease. His eyes used to sparkle when he talked. And another odd thing he told me. He was a keen rock-climber, but, curiously enough, he had never a very good head. Dizzy heights always worried him, though he managed to keep hold on himself. But now all that had gone. The sense of the fulness of Space made him as happy – happier I believe – with his legs dangling into eternity, as sitting before his own study fire.

'I remember saying that it was all rather like the mediaeval wizards who made their spells by means of numbers and figures.

'He caught me up at once. "Not numbers," he said. "Number has no place in Nature. It is an invention of the human mind to atone for a bad memory. But figures are a different matter. All the mysteries of the world are in them, and the old magicians knew that at least, if they knew no more."

'He had only one grievance. He complained that it was terribly lonely. "It is the Desolation," he would quote, "spoken of by Daniel the prophet." He would spend hours travelling those eerie shifting corridors of Space with no hint of another human soul. How could there be? It was a world of pure reason, where human personality had no place. What puzzled me was why he should feel the absence of this. One wouldn't, you know, in an intricate problem of geometry or a game of chess. I asked him, but he didn't understand the question. I puzzled over it a good deal, for it seemed to me that if Hollond felt lonely, there must be more in this world of his than we imagined. I began to wonder if there was any truth in fads like psychical research. Also, I was not so sure that he was as normal as I had thought: it looked as if his nerves might be going bad.

'Oddly enough, Hollond was getting on the same track himself. He had discovered, so he said, that in sleep everybody now and then lived in this new world of his. You know how one dreams of triangular railway platforms with trains running simultaneously down all three sides and not colliding. Well, this sort of cantrip was "common form," as we say at the Bar, in Hollond's Space, and he was very curious about the why and wherefore of Sleep. He began to haunt psychological laboratories, where they experiment with the charwoman and the odd man, and he used to go up to Cambridge for *séances*. It was a foreign atmosphere to him, and I don't think he was very happy in it. He found so many charlatans that he used to get angry, and declare he would be better employed at Mothers' Meetings!'

FROM far up the Glen came the sound of the pony's hoofs. The stag had been loaded up, and the gillies were returning. Leithen looked at his watch. 'We'd better wait and see the beast,' he said.

'... Well, nothing happened for the better part of a year. Then one evening in May he burst into my rooms in high excitement. You understand quite clearly that there was no suspicion of horror or fright or anything unpleasant about this world he had discovered. It was simply a series of interesting and difficult problems. All this time Hollond had been rather extra well and cheery. But when he came in I thought I noticed a different look in his eyes, something puzzled and diffident and apprehensive.

' "There's a queer performance going on in the other world," he said. "It's unbelievable. I never dreamed of such a thing. I – I don't quite know how to put it, and I don't know how to explain it, but – but I am becoming aware that there are other beings – other minds – moving in Space besides mine."

'I suppose I ought to have realised then that things were beginning to go wrong. But it was very difficult, he was so rational and anxious to make it all clear. I asked him how he knew. There could, of course, on his own showing be no *change* in that world, for the forms of Space moved and existed under inexorable laws. He said he found his own mind failing him at points. There would come over him a sense of fear – intellectual fear – and weakness, a sense of something else, quite alien to Space, thwarting him. Of course he could only describe his impressions very lamely, for they were purely of the mind, and he had no material peg to hang them on, so that I could realise them. But the gist of it was that he had been gradually becoming conscious of what he called "Presences" in his world. They had no effect on Space – did not leave footprints in its corridors, for instance – but they affected his mind. There was some mysterious contact established between him and them. I asked him if the affection was unpleasant, and he said. "No, not exactly." But I could see a hint of fear in his eyes.

'Think of it. Try to realise what intellectual fear is. I can't, but it is conceivable. To you and me fear implies pain to ourselves or some other, and such pain is always in the last resort pain of the flesh. Consider it carefully and you will see that it is so. But imagine fear so sublimated and transmuted as to be the tension of pure spirit. I can't realise it, but I think it possible. I don't pretend to understand how Hollond got to know about these Presences. But there was no doubt about the fact. He was positive, and he wasn't in the least mad – not in our sense. In that very month he published his book on Number, and gave a German professor who attacked it a most tremendous public trouncing.

'I know what you are going to say – that the fancy was a weakening of the mind from within. I admit I should have thought of that, but he looked so confoundedly sane and able that it seemed ridiculous. He kept asking me my opinion, as a lawyer, on the facts he offered. It was the oddest case ever put before me, but I did my best for him. I dropped all my own views of sense and nonsense. I told him that, taking all that he had told me as fact, the Presences might be either ordinary minds traversing Space in sleep; or minds such as his which had independently captured the sense of Space's quality; or, finally, the spirits of just men made perfect, behaving as psychical researchers think they do. It was a ridiculous task to set a prosaic man, and I wasn't quite serious. But Hollond was serious enough.

'He admitted that all three explanations were conceivable, but he was very doubtful about the first. The projection of the spirit into Space during sleep, he thought, was a faint and feeble thing, and these were powerful Presences. With the second and the third he was rather impressed. I suppose I should have seen what was happening and tried to stop it; at least, looking back that seems to have been my duty. But it was difficult to think that anything was wrong with Hollond; indeed the odd thing is that all this time the idea of madness never entered my head. I rather backed him up. Somehow the thing took my fancy, though I thought it moonshine at the bottom of my heart. I enlarged on the pioneering before him. "Think," I told him, "what may be waiting for you. You may discover the meaning of Spirit. You may open up a new world, as rich as the old one, but imperishable. You may prove to mankind their immortality and deliver them for ever from the fear of death. Why, man, you are picking at the lock of all the world's mysteries."

'But Hollond did not cheer up. He seemed strangely languid and dispirited. "That is all true enough," he said, "if you are right, if your alternatives are exhaustive. But suppose they are something else, something ..." What that "something" might be he had apparently no idea, and very soon he went away.

'He said another thing before he left. He asked me if I ever read poetry, and I said, Not often. Nor did he: but he had picked up a little book somewhere and found a man who knew about the Presences. I think his name was Traherne, one of the seventeenth-century fellows. He quoted a verse which stuck to my fly-paper memory. It ran something like this:

> 'Within the region of the air,
> Compassed about with Heavens fair,
> Great tracts of land there may be found,
>   Where many numerous hosts,
>   In those far distant coasts,
> For other great and glorious ends
> Inhabit, my yet unknown friends.

Hollond was positive he did not mean angels or anything of the sort. I told him that Traherne evidently took a cheerful view of them. He admitted that, but added: "He had religion, you see. He believed that everything was for the best. I am not a man of faith, and can only take comfort from what I understand. I'm in the dark, I tell you ..."

'Next week I was busy with the Chilian Arbitration case, and saw nobody for a couple of months. Then one evening I ran against Hollond on the Embankment, and thought him looking horribly ill. He walked back with me to my rooms, and hardly uttered one word all the way. I gave him a stiff whisky-and-soda, which he gulped down absent-mindedly. There was that strained, hunted look in his eyes that you see in a frightened animal's. He was always lean, but now he had fallen away to skin and bone.

' "I can't stay long," he told me, "for I'm off to the Alps tomorrow and I have a lot to do." Before then he used to plunge readily into his story, but now he seemed shy about beginning. Indeed I had to ask him a question.

' "Things are difficult," he said hesitatingly, "and rather distressing. Do you know, Leithen, I think you were wrong about – about what I spoke to you of. You said there must be one of three explanations. I am beginning to think that there is a fourth ..."

'He stopped for a second or two, then suddenly leaned forward and gripped my knee so fiercely that I cried out. "That world is the Desolation," he said in a choking voice, "and perhaps I am getting near the Abomination of the Desolation that the old prophet spoke of. I tell you, man, I am on the edge of a terror, a terror," he almost screamed, "that no mortal can think of and live."

'You can imagine that I was considerably startled. It was lightning out of a clear sky. How the devil could one associate horror with mathematics? I don't see it yet ... At any rate, I – You may be sure I cursed my folly for ever pretending to take him seriously. The only way would have been to have laughed him out of it at the start. And yet I couldn't, you know – it was too real and reasonable. Anyhow, I tried a firm tone now, and told him the whole thing was arrant raving bosh. I bade him be a man and pull himself together. I made him dine with me, and took him home, and got him into a better state of mind before he went to bed. Next morning I saw him off at Charing Cross, very haggard still, but better. He promised to write to me pretty often ...'

━━━━━━━━━━━━

THE pony, with a great eleven-pointer lurching athwart its back, was abreast of us, and from the autumn mist came the sound of soft Highland voices. Leithen and I got up to go, when we heard that the rifle had made direct for the Lodge by a short cut past the Sanctuary. In the wake of the gillies we descended the Correi road into a glen all swimming with dim purple shadows. The pony minced and boggled; the stag's antlers stood out sharp on the rise against a patch of sky, looking like a skeleton tree. Then we dropped into a covert of birches and emerged on the white glen highway.

Leithen's story had bored and puzzled me at the start, but now it had somehow gripped my fancy. Space a domain of endless corridors and Presences moving in them! The world was not quite the same as an hour ago. It was the hour, as the French say, 'between dog and wolf,' when the mind is disposed to marvels. I thought of my stalking on the morrow, and was miserably conscious that I would miss my stag. Those airy forms would get in the way. Confound Leithen and his yarns!

'I want to hear the end of your story,' I told him, as the lights of the Lodge showed half a mile distant.

'The end was a tragedy,' he said slowly; 'I don't much care to talk about it. But how was I to know? I couldn't see the nerve going. You see I couldn't believe it was all nonsense. If I could I might have seen.

But I still think there was something in it – up to a point. Oh, I agree he went mad in the end. It is the only explanation. Something must have snapped in that fine brain, and he saw the little bit more which we call madness. Thank God, you and I are prosaic fellows ...

'I was going out to Chamonix myself a week later. But before I started I got a postcard from Hollond, the only word from him. He had printed my name and address, and on the other side had scribbled six words – "*I know at last – God's mercy. – H.G.H.*" The handwriting was like a sick man of ninety. I knew that things must be pretty bad with my friend.

'I got to Chamonix in time for his funeral. An ordinary climbing accident – you probably read about it in the papers. The Press talked about the toll which the Alps took from intellectuals – the usual rot. There was an inquiry, but the facts were quite simple. The body was only recognised by the clothes. He had fallen several thousand feet.

'It seems that he had climbed for a few days with one of the Kronigs and Dupont, and they had done some hair-raising things on the Aiguilles. Dupont told me that they had found a new route up the Montanvert side of the Charmoz. He said that Hollond climbed like a '*diable fou*,' and if you know Dupont's standard of madness you will see that the pace must have been pretty hot. "But Monsieur was sick," he added; "his eyes were not good. And I and Franz, we were grieved for him and a little afraid. We were glad when he left us."

'He dismissed the guides two days before his death. The next day he spent in the hotel, getting his affairs straight. He left everything in perfect order, but not a line to a soul, not even to his sister. The following day he set out alone about three in the morning for the Grèpon. He took the road up the Nantillons glacier to the Col, and then he must have climbed the Mummery crack by himself. After that he left the ordinary route and tried a new traverse across the Mer de Glace face. Somewhere near the top he fell, and next day a party going to the Dent du Requin found him on the rocks thousands of feet below.

'He had slipped in attempting the most foolhardy course on earth, and there was a lot of talk about the dangers of guideless climbing. But I guessed the truth, and I am sure Dupont knew, though he held his tongue ...'

We were now on the gravel of the drive, and I was feeling better. The thought of dinner warmed my heart and drove out the eeriness of the twilight glen. The hour between dog and wolf was passing. After all, there was a gross and jolly earth at hand for wise men who had a mind to comfort.

Leithen, I saw, did not share my mood. He looked glum and puzzled, as if his tale had aroused grim memories. He finished it at the Lodge door.

'... For, of course, he had gone out that day to die. He had seen the something more, the little bit too much, which plucks a man from his moorings. He had gone so far into the land of pure spirit that he must needs go further and shed the fleshly envelope that cumbered him. God send that he found rest! I believe that he chose the steepest cliff in the Alps for a purpose. He wanted to be unrecognisable. He was a brave man and a good citizen. I think he hoped that those who found him might not see the look in his eyes.'

Basilissa

WHEN Vernon was a very little boy he was the sleepiest of mortals, but in the spring he had seasons of bad dreams, and breakfast became an idle meal. Mrs Ganthony, greatly concerned, sent for Dr Moreton from Axby, and homely remedies were prescribed.

'It is the spring fever,' said the old man. 'It gives the gout to me and nightmares to this baby; it brings lads and lasses together, and scatters young men about the world. An antique complaint, Mrs Ganthony. But it will right itself, never fear. *Ver non semper viret.*' Chuckling at his ancient joke, the doctor mounted his horse, leaving the nurse only half comforted. 'What fidgets me,' she told the housekeeper, 'is the way his lordship holds his tongue. For usual he'll shout as lusty as a whelp. But now I finds him in the morning with his eyes like moons and his skin white and shiny, and never a cheep has he given the whole blessed night, with me laying next door, and it open, and a light sleeper at all times, Mrs Wace, ma'am.'

Every year the dreams came, generally – for his springs were spent at Severns – in the big new night-nursery at the top of the west wing, which his parents had built not long before their death. It had three windows looking over the moorish flats which run up to the Lancashire fells, and from one window, by craning your neck, you could catch a glimpse of the sea. It was all hung, too, with a Chinese paper whereon pink and green parrots squatted in wonderful blue trees, and there seemed generally to be a wood fire burning. Vernon's recollections of his childish nightmare are hazy. He always found himself in a room different from the nursery and bigger, but with the same smell of wood smoke. People came and went, such as his nurse, the butler, Simon the head-keeper, Uncle Appleby his guardian, Cousin Jennifer, the old woman who sold oranges in Axby, and a host of others. Nobody hindered them from going away, and they seemed to be pleading with him to come too. There was danger in the place; something was going to happen in that big room, and if by that time he was not gone there would be mischief. But it was quite clear to him that he could not go.

He must stop there, with the wood smoke in his nostrils, and await the advent of a terrible Something. But he was never quite sure of the nature of the compulsion. He had a notion that if he made a rush for the door at Uncle Appleby's heels he would be allowed to escape, but that somehow he would be behaving badly. Anyhow, the place put him into a sweat of fright, and Mrs Ganthony looked darkly at him in the morning.

Vernon was nine before this odd spring dream began to take definite shape – at least he thinks he must have been about that age. The dream-stage was emptying. There was nobody in the room now but himself, and he saw its details a little more clearly. It was not any apartment in the modern magnificence of Severns. Rather it looked like one of the big old panelled chambers which the boy remembered from visits to Midland country-houses, where he had arrived after dark and had been put to sleep in a great bed in a place lit with dancing firelight. In the morning it had looked only an ordinary big room, but at that hour of the evening it had seemed an enchanted citadel. The dream-room was not unlike these, for there was the scent of a wood fire and there were dancing shadows, but he could not see clearly the walls or the ceiling, and there was no bed. In one corner was a door which led to the outer world, and through this he knew that he might on no account pass. Another door faced him, and he knew that he had only to turn the handle and enter it. But he did not want to, for he understood quite clearly what was beyond. There was another room like the first one, but he knew nothing about it, except that opposite the entrance another door led out of it. Beyond was a third chamber, and so on interminably. There seemed to the boy no end to this fantastic suite. He thought of it as a great snake of masonry, winding up hill and down dale away to the fells or the sea. Yes, but there was an end. Somewhere far away in one of the rooms was a terror waiting on him, or, as he feared, coming towards him. Even now it might be flitting from room to room, every minute bringing its soft tread nearer to the chamber of the wood fire.

About this time of life the dream was an unmitigated horror. Once it came while he was ill with a childish fever, and it sent his temperature up to a point which brought Dr Moreton galloping from Axby. In his waking hours he did not, as a rule, remember it clearly; but during the fever, asleep and awake, that sinuous building, one room thick, with each room opening from the other, was never away from his thoughts. It fretted him to think that outside were the cheerful moors where he hunted for plovers' eggs, and that only a thin wall of stone kept him from pleasant homely things. The thought used to comfort him for a moment when he was awake, but in the dream it never came near him. Asleep, the whole world seemed one suite of rooms, and he, a forlorn little prisoner, doomed to wait grimly on the slow coming through the many doors of a Fear which transcended word and thought.

He was a silent, self-absorbed boy, and though the fact of his nightmares was patent to the little household, the details remained locked in his heart. Not even to Uncle Appleby would he tell them when that gentleman, hurriedly kind, came down to visit his convalescent ward. His illness made Vernon grow, and he shot up into a lanky, leggy boy – weakly, too, till the hills tautened his sinews again. His Greek blood – his grandmother had been a Karolides – had given him a face curiously like the young Byron, with a finely-cut brow and nostrils, and hauteur in the full lips. But Vernon had no Byronic pallor, for his upland home kept him sunburnt and weather-beaten, and below his straight Greek brows shone a pair of grey and steadfast and very English eyes.

He was about fifteen – so he thinks – when he made the great discovery. The dream had become almost a custom now. It came in April at Severns during the Easter holidays – a night's discomfort (it was now scarcely more) in the rush and glory of the spring fishing. There was a moment of the old wild heart-fluttering; but a boy's fancy is quickly dulled, and the endless corridors were now more of a prison than a witch's ante-chamber. By this time, with the help of his diary, he had fixed the date of the dream: it came regularly on the night of the first Monday of April. Now the year I speak of he had been on a long expedition into the hills, and had stridden homewards at a steady four miles an hour among the gleams and shadows of an April twilight. He was alone at Severns, so he had his supper in the big library, where afterwards he sat watching the leaping flames in the open stone hearth. He was very weary, and sleep fell upon him in his chair. He found himself in the wood-smoke chamber, and before him the door leading to the unknown. But it was no indefinite fear that lay beyond. He knew clearly – though how he knew he could not tell – that each year the Something came one room nearer, and was even now but ten rooms off. In ten years his own door would open, and then –

He woke in the small hours, chilled and mazed, but with a curious new assurance in his heart. Hitherto the nightmare had left him in gross terror, unable to endure the prospect of its recurrence, till the kindly forgetfulness of youth had soothed him. But now, though his nerves were tense with fright, he perceived that there was a limit to the mystery. Some day it must declare itself, and fight on equal terms. As he thought over the matter in the next few days he had the sense of being forewarned and prepared for some great test of courage. The notion exhilarated as much as it frightened him. Late at night, or on soft dripping days, or at any moment of lessened vitality, he would bitterly wish that he had been born an ordinary mortal. But on a keen morning of frost, when he rubbed himself warm after a cold tub, or at high noon of summer, the adventure of the dream almost pleased him. Unconsciously he braced himself to a harder discipline. His fitness, moral and physical, became his chief interest, for reasons which would have been unintelligible to his friends and more so to his masters. He passed through school an aloof and splendid figure, magnificently athletic, with a brain as well as a perfect body – a good fellow in everybody's opinion, but a grave one. He had no intimates, and never shared the secret of the spring dream. For some reason which he could not tell, he would have burned his hand off rather than breathe a hint of it. Pure terror absolves from all conventions and demands a confidant, so terror, I think, must have largely departed from the nightmare as he grew older. Fear, indeed, remained, and awe and disquiet, but these are human things, whereas terror is of hell.

Had he told any one, he would no doubt have become self-conscious and felt acutely his difference from other people. As it was, he was an ordinary schoolboy, much beloved, and, except at odd moments, unaware of any brooding destiny. As he grew up and his ambition awoke, the moments when he remembered the dream were apt to be disagreeable, for a boy's ambitions are strictly conventional and his soul revolts at the abnormal. By the time he was ready for the University he wanted above all things to run the mile a second faster than any one else, and had vague hopes of exploring wild countries. For most of the year he lived with these hopes and was happy; then came April, and for a short season he was groping in dark places. Before and after each dream he was in a mood of exasperation; but when it came he plunged into a different atmosphere, and felt the quiver of fear and the quick thrill of expectation. One year, in the unsettled moods of nineteen, he made an attempt to avoid it. He and three others were on a walking tour in Brittany in gusty spring weather, and came late one evening to an inn by an estuary where seagulls clattered about the windows. Youth – like they ordered a great and foolish feast, and sat all night round a bowl of punch, while school songs and 'John Peel' contended with the dirling of the gale. At daylight they took the road again, without having closed an eye, and Vernon told himself that he was rid of his incubus. He wondered at the time why he was not more cheerful. Next April he was at Severns,

reading hard, and on the first Monday of the month he went to bed
with scarcely a thought of what that night used to mean. The dream
did not fail him. Once more he was in the chamber with the wood fire;
once again he was peering at the door and wondering with tremulous
heart what lay beyond. For the Something had come nearer by two
rooms, and was now only five doors away. He wrote in his diary at that
time some lines from Keats' 'Indian Maid's Song':

> 'I would deceive her,
> And so leave her,
> But ah! she is so constant and so kind.'

And there is a mark of exclamation against the 'she,' as if he found
some irony in it.

From that day the boy in him died. The dream would not suffer
itself to be forgotten. It moulded his character and determined his
plans like the vow of the young Hannibal at the altar. He had forgotten
now either to fear or to hope; the thing was part of him, like his
vigorous young body, his slow kindliness, his patient courage. He left
Oxford at twenty-two with a prodigious reputation which his
remarkable athletic record by no means explained. All men liked him,
but no one knew him; he had a thousand acquaintances and a hundred
friends, but no comrade. There was a sense of brooding power about
him which attracted and repelled his little world. No one forecast any
special career for him; indeed, it seemed almost disrespectful to
condescend upon such details. It was not what Vernon would do that
fired the imagination of his fellows, but what they dimly conceived that
he already was. I remember my first sight of him about that time, a tall
young man in his corner of a club smoking-room, with a head like
Apollo's and eyes which received much but gave nothing. I guessed at
once that he had foreign blood in him, not from any oddness of
colouring or feature but from his silken reserve. We of the North are
angular in our silences; we have not learned the art of gracious
reticence.

His twenty-third April was spent in a hut on the Line, somewhere
between the sources of the Congo and the Nile, in the trans-African
expedition when Waldemar found the new variety of okapi. The
following April I was in his company in a tent far up on the shoulder of
a Kashmir mountain. On the first Monday of the month we had had a
heavy day after ovis, and that night I was asleep almost before my
weary limbs were tucked into my kaross. I knew nothing of Vernon's

dream, but next morning I remember that I remarked a certain heaviness of eye, and wondered idly if the frame of this Greek divinity was as tough as it was shapely.

———

NEXT year Vernon left England early in March. He had resolved to visit again his grandmother's country and to indulge his passion for cruising in new waters.

His 20-ton yawl was sent as deck cargo to Patras, while he followed by way of Venice. He brought one man with him from Wyvenhoe, a lean gypsy lad called Martell, and for his other hand he found an Epirote at Corfu, who bore a string of names that began with Constantine. From Patras with a west wind they made good sailing up the Gulf of Corinth, and, passing through the Canal, came in the last days of March to the Piraeus. In that place of polyglot speech, whistling engines, and the odour of gas-works, they delayed only for water and supplies, and presently had rounded Sunium, and were beating up the Euripus with the Attic hills rising sharp and clear in the spring sunlight. Vernon had no plan. It was a joy to him to be alone with the racing seas and the dancing winds, to scud past little headlands, pink and white with blossom, or to lie of a night in some hidden bay beneath the thymy crags. It was his habit on his journeys to discard the clothes of civilisation. In a blue jersey and old corduroy trousers, bare-headed and barefooted, he steered his craft and waited on the passing of the hours. Like an acolyte before the temple gate, he believed himself to be on the threshold of a new life.

Trouble began under the snows of Pelion as they turned the north end of Euboea. On the morning of the first Monday in April the light west winds died away, and scirocco blew harshly from the south. By midday it was half a gale, and in those yeasty shallow seas with an iron coast on the port the prospect looked doubtful. The nearest harbour was twenty miles distant, and as no one of the crew had been there before it was a question if they could make it by nightfall. With the evening the gale increased, and Constantine advised a retreat from the maze of rocky islands to the safer deeps of the Ægean. It was a hard night for the three, and there was no chance of sleep. More by luck than skill they escaped the butt of Skiathos, and the first light found them far to the east among the long seas of the North Ægean, well on the way to Lemnos. By eight o'clock the gale had blown itself out, and three soaked and chilly mortals relaxed their vigil. Soon bacon was frizzling on the cuddy-stove, and hot coffee and dry clothes restored them to comfort.

The sky cleared, and in bright sunlight, with the dregs of the gale behind him, Vernon stood in for the mainland, where the white crest of Olympus hung in the northern heavens. In the late afternoon they came into a little bay carved from the side of a high mountain. The slopes were gay with flowers, yellow and white and scarlet, and the young green of crops showed in the clearings. Among the thyme a flock of goats was browsing, shepherded by a little girl in a saffron skirt, who sang shrilly in snatches. Midway in the bay and just above the anchorage rose a great white building, which showed to seaward a blank white wall pierced with a few narrow windows. At first sight Vernon took it for a monastery, but a look through the glasses convinced him that its purpose was not religious. Once it had been fortified, and even now a broad causeway ran between it and the sea, which looked as if it had once held guns. The architecture was a jumble, showing here the enriched Gothic of Venice and there the straight lines and round arches of the East. It had once, he conjectured, been the hold of some Venetian sea-king, then the palace of a Turkish conqueror, and now was, perhaps, the homely manor-house of this pleasant domain.

A fishing-boat was putting out from the shore. He hailed its occupant and asked who owned the castle.

The man crossed himself and spat overboard. 'Basilissa,' he said, and turned his eyes seaward.

Vernon called Constantine from the bows and asked him what the word might mean. The Epirote crossed himself also before he spoke. 'It is the Lady of the Land,' he said, in a hushed voice. 'It is the great witch who is the Devil's bride. In old days in spring they made sacrifice to her, but they say her power is dying now. In my country we do not speak her name, but elsewhere they call her "Queen".' The man's bluff sailorly assurance had disappeared, and as Vernon stared at him in bewilderment he stammered and averted his eyes.

By supper-time he had recovered himself, and the weather-beaten three made such a meal as befits those who have faced danger together. Afterwards Vernon, as was his custom, sat alone in the stern, smoking and thinking his thoughts. He wrote up his diary with a ship's lantern beside him, while overhead the starless velvet sky seemed to hang low and soft like an awning. Little fires burned on the shore at which folk were cooking food – he could hear their voices, and from the keep one single lit window made an eye in the night.

He had leisure now for the thought which had all day been at the back of his mind. The night had passed and there had been no dream.

The adventure for which he had prepared himself had vanished into the Ægean tides. He told himself that it was a relief, that an old folly was over, but he knew in his heart that he was bitterly disappointed. The fates had prepared the stage and rung up the curtain without providing the play. He had been fooled, and somehow the zest and savour of life had gone from him. No man can be strung high and then find his preparation idle without suffering a cruel recoil.

As he scribbled idly in his diary he found some trouble about dates. Down in his bunk was a sheaf of Greek papers bought at the Piraeus and still unlooked at. He fetched them up and turned them over with a growing mystification. There was something very odd about the business. One gets hazy about dates at sea, but he could have sworn that he had made no mistake. Yet here it was down in black and white, for there was no question about the number of days since he left the Piraeus. The day was not Tuesday, as he had believed, but Monday, the first Monday of April.

He stood up with a beating heart and that sense of unseen hands which comes to all men once or twice in their lives. The night was yet to come, and with it the end of the dream. Suddenly he was glad, absurdly glad, he could almost have wept with the joy of it. And then he was conscious for the first time of the strangeness of the place in which he had anchored. The night was dark over him like a shell, enclosing the half-moon of bay and its one lit dwelling. The great hills, unseen but felt, ran up to snows, warding it off from a profane world. His nerves tingled with a joyful anticipation. Something, some wonderful thing, was coming to him out of the darkness.

Under an impulse for which he could give no reason, he called Constantine and gave his orders. Let him be ready to sail at any moment – a possible thing, for there was a light breeze off shore. Also let the yacht's dinghy be ready in case he wanted it. Then Vernon sat himself down again in the stern beside the lantern, and waited ...

He was dreaming, and did not hear the sound of oars or the grating of a boat alongside. Suddenly he found a face looking at him in the ring of lamplight – an old bearded face curiously wrinkled. The eyes, which were grave and penetrating, scanned him for a second or two, and then a voice spoke–

'Will the Signor come with me? There is work for him to do this night.'

Vernon rose obediently. He had waited for this call these many years, and he was there to answer it. He went below and put a loaded revolver in his trouser-pocket, and then dropped over the yacht's side into a cockleshell of a boat. The messenger took the oars and rowed for the point of light on shore.

A middle-aged woman stood on a rock above the tide, holding a small lantern. In its thin flicker he made out a person with the air and dress of a French maid. She cast one glance at Vernon, and then turned wearily to the other. 'Fool, Mitri!' she said. 'You have brought a peasant.'

'Nay,' said the old man, 'he is no peasant. He is a Signor, and as I judge, a man of his hands.'

The woman passed the light of her lantern over Vernon's form and face. 'His dress is a peasant's, but such clothes may be a nobleman's whim. I have heard it of the English.'

'I am English,' said Vernon in French.

She turned on him with a quick movement of relief.

'You are English and a gentleman? But I know nothing of you, only that you have come out of the sea. Up in the House we women are alone, and my mistress has death to face, or a worse than death. We have no claim on you, and if you give us your service it means danger – ah, what danger! The boat is waiting. You have time to go back and go away and forget that you have seen this accursed place. But, O Monsieur, if you hope for Heaven and have pity on a defenceless angel, you will not leave us.'

'I am ready,' said Vernon.

'God's mercy,' she sighed, and, seizing his arm, drew him up the steep causeway, while the old man went ahead with the lantern. Now and then she cast anxious glances to the right where the little fires of the fishers twinkled along the shore. Then came a point when the three entered a narrow uphill road, where rocky steps had been cut in a tamarisk thicket. She spoke low in French to Vernon's ear –

'My mistress is the last of her line, you figure; a girl with a wild estate and a father long dead. She is good and gracious, as I who have tended her can witness, but she is young and cannot govern the wolves who are the men of these parts. They have a long hatred of her house, and now they have rumoured it that she is a witch and blights the crops and slays the children. No one will look at her; the priest – for they are all in the plot – signs himself and crosses the road; the little ones run screaming to their mothers. Once, twice, they have cursed our threshold and made the blood mark on the door. For two years we have been prisoners in the House, and only Mitri is true. They name her Basilissa, meaning the Queen of Hell, whom the ancients called Proserpine. There is no babe but will faint with fright if it casts eyes on her, and she as mild and innocent as Mother Mary ...'

The woman stopped at a little door and in a high wall of masonry. 'Nay, wait and hear me out. It is better that you hear the tale from me than from her. Mitri has the gossip of the place through his daughter's husband, and the word has gone round to burn the witch out. The winter in the hills has been cruel, and they blame their sorrow on her. The dark of the moon in April is the time fixed, for they say that a witch has power only in moonlight. This is the night, and down on the shore the fishers are gathered. The men from the hills are in the higher woods.'

'Have they a leader?' Vernon asked.

'A leader?' her voice echoed shrilly. 'But that is the worst of our terrors. There is one Vlastos, a lord in the mountains, who saw my mistress a year ago as she looked from the balcony at the Swallow-singing, and was filled with a passion for her. He has persecuted her since with his desires. He is a king among these savages, being himself a very wolf in man's flesh. We have denied him, but he persists, and this night he announces that he comes for an answer. He offers to save her if she will trust him, but what is the honour of his kind? He is like a brute out of a cave. It were better for my lady to go to God in the fire than to meet all Hell in his arms. But this night we must choose, unless you prove a saviour.'

'Did you see my boat anchor in the bay?' Vernon asked, though he already knew the answer.

'But no,' she said. 'We live only to the landward side of the House. My lady told me that God would send a man to our aid. And I bade Mitri fetch him.'

The door was unlocked and the three climbed a staircase which seemed to follow the wall of a round tower. Presently they came into a stone hall with curious hangings like the old banners in a church. From the open flame of the lantern another was kindled, and the light showed a desolate place with crumbling mosaics on the floor and plaster dropping from the cornices. Through another corridor they went, where the air blew warmer and there was that indefinable scent which comes from human habitation. Then came a door which the woman held open for Vernon to enter. 'Wait there, Monsieur,' she said. 'My mistress will come to you.'

It was his own room, where annually he had waited with a fluttering heart since he was a child at Severns. A fire of wood – some resinous thing like juniper – burned on the hearth, and spirals of blue smoke escaped the stone chimney and filled the air with their pungent fragrance. On a Spanish cabinet stood an antique silver lamp, and there was a great blue Chinese vase filled with spring flowers. Soft

Turcoman rugs covered the wooden floor – Vernon noted every detail for never before had he been able to see his room clearly. A woman had lived here, for an embroidery frame lay on a table and there were silken cushions on the low divans. And facing him in the other wall there was a door.

In the old days he had regarded it with vague terror in his soul. Now he looked at it with the hungry gladness with which a traveller sees again the familiar objects of home. The hour of his destiny had struck. The thing for which he had trained himself in body and spirit was about to reveal itself in that doorway …

It opened, and a girl entered. She was tall and very slim, and moved with the free grace of a boy. She trod the floor like one walking in spring meadows. Her little head on the flower-like neck was bent sideways as if she were listening, and her eyes had the strange disquieting innocence of a child's. Yet she was a grown woman, nobly made, and lithe and supple as Artemis herself when she ranged with her maidens through the moonlit gades. Her face had the delicate pallor of pure health, and above it the masses of dark hair were bound with a thin gold circlet. She wore a gown of some soft white stuff, and had thrown over it a cloak of russet furs.

For a second – or so it seemed to Vernon – she looked at him as he stood tense and expectant like a runner at the start. Then the hesitation fled from her face. She ran to him with the confidence of a child who has waited long for the coming of a friend and has grown lonely and fearful. She gave him both her hands and in her tall pride looked him full in the eyes. 'You have come,' she sighed happily. 'I did not doubt it. They told me there was no help, but, you see, they did not know about you. That was my own secret. The Monster had nearly gobbled me, Perseus, but of course you could not come quicker. And now you will take me away with you? See, I am ready. And Elise will come too, and old Mitri, for they could not live without me. We must hurry, for the Monster is very near.'

In that high moment of romance, when young love had burst upon him like spring, Vernon retained his odd discipline of soul. The adventure of the dream could not be satisfied by flight, even though his companion was a goddess.

'We will go, Andromeda, but not yet. I have something to say to the Monster.'

She broke into a ripple of laughter. 'Yes, that is the better way. Mitri will admit him alone, and he will think to find us women. But you will be here and you will speak to him.' Then her eyes grew solemn. 'He is very cruel, Perseus, and he is full of evil. He may devour us both. Let us begone before he comes.'

It was Vernon's turn to laugh. At the moment no enterprise seemed too formidable, and a price must be paid for this far-away princess. And even as he laughed the noise of a great bell clanged through the house.

Mitri stole in with a scared face, and it was from Vernon that he took his orders. 'Speak them fair, but let one man enter and no more. Bring him here, and see that the gate is barred behind him. After that make ready for the road.' Then to the girl: 'Take off your cloak and wait here as if you were expecting him. I will stand behind the screen. Have no fear, for I will have him covered, and I will shoot him like a dog if he lays a finger on you.'

From the shelter of the screen Vernon saw the door open and a man enter. He was a big fellow of the common mountain type, gorgeously dressed in a uniform of white and crimson, with boots of yellow untanned leather, and a beltful of weapons. He was handsome in a coarse way, but his slanting eyes and the heavy lips scarcely hidden by the curling moustaches were ugly and sinister. He smiled, showing his white teeth, and spoke hurriedly in the guttural Greek of the north. The girl shivered at the sound of his voice, and to the watcher it seemed like Pan pursuing one of Dian's nymphs.

'You have no choice, my Queen,' he was saying. 'I have a hundred men at the gate who will do my bidding, and protect you against these fools of villagers till you are safe with me at Louko. But if you refuse me I cannot hold the people. They will burn the place over your head, and by to-morrow's morn these walls will be smouldering ashes with your fair body in the midst of them.'

Then his wooing became rougher. The satyr awoke in his passionate eyes. 'Nay, you are mine, whether you will it or not. I and my folk will carry you off when the trouble begins. Take your choice, my girl, whether you will go with a good grace, or trussed up behind a servant. We have rough ways in the hills with ungracious wenches.'

'I am going away,' she whispered, 'but not with you!'

The man laughed. 'Have you fetched down friend Michael and his angels to help you? By Saint John the Hunter, I would I had a rival. I would carve him prettily for the sake of your sweet flesh.'

Vernon kicked aside the screen. 'You will have your chance,' he said. 'I am ready.'

Vlastos stepped back with his hand at his belt. 'Who in the devil's name are you?' he asked.

'One who would dispute the lady with you,' said Vernon.

The man had recovered his confidence. 'I know nothing of you or whence you come, but to-night I am merciful. I give you ten seconds to disappear. If not, I will spit you, my fine cock, and you will roast in this oven.'

'Nevertheless the lady goes with me,' said Vernon, smiling.

Vlastos plucked a whistle from his belt, but before it reached his mouth he was looking into the barrel of Vernon's revolver. 'Pitch that thing on the floor,' came the command. 'Not there! Behind me! Off with that belt and give it to the lady. Quick, my friend.'

The dancing grey eyes dominated the sombre black ones. Vlastos flung down the whistle, and slowly removed the belt with its silver-mounted pistols and its brace of knives.

'Put up your weapon,' he muttered, 'and fight me for her, as a man should.'

'I ask nothing better,' said Vernon, and he laid his revolver in the girl's lap.

He had expected a fight with fists, and was not prepared for what followed. Vlastos sprang at him like a wild beast and clasped him round the waist. He was swung off his feet in a grip that seemed more than human. For a second or two he swayed to and fro, recovered himself, and by a back-heel stroke forced his assailant to relax a little. Then, locked together in the middle of the room, the struggle began. Dimly out of a corner of his eye he saw the girl pick up the silver lamp and stand by the door holding it high.

Vernon had learned the rudiments of wrestling among the dalesmen of the North, but now he was dealing with one who followed no ordinary methods. It was a contest of sheer physical power. Vlastos was a stone or two heavier, and had an uncommon length of arm; but he was clumsily made, and flabby from gross living. Vernon was spare and hard and clean, but he lacked one advantage – he had never striven with a man save in friendly games, and the other was bred to kill. For a minute or two they swayed and stumbled, while Vernon strove for the old Westmorland 'inside click.' Every second brought him nearer to it, while the other's face was pressed close to his shoulder.

Suddenly he felt a sharp pain. Teeth met in his flesh, and there was the jar and shiver of a torn muscle. The thing sickened him, and his grip slackened. In a moment Vlastos had swung him over in a strangle-hold, and had his neck bent almost to breaking.

On the sickness followed a revulsion of fierce anger. He was contending not with a man, but with some shaggy beast from the thicket. The passion brought out the extra power which is dormant in us all against the last extremity. Two years before he had been mauled by a leopard on the Congo, and had clutched its throat with his hand

and torn the life out. Such and no other was his antagonist. He was fighting with one who knew no code, and would gouge his eyes if he got the chance. The fear which had sickened him was driven out by fury. This wolf should go the way of other wolves who dared to strive with man.

By a mighty effort he got his right arm free, and though his own neck was in torture, he forced Vlastos' chin upward. It was a struggle of sheer endurance, till with a snarl the other slackened his pressure. Vernon slipped from his grasp, gave back a step, and then leaped for the under-grip. He seemed possessed with unholy strength, for the barrel of the man gave in his embrace. A rib cracked, and as they swayed to the breast-stroke, he felt the breath of his opponent coming in harsh gasps. It was the end, for with a twist which unlocked his arms he swung him high, and hurled him towards the fireplace. The head crashed on the stone hearth, and the man lay stunned among the blue jets of wood-smoke.

Vernon turned dizzily to the girl. She stood, statue-like, with the lamp in her hand, and beside her huddled Mitri and Elise.

'Bring ropes,' he cried to the servants. 'We will truss up this beast. The other wolves will find him and learn a lesson.' He bound his legs and arms and laid him on a divan.

The fire of battle was still in his eyes, but it faded when they fell upon the pale girl. A great pity and tenderness filled him. She swayed to his arms, and her head dropped on his shoulder. He picked her up like a child, and followed the servants to the sea-stair.

But first he found Vlastos' whistle, and blew it shrilly. The answer was a furious hammering at the castle door …

Far out at sea, in the small hours, the yacht sped eastward with a favouring wind. Behind in the vault of night at a great distance shone a point of brightness, which flickered and fell as if from some mighty fire.

The two sat in the stern in that first rapture of comradeship which has no words to fit it. Her head lay in the crook of his arm, and she sighed happily, like one awakened to a summer's dawn from a night of ill dreams. At last he spoke.

'Do you know that I have been looking for you for twenty years?'

She nestled closer to him.

'And I,' she said, 'have been waiting on you from the beginning of the world.'

Tendebant Manus

ONE night we were discussing Souldern, who had died a week before and whose memorial service had been held that morning in St. Margaret's. He had come on amazingly in Parliament, one of those sudden rises which were common in the immediate post-war years, when the older reputations were being questioned and the younger men were too busy making a livelihood to have time for hobbies. His speeches, his membership of a commission where he had shown both originality and courage, and his reputed refusal, on very honourable grounds, of a place in the Cabinet, had given him in the popular mind a flavour of mystery and distinction. The papers had devoted a good deal of space to him, and there was a general feeling that his death – the result of a motor smash – was a bigger loss to the country than his actual achievement warranted.

'I never met him,' Palliser-Yates said. 'But I was at school with his minor. You remember Reggie Souldern, Charles? An uncommon good fellow – makings of a fine soldier, too – disappeared with most of his battalion in March '18, and was never heard of again. Body committed to the pleasant land of France but exact spot unknown – rather like a burial at sea.'

'I knew George Souldern well enough,' said Lamancha, whom he addressed. 'I sat in the House with him for two years before the War. That is to say, I knew as much of him as anybody did, but there was very little you could lay hold of. He used to be a fussy, ineffective chap, very fertile in ideas which he never thought out, and always starting hares that he wouldn't hunt. But just lately he seems to have had a call, and he looked as if he might have a career. Rotten luck that a sharp corner and a lout of a motor-cyclist should have put an end to it.'

He turned to his neighbour. 'Wasn't he a relation of yours, Sir Arthur?'

The man addressed was the oldest member of the Club and by far the most distinguished. Sir Arthur Warcliff had been a figure of note when most of us were in our cradles. He began life in the Sappers, and before he was thirty had been in command of a troublesome little Somaliland expedition; then he had governed a variety of places with such success that he was seriously spoken of for India. In the War he would have liked to have returned back to soldiering, but they used him as the Cabinet handy-man, and he had all the worst diplomatic and administrative jobs to tackle. You see, he was a master of detail and had to translate the generalities of policy into action. He had never, as the jargon goes, got his personality over the footlights, so he was only a name to the public – but a tremendous name, of which every party spoke respectfully. He had retired now, and lived alone with his motherless boy. Usually, for all his sixty-five years, he seemed a contemporary, for he was curiously young at heart, but every now and then we looked at his wise, worn face, realised what he had been and was, and sat at his feet.

'Yes,' he said in reply to Lamancha. 'George Souldern was my wife's cousin, and I knew him well for the last twenty years. Since the War I knew him better, and in the past eighteen months I was, I think, his only intimate friend.'

'Was he a really big man?' Sandy Arbuthnot asked. 'I don't take much stock in his profession – but I thought – just for a moment – in that Irish row – that I got a glimpse of something rather out of the ordinary.'

'He had first-class brains.'

Sandy laughed. 'That doesn't get you very far,' he said. The phrase "first-class brains" had acquired at the time a flavour of comedy.

'No. It doesn't. If you had asked me the question six years ago I should have said that George was a brilliant failure. Immensely clever in his way, really well educated – which very few of us are – laborious as a beaver, but futile. The hare that is always being passed by every kind of tortoise. He had everything in his favour, but nothing ever came out as he wanted it. I only knew him after he came down from Oxford, but I believe that at the University he was a nonpareil.'

'I was up with him,' said Peckwether, the historian. 'Oh, yes, he was a big enough figure there. He was head of Winchester, and senior scholar of Balliol, and took two Firsts and several University prizes in his stride. He must have sat up all night, for he never appeared to work – you see, it was his pose to do things easily – a variety of the Grand Manner. He was a most disquieting undergraduate. In his political speeches he had the air of having just left a Cabinet meeting.'

'Was he popular?' someone asked.

'Not a bit,' said Peckwether. 'And for all his successes we didn't believe in him. He was too worldly-wise – what we used to call 'banausic' – too bent on getting on. We felt that he had all his goods in the shop window, and that there was no margin to him.'

Sir Arthur smiled. 'A young man's contemporaries are pretty shrewd judges. When I met him first I felt the same thing. He wasn't a prig, and he had a sense of humour, and he had plenty of ordinary decent feeling. But he was the kind of man who could never forget himself and throw his cap over the moon. One couldn't warm to him ... But, unlike you, I thought he would succeed. The one thing lacking was money, and within two years he had remedied that. He married a rich wife; the lady died, but the fortune remained. I believe it was an honest love match, and for a long time he was heart-broken, and when he recovered he buried himself in work. You would have said that something was bound to happen. Young, rich, healthy, incredibly industrious, able, presentable – you would have said that any constituency would have welcomed him, that his party would have jumped at him, that he would have been a prodigious success.

'But he wasn't. He made a bad candidate, and had to stand three times before he got into the House. And there he made no kind of impression, though he spoke conscientiously and always on matters he knew about. He wrote a book on the meaning of colonial nationalism – fluent, well expressed, sensible, even in parts eloquent, but somehow it wasn't read. He was always making speeches at public dinners and at the annual meetings of different kinds of associations, but it didn't seem to signify what he said, and he was scarcely reported. There was no conspiracy of silence to keep him down, for people rather liked him. He simply seemed to have no clear boundary lines and to be imperfectly detached from the surrounding atmosphere. I could never understand why.'

'Lack of personality,' said Lamancha. 'I remember, feeling that.'

'Yes, but what is personality? He had the things that make it – brains and purpose. One liked him – was impressed by his attainments, but, if you understand me, one wasn't impressed by the man ... It wasn't ordinary lack of confidence, for on occasion he could be aggressive. It was the lack of a continuity of confidence – in himself and in other things. He didn't *believe* enough. That was why, as you said, he was always starting hares that he wouldn't hunt. Some excellent and unanswerable reason would occur to him why he should slack off. He was what I believe you call a good party man and always voted orthodoxly, but, after four years in the House, instead of being a leader he was rapidly becoming a mere cog in the machine. He didn't seem to be able to make himself count.

'That was his position eight years ago, and it was not far from a tragedy. He was as able as any man in the Cabinet, but he lacked the dæmonic force which even stupid people sometimes possess. I can only describe him in paradoxes. He was at once conceited and shy, inordinately ambitious and miserably conscious that he never got the value of his abilities out of life. ... Then came the War.'

'He served, didn't he?' Leithen asked. 'I remember running across him at G.H.Q.'

'You may call it serving, if you mean that he was never out of uniform for four years. But he didn't fight. I wanted him to. I thought a line battalion might make a man of him, but he shrank from the notion. It wasn't lack of courage – I satisfied myself of that. But he hadn't the nerve to sink himself into the ranks of ordinary men. You understand why? It would have meant the realisation of what was the inmost fear of his heart. He had to keep up the delusion that he was some sort of a swell – had to have authority to buttress his tottering vanity.

'So he had a selection of footling staff jobs – *liaison* with this and that, deputy-assistant to Tom, Dick and Harry, quite futile, but able to command special passes and staff cars. He ranked, I think, as a full colonel, but an Army Service Corps private was more useful than ten of him. And he was as miserable as a man could be. He liked people to think that his trouble was the strain of the War, but the real strain was that there was no strain. He knew that he simply didn't matter. At least he was candid with himself, and he was sometimes candid with me. He rather hoped, I think, that I would inspan him into something worth doing, but in common honesty I couldn't, for you see I too had come to disbelieve in him utterly.

'Well, that went on till March 1918, when his brother Reggie was killed in the German push. Ninth Division, wasn't it?'

Palliser-Yeates nodded. 'Ninth. South African Brigade. He went down at Marrières Wood, but he and his lot stuck up the enemy for the best part of a Sunday, and I solemnly believe, saved our whole front. They were at the critical point, you see, the junction of Gough and Byng. His body was never found.'

'I know,' said Sir Arthur, 'and that is just the point of my story.'

He stopped. 'I suppose I'm right to tell you this. He left instructions that if anything happened to him I was to have his diary. He can't have meant me to keep it secret ... No, I think he would have liked one or two people to know.'

He looked towards, Palliser-Yeates. 'You knew Reggie Souldern? How would you describe him?'

'The very best stamp of British regimental officer,' was the emphatic reply.

'Clever?'

'Not a bit. Only average brains, but every ounce of them useful. Always cheery and competent, and a born leader of men. He was due for a brigade when he fell, and if the War had lasted another couple of years he might have had a corps. I never met the other Souldern, but from what you say he must have been the plumb opposite of Reggie.'

'Just so. George had a great opinion of his brother – in addition to the ordinary brotherly love, for there were only the two of them. I thought the news of his death would break him altogether. But it didn't. He took it with extraordinary calm, and presently it looked as if he were actually more cheerful ... You see, they never found the body. He never saw him lying dead, or even the grave where he was buried, and he never met anybody who had. Reggie had been translated mysteriously out of the world, but the melancholy indisputable signs of death were lacking.'

'You mean he thought he was only missing and might turn up some day?'

'No. He *knew* he was dead – the proof was too strong, the presumption was too heavy ... But while there was enough to convince his reason, there was too little for his imagination – no white face and stiff body, no wooden cross in the cemetery. He could *picture* him as still alive, and George had a queer sensitive imagination about which most people knew nothing.'

Sir Arthur looked round the table and saw that we were puzzled.

'It is a little difficult to explain ... Do you remember a story of the French at Verdun making an attack over ground they had been fighting on for months? They shouted "En avant, les morts," and they believed that the spirits of the dead responded and redressed the balance. I think it was the last action at Vaux ... I don't suppose the *poilu* thought the dead came back to help him, but he pretended they were still combatants, and got a moral support from the fancy ... That was something like George Souldern's case. If you had asked him, you would have found that he had no doubt that what was left of Reggie was somewhere in the churned-up wilderness north of Péronne. And there was never any nonsense about visitations or messages from the dead ... But the lack of *visible* proofs enabled his imagination to picture Reggie as still alive, and going from strength to strength. He nursed the fancy till it became as real to him as anything in his ordinary life ... Reggie was becoming a great man and would soon be the most famous man in the world, and something of Reggie went into him and he shared in Reggie's glory. In March '18 a partnership began for George Souldern with his dead brother, and the dead, who in his imagination was alive and triumphant, lifted him out of the sticky furrow which he had been ploughing since he left Oxford.'

We were all silent except Pugh, who said that he had come across the same thing in the East – some Rajput prince, I think.

'How did you know this?' Lamancha asked.

'From the diary. George set down very fully every stage of his new career. But I very nearly guessed the truth for myself. You see, knowing him as I did, I had to admit a sudden and staggering change.'

'How soon?'

'The week after the news came. I had been in Paris, and on my return ran across George in the Travellers' and said the ordinary banal words of sympathy. He looked at me queerly, as he thanked me, and if I had not known how deeply attached the brothers were, I would have said that he was exhilarated by his loss. It was almost as if he had been given a drug to strengthen his arteries. He seemed to me suddenly a more substantial fellow, calmer, more at peace with himself. He said an odd thing too. "Old Reggie has got his chance," he said, and then, as if pulling himself up, "I mean, he had the chance he wanted."

'In June it was clear that something had happened to George Souldern. Do you remember how about that time a wave of dejection passed over all the Allied countries? It was partly the mess in Russia, partly in this country a slight loss of confidence in the Government, which seemed to have got to loggerheads with the soldiers, but mainly the 'drag' that comes in all wars. It was the same in the American Civil War before Gettysburg. Foch was marking time, but he was doing it by retreating pretty fast on the Aisne. Well, our people needed a little cheering up, and our politicians tried their hand at it. There was a debate in Parliament, and far the best speech was George's. The rest was mere platitude and rhetoric, but he came down on the point like a steam-hammer.'

'I know,' said Lamancha. 'I read it in the *Times* in a field hospital in Palestine.'

'In his old days nobody would have paid much attention. He would have been clever and epigrammatic – sound enough, but "precious." His speech would have read well, if it had been reported, but it wouldn't have mattered a penn'orth to anybody … Instead he said just the wise, simple, stalwart thing that every honest man had at the back of his head, and he said it with an air which made everybody sit up. For the first time in his life he spoke as one having authority. The press reported him nearly verbatim, for the journalists in the Gallery have a very acute sense of popular values.

'The speech put George, as the phrase goes, on the political map.

The Prime Minister spoke to me about him, and there was some talk of employing him on a mission which never materialised. I met him one day in the street and congratulated him, and I remember that I was struck by the new vigour in his personality. He made me come home with him to tea, and to talk to him was like breathing ozone. He asked me one or two questions about numbers, and then he gave me his views on the War. At the time it was fashionable to think that no decision would be reached till the next summer, but George maintained that, if we played our cards right, victory was a mathematical certainty before Christmas. He showed a knowledge of the military situation which would have done credit to any soldier, and he could express himself, which few soldiers can do. His arguments stuck in my head, and I believe I used them in the War Cabinet. I left with a very real respect for one whom I had written off as a failure.

'Well, then came the last battle of the Marne, and Haig's great advance, and all the drama and confusion of the autumn months. I lost sight of George, for I was busy with the peace overtures, and I don't think I even heard of him again till the new year ... But the diary tells all about those months. I am giving you the bones of the story, but I am going to burn the diary, for it is too intimate for other eyes ... According to it Reggie finished the War as a blazing hero. It was all worked out in detail with maps and diagrams. He had become a corps commander by August, and in October he was the chief fighting figure on the British front, the conduit pipe of Foch's ideas, for he could work out in practice what the great man saw as a vision. It sounds crazy, but it was so convincingly done that I had to rub my eyes and make myself remember that Reggie was lying in a nameless grave on the Somme and not a household word in two hemispheres ... George, too, shared in his glory, but just how was not very clear. Anyway, the brothers were in the front of the stage, Reggie the bigger man and George his civilian adviser and opposite number. I can see now how he got his confidence. He was no longer a struggler, but a made man; he had arrived, he was proved, the world required him. Whatever he said or did must be attended to, and, because he believed this, it was.'

Lamancha whistled long and low. 'But how could his mind work, if he lived among fairy tales?' he asked.

'He didn't,' said Sir Arthur. 'He lived very much in the real world. But he had all the time his private imaginative preserve, into which his normal mind did not penetrate. He drew his confidence from this preserve, and, having once got it, could carry it also into the real world.'

'Wasn't he intolerably conceited?' someone asked.

'No, for the great man was Reggie and he was only a satellite. He was Reggie's prophet, and assured enough on that side, but there was no personal arrogance. His dead brother had become, so to speak, his familiar spirit, his *dæmon*. The fact is that George was less of an egotist than he had ever been before. His vanity was burned up in a passion of service.

'I saw him frequently during the first half of '19, and had many talks with him. He had been returned to Parliament by a big majority, but he wasn't much in the public eye. He didn't like the way things were going, but at the same time as a good citizen he declined to make things more difficult for the Government. The diary gives his thoughts at that time. He considered that the soldiers should have had the chief share in the settlement of the world – Foch and Haig and Hindenburg – and Reggie. He held that they would have made a cleaner and fairer job of it than the kind of circus that appeared at Versailles. Perhaps he was right – I can't be dogmatic, for I was a performer in the circus.

'That, of course, I didn't know till the other day. But the change in George Souldern was soon manifest to the whole world. There was the Irish business, when he went down to the worst parts of the South and West, and seemed to be simply asking for a bullet in his head. He was half Irish, you know. He wrote and said quite frankly that he didn't care a straw whether Ireland was inside or outside the British Empire, that the only thing which mattered was that she should find a soul, and that she had a long road to travel before she got one. He told her that at present she was one vast perambulating humbug, and that till she got a little discipline and sense of realities she would remain on the level of Hayti. Why some gunman didn't have a shot at him I can't imagine, except that such naked candour and courage was a new thing and had to be respected. ... Then there was the Unemployment Commission. You remember the majority report – pious generalities and futile compromises, George's dissenting report made him for a month the best abused man in Britain, for he was impartially contemptuous of all sides. To-day – well, I fancy most of us would agree with George, and I observe that he is frequently quoted by the Labour people.

'What struck me about his line of country was that it was like that of a good soldier's. He had the same power of seeing simple facts and of making simple syllogisms, which the clever intellectual – such as George used to be – invariably misses. And there was the soldier's fidelity and sense of service. George plainly had no axe to grind. He had intellectual courage and would back his views as a general backs his strategy, but he kept always a curious personal modesty. I tell you it seemed nothing short of a miracle to one who had known him in the old days.

'I accepted it as the act of God and didn't look for any further explanation. I think that what first set me questioning was his behaviour about Reggie's memorial. The family wanted a stone put up in the churchyard of the family place in Gloucestershire. George absolutely declined. He stuck his toes into the ground and gave nothing but a flat refusal. One might have thought that the brothers had been estranged, but it was common knowledge that they had been like twins and had written to each other every day.

'Then there was the business about a memoir of Reggie. The regiment wanted one, and his Staff College contemporaries. Tollett – you remember him, the man on the Third Army Staff – volunteered to write it, of course with George's assistance. George refused bluntly and said that he felt the strongest distaste for the proposal. Tollett came to me about it, and I had George to luncheon and thrashed it out with him. I found his reasons very difficult to follow, for he objected even to a regimental history being compiled. He admitted that Tollett was as good a man as could be found for the job, but he said he hated the idea. Nobody understood Reggie but himself. Someday, he suggested, he might try to do justice to him in print – but not yet. I put forward all the arguments I could think of, but George was adamant.

'Walking home, I puzzled a good deal about the affair. It couldn't be merely the jealousy of a writer who wanted to reserve a good subject for himself – that wasn't George's character, and he had no literary vanity. Besides, that wouldn't explain his aversion to a prosaic regimental chronicle, and still less his objection to the cenotaph in the Gloucestershire churchyard. I wondered if there was not some quirk in George, some odd obsession about his brother. For a moment I thought that he might have been dabbling in spiritualism and have got some message from Reggie, till I remembered that I had heard him a week before declare his unbridled contempt for such mumbo-jumbo.

'I thought a good deal about it, and the guess I made was that George was living a double life – that in his subconsciousness Reggie was still alive for him. It was only a guess, but it was fairly near the truth, and last year I had it from his own lips.

'We were duck-shooting together on Croftsmoor, the big marsh near his home. That had been Reggie's pet game; he used to be out at all hours in the winter dawns and dusks stalking wildfowl. George never cared for it, or indeed for any field sport. He would take his place at a covert shoot or a grouse drive and was useful enough with a gun, but he would have been the first to disclaim the title of sportsman. But now he was as keen and tireless as Reggie. He kept me out for eight hours in a filthy day of rain wading in trench boots in Gloucestershire mud.

'We did fairly well, and just before sunset the weather improved. The wind had gone into the north, and promised frost, and as we sat on an old broken-backed stone bridge over one of the dykes, waiting for the birds to be collected from the different stands, the western sky was one broad band of palest gold. We were both tired, and the sudden change from blustering rain to a cold stillness, and from grey mist to colour and light, had a strange effect upon my spirits. I felt peaceful and solemnised. I lit a pipe, but let it go out, for my attention was held by the shoreless ocean in the west, against which the scarp of the Welsh hills showed in a dim silhouette. The sharp air, the wild marsh scents, the faint odour of tobacco awoke in me a thousand half-sad and half-sweet recollections.

'I couldn't help it. I said something about Reggie.

'George was sitting on the bridge with his eyes fixed on the sky. I thought he hadn't heard me, till suddenly he repeated "Reggie. Yes, old Reggie."

' "This was what he loved," I said.

' "He still loves it," was the answer, spoken very low. And then he repeated – to himself as it were:

> ' "Fight on, fight on," said Sir Andrew Barton.
> "Though I be wounded I am not slain.
> I'll lay me down and bleed awhile
> And then I'll rise and fight again." '

'HE turned his fine-drawn face to me.

' "You think Reggie is dead?"

'I didn't know what to say. "Yes," I stammered, "I suppose –"

' "What do you mean by death?" His voice was almost shrill. "We know nothing about it. What does it matter if the body is buried in a shell-hole–?"

'He stopped suddenly, as a lamp goes out when you press the switch. I had the impression that those queer shrill words came not from George but from some other who had joined us.

' "I believe that the spirit is immortal," I began.

' "The spirit –" again the shrill impersonal voice – "I tell you the whole man lives ... He is nearer to me than he ever was ... we are never parted ..."

'Again the light went out. He seemed to gulp, and when he spoke it was in his natural tones.

' "I apologise," he said, "I must seem to you to be talking nonsense

... You don't understand. *You* would understand, if anyone could, but I can't explain – yet – someday ..."

'The head-keeper, the beaters and the dogs came out of the reed beds, and at the same time the uncanny glow in the west was shrouded with the film of the coming night. It was almost dark when we turned to walk home, and I was glad of it, for neither of us wished to look at the other's face.

'I felt at once embarrassed and enlightened. I had been given a glimpse into the cloudy places of a man's soul, and had surprised his secret. My guess had been right. In George's subconscious mind Reggie was still alive – nay more, was progressing in achievement as if he had never disappeared in the March battle. It was no question of a disembodied spirit establishing communication with the living – that was a business I knew nothing about, nor George either. It was a question of life, complete life, in a peculiar world, companionship in some spiritual fourth dimension, and from that companionship he was drawing sustenance. He had learned Reggie's forthrightness and his happy simplicity ... I wondered and I trembled. There is a story of an early Victorian statesman who in his leisure moments played at being Emperor of Byzantium. The old Whig kept the two things strictly separate – he was a pious humanitarian in his English life, though he was a ruthless conqueror in the other. But in George's case the two were mingling. He was going about his daily duties with the power acquired from his secret world; that secret world, in which, with Reggie, he had become a master, was giving him a mastery over our common life. ... I did not believe it would last. It was against nature that a man could continue to live as a parasite on the dead.

'I am almost at the end of my story.' Two months later, George became a figure of national importance. It was he who chiefly broke up the Coalition at the Grafton House meeting, and thereby, I suppose, saved his party. His speech, you remember, clove through subtleties and irrelevances with the simple declaration that he could not work with what he could not trust, and unless things changed, must go out of public life. That was Reggie's manner, you know – pure Reggie. Then came the general election and the new Government, and George, very much to people's surprise, refused Cabinet office. The reason he gave was that on grounds of principle he had taken a chief part in wrecking the late Ministry, and he felt he could not allow himself to benefit personally by his action. We all thought him high-minded, if finical and quixotic, but the ordinary man liked it – it was a welcome change from the old gang of *arrivistes*. but it was not the real reason. I found that in the diary.'

Sir Arthur stopped, and there was a silence while he seemed to be fumbling for words.

'Here we are walking on the edge of great mysteries,' he continued. 'The reason why he refused the Prime Minister's offer was Reggie. ... Somehow the vital force in that subconscious world of his was ebbing ... I cannot explain how, but Reggie was moving away from what we call realities and was beckoning him to follow. ... The Grafton House speech was George's last public utterance. Few people saw him after that, for he rarely attended the House. I saw him several times in Gloucestershire ... Was he happy? Yes, I should say utterly happy, but too detached, too peaceful, as if he had done with the cares of his world ... I think I guessed what was happening, when he told me that he had consented to the cenotaph in the churchyard. He took a good deal of pains about it, too, and chose an inscription, which his maiden aunts thought irreligious. It was Virgil's *"Tendebant manus ripæ ulterioris amore"* ... He withdrew his objection to the memoir, too, and Tollett got to work, but he gave him no help – it was as if he had lost interest ... It is an odd thing to say, but I have been waiting for the news which was in last week's paper.'

'You don't mean that he engineered the motor smash?' Lamancha asked.

'Oh no,' said Sir Arthur gently. 'As I said, we are treading on the brink of great mysteries. Say that it was predestined, fore-ordained, decreed by the Master of Assembly ... I know that it had to be. If you join hands with the dead they will pull you over the stream.'

The Wind in the Portico

THERE is a place in Shropshire which I do not propose to visit again. It lies between Ludlow and the hills, in a shallow valley full of woods. Its name is St. Sant, a village with a big house and park adjoining, on a stream called the Vaun, about five miles from the little town of Faxeter. They have queer names in those parts, and other things queerer than the names.

I was motoring from Wales to Cambridge at the close of the long vacation. All this happened before the War, when I had just got my fellowship and was settling down to academic work. It was a fine night in early October, with a full moon, and I intended to push on to Ludlow for supper and bed. The time was about half-past eight, the road was empty and good going, and I was trundling pleasantly along when something went wrong with my headlights. It was a small thing, and I stopped to remedy it beyond a village and just at the lodge-gates of a house.

On the opposite side of the road a carrier's cart had drawn up, and two men, who looked like indoor servants, were lifting some packages from it on a big barrow. The moon was up, so I didn't need the feeble light of the carrier's lamp to see what they were doing. I suppose I wanted to stretch my legs for a moment, for when I had finished my job I strolled over to them. They did not hear me coming, and the carrier on his perch seemed to be asleep.

The packages were the ordinary consignments from some big shop in town. But I noticed that the two men handled them very gingerly, and that, as each was laid in the barrow, they clipped off the shop label and affixed one of their own. The new labels were odd things, large and square, with some address written on them in very black capital letters. There was nothing in that, but the men's faces puzzled me. For they seemed to do their job in a fever, longing to get it over and yet in a sweat lest they should make some mistake. Their commonplace task seemed to be for them a matter of tremendous importance. I moved so as to get a view of their faces, and I saw that they were white and strained. The two were of the butler or valet class, both elderly, and I could have sworn that they were labouring under something like fear.

I shuffled my feet to let them know of my presence and remarked that it was a fine night. They started as if they had been robbing a corpse. One of them mumbled something in reply, but the other caught a package which was slipping, and in a tone of violent alarm growled to his mate to be careful. I had a notion that they were handling explosives.

I had no time to waste, so I pushed on. That night, in my room at Ludlow, I had the curiosity to look up my map and identify the place were I had seen the men. The village was St. Sant, and it appeared that the gate I had stopped at belonged to a considerable demesne called Vauncastle. That was my first visit.

At that time I was busy on a critical edition of Theocritus, for which I was making a new collation of the manuscripts. There was a variant of the Medicean Codex in England, which nobody had seen since Gaisford, and after a good deal of trouble I found that it was in the library of a man called Dubellay. I wrote to him at his London club, and got a reply to my surprise from Vauncastle Hall, Faxeter. It was an odd letter, for you could see that he longed to tell me to go to the devil, but couldn't quite reconcile it with his conscience. We exchanged several letters, and the upshot was that he gave me permission to examine his manuscript. He did not ask me to stay, but mentioned that there was a comfortable little inn in St. Sant.

My second visit began on the 27th of December, after I had been home for Christmas. We had had a week of severe frost, and then it had thawed a little; but it remained bitterly cold, with leaden skies that threatened snow. I drove from Faxeter, and as we ascended the valley I remember thinking that it was a curiously sad country. The hills were too low to be impressive, and their outlines were mostly blurred with woods; but the tops showed clear, funny little knolls of grey bent that suggested a volcanic origin. It might have been one of those backgrounds you find in Italian primitives, with all the light and colour left out. When I got a glimpse of the Vaun in the bleached meadows it looked like the 'wan water' of the Border ballads. The woods, too, had not the friendly bareness of English copses in wintertime. They remained dark and cloudy, as if they were hiding secrets. Before I reached St. Sant, I decided that the landscape was not only sad, but ominous.

I was fortunate in my inn. In the single street of one-storied cottages it rose like a lighthouse, with a cheery glow from behind the red curtains of the bar parlour. The inside proved as good as the outside. I found a bedroom with a bright fire, and I dined in a wainscoted room full of preposterous old pictures of lanky hounds and hollow-backed horses. I had been rather depressed on my journey, but my spirits were raised by this comfort, and when the house produced a most respectable bottle of port I had the landlord in to drink a glass. He was an ancient man who had been a gamekeeper, with a much younger wife, who was responsible for the management. I was curious to hear something about the owner of my manuscript, but I got little from the landlord. He had been with the old squire, and had never served the present one. I heard of Dubellays in plenty – the landlord's master, who had hunted his own hounds for forty years, the Major his brother, who had fallen at Abu Klea; Parson Jack, who had had the living till he died, and of all kinds of collaterals. The 'Deblays' had been a high-spirited, open-handed stock, and much liked in the place. But of the present master of the Hall he could or would tell me nothing. The Squire was a 'great scholard,' but I gathered that he followed no sport and was not a convivial soul like his predecessors. He had spent a mint of money on the house, but not many people went there. He, the landlord, had never been inside the grounds in the new master's time, though in the old days there had been hunt breakfasts on the lawn for the whole countryside, and mighty tenantry dinners. I went to bed with a clear picture in my mind of the man I was to interview on the morrow. A scholarly and autocratic recluse, who collected treasures and beautified his dwelling and probably lived in his library. I rather looked forward to meeting him, for the bonhomous sporting squire was not much in my line.

After breakfast next morning I made my way to the Hall. It was the same leaden weather, and when I entered the gates the air seemed to grow bitterer and the skies darker. The place was muffled in great trees which even in their winter bareness made a pall about it. There was a long avenue of ancient sycamores, through which one caught only rare glimpses of the frozen park. I took my bearings, and realised that I was walking nearly due south, and was gradually descending. The house must be in a hollow. Presently the trees thinned, I passed through an iron gate, came out on a big untended lawn, untidily studden with laurels and rhododendrons, and there before me was the house front.

I had expected something beautiful – an old Tudor or Queen Anne façade or a dignified Georgian portico. I was disappointed, for the front was simply mean. It was low and irregular, more like the back parts of a house, and I guessed that at some time or another the building had been turned round, and the old kitchen door made the chief entrance. I was confirmed in my conclusion by observing that the roofs rose in tiers, like one of those recessed New York sky-scrapers, so that the present back parts of the building were of an impressive height.

The oddity of the place interested me, and still more its dilapidation. What on earth, could the owner have spent his money on? Everything – lawn, flower-beds, paths – was neglected. There was a new stone doorway, but the walls badly needed pointing, the window woodwork had not been painted for ages, and there were several broken panes. The bell did not ring, so I was reduced to hammering on the knocker, and it must have been ten minutes before the door opened. A pale butler, one of the men I had seen at the carrier's cart the October before, stood blinking in the entrance.

He led me in without question, when I gave my name, so I was evidently expected. The hall was my second surprise. What had become of my picture of the collector? The place was small and poky, and furnished as barely as the lobby of a farm-house. The only thing I approved was its warmth. Unlike most English country houses there seemed to be excellent heating arrangements.

I was taken into a little dark room with one window that looked out on a shrubbery, while the man went to fetch his master. My chief feeling was of gratitude that I had not been asked to stay, for the inn was paradise compared with this sepulchre. I was examining the prints on the wall, when I heard my name spoken and turned round to greet Mr. Dubellay.

He was my third surprise. I had made a portrait in my mind of a fastidious old scholar, with eye-glasses on a black cord, and a finical *weltkind*-ish manner. Instead I found a man still in early middle age, a heavy fellow dressed in the roughest country tweeds. He was as untidy as his demesne, for he had not shaved that morning, his flannel collar was badly frayed, and his fingernails would have been the better for a scrubbing brush. His face was hard to describe. It was high-coloured, but the colour was not healthy; it was friendly, but it was also wary; above all, it was *unquiet*. He gave me the impression of a man whose nerves were all wrong, and who was perpetually on his guard.

He said a few civil words, and thrust a badly tied brown paper parcel at me.

'That's your manuscript,' he said jauntily.

I was staggered. I had expected to be permitted to collate the codex in his library, and in the last few minutes had realised that the prospect was distasteful. But here was this casual owner offering me the priceless thing to take away.

I stammered my thanks, and added that it was very good of him to trust a stranger with such a treasure.

'Only as far as the inn,' he said. 'I wouldn't like to send it by post. But there's no harm in your working at it at the inn. There should be confidence among scholars.' And he gave an odd cackle of a laugh.

'I greatly prefer your plan,' I said. 'But I thought you would insist on my working at it here.'

'No, indeed,' he said earnestly. 'I shouldn't think of such a thing ... Wouldn't do at all. ... An insult to our freemasonry ... That's how I should regard it.'

We had a few minutes' further talk. I learned that he had inherited under the entail from a cousin, and had been just over ten years at Vauncastle. Before that he had been a London solicitor. He asked me a question or two about Cambridge – wished he had been at the University – much hampered in his work by a defective education. I was a Greek scholar? – Latin, too, he presumed. Wonderful people the Romans. ... He spoke quite freely, but all the time his queer restless eyes were darting about, and I had a strong impression that he would have liked to say something to me very different from these commonplaces – that he was longing to broach some subject but was held back by shyness or fear. He had such an odd appraising way of looking at me.

I left without his having asked me to a meal, for which I was not sorry, for I did not like the atmosphere of the place. I took a short cut over the ragged lawn, and turned at the top of the slope to look back. The house was in reality a huge pile, and I saw that I had been right and that the main building was all at the back. Was it, I wondered, like the Alhambra, which behind a front like a factory concealed a treasure-house? I saw, too, that the woodland hollow was more spacious than I had fancied. The house, as at present arranged, faced due north, and behind the south front was an open space in which I guessed that a lake might lie. Far beyond I could see in the December dimness the lift of high dark hills.

That evening the snow came in earnest, and fell continuously for the better part of two days. I banked up the fire in my bedroom and spent a happy time with the codex. I had brought only my working books with me and the inn boasted no library, so when I wanted to relax I went down to the tap-room, or gossiped with the landlady in the bar parlour. The yokels who congregated in the former were pleasant fellows, but, like all the folk on the Marches, they did not talk readily to a stranger and I heard little from them of the Hall. The old squire had reared every year three thousand pheasants, but the present squire would not

allow a gun to be fired on his land and there were only a few wild birds
left. For the same reason the woods were thick with vermin. This they
told me when I professed an interest in shooting. But of Mr. Dubellay
they would not speak, declaring that they never saw him. I daresay
they gossiped wildly about him, and their public reticence struck me as
having in it a touch of fear.

The landlady, who came from a different part of the shire, was more
communicative. She had not known the former Dubellays and so had
no standard of comparison, but she was inclined to regard the present
squire as not quite right in the head. 'They do say,' she would begin,
but she, too, suffered from some inhibition, and what promised to be
sensational would tail off into the commonplace. One thing apparently
puzzled the neighbourhood above others, and that was his
rearrangement of the house, 'They do say,' she said in an awed voice,
'that he have built a great church.' She had never visited it – no one in
the parish had, for Squire Dubellay did not allow intruders – but from
Lyne Hill you could see it through a gap in the woods. 'He's no good
Christian,' she told me, 'and him and Vicar has quarrelled this many a
day. But they do say as he worships summat there.' I learned that there
were no women servants in the house, only the men he had brought
from London, 'Poor benighted souls, they must live in a sad hobble,'
and the buxom lady shrugged her shoulders and giggled.

On the last day of December I decided that I needed exercise and
must go for a long stride. The snow had ceased that morning, and the
dull skies had changed to a clear blue. It was still very cold, but the sun
was shining, the snow was firm and crisp underfoot, and I proposed to
survey the country. So after luncheon I put on thick boots and gaiters,
and made for Lyne Hill. This meant a considerable circuit, for the
place lay south of the Vauncastle park. From it I hoped to get a view of
the other side of the house.

I was not disappointed. There was a rift in the thick woodlands, and
below me, two miles off, I suddenly saw a strange building, like a
classical temple. Only the entablature and the tops of the pillars
showed above the trees, but they stood out vivid and dark against the
background of snow. The spectacle in that lonely place was so startling
that for a little I could only stare. I remember that I glanced behind me
to the snowy line of the Welsh mountains, and felt that I might have
been looking at a winter view of the Apennines two thousand years ago.

My curiosity was now alert, and I determined to get a nearer view of
this marvel. I left the track and ploughed through the snowy fields down
to the skirts of the woods. After that my troubles began. I found myself in
a very good imitation of a primeval forest, where the undergrowth had

been unchecked and the rides uncut for years. I sank into deep pits, I was savagely torn by briars and brambles, but I struggled on, keeping a line as best I could. At last the trees stopped. Before me was a flat expanse which I knew must be a lake, and beyond rose the temple.

It ran the whole length of the house, and from where I stood it was hard to believe that there were buildings at its back where men dwelt. It was a fine piece of work – the first glance told me that – admirably proportioned, classical, yet not following exactly any of the classical models. One could imagine a great echoing interior dim with the smoke of sacrifice, and it was only by reflecting that I realised that the peristyle could not be continued down the two sides, that there was no interior, and that what I was looking at was only a portico.

The thing was at once impressive and preposterous. What madness had been in Dubellay when he embellished his house with such a grandiose garden front? The sun was setting and the shadow of the wooded hills darkened the interior, so I could not even make out the back wall of the porch. I wanted a nearer view, so I embarked on the frozen lake.

Then I had an odd experience. I was not tired, the snow lay level and firm, but I was conscious of extreme weariness. The biting air had become warm and oppressive. I had to drag boots that seemed to weigh tons across that lake. The place was utterly silent in the stricture of the frost, and from the pile in front no sign of life came.

I reached the other side at last and found myself in a frozen shallow of bulrushes and skeleton willow-herbs. They were taller than my head, and to see the house I had to look upward through their snowy traceries. It was perhaps eighty feet above me and a hundred yards distant, and, since I was below it, the delicate pillars seemed to spring to a great height. But it was still dusky, and the only detail I could see was on the ceiling, which seemed either to be carved or painted with deeply-shaded monochrome figures.

Suddenly the dying sun came slanting through the gap in the hills, and for an instant the whole portico to its farthest recesses was washed in clear gold and scarlet. That was wonderful enough, but there was something more. The air was utterly still with not the faintest breath of wind – so still that when I had lit a cigarette half an hour before the flame of the match had burned steadily upward like a candle in a room. As I stood among the sedges not a single frost crystal stirred … But there was a wind blowing in the portico.

I could see it lifting feathers of snow from the base of the pillars and fluffing the cornices. The floor had already been swept clean, but tiny flakes drifted on to it from the exposed edges. The interior was filled with a furious movement, though a yard from it was frozen peace. I felt nothing of the action of the wind, but I knew that it was hot, hot as the breath of a furnace.

I had only one thought, dread of being overtaken by night near that place. I turned and ran. Ran with labouring steps across the lake, panting and stifling with a deadly hot oppression, ran blindly by a sort of instinct in the direction of the village. I did not stop till I had wrestled through the big wood, and come out on some rough pasture above the highway. Then I dropped on the ground, and felt again the comforting chill of the December air.

The adventure left me in an uncomfortable mood. I was ashamed of myself for playing the fool, and at the same time hopelessly puzzled, for the oftener I went over in my mind the incidents of that afternoon the more I was at a loss for an explanation. One feeling was uppermost, that I did not like this place and wanted to be out of it. I had already broken the back of my task, and by shutting myself up for two days I completed it; that is to say, I made my collation as far as I had advanced myself in my commentary on the text. I did not want to go back to the Hall, so I wrote a civil note to Dubellay, expressing my gratitude and saying that I was sending up the manuscript by the landlord's son, as I scrupled to trouble him with another visit.

I got a reply at once, saying that Mr. Dubellay would like to give himself the pleasure of dining with me at the inn before I went, and would receive the manuscript in person.

It was the last night of my stay in St. Sant, so I ordered the best dinner the place could provide, and a magnum of claret, of which I discovered a bin in the cellar. Dubellay appeared promptly at eight o'clock, arriving to my surprise in a car. He had tidied himself up and put on a dinner jacket, and he looked exactly like the city solicitors you see dining in the Junior Carlton.

He was in excellent spirits, and his eyes had lost their air of being on guard. He seemed to have reached some conclusion about me, or decided that I was harmless. More, he seemed to be burning to talk to me. After my adventure I was prepared to find fear in him, the fear I had seen in the faces of the men-servants. But there was none; instead there was excitement, overpowering excitement.

He neglected the courses in his verbosity. His coming to dinner had considerably startled the inn, and instead of a maid the landlady herself waited on us. She seemed to want to get the meal over, and hustled the biscuits and the port on to the table as soon as she decently could. Then Dubellay became confidential.

He was an enthusiast, it appeared, an enthusiast with a single hobby.

All his life he had pottered among antiquities, and when he succeeded to Vauncastle he had the leisure and money to indulge himself. The place, it seemed, had been famous in Roman Britain – Vauni Castra – and Faxeter was a corruption of the same. 'Who was Vaunus?' I asked. He grinned, and told me to wait.

There had been an old temple up in the high woods. There had always been a local legend about it, and the place was supposed to be haunted. Well, he had had the site excavated and he had found – Here he became the cautious solicitor, and explained to me the law of treasure trove. As long as the objects found were not intrinsically valuable, not gold or jewels, the finder was entitled to keep them. He had done so – had not published the results of his excavations in the proceedings of any learned society – did not want to be bothered by tourists. I was different, for I was a scholar.

What had he found? It was really rather hard to follow his babbling talk, but I gathered that he had found certain carvings and sacrificial implements. And – he sunk his voice – most important of all, an altar, an altar of Vaunus, the tutelary deity of the vale.

When he mentioned this word his face took on a new look – not of fear but of secrecy, a kind of secret excitement. I have seen the same look on the face of a street-preaching Salvationist.

Vaunus had been a British god of the hills, whom the Romans in their liberal way appear to have identified with Apollo. He gave me a long confused account of him, from which it appeared that Mr. Dubellay was not an exact scholar. Some of his derivations of place-names were absurd – like St. Sant from Sancta Sanctorum – and in quoting a line of Ausonius he made two false quantities. He seemed to hope that I could tell him something more about Vaunus, but I said that my subject was Greek, and that I was deeply ignorant about Roman Britain. I mentioned several books, and found that he had never heard of Haverfield.

One word he used, 'hypocaust,' which suddenly gave me a clue. He must have heated the temple, as he heated his house, by some very efficient system of hot air. I know little about science, but I imagined that the artificial heat of the portico, as contrasted with the cold outside, might create an air current. At any rate that explanation satisfied me, and my afternoon's adventure lost its uncanniness. The reaction made me feel friendly towards him, and I listened to his talk with sympathy, but I decided not to mention that I had visited his temple.

He told me about it himself in the most open way. 'I couldn't leave the altar on the hillside,' he said. 'I had to make a place for it, so I turned the old front of the house into a sort of temple. I got the best advice, but architects are ignorant people, and I often wished I had been a better scholar. Still the place satisfies me.'

'I hope it satisfies Vaunus,' I said jocularly.

'I think so,' he replied quite seriously, and then his thoughts seemed to go wandering, and for a minute or so he looked through me with a queer abstraction in his eyes.

'What do you do with it now you've got it?' I asked.

He didn't reply, but smiled to himself.

'I don't know if you remember a passage in Sidonius Apollinaris,' I said, 'a formula for consecrating pagan altars to Christian uses. You begin by sacrificing a white cock or something suitable, and tell Apollo with all friendliness that the old dedication is off for the present. Then you have a Christian invocation –'

He nearly jumped out of his chair.

'That wouldn't do – wouldn't do at all! … Oh Lord, no! … Couldn't think of it for one moment!'

It was as if I had offended his ears by some horrid blasphemy, and the odd thing was that he never recovered his composure. He tried, for he had good manners, but his ease and friendliness had gone. We talked stiffly for another half-hour about trifles, and then he rose to leave. I returned him his manuscript neatly parcelled up, and expanded in thanks, but he scarcely seemed to heed me. He stuck the thing in his pocket, and departed with the same air of shocked absorption.

After he had gone I sat before the fire and reviewed the situation. I was satisfied with my hypocaust theory, and had no more perturbation in my memory about my afternoon's adventure. Yet a slight flavour of unpleasantness hung about it, and I felt that I did not quite like Dubellay. I set him down as a crank who had tangled himself up with a half-witted hobby, like an old maid with her cats, and I was not sorry to be leaving the place.

———————

MY third and last visit to St. Sant was in the following June – the midsummer of 1914. I had all but finished my Theocritus, but I needed another day or two with the Vauncastle manuscript, and, as I wanted to clear the whole thing off before I went to Italy in July, I wrote to Dubellay and asked if I might have another sight of it. The thing was a bore, but it had to be faced, and I fancied that the valley would be a pleasant place in that hot summer.

I got a reply at once, inviting, almost begging me to come, and insisting that I should stay at the Hall. I couldn't very well refuse, though

I would have preferred the inn. He wired about my train, and wired again saying he would meet me. This time I seemed to be a particularly welcome guest.

I reached Faxeter in the evening, and was met by a car from a Faxeter garage. The driver was a talkative young man, and, as the car was a closed one, I sat beside him for the sake of fresh air. The term had tired me, and I was glad to get out of stuffy Cambridge, but I cannot say that I found it much cooler as we ascended the Vaun valley. The woods were in their summer magnificence but a little dulled and tarnished by the heat, the river was shrunk to a trickle, and the curious hill-tops were so scorched by the sun that they seemed almost yellow above the green of the trees. Once again I had the feeling of a landscape fantastically un-English.

'Squire Dubellay's been in a great way about your coming, sir,' the driver informed me. 'Sent down three times to the boss to make sure it was all right. He's got a car of his own, too, a nice little Daimler, but he don't seem to use it much. Haven't seen him about in it for a month of Sundays.'

As we turned in at the Hall gates he looked curiously about him. 'Never been here before, though I've been in most gentlemen's parks for fifty miles round. Rum old-fashioned spot, isn't it, sir?'

If it had seemed a shuttered sanctuary in midwinter, in that June twilight it was more than ever a place enclosed and guarded. There was almost an autumn smell of decay, a dry decay like touchwood. We seemed to be descending through-layers of ever-thickening woods. When at last we turned through the iron gate I saw that the lawns had reached a further stage of neglect, for they were as shaggy as a hayfield.

The white-faced butler let me in, and there, waiting at his back, was Dubellay. But he was not the man whom I had seen in December. He was dressed in an old baggy suit of flannels, and his unwholesome red face was painfully drawn and sunken. There were dark pouches under his eyes, and these eyes were no longer excited, but dull and pained. Yes, and there was more than pain in them – there was fear. I wondered if his hobby were becoming too much for him.

He greeted me like a long-lost brother. Considering that I scarcely knew him, I was a little embarrassed by his warmth. 'Bless you for coming, my dear fellow,' he cried. 'You want a wash and then we'll have dinner. Don't bother to change, unless you want to. I never do.' He led me to my bedroom, which was clean enough but small and shabby like a servant's room. I guessed that he had gutted the house to build his absurd temple.

We dined in a fair-sized room which was a kind of library. It was lined with old books, but they did not look as if they had been there long; rather it seemed like a lumber room in which a fine collection had been stored. Once no doubt they had lived in a dignified Georgian chamber. There was nothing else, none of the antiques which I had expected.

'You have come just in time,' he told me. 'I fairly jumped when I got your letter, for I had been thinking of running up to Cambridge to insist on your coming down here. I hope you're in no hurry to leave.'

'As it happens,' I said, 'I *am* rather pressed for time, for I hope to go abroad next week. I ought to finish my work here in a couple of days. I can't tell you how much I'm in your debt for your kindness.'

'Two days,' he said. 'That will get us over midsummer. That should be enough.' I hadn't a notion what he meant.

I told him that I was looking forward to examining his collection. He opened his eyes. 'Your discoveries, I mean,' I said, 'the altar of Vaunus …'

As I spoke the words his face suddenly contorted in a spasm of what looked like terror. He choked and then recovered himself. 'Yes, yes,' he said rapidly. 'You shall see it – you shall see everything – but not now – not to-night. Tomorrow – in broad daylight – that's the time.'

After that the evening became a bad dream. Small talk deserted him, and he could only reply with an effort to my commonplaces. I caught him often looking at me furtively, as if he were sizing me up and wondering how far he could go with me. The thing fairly got on my nerves, and to crown all it was abominably stuffy. The windows of the room gave on a little paved court with a background of laurels, and I might have been in Seven Dials for all the air there was.

When coffee was served I could stand it no longer. 'What about smoking in the temple?' I said. 'It should be cool there with the air from the lake.'

I might have been proposing the assassination of his mother. He simply gibbered at me. 'No, no,' he stammered. 'My God, no!' It was half an hour before he could properly collect himself. A servant lit two oil lamps, and we sat on in the frowsty room.

'You said something when we last met,' he ventured at last, after many a sidelong glance at me. 'Something about a ritual for re-dedicating an altar.'

I remembered my remark about Sidonius Apollinaris.

'Could you show me the passage? There is a good classical library here, collected by my great-grandfather. Unfortunately my scholarship is not equal to using it properly.'

I got up and hunted along the shelves, and presently found a copy of Sidonius, the Plantin edition of 1609. I turned up the passage, and

roughly translated it for him. He listened hungrily and made me repeat
it twice.

'He says a cock,' he hesitated. 'Is that essential?'

'I don't think so. I fancy any of the recognised ritual stuff would do.'

'I am glad,' he said simply. 'I am afraid of blood.'

'Good God, man,' I cried out, 'are you taking my nonsense
seriously? I was only chaffing. Let old Vaunus stick to his altar!'

He looked at me like a puzzled and rather offended dog.

'Sidonius was in earnest …'

'Well, I'm not,' I said rudely. 'We're in the twentieth century and not
in the third. Isn't it about time we went to bed?'

He made no objection, and found me a candle in the hall. As I
undressed I wondered into what kind of lunatic asylum I had strayed. I
felt the strongest distaste for the place, and longed to go straight off to
the inn; only I couldn't make use of a man's manuscripts and insult his
hospitality. It was fairly clear to me that Dubellay was mad. He had
ridden his hobby to the death of his wits and was now in its bondage.
Good Lord! he had talked of his precious Vaunus as a votary talks of a
god. I believed he had come to worship some figment of his half-
educated fancy.

I think I must have slept for a couple of hours. Then I woke dripping
with perspiration, for the place was simply an oven. My window was as
wide open as it would go, and, though it was a warm night, when I
stuck my head out the air was fresh. The heat came from indoors. The
room was on the first floor near the entrance and I was looking on to
the overgrown lawns. The night was very dark and utterly still, but I
could have sworn that I heard wind. The trees were as motionless as
marble, but somewhere close at hand I heard a strong gust blowing.
Also, though there was no moon, there was somewhere near me a
steady glow of light; I could see the reflection of it round the end of the
house. That meant that it came from the temple. What kind of
saturnalia was Dubellay conducting at such an hour?

When I drew in my head I felt that if I was to get any sleep
something must be done. There could be no question about it; some
fool had turned on the steam heat, for the room was a furnace. My
temper was rising. There was no bell to be found, so I lit my candle
and set out to find a servant.

I tried a cast downstairs and discovered the room where we had
dined. Then I explored a passage at right angles, which brought me up
against a great oak door. The light showed me that it was a new door,
and that there was no apparent way of opening it. I guessed that it led
into the temple, and, though it fitted close and there seemed to be no

key-hole, I could hear through it a sound like a rushing wind ... Next I opened a door on my right and found myself in a big store cupboard. It had a funny, exotic, spicy smell, and, arranged very neatly on the floor and shelves, was a number of small sacks and coffers. Each bore a label, a square of stout paper with very black lettering. I read '*Pro servitio Vauni.*'

I had seen them before, for my memory betrayed me if they were not the very labels that Dubellay's servants had been attaching to the packages from the carrier's cart that evening in the past autumn. The discovery made my suspicions an unpleasant certainty. Dubellay evidently meant the labels to read 'For the service of Vaunus.' He was no scholar, for it was an impossible use of the word 'servitium,' but he was very patently a madman.

However, it was my immediate business to find some way to sleep, so I continued my quest for a servant. I followed another corridor, and discovered a second staircase. At the top of it I saw an open door and looked in. It must have been Dubellay's, for his flannels were tumbled untidily on a chair, but Dubellay himself was not there and the bed had not been slept in.

I suppose my irritation was greater than my alarm – though I must say I was getting a little scared – for I still pursued the evasive servant. There was another stair which apparently led to attics, and in going up it I slipped and made a great clatter. When I looked up the butler in his nightgown was staring down at me, and if ever a mortal face held fear it was his. When he saw who it was he seemed to recover a little.

'Look here,' I said, 'for God's sake turn off that infernal hot air. I can't get a wink of sleep. What idiot set it going?'

He looked at me owllishly, but he managed to find his tongue.

'I beg your pardon, sir,' he said, 'but there is no heating apparatus in this house.'

There was nothing more to be said. I returned to my bedroom and it seemed to me that it had grown cooler. As I leaned out of the window, too, the mysterious wind seemed to have died away, and the glow no longer showed from beyond the corner of the house. I got into bed and slept heavily till I was roused by the appearance of my shaving water about half-past nine. There was no bathroom, so I bathed in a tin pannikin.

It was a hazy morning which promised a day of blistering heat. When I went down to breakfast I found Dubellay in the dining-room. In the daylight he looked a very sick man, but he seemed to have taken a pull on himself, for his manner was considerably less nervy than the night before. Indeed, he appeared almost normal, and I might have reconsidered my view but for the look in his eyes.

I told him that I proposed to sit tight all day over the manuscript, and get the thing finished. He nodded. 'That's all right. I've a lot to do myself, and I won't disturb you.'

'But first,' I said, 'you promised to show me your discoveries.'

He looked at the window where the sun was shining on the laurels and on a segment of the paved court.

'The light is good,' he said – an odd remark. 'Let us go there now. There are times and seasons for the temple.'

He led me down the passage I had explored the previous night. The door opened not by a key but some lever in the wall. I found myself looking suddenly at a bath of sunshine with the lake below as blue as a turquoise.

It is not easy to describe my impressions of that place. It was unbelievably light and airy, as brilliant as an Italian colonnade in midsummer. The proportions must have been good, for the columns soared and swam, and the roof (which looked like cedar) floated as delicately as a flower on its stalk. The stone was some local limestone, which on the floor took a polish like marble. All around was a vista of sparkling water and summer woods and far blue mountains. It should have been as wholesome as the top of a hill.

And yet I had scarcely entered before I knew that it was a prison. I am not an imaginative man, and I believe my nerves are fairly good, but I could scarcely put one foot before the other, so strong was my distaste. I felt shut off from the world, as if I were in a dungeon or on an ice-floe. And I felt, too, that though far enough from humanity, we were not alone.

On the inner wall there were three carvings. Two were imperfect friezes sculptured in low-relief, dealing apparently with the same subject. It was a ritual procession, priests bearing branches, the ordinary *dendrophori* business. The faces were only half-human, and that was from no lack of skill, for the artist had been a master. The striking thing was that the branches and the hair of the hierophants were being tossed by a violent wind, and the expression of each was of a being in the last stage of endurance, shaken to the core by terror and pain.

Between the friezes was a great roundel of a Gorgon's head. It was not a female head, such as you commonly find, but a male head, with the viperous hair sprouting from chin and lip. It had once been coloured, and fragments of a green pigment remained in the locks. It was an awful thing, the ultimate horror of fear, the last dementia of cruelty made manifest in stone. I hurriedly averted my eyes and looked at the altar.

That stood at the west end on a pediment with three steps. It was a beautiful piece of work, scarcely harmed by the centuries, with two words inscribed on its face – APOLL. VAUN. It was made of some foreign marble, and the hollow top was dark with ancient sacrifices. Not so ancient either, for I could have sworn that I saw there the mark of recent flame.

I do not suppose I was more than five minutes in the place. I wanted to get out, and Dubellay wanted to get me out. We did not speak a word till we were back in the library.

'For God's sake give it up!' I said. 'You're playing with fire, Mr. Dubellay. You're driving yourself into Bedlam. Send these damned things to a museum and leave this place. Now, now, I tell you. You have no time to lose. Come down with me to the inn straight off and shut up this house.'

He looked at me with his lip quivering like a child about to cry.

'I will. I promise you I will … But not yet … After to-night … To-morrow I'll do whatever you tell me … You won't leave me?'

'I won't leave you, but what earthly good am I to you if you won't take my advice?'

'Sidonius …' he began.

'Oh, damn Sidonius! I wish I had never mentioned him. The whole thing is arrant nonsense, but it's killing you. You've got it on the brain. Don't you know you're a sick man?'

'I'm not feeling very grand. It's so warm to-day. I think I'll lie down.'

It was no good arguing with him, for he had the appalling obstinacy of very weak things. I went off to my work in a shocking bad temper.

The day was what it had promised to be, blisteringly hot. Before midday the sun was hidden by a coppery haze, and there was not the faintest stirring of wind. Dubellay did not appear at luncheon – it was not a meal he ever ate, the butler told me. I slogged away all the afternoon, and had pretty well finished my job by six o'clock. That would enable me to leave next morning, and I hoped to be able to persuade my host to come with me.

The conclusion of my task put me into a better humour, and I went for a walk before dinner. It was a very close evening, for the heat haze had not lifted; the woods were as silent as a grave, not a bird spoke, and when I came out of the cover to the burnt pastures the sheep seemed too languid to graze. During my walk I prospected the environs of the house, and saw that it would be very hard to get access to the temple except by a long circuit. On one side was a mass of outbuildings, and then a high wall, and on the other the very closest and highest quickset hedge I have ever seen, which ended in a wood with savage spikes on its containing wall. I returned to my room, had a cold bath in the exiguous tub, and changed.

Dubellay was not at dinner. The butler said that his master was feeling unwell and had gone to bed. The news pleased me, for bed was the best place for him. After that I settled myself down to a lonely evening in the library. I browsed among the shelves and found a number of rare editions which served to pass the time. I noticed that the copy of Sidonious was absent from its place.

I think it was about ten o'clock when I went to bed, for I was unaccountably tired. I remember wondering whether I oughtn't to go and visit Dubellay, but decided that it was better to leave him alone. I still reproach myself for that decision. I know now I ought to have taken him by force and haled him to the inn.

Suddenly I came out of heavy sleep with a start. A human cry seemed to be ringing in the corridors of my brain. I held my breath and listened. It came again, a horrid scream of panic and torture.

I was out of bed in a second, and only stopped to get my feet into slippers. The cry must have come from the temple. I tore downstairs expecting to hear the noise of an alarmed household. But there was no sound, and the awful cry was not repeated.

The door in the corridor was shut, as I expected. Behind it pandemonium seemed to be loose, for there was a howling like a tempest – and something more, a crackling like fire. I made for the front door, slipped off the chain, and found myself in the still, moonless night. Still, except for the rending gale that seemed to be raging in the house I had left.

From what I had seen on my evening's walk I knew that my one chance to get to the temple was by way of the quickset hedge. I thought I might manage to force a way between the end of it and the wall. I did it, at the cost of much of my raiment and my skin. Beyond was another rough lawn set with tangled shrubberies, and then a precipitous slope to the level of the lake. I scrambled along the sedgy margin, not daring to lift my eyes till I was on the temple steps.

The place was brighter than day with a roaring blast of fire. The very air seemed to be incandescent and to have become a flaming ether. And yet there were no flames – only a burning brightness. I could not enter, for the waft from it struck my face like a scorching hand and I felt my hair singe ...

I am short-sighted, as you know, and I may have been mistaken, but this is what I think I saw. From the altar a great tongue of flame seemed to shoot upwards and lick the roof, and from its pediment ran flaming streams. In front of it lay a body – Dubellay's – a naked body, already charred and black. There was nothing else, except that the Gorgon's head in the wall seemed to glow like a sun in hell.

I suppose I must have tried to enter. All I know is that I found myself staggering back, rather badly burned. I covered my eyes, and as I looked through my fingers I seemed to see the flames flowing under the wall, where there may have been lockers, or possibly another entrance. Then the great oak door suddenly shrivelled like gauze, and with a roar the fiery river poured into the house.

I ducked myself in the lake to ease the pain, and then ran back as hard as I could by the way I had come. Dubellay, poor devil, was beyond my aid. After that I am not very clear what happened. I know that the house burned like a haystack. I found one of the men-servants on the lawn, and I think I helped to get the other down from his room by one of the rain-pipes. By the time the neighbours arrived the house was ashes, and I was pretty well mother-naked. They took me to the inn and put me to bed, and I remained there till after the inquest. The coroner's jury were puzzled, but they found it simply death by misadventure; a lot of country houses were burned that summer. There was nothing found of Dubellay; nothing remained of the house except a few blackened pillars; the altar and the sculptures were so cracked and scarred that no museum wanted them. The place has not been rebuilt, and for all I know they are there to-day. I am not going back to look for them.

─────────

Fullcircle

'Between the Windrush and the Colne
I found a little house of stone –
A little wicked house of stone.'

THE October day was brightening toward late afternoon when Leithen and I climbed the hill above the stream and came in sight of the house. All morning a haze with the sheen of pearl in it had lain on the folds of downland, and the vision of far horizons, which is the glory of Cotswold, had been veiled, so that every valley seemed as a place inclosed and set apart. But now a glow had come into the air, and for a little the autumn lawns stole the tints of summer. The gold of sunshine was warm on the grasses, and only the riot of color in the berry-laden edges of the fields and the slender woodlands told of the failing year.

We were looking into a green cup of the hills, and it was all a garden. A little place, bounded by slopes that defined its graciousness with no hint of barrier, so that a dweller there, though his view was but half a mile on any side, would yet have the sense of dwelling on uplands and commanding the world. Round the top edge ran an old wall of stones, beyond which the October bracken flamed to the skyline. Inside were folds of ancient pasture, with here and there a thorn-bush, falling to rose gardens and, on one side, to the smooth sward of a terrace above a tiny lake.

At the heart of it stood the house like a jewel well-set. It was a miniature, but by the hand of a master. The style was late seventeenth century, when an agreeable classic convention had opened up to sunlight and comfort the dark magnificence of the Tudor fashion. The place had the spacious air of a great mansion, and was furnished in every detail with a fine scrupulousness. Only when the eye measured its proportions with the woods and the hillside did the mind perceive that it was a small dwelling.

The stone of Cotswold takes curiously the color of the weather. Under thunderclouds it will be as dark as basalt; on a gray day it will be

204

gray like lava but in sunshine it absorbs the sun. At the moment the little house was pale gold, like honey.

Leithen swung a long leg across the stile.

'Pretty good, isn't it?' he said. 'It's pure, authentic Sir Christopher Wren. The name is worthy of it, too. It is called Fullcircle.'

He told me its story. It had been built after the Restoration by the Carteron family, whose wide domains ran into these hills. The Lord Carteron of the day was a friend of the Merry Monarch; but it was not as a sanctuary for orgies that he built the house. Perhaps he was tired of the gloomy splendor of Minster Carteron, and wanted a home of his own and not of his ancestors' choosing. He had an elegant taste in letters, as we can learn from his neat imitations of Martial, his pretty *Bucolics* and the more than respectable Latin hexameters of his *Ars Vivendi*. Being a great nobleman, he had the best skill of the day to construct his hermitage, and thither he would retire for months at a time, with like-minded friends, to a world of books and gardens. He seems to have had no ill-wishers; contemporary memoirs speak of him charitably and Dryden spared him four lines of encomium. 'A selfish old dog,' Leithen called him. 'He had the good sense to eschew politics and enjoy life. His soul is in that little house. He only did one rash thing in his career – he anticipated the King, his master, by some years in turning Papist.'

I asked about its later history.

'After his death it passed to a younger branch of the Carterons. It left them in the eighteenth century, and the Applebys got it. They were a jovial lot of hunting squires and let the library go to the dogs. Old Colonel Appleby wsa still alive when I came to Borrowby. Something went wrong in his inside when he was nearly seventy, and the doctors knocked him off liquor. Not that he drank too much, though he did himself well. That finished the poor old boy. He told me that it revealed to him the amazing truth that during a long and, as he hoped, publicly useful life he had never been quite sober. He was a good fellow and I missed him when he died. The place went to a remote cousin called Giffen.'

Leithen's eyes as they scanned the prospect, seemed amused.

'Julian and Ursula Giffen – I dare say you know the names. They always hunt in couples, and write books about sociology and advanced ethics and psychics – books called either "The New This or That" or "The Truth about Something or Other." You know the sort of thing. They're deep in all the pseudo-sciences. They're decent souls, but you can guess the type. I came across them in a case I had at the Old Bailey – defending a ruffian who was charged with murder. I hadn't a doubt he deserved hanging on twenty counts, but there wasn't enough evidence to convict him on this one. Dodderidge was at his worst – it was just before they induced him to retire – and his handling of the jury was a masterpiece of misdirection. Of course, there was a shindy. The thing was a scandal, and it stirred up all the humanitarians till the murderer was almost forgotten in the iniquities of old Dodderidge. You must remember the case. It filled the papers for weeks. Well, it was in that connection that I fell in with the Giffens. I got rather to like them, and I've been to see them at their house in Hampstead. Golly, what a place! Not a chair fit to sit down on, and colors that made you want to howl. I never met people whose heads were so full of feathers.'

I said something about that being an odd *milieu* for him.

'Oh, I like human beings, all kinds. It's my profession to study them, for without that the practice of the law would be a dismal affair. There are hordes of people like the Giffens – only not so good, for they really have hearts of gold. They are the rootless stuff in the world to-day. In revolt against everything and everybody with any ancestry. A kind of innocent self-righteousness – wanting to be the people with whom wisdom begins and ends. They are mostly sensitive and tender-hearted, but they wear themselves out in an eternal dissidence. Can't build, you know, for they object to all tools, but very ready to crab. They scorn any form of Christianity, but they'll walk miles to patronize some wretched sect that has the merit of being brand-new. "Pioneers" they call themselves – funny little unclad people adventuring into the cold desert with no maps. Giffen once described himself and his friends to me as "forward-looking," but that, of course, is just what they are not. To tackle the future you must have a firm grip of the past, and for them, the past is only a pathological curiosity. They're up to their necks in the mud of the present – but good, after a fashion; and innocent – sordidly innocent. Fate was in an ironical mood when she saddled them with that wicked little house.'

'Wicked' did not seem to me to be a fair word. It sat honey-colored among its gardens with the meekness of a dove.

The sound of a bicycle on the road behind made us turn round, and Leithen advanced to meet a dismounting rider.

He was a tallish fellow, some forty years old, perhaps, with one of those fluffy blond beards that have never been shaved. Short-sighted, of course, and wore glasses. Biscuit-colored knickerbockers and stockings clad his lean limbs.

Leithen introduced me. 'We are walking to Borrowby and stopped to admire your house. Could we have just a glimpse inside? I want Jardine to see the staircase.'

Mr. Giffen was very willing. 'I've been over to Clyston to send a telegram. We have some friends for the week-end who might interest you. Won't you stay to tea?'

He had a gentle, formal courtesy about him, and his voice had the facile intonations of one who loves to talk. He led us through a little gate, and along a shorn green walk among the bracken, to a postern which gave entrance to the garden. Here, though it was October, there was still a bright show of roses, and the jet of water from the leaden Cupid dripped noiselessly among fallen petals. And then we stood before the doorway above which the old Carteron had inscribed a line of Horace.

I have never seen anything quite like the little hall. There were two, indeed, separated by a staircase of a wood that looked like olive. Both were paved with black-and-white marble, and the inner was oval in shape, with a gallery supported on slender walnut pillars. It was all in miniature, but it had a spaciousness which no mere size could give. Also it seemed to be permeated by the quintessence of sunlight. Its air was of long-descended, confident, equable happiness.

There were voices on the terrace beyond the hall. Giffen led us into a little room on the left. 'You remember the house in Colonel Appleby's time, Leithen. This was the chapel. It had always been the chapel. You see the change we have made. – I beg your pardon, Mr. Jardine. You're not by any chance a Roman Catholic?'

The room had a white paneling and, on two sides, deep windows. At one end was a fine Italian shrine of marble, and the floor was mosaic, blue and white, in a quaint Byzantine pattern. There was the same air of sunny cheerfulness as in the rest of the house. No mystery could find a lodgment here. It might have been a chapel for three centuries, but the place was pagan. The Giffens' changes were no sort of desecration. A green baize table filled most of the floor, surrounded by chairs like a committee room. On new raw-wood shelves were files of papers and stacks of blue-books and those desiccated works into which reformers of society torture the English tongue. Two typewriters stood on a side table.

'It is our workroom,' Giffen explained. 'We hold our Sunday moots here. Ursula thinks that a week-end is wasted unless it produces some piece of real work. Often a quite valuable committee has its beginning here. We try to make our home a refuge for busy workers, where they need not idle but can work under happy conditions.'

' "A college situate in a clearer air," ' Leithen quoted.

But Giffen did not respond except with a smile; he had probably never heard of Lord Falkland.

A woman entered the room, a woman who might have been pretty if she had taken a little pains. Her reddish hair was drawn tightly back and dressed in a hard knot, and her clothes were horribly incongruous in a remote manor-house. She had bright eager eyes, like a bird, and hands that fluttered nervously. She greeted Leithen with warmth.

'We have settled down marvelously,' she told him. 'Julian and I feel as if we had always lived here, and our life has arranged itself so perfectly. My mothers' cottages in the village will soon be ready, and the Club is to be opened next week. Julian and I will carry on the classes ourselves for the first winter. Next year we hope to have a really fine programme. And then it is so pleasant to be able to entertain one's friends. Won't you stay to tea? Dr. Swope is here, and Mary Elliston, and Mr. Percy Blaker – you know, the Member of Parliament. Must you hurry off? I'm so sorry. – What do you think of our workroom? It was utterly terrible when we first came here – a sort of decayed chapel, like a withered tuberose. We have let the air of heaven into it.'

I observed that I had never seen a house so full of space and light.

'Ah, you notice that? It is a curiously happy place to live in. Sometimes I'm almost afraid to feel so light-hearted. But we look on ourselves as only trustees. It is a trust we have to administer for the common good. You know, it's a house on which you can lay your own impress. I can imagine places which dominate the dwellers, but Fullcircle is plastic, and we can make it our own as much as if we had planned and built it. That's our chief piece of good fortune.'

We took our leave, for we had no desire for the company of Dr. Swope and Mr. Percy Blaker. When we reached the highway we halted and looked back on the little jewel. Shafts of the westering sun now caught the stone and turned the honey to ripe gold. Thin spires of amethyst smoke rose into the still air. I thought of the well-meaning, restless couple inside its walls, and somehow they seemed out of the picture. They simply did not matter. The house was the thing, for I had never met in inanimate stone such an air of gentle masterfulness. It had a personality of its own, clean-cut and secure, like a high-born old dame among the females of profiteers. And Mrs. Giffen claimed to have given it her impress!

That night, in the library at Borrowby, Leithen discoursed of the Restoration. Borrowby, of which, by the expenditure of much care and a good deal of money, he had made a civilized dwelling, is a Tudor manor of the Cotswold type, with its high-pitched narrow roofs and tall stone chimneys, rising sheer from the meadows with something of the massiveness of a Border keep.

He nodded toward the linen-fold paneling and the great carved chimney-piece.

'In this kind of house you have the mystery of the elder England. What was Raleigh's phrase? "High thoughts and divine contemplations." The people who built this sort of thing lived close to another world, and thought bravely of death. It doesn't matter who they were – Crusaders or Elizabethans or Puritans – they all had poetry in them and the heroic and a great unworldliness. They had marvelous spirits, and plenty of joys and triumphs; but they had also their hours of black gloom. Their lives were like our weather – storm and sun. One thing they never feared – death. He walked too near them all their days to be a bogey.

'But the Restoration was a sharp break. It brought paganism into England; paganism and the art of life. No people have ever known better the secret of bland happiness. Look at Fullcircle. There are no dark corners there. The man that built it knew all there was to be known about how to live. The trouble was that they did not know how to die. That was the one shadow on the glass. So they provided for it in a pagan way. They tried magic. They never become true Catholics – they were always pagan to the end, but they smuggled a priest into their lives. He was a kind of insurance premium against unwelcome mystery.'

It was not till nearly two years later that I saw the Giffens again. The May-fly season was about at its close, and I had snatched a day on a certain limpid Cotswold river. There was another man on the same beat, fishing from the opposite bank, and I watched him with some anxiety, for a duffer would have spoiled my day. To my relief I recognized Giffen. With him it was easy to come to terms, and presently the water was parceled out between us.

We foregathered for luncheon, and I stood watching while he neatly stalked, rose, and landed a trout. I confessed to some surprise – first that Giffen should be a fisherman at all, for it was not in keeping with my old notion of him; and second, that he should cast such a workmanlike line. As we lunched together, I observed several changes. He had shaved his fluffy beard, and his face was notably less lean, and had the clear even sunburn of the countryman. His clothes, too, were different. They also were workmanlike, and looked as if they belonged to him – he no longer wore the uneasy knickerbockers of the Sunday golfer.

'I'm desperately keen,' he told me. 'You see it's only my second

May-fly season, and last year I was no better than a beginner. I wish I had known long ago what good fun fishing was. Isn't this a blessed place?' And he looked up through the canopy of flowering chestnuts to the June sky.

'I'm glad you've taken to sport,' I said, 'even if you only come here for the week-ends. Sport lets you into the secrets of the countryside.'

'Oh, we don't go much to London now,' was his answer. 'We sold our Hampstead house a year ago. I can't think how I ever could stick that place. Ursula takes the same view. I wouldn't leave Oxfordshire just now for a thousand pounds. Do you smell the hawthorn? Last week this meadow was scented like Paradise. – D'you know, Leithen's a queer fellow?'

I asked why.

'He once told me that this countryside in June made him sad. He said it was too perfect a thing for fallen humanity. I call that morbid. Do you see any sense in it?'

I knew what Leithen meant, but it would have taken too long to explain.

'I feel warm and good and happy here,' he went on. 'I used to talk about living close to nature. Rot! I didn't know what nature meant. Now –' He broke off. 'By Jove, there's a kingfisher. That is only the second I've seen this year. They're getting uncommon with us.'

'With us.' I liked the phrase. He was becoming a true countryman.

We had a good day, – not extravagantly successful, but satisfactory, – and he persuaded me to come home with him to Fullcircle for the night, explaining that I could catch an early train next morning at the junction. So we extricated a little two-seater from the midst of a clump of lilacs, and drove through four miles of sweet-scented dusk, with nightingales shouting in every thicket.

I changed into a suit of his flannels in a room looking out on the little lake where trout were rising, and I remember that I whistled from pure light-heartedness. In that adorable house one seemed to be still breathing the air of the spring meadows.

Dinner was my first big surprise. It was admirable – plain, but perfectly cooked, and with that excellence of basic material which is the glory of a well-appointed country house. There was wine, too, which I am certain was a new thing. Giffen gave me a bottle of sound claret, and afterwards some more than decent port. My second surprise was my hostess. Her clothes, like her husband's, must have changed, for I did not notice what she was wearing, and I had noticed it only too clearly the last time we met. More remarkable still was the difference in her face. For the first time I realized that she was a pretty woman. The contours had softened and rounded, and there was a charming well-being in her eyes, very different from the old restlessness. She looked content, infinitely content.

I asked about her mothers' cottages. She laughed cheerfully.

'I gave them up after the first year. They didn't mix well with the village people. I'm quite ready to admit my mistake, and it was the wrong kind of charity. The Londoners didn't like it – felt lonesome and sighed for the fried-fish shop; and the village women were shy of them – afraid of infectious complaints, you know. Julian and I have decided that our business is to look after our own people.'

It may have been malicious, but I said something about the wonderful scheme of village education.

'Another relic of Cockneyism,' laughed the lady, but Giffen looked a trifle shy.

'I gave it up because it didn't seem worth while. What is the use of spoiling a perfectly wholesome scheme of life by introducing unnecessary complications? Medicine is no good unless a man is sick, and these people are not sick. Education is the only cure for certain diseases the modern world has engendered, but if you don't find the disease, the remedy is superfluous. The fact is, I hadn't the face to go on with the thing. I wanted to be taught rather than to teach. There's a whole world round me of which I know very little, and my first business is to get to understand it. Any village poacher can teach me more of the things that matter than I have to tell him.'

'Besides, we have so much to do,' his wife added. 'There's the house and the garden and the home farm and the property. It isn't large, but it takes a lot of looking after.'

The dining-room was long and low-ceilinged, and had a white paneling in bold relief. Through the deep windows came odors of the garden and a faint tinkle of water. The dusk was deepening and the engravings in their rosewood frames were dim, but sufficient light remained to reveal the picture above the fireplace. It showed a middle-aged man in the clothes of the later Stuarts. The plump tapering fingers of one hand held a book; the other was hidden in the folds of a flowered waistcoat. The long curled wig framed a delicate face with something of the grace of youth left to it. There were quizzical lines about the mouth, and the eyes smiled pleasantly yet very wisely. It was the face of a man I should have liked to dine with. He must have been the best of company.

Giffen answered my question.

'That's the Lord Carteron who built the house. No – no relation. Our people were the Applebys, who came in 1753. We've both fallen so deep in love with Fullcircle that we wanted to see the man who conceived it. I had some trouble getting it. It came out of the Minster Carteron sale, and I had to give a Jew dealer twice what he paid for it. It's a jolly thing to live with.'

It was indeed a curiously charming picture. I found my eyes straying to it till the dusk obscured the features. It was the face of one wholly at home in a suave world, learned in all the urbanities. A good friend, I thought, the old lord must have been, and a superlative companion. I could imagine neat Horatian tags coming ripely from his lips. Not a strong face, but somehow a dominating one. The portrait of the long-dead gentleman had still the atmosphere of life. Giffen raised his glass of port to him as we rose from table, as if to salute a comrade.

We moved to the room across the hall which had once been the Giffens' workroom, the cradle of earnest committees and weighty memoranda. This was my third surprise. Baize-covered table and raw-wood shelves had disappeared. The place was now half smoking-room, half library. On the walls hung a fine collection of colored sporting prints, and below them were ranged low Hepplewhite bookcases. The lamplight glowed on the ivory walls, and the room, like everything else in the house, was radiant.

Above the mantelpiece was a stag's head – a fair eleven-pointer.

Giffen nodded proudly toward it. 'I got that last year at Machray. My first stag.'

There was a little table with an array of magazines and weekly papers. Some amusement must have been visible in my face, as I caught sight of various light-hearted sporting journals, for he laughed apologetically. 'You mustn't think that Ursula and I take in that stuff for ourselves. It amuses our guests, you know.'

I dared say it did, but I was convinced that the guests were no longer Dr. Swope and Mr. Percy Blaker.

One of my many failings is that I can never enter a room containing books without scanning the titles. Giffen's collection won my hearty approval. There were the very few novelists I can read myself – Miss Austen and Sir Walter and the admirable Marryat; there was a shelf full of memoirs, and a good deal of seventeenth – and eighteenth-century poetry; there was a set of the classics in fine editions. Bodonis and Baskervilles and such like; there was much county history and one or two valuable old Herbals and Itineraries. I was certain that two years earlier Giffen would have had no use for literature except some muddy Russian oddments, and I am positive that he would not have known the name of Surtees. Yet there stood the tall octavos recording the unedifying careers of Mr. Jorrocks, Mr.

Facey Romford, and Mr. Soapy Sponge.

I was a little bewildered as I stretched my legs in a very deep armchair. Suddenly I had a strong impression of looking on at a play. My hosts seemed to be automata, moving docilely at the orders of a masterful stage manager, and yet with no sense of bondage. And as I looked on, they faded off the scene, and there was only one personality – that house so serene and secure, smiling at our modern antics, but weaving all the while an iron spell around its lovers.

For a second I felt an oppression as of something to be resisted. But no. There was no oppression. The house was too well-bred and disdainful to seek to captivate. Only those who fell in love with it could know its mastery, for all love exacts a price. It was far more than a thing of stone and lime: it was a creed, an art, a scheme of life – older than any Carteron, older than England. Somewhere far back in time, in Rome, in Attica, or in an Ægean island, there must have been such places; and then they called them temples, and gods dwelt in them.

I was roused by Giffen's voice discoursing of his books. 'I've been rubbing up my classics again,' he was saying. 'Queer thing, but ever since I left Cambridge I have been out of the mood for them. And I'm shockingly ill-read in English literature. I wish I had more time for reading, for it means a lot to me.'

'There is such an embarrassment of riches here,' said his wife. 'The days are far too short for all there is to do. Even when there is nobody staying in the house I find every hour occupied. It's delicious to be busy over things one really cares for.'

'All the same I wish I could do more reading,' said Giffen. 'I've never wanted to so much before.'

'But you come in tired from shooting and sleep sound till dinner,' said the lady, laying an affectionate hand on his shoulder.

They were happy people, and I like happiness. Self-absorbed, perhaps, but I prefer selfishness in the ordinary way of things. We are most of us selfish dogs, and altruism makes us uncomfortable. But I had somehow in my mind a shade of uneasiness, for I was the witness of a transformation too swift and violent to be wholly natural. Years, no doubt, turn our eyes inward and abate our heroics, but not a trifle of two or three. Some agency had been at work here, some agency other and more potent than the process of time. The thing fascinated and partly frightened me. For the Giffens – though I scarcely dared to admit it – had deteriorated. They were far pleasanter people, I liked them infinitely better, I hoped to see them often again. I detested the type they used to represent, and shunned it like the plague. They were wise now, and mellow, and most agreeable human beings. But some virtue had gone out of them. An uncomfortable virtue, no doubt, but still a virtue; something generous and adventurous. In the earlier time, their faces had had a sort of wistful kindness. Now they had geniality – which is not the same thing.

What was the agency of this miracle? It was all around me: the ivory paneling, the olive-wood staircase, the lovely pillared hall.

I got up to go to bed with a kind of awe on me. As Mrs. Giffen lit my candle, she saw my eyes wandering among the gracious shadows.

'Isn't it wonderful,' she said, 'to have found a house which fits us like a glove? No! Closer. Fits us as a bearskin fits the bear. It has taken our impress like wax.'

Somehow I didn't think that impress had come from the Giffens' side.

A November afternoon found Leithen and myself jogging homeward from a run with the Heythrop. It had been a wretched day. Twice we had found and lost, and then a deluge had set in which scattered the field. I had taken a hearty toss into a swamp, and got as wet as a man may be, but the steady downpour soon reduced everyone to a like condition. When we turned toward Borrowby the rain ceased, and an icy wind blew out of the east which partially dried our sopping clothes. All the grace had faded from the Cotswold valleys. The streams were brown torrents, the meadows lagoons, the ridges bleak and gray, and a sky of scurrying clouds cast leaden shadows. It was a matter of ten miles to Borrowby; we had long ago emptied our flasks, and I longed for something hot to take the chill out of my bones.

'Let's look in at Fullcircle,' said Leithen, as we came out on the highroad from a muddy lane. 'We'll make the Giffens give us tea. You'll find changes there.'

I asked what changes, but he only smiled and told me to wait and see.

My mind was busy with surmises as we rode up the avenue. I thought of drink or drugs, and promptly discarded the notion. Fullcircle was, above all things, decorous and wholesome. Leithen could not mean the change in the Giffens' ways which had so impressed me a year before, for he and I had long ago discussed that. I was still puzzling over his words when we found ourselves in the inner hall, with the Giffens making a hospitable fuss over us.

The place was more delectable than ever. Outside was a dark November day, yet the little house seemed to be transfused with sunshine. I do not know by what art the old builders had planned it; but the airy pilasters, the perfect lines of the ceiling, the soft coloring of the wood seemed to lay open the house to a clear sky. Logs burned brightly on the massive steel andirons, and the scent and the fine blue smoke of them strengthened the illusion of summer.

Mrs. Giffen would have us change into dry things, but Leithen pleaded a waiting dinner at Borrowby. The two of us stood by the fireplace, drinking tea, the warmth drawing out a cloud of vapor from our clothes to mingle with the wood-smoke. Giffen lounged in an armchair and his wife sat by the tea-table. I was looking for the changes of which Leithen had spoken.

I did not find them in Giffen. He was much as I remembered him on the June night when I had slept here – a trifle fuller in the face, perhaps, a little more placid about the mouth and eyes. He looked a man completely content with life. His smile came readily, and his easy laugh. Was it my fancy, or had he acquired a look of the picture in the dining-room? I nearly made an errand to go and see it. It seemed to me that his mouth had now something of the portrait's delicate complacence. Lely would have found him a fit subject, though he might have boggled at his lean hands.

But his wife! Ah, there the changes were unmistakable. She was comely now rather than pretty, and the contours of her face had grown heavier. The eagerness had gone from her eyes and left only comfort and good humor. There was a suspicion, ever so slight, of rouge and powder. She had a string of good pearls – the first time I had seen her wear jewels. The hand that poured out the tea was plump, shapely, and well cared for. I was looking at a most satisfactory mistress of a country house, who would see that nothing was lacking to the part.

She talked more and laughed oftener. Her voice had an airy lightness which would have made the silliest prattle charming.

'We are going to fill the house with young people and give a ball at Christmas,' she announced. 'This hall is simply clamoring to be danced in. You must come, both of you. Promise me. And, Mr. Leithen, it would be very nice if you brought a party from Borrowby. Young men, please. We are overstocked with girls in these parts. We must do something to make the country cheerful in winter-time.'

I observed that no season could make Fullcircle other than cheerful.

'How nice of you!' she cried. 'To praise a house is to praise the householders, for a dwelling is just what its inmates make it. Borrowby is you, Mr. Leithen, and Fullcircle us.'

'Shall we exchange?' Leithen asked.

She made a mouth. 'Borrowby would crush me, but it suits a Gothic survival like you. Do you think you would be happy here?'

'Happy?' said Leithen thoughtfully. 'Happy? Yes, undoubtedly. But it might be bad for my soul. – There's just time for a pipe, Giffen, and then we must be off.'

I was filling my pipe as we crossed the outer hall, and was about to enter the smoking-room that I so well remembered, when Giffen laid a hand on my arm.

'We don't smoke there now,' he said hastily.

He opened the door and I looked in. The place had suffered its third metamorphosis. The marble shrine which I had noticed on my first visit had been brought back, and the blue mosaic pavement and the ivory walls were bare. At the eastern end stood a little altar, with, above it, a copy of a Correggio Madonna.

A faint smell of incense hung in the air, and the fragrance of hothouse flowers. It was a chapel, but, I swear, it was a more pagan place than when it had been workroom or smoking-room.

Giffen gently shut the door. 'Perhaps you may not have heard, but some months ago my wife became a Catholic. It is a good thing for women, I think. It gives them a regular ritual for their lives. So we restored the chapel, which had always been there in the days of the Carterons and the Applebys.'

'And you?' I asked.

He shrugged his shoulders.

'I don't bother much about that sort of thing. But I propose to follow suit. It will please Ursula and do no harm to anybody.'

We halted on the brow of the hill and looked back on the garden valley. Leithen's laugh, as he gazed, had more awe than mirth in it.

'That wicked little house! I'm going to hunt up every scrap I can find about old Tom Carteron. He must have been an uncommon clever fellow. He's still alive down there and making people do as he did. In that kind of place you may expel the priest and sweep it and garnish it, but he always returns.'

The wrack was lifting before the wind, and a shaft of late watery sun fell on the gray walls. It seemed to me that the little house wore an air of gentle triumph.

The Magic Walking Stick

WHEN Bill came back for long-leave that autumn half he had before him a complex programme of entertainment. Thomas, the Keeper, whom he revered more than anyone else in the world, was to take him in the afternoon to try for a duck in the big marsh called Alemoor. In the evening Hallowe'en would be celebrated in the nursery with his small brother Peter, and he would be permitted to sit up after dinner till ten o'clock. Next day, which was Sunday, would be devoted to wandering about with Peter, hearing from him all the appetising home news, and pouring into his greedy ears the gossip of the foreign world of school. On Monday morning, after a walk with the dogs, he was to motor to London, lunch with Aunt Alice, go to a conjuring show, and then, after a noble tea, return to school in time for lock-up.

It seemed to Bill all that could be desired in the way of excitement. But he did not know just how exciting that long leave was destined to be.

The first shadow of a cloud appeared after luncheon, when he had changed into knickerbockers, and Peter and the dogs were waiting at the gun-room door. Bill could not find his own proper stick. It was a long hazel staff, given him by the second stalker in a Scotch deer-forest the year before – a staff rather taller than Bill, of glossy hazel, with a shapely polished crook, and without a ferrule, like all stalking sticks. He hunted for it high and low, but it could not be found. Without it in his hand Bill felt that an expedition lacked something vital, and he was not prepared to take instead one of his father's shooting sticks, as Groves, the butler, recommended. Nor would he accept a knubbly cane proffered by Peter. Feeling a little aggrieved and imperfectly equipped, he rushed out to join Thomas. He would cut himself an ashplant in the first hedge.

But as the two ambled down the lane which led to Alemoor, they came on an old man sitting under a hornbeam. He was a funny little wizened old man, in a shabby long green overcoat, which had once been black, and he wore on his head the oldest and tallest and greenest bowler hat that ever graced a human head. Thomas walked on as if he did not see him, and Gyp, the spaniel, and Shawn, the Irish setter, at the sight of him dropped their tails between their legs, and remembered an engagement a long way off. But Bill stopped, for he saw that the old man had a bundle under his arm, a bundle of ancient umbrellas and queer ragged sticks.

The old man smiled at him, and he had very bright eyes. He seemed to know what was wanted, for he at once took from his bundle a stick. You would not have said that it was the kind of stick Bill was looking for. It was short, and heavy, and made of some dark foreign wood, and instead of a crook it had a handle shaped like a crescent, cut out of some white substance which was neither bone nor ivory. Yet Bill, as soon as he saw it, felt that it was the one stick in the world for him.

'How much?' he asked.

'One farthing,' said the old man, and his voice squeaked like a winter wind in a chimney.

Now a farthing is not a common coin, but Bill happened to have one – a gift from Peter on his arrival that day, along with a brass cannon, five empty cartridges, a broken microscope, and a badly-printed brightly-illustrated narrative called 'Two Villains Foiled.' But a farthing sounded too little, so Bill proffered one of his scanty shillings.

'I said one farthing,' said the old man rather snappily.

The small coin changed hands, and the little old wizened face seemed to light up with an elfish glee. ''Tis a fine stick, young sir,' he squeaked, 'a noble stick, when you gets used to the ways of it.'

Bill had to run to catch up Thomas, who was plodding along with the dogs, now returned from their engagement.

'That's a queer chap – the old stick-man, I mean,' he said.

'I ain't seen no old man, Maaster Bill,' said Thomas. 'What be 'ee talkin' about?'

'The fellow back there. I bought this stick of him.'

Thomas cast a puzzled glance at the stick. 'That be a craafty stick, Maaster Bill –' but he said no more, for Bill had shaken it playfully at the dogs. As soon as they saw it they set off to keep another engagement – this time, apparently, with a hare – and Thomas was yelling and whistling for ten minutes before he brought them to heel.

It was a soft grey afternoon, and Bill was stationed beside one of the deep dykes in the moor, well in cover of a thorn bush, while Thomas and the dogs went off on a long circuit to show themselves beyond the big mere, so that the duck might move in Bill's direction. It was rather cold, and very wet underfoot, for a lot of rain had fallen in the past week, and the mere, which was usually only a sedgy pond, had now grown to a great expanse of shallow floodwater. Bill began his vigil in high excitement. He drove his new stick into the ground, and used the handle as a seat, while he rested his gun in the orthodox way in the crook of his arm. It was a double-barrelled, sixteen bore, and Bill knew that he would be lucky if he got a duck with it; but a duck was to him a bird of mystery, true wild game, and he preferred the chance of one to the certainty of many rabbits.

The minutes passed, the grey afternoon sky darkened towards twilight, but no duck came. Bill saw a wedge of geese high up in the sky and longed to salute them; also he heard snipe, but could not locate them in the dim weather. Far away he thought he detected the purring noise which Thomas made to stir the duck, but no overhead beat of wings followed. Soon the mood of eager anticipation died away, and he grew bored and rather despondent. He scrambled up the bank of the dyke and strained his eyes over the moor between the bare boughs of the thorn. He thought he saw duck moving – yes, he was certain of it – they were coming from the direction of Thomas and the dogs. It was perfectly clear what was happening. There was far too much water on the moor, and the birds, instead of flighting across the mere to the boundary slopes, were simply settling on the flood. From the misty grey water came the rumour of many wildfowl.

Bill came back to his wet stand grievously disappointed. He did not dare to leave it in case a flight did appear, but he had lost all hope. He tried to warm his feet by moving them up and down in the squelchy turf. His gun was now under his arm, and he was fiddling idly with the handle of the stick which was still embedded in earth. He made it revolve, and as it turned he said aloud: 'I wish I was in the middle of the big flood.'

Then a remarkable thing happened. Bill was not conscious of any movement, but suddenly his surroundings were completely changed. He had still his gun under his left arm and the stick in his right hand, but instead of standing on wet turf he was up to the waist in water ... And all around him were duck – shovellers, pintail, mallard, teal, widgeon, pochard, tufted – and bigger things that might be geese – swimming or diving or just alighting from the air. In a second Bill realised that his wish had been granted. He was in the very middle of the flood water.

He got a right and left at mallards, missing with his first barrel. Then the birds rose in alarm, and he shoved in fresh cartridges and fired wildly into the brown. His next two shots were at longer range, but he was certain that he had hit something. And then the duck vanished in the brume, and he was left alone with the grey waters running out to the dimness.

He lifted up his voice and shouted wildly for Thomas and the dogs, and looked about him to retrieve what he had shot. He had got two anyhow – a mallard drake and a young teal, and he collected them. Presently he heard whistling and splashing, and Gyp the spaniel appeared half swimming, half wading. Gyp picked up a second mallard, and Bill left it at that. He thought he knew roughly where the deeper mere lay so as to avoid it, and with his three duck he started for where he believed Thomas to be. The water was often up to his armpits and once he was soused over his head, and it was a very wet, breathless and excited boy that presently confronted the astounded keeper.

'Where in goodness ha' ye been, Maaster Bill? Them ducks was tigglin' out to the deep water and I was feared ye wouldn't get a shot. Three on 'em, no less! My word, ye 'ave poonished 'em.'

'I was in the deep water,' said Bill, but he explained no more, for it had just occurred to him that he couldn't. It was a boy not less puzzled than triumphant that returned to show his bag to his family, and at dinner he was so abstracted that his mother thought he was ill and sent him early to bed. Bill made no complaint, for he wanted to be alone to think things out.

It was plain that a miracle had happened, and it must be connected with the stick. He had wished himself in the middle of the flood-water – he remembered that clearly – and at the time he had been doing something to the stick. What was it? It had been stuck in the ground, and he had been playing with the handle. Yes, he had it. He had been turning it round when he uttered the wish. Bill's mind was better stored wth fairy tales than with Latin and Greek, and he remembered many precedents. The stick was in the rack in the hall, and he had half a mind to slip downstairs and see if he could repeat the performance. But he reflected that he might be observed, and that this was a business demanding profound secrecy. So he resolutely composed himself to sleep. He had been allowed for a treat to have his old bed in the night-nursery, next to Peter, and he realised that he must be up bright and early to frustrate that alert young inquirer.

HE woke before dawn, and at once put on socks and fives-shoes and a dressing-gown, and tiptoed downstairs. He heard a housemaid moving in the direction of the dining-room, and Groves opening the library shutters, but the hall was deserted. He groped in the rack and found the stick, struggled with the key of the garden door, and emerged into the foggy winter half-light. It was very cold, as he padded down the lawn to a retired half-moon of shrubbery beside the pond, and his shoes were soon soaked with hoar-frost. He shivered and drew his dressing-gown around him, but he had decided what to do. In this kind of weather he wished to be warm. He planted his stick in the turf.

'I want to be on the beach in the Solomon Islands,' said Bill, and three times twisted the handle.

In a second his eyes seemed to dazzle with excess of light and something beat on his body like a blast from an open furnace. ... He was standing on an expanse of blinding white sand at which a lazy blue sea was licking. Behind him at a distance of perhaps two hundred yards was a belt of high green forest, out of which stuck a tall crest of palms. A hot wind was blowing and tossing the tree-tops, but it only crisped the sea.

Bill gasped with joy to find his dream realised. He was in the far Pacific where he had always longed to be ... But he was very hot, and could not endure the weight of winter pyjamas and winter dressing-gown. Also he longed to bathe in those inviting waters. So he shed everything and hopped gaily down to the tide's edge, leaving the stick still upright in the sand.

The sea was as delicious as it looked, but Bill, though a good swimmer, kept near the edge for fear of sharks. He wallowed and splashed, with the fresh salt smell which he loved in his nostrils. Minutes passed rapidly, and he was just on the point of striking out for a little reef, when he cast a glance towards the shore ...

At the edge of the forest stood men – dark-skinned men, armed with spears.

Bill scrambled to his feet with a fluttering heart, and as he rose the men moved forward. He was, perhaps, fifty yards from the stick, which cast its long morning shadow on the sand, and they were two hundred yards on the farther side. At all costs he must get there first. He sprang out of the sea, and as he ran he saw to his horror that the men ran also – ran in great bounds – shouting and brandishing their spears.

Those fifty yards seemed miles, but Bill won the race. No time to put on his clothes. He seized his dressing-gown with one hand and the stick with the other, and as he twirled the handle a spear whizzed by his ear. 'I want to be home,' he gasped, and the next second he stood naked between the shrubbery and the pond, clutching his dressing-gown. The Solomon Islands had got his fives-shoes and his pyjamas.

The cold of a November morning brought him quickly to his senses. He clothed his shivering body in his dressing-gown and ran by devious paths to the house. Happily the gun-room door was unlocked, and he

was able to ascend by way of empty passages and back-stairs to the
nursery floor. He did not, however, escape the eagle eye of Elsie, the
nurse, who read a commination service over a boy who went out of doors
imperfectly clad on such a morning. She prophesied pneumonia, and
plumped him into a hot bath.

Bill applied his tongue to the back of his hand. Yes. It tasted salt, and
the salt smell was still in his nose. It had not been a dream ... He hugged
himself in the bath and made strange gurgling sounds of joy. Life had
suddenly opened up for him in dazzling vistas of adventure.

———

HIS conduct in church that morning was exemplary, for while Peter at
his side had his usual Sunday attack of St. Vitus's Dance, Bill sat
motionless as a mummy. On the way home his mother commented on
it and observed that Lower Chapel seemed to have taught him how to
behave. But his thoughts during the service had not been devotional.
The stick lay beside him on the floor, and for a moment he had a wild
notion of twisting it during the Litany and disappearing for a few
minutes to Kamschatka. Then prudence supervened. He must go very
cautiously in this business, and court no questions. That afternoon he
and Peter would seek a secluded spot and make experiments. He
would take the stick back to school and hide it in his room – he had a
qualm when he thought what a 'floater' it would be if a lower boy
appeared with it in public! For him no more hours of boredom. School
would no longer be a place of exile, but a rapturous holiday. He would
slip home now and then and see what was happening – he would go
often to Glenmore – he would visit any spot in the globe which took his
fancy. His imagination reeled at the prospect, and he cloaked his
chortles of delight in a fervent Amen.

At luncheon it was decided that Peter and he should go for a walk
together, and should join the others at a place called the Roman Camp.
'Let the boys have a chance of being alone,' his father had said. This
exactly suited Bill's book, and as they left the dining-room he clutched
his small brother. 'Shrimp,' he said in his ear, 'You're going to have
the afternoon of your life.'

It was a mild, grey day, with the leafless woods and the brown
ploughlands lit by a pale November sun. Peter, as he trotted beside
him, jerked out breathless inquiries about what Bill proposed to do,
and was told to wait and see.

Arrived at a clump of beeches which promised privacy, Bill first
swore his brother to secrecy by the most awful oaths which he could

imagine.

'Put your arm round my waist and hang on to my belt,' he told him. 'I'm going to take you to have a look at Glenmore.'

'Don't be silly,' said Peter. 'That only happens in Summer, and we haven't packed yet.'

'Shut up and hold tight,' said Bill as he twirled the stick and spoke the necessary words...

The boys were looking not at the smooth boles of beeches, but at a little coppice of rowans and birches above the narrow glen of the hill burn. It was Glenmore in very truth. There was the strip of mossy lawn, the white-washed gable end of the lodge; there to the left beside the walled garden was the smoking chimney of the keeper's cottage; there beyond the trees was the long lift of brown moorland and the blue top of Stob Ghabhar. To the boys Glenmore was the true home of the soul, but they had seen it only in the glory of late summer and early autumn. In its winter dress it seemed for a moment strange. Then the sight of an old collie waddling across the lawn gave the connecting link.

'There's Wattie,' Peter gasped, and lifted up his voice in an excited summons. His brother promptly scragged him.

'Don't be an ass, Shrimp,' he said fiercely. 'This is a secret, you fathead. This is magic. Nobody must know we are here. Come on and explore.'

For an hour – it must have been an hour, Bill calculated afterwards, but it seemed like ten minutes – the two visited their favourite haunts. They found the robbers' cave in the glen where a raven nested, and the pool where Bill had caught his first pound trout, and the stretch in the river where their father that year had had the thirty pound salmon. There were no blaeberries or crowberries in the woods, but there were many woodcock, and Bill had a shot with his catapult at a wicked old blackcock on a peat-stack. Also they waylaid Wattie, the collie, and induced him to make a third in the party. All their motions were as stealthy as an Indian's, and the climax of the adventure was reached when they climbed the garden wall and looked in at the window of the keeper's cottage.

Tea was laid before a bright peat fire in the parlour, so Mrs. Macrae must be expecting company. It looked a very good tea, for there were scones and pancakes, and shortbread and currant-loaf and heather honey. Both boys felt suddenly famished at the sight.

'Mrs. Macrae always gives me a scone and honey,' Peter bleated. 'I'm hungry. I want one.'

So did Bill. His soul longed for food, but he kept hold of his prudence. 'We daren't show ourselves,' he whispered. 'But, perhaps, we might pinch a scone. It wouldn't be stealing, for if Mrs. Macrae saw us she would say "Come awa in, laddies, and get a jeely piece." I'll give you a back, Shrimp, and in you get.'

The window was open, and Peter was hoisted through, falling with a bang on a patch-work rug. But he never reached the table, for at that moment the parlour door opened and someone entered. After that things happened fast. Peter, urged by Bill's anguished whisper, turned back to the window, and was hauled through by the scruff of the neck. A woman's voice was heard crying, 'Mercy on us, it's the bairns,' as the culprits darted to the shelter of the gooseberry bushes.

Billy realised that there was no safety in the garden, so he dragged Peter over the wall by the way they had come, thereby seriously damaging a pear tree. But they had been observed, and as they scrambled out of a rose-bed, they heard cries and saw Mrs. Macrae appearing round the end of the wall, having come through the stable yard. Also a figure, which looked like Angus, the river gillie, was running from the same direction.

There was nothing for it but to go. Bill seized Peter with one hand and the stick with the other, and spoke the words, with Angus not six yards away … As he looked once more at the familiar beech boles, his ears were still full of the cries of an excited woman and the frenzied howling of Wattie, the dog.

The two boys, very warm and flustered and rather scratched about the hands and legs, confronted their father and mother and their sister, Barabara, who was sixteen and very proud.

'Hullo, hullo,' they heard their father say. 'I thought you'd be hiding somewhere hereabouts. You young rascals know how to take cover, for you seemed to spring out of the ground. You look as if you'd been playing football. Better walk home with us and cool down … Bless my soul, Peter, what's that you've got? It's bog myrtle! Where on earth did you find it? I've never seen it before in Oxfordshire.'

Then Barbara raised a ladylike voice. 'Oh, Mummy, look at the mess they've made of themselves. They've been among the brambles, for Peter has two holes in his stockings. Just look at Bill's hands!' And she wrinkled her finical nose, and sniffed.

Bill kept a diplomatic silence, and Peter, usually garrulous, did the same, for his small wrist was in his brother's savage clutch.

———

THAT night, before Peter went to bed, he was compelled once more to swear solemn oaths, and Bill was so abstracted that his mother thought that he was sickening for some fell disease. He lay long awake, planning out the best way to use his marvellous new possession. His thoughts were still on the subject next morning, and to his family's amazement he made no protest when, to suit his mother's convenience, it was decided to start for London soon after breakfast, and the walk with the dogs was cancelled. He departed in high spirits, most unlike his usual leave-takings, and his last words to Peter were fierce exhortations to secrecy.

All the way to London he was in a happy dream, and at luncheon he was so urbane that Aunt Alice, who had strong and unorthodox views about education, announced that in Bill's case, at any rate, the public school system seemed to answer, and gave him double her customary tip.

Then came the conjuring show at the Grafton Hall. Bill in the past had had an inordinate appetite for such entertainments, and even in his new ecstasy he looked forward to this one. But at the door of the hall he had a shock. Hitherto he had kept close to his stick, but it was now necessary to give it up and receive a metal check for it. To his mother's surprise he protested hotly. 'It won't do any harm,' he pleaded. 'It will stay beside me under the seat.' But the rule was inexorable and he had to surrender it. 'Don't be afraid, darling,' his mother told him. 'That funny new stick of yours won't be lost. The check is a receipt for it, and they are very careful.'

The show was not up to his expectations. What were all these disappearing donkeys and vanishing ladies compared to the performances he had lately staged? Bill was puffed up with a great pride. With the help of his stick he could make rings round this trumpery cleverness. He was the true magician ... He wished that the thing would end that he might feel the precious stick again in his hand.

At the counter there was no sign of the man who had given him the check. Instead there was a youth who seemed to be new to the business, and who was very slow in returning the sticks and umbrellas. When it came to Bill's turn he was extra slow, and presently announced that he could find no Number 229.

Bill's mother, seeing his distress, intervened, and sent the wretched youth to look again, while other people were kept waiting, but he came back with the same story. There was no duplicate Number 229, or any article to correspond to the check. After that he had to be allowed to attend to the others, and Bill, almost in tears, waited hysterically till the crowd had gone. Then there was a thorough search, and Bill and his mother were allowed to go behind the counter. But no Number 229 could be found, and there were no sticks left, only three umbrellas.

Bill was now patently in tears.

'Never mind, darling,' his mother said, 'we must be off now, or you will be late for lock-up. I promise that your father will come here to-morrow and clear up the whole business. Never fear – the stick will be found.'

But it is still lost.

━━━━━━━━━━━━

WHEN Bill's father went there next day, and cross-examined the wretched youth – for he had once been a barrister – he extracted a curious story. If the walking-stick was lost, so also was the keeper of the walking-sticks, for the youth was only an assistant. The keeper – his name was Jukes and he lived in Hammersmith – had not been seen since yesterday afternoon during the performance, and Mrs. Jukes had come round and made a scene last night, and that morning the police had been informed. Mr. Jukes, it appeared, was not a very pleasant character, and he had had too much beer at luncheon. When the audience had all gone in, he had expressed to his assistant his satiety of life. The youth's testimony ran as follows: 'Mr. Jukes, 'e was wavin' his arm something chronic and carryin' on about 'ow this was no billet for a man like 'im. He picks up a stick, and I thought he was goin' to 'it me. "Percy, me lad," says 'e, "I'm fed up – fed up to the back teeth." He starts twisting the stick, and says 'e "I wish to 'eaven I was out of 'ere." After that I must 'ave come over faint, for when I looks again, 'e 'ad 'opped it.'

Mr. Jukes' case is still a puzzle to Mrs. Jukes and the police, but Bill understands only too clearly what happened. Mr. Jukes and the stick have gone 'out of 'ere', and where that may be neither Bill nor I can guess.

But he still lives in hope, and he wants me to broadcast this story in case the stick may have come back to earth. So let every boy and girl keep a sharp eye on shops where sticks are sold. The magic walking-stick is not quite four feet long, and about one inch and a quarter thick. It is made of a heavy dark-red wood, rather like the West Indian purpleheart. Its handle is in the shape of a crescent with the horns uppermost, made of some white substance which is neither bone nor ivory. If anyone sees such a stick, then Bill will give all his worldly wealth for news of it.

Failing that, he would like information about the man who sold it to him. He is very old, small and wizened, but his eyes are the brightest you ever saw in a human head. He wears a shabby, greeny-black overcoat which reaches down to his heels, and a tall, greeny-black bowler hat. It is possible that the stick may have returned to him. So if you meet anyone like him, look sharply at his bundle, and if it is there and he is willing to sell, *buy it – buy it – buy it*, or you will regret it all your days. For this purpose it is wiser always to have a farthing in your pocket, for he won't give change.

The Strange Adventure of Mr. Andrew Hawthorn

ANY disappearance is a romantic thing, especially if it be unexpected and inexplicable. To vanish from the common world and leave no trace, and to return with the same suddenness and mystery, satisfies the eternal human sense of wonder. That is why the old stories make so much of it. Tamlane and Kilmeny and Ogier the Dane retired to Fairyland, and Oisin to the Land of the Ever Living, and no man knows the manner of their going or their return. The common world goes on, but they are far away in a magic universe of their own.

But even ordinary folk can disappear. Sometimes they never come back and leave only blank mystery behind them. But sometimes they return and can explain what happened. Here is a true tale of what befell a most prosaic Scots gentleman rather less than two centuries ago.

Let us call him Andrew Hawthorn. He was thirty-two years of age and had no wife, but lived with his sister, Barbara, in a steep-roofed, stone house a dozen miles from Edinburgh. The house stood above a narrow wooded glen, what is called in Scotland a 'dean,' at the bottom of which ran a brawling stream.

Mr. Hawthorn was a stiff gentleman, very set in his ways. His wig was always carefully powdered, his clothes were trim, and his buckles bright. He enjoyed a modest competence, which enabled him to devote his life to his hobbies. These were principally antiquities, and he had been busy for some years on a great work on the Antonines.

He was in the habit of breakfasting at seven with his sister, and being particular in his habits, he liked to have his meal served punctually at that hour. He was always in the little dining-room as the clock struck, while his sister was usually a few minutes late. His custom was to take a walk after breakfast and be at his books at eight o'clock. Therefore he liked to finish his meal by a quarter after seven, and this meant punctilious service. In especial he disliked having his porridge so hot that he had to delay some minutes before he could begin on it.

On a fine May morning, Mr. Hawthorn appeared in the breakfast room at the exact hour. His sister was not down, but two steaming bowls of porridge stood on the table. Mr. Hawthorn was annoyed. He strode into the little hall and shouted upstairs.

'Babbie,' he cried, 'how often have I told you the porridge should be dished up earlier? They are scalding hot again. I am going out of doors until they cool.'

He walked out into the garden. He also walked out of the world for five years and seven months.

There was a great hue and cry in the countryside. The Procurator Fiscal made his precognitions, and even the capital city was stirred by the mystery, but no trace could be found of Mr. Andrew Hawthorn. His footsteps were followed on the coarse dewy turf which ran along tht edge of the dean, and there they disappeared. In the dean itself there were signs of an old fire on a little shelf of ground, and a good deal of trampled grass and broken underwood; but the latter might have been due to the cattle-beasts that were always straying in from the neighbouring hillside.

Mr. Hawthorn had no near kin besides his sister, but his lawyers offered a considerable reward for news of him. None came, and most people assumed that he was dead. His sister, who was his heir-at-law, would have succeeded to his estate had his death been presumed, but she resolutely refused to admit the presumption. Andrew, she said, would come back, though she would give no grounds for her belief. She conducted the household as usual, and every morning she had a plate of porridge set for him at breakfast, as if at any moment he might appear from the garden. She even remembered his wishes and saw to it that the porridge was dished up a little earlier.

MR. Hawthorn went out into the bright sunshine and impatiently sniffed the morning freshness. He walked to the edge of the dean, and there, on the well trodden path among the fir trees, he saw one Bauldy Grieve, a packman, whose rounds took him up and down the Lowlands. Bauldy was an old friend who had often provided him with minor antiquities. It appeared that he had something important to communicate, for he was sitting there to intercept the laird on his morning walk.

'I've some michty wonders to show your honour,' he announced.

'The pleughman at the Back o' the Buss turned up an auld kist in the field. He didn't let on to his master, but he telled me. I bocht what was in it, a wheen auld siller coins and some muckle flaigons. The pleughman – Tam Dod is his name – thocht the flaigons were brass, so I got them cheap, though he haggled sair over the siller. But they are no brass, your honour – they're gowd, as sure as I'm a living man. Nae doot they were buried by the ancient Romans. So I cam off post haste to see ye, and have gotten them in my pack. Will your honour step doun wi' me and hae a look at them?'

Mr. Hawthorn was excited and forgot all about breakfast. He followed the packman down through the bracken to a shelf above the burn, where Bauldy had spent the night. At the first sight of the flagons his eyes opened wide. They were amphoræ of exquisite design, probably vessels used for some ceremonial rite. He scraped off a little of the encrusted dirt, and saw the gleam of bright metal.

Now, as ill-luck would have it, news of the find had got abroad, perhaps because Bauldy had gossiped in his cups. Anyhow three tinkler ruffians of the Baillie clan were on the trail, and had followed Bauldy to his camp for the night. They had seen him speak to the laird and were now lurking in the undergrowth.

'Guid save us, Bauldy,' said Mr. Hawthorn. 'This is a most remarkable discovery. The like has not been seen in Scotland.'

'Are they gowd, your honour?' the packman asked.

'I have little doubt of it,' said Mr. Hawthorn. 'Things so beautiful could be made of no baser metal.'

This was enough for the tinklers. They leaped out upon the two, and one, with his big staff, or 'kent,' struck the packman a savage blow on the back of his head. Mr. Hawthorn, though taken by surprise, put up a stout fight, for the passion of the antiquarian put fire into his manhood. But he was soon overpowered and knocked senseless by a blow from behind.

After that Mr. Hawthorn's memory became confused. The tinklers were men of caution and foresight. It was not enough to annex the contents of the pedlar's pack, they must get rid of compromising evidence. The pedlar looked pretty bad, and the gentleman not much better. It would never do to leave them on the scene of the assault, for they had seen too much of their assailants.

Now, on the highway on the other side of the dean, the tinklers had a covered cart, which they were accustomed to use for nefarious business. They swung their two victims on their shoulders and cautiously made their way to the cart, and some time that evening were safe in a hovel near the water-front in Leith.

The pedlar never recovered, for his neck had been broken. Mr. Hawthorn came back to consciousness with an intolerable headache and a raging thirst; he was given a drink, which must have been hocussed, for he lost his senses again. The body of the pedlar was secretly buried, a ceremony for which the tinklers had their own contrivances, and it was not likely that a wandering packman would be missed.

But Mr. Hawthorn was a different matter. The hue and cry over his loss alarmed them, and they saw no other course but to get rid of him too. Murder was their first idea, but presently a better presented itself. They had already done some traffic in kidnapping and exporting the able-bodied to the American plantations, and they had a shipmaster who was in their secret. One dark night Mr. Hawthorn, still hocussed, was smuggled aboard a vessel, and when his wits fully returned to him he was a prisoner on the broad Atlantic.

———

IT would take a long time to tell the full story of Mr. Hawthorn's life in the Carolinas. He was sold under an indenture to a tobacco planter, which meant that till the period of his indenture expired he was virtually a slave. His ill-treatment at the hands of the tinklers had affected both his memory and his wits, and it was a long time before his head cleared. Bit by bit, however recollection came back to him, but the last scene he remembered clearly was leaving his steaming porridge in the little dining-room of his house. All that had happened in the dean remained in a misty confusion.

He was strong in body and of careful habits, and this stood him well in the hard toil of the plantation. Also he was a prudent soul, and, having decided that there was nothing for it but to submit, he did his work and kept his thoughts to himself. His companions were mostly the scum of British prisons, and he might have endured a good deal of rough usage at their hands. But Mr. Hawthorn had a stiff temper of his own, and his fellows realised that there was a point when he would show fight and defend himself. So slowly he won a position of some respect among the others, while his industry and docility secured him reasonable treatment from the overseer.

His master was a man of pleasure who spent his days chiefly in horse-racing and card-playing. Several times Mr. Hawthorn, after his memory returned to him, tried to approach him to state his case, but it was long before he got an opportunity. When it came he found that he was not believed. Such yarns had often been heard before from redemptioners. But the superior breeding of Mr. Hawthorn impressed his master. Here was one who in deportment and speech appeared to be a gentleman, though he looked a dull dog and spoke with a strong Scots accent. The upshot was that when the butler broke his neck one dark night Mr. Hawthorn was promoted to fill his place. Among his other gifts it appeared that he had a very fair knowledge of wine.

Now it happened some months later, when the household under Mr. Hawthorn's sway had acquired a new precision, that a neighbouring squire came to dinner. The guest was of a very different type from the master of the house, for he was something of a politician and something of a scholar. During the meal he quoted a tag from Horace, but could not remember its conclusion. His host could not help him out, but, to his surprise, the butler volunteered the missing line.

The result was that the guest had some speech with Mr. Hawthorn before he left, heard his story, and believed it. He was a man of a philanthropic spirit, and his first aim was to remove this unhappy scholar to more congenial surroundings. So after various negotiations, which had something to do with a young thoroughbred filly, Mr. Hawthorn was transferred to the establishment of his new-found friend.

There he dwelt not unhappily for a considerable time. At his request his new master wrote to a Scottish correspondent, and, without revealing Mr. Hawthorn's existence, secured the full details of the events which had mystified all Lothian. He learned that Miss Barbara was living in the house, confident that her brother would some day return. Mr. Hawthorn would not let him proceed further. Somewhere in his sober bosom was a spark of romance; as he had departed mysteriously, so he would return. His new life interested him, he had formed an attachment to his new master, and he had almost forgotten about his great work on the Antonines. Also, Mr. Hawthorn was proud. He was determined to be beholden to no man for the cost of his return, and he was waiting until he had saved sufficient money from his wages.

———————

AT last the day arrived when he was ready and willing to leave. But in those days of continuous war with France it was no slight business to cross the Atlantic, and there were many adventures in store for him before he reached his native land.

He embarked on a ship which was taken off Land's End by a French privateer. He was carried to Havre and found himself a prisoner in the enemy's hands. This misfortune achieved what none of his sufferings in Carolina had achieved – it broke Mr. Hawthorn's temper. He managed to escape, and for several months was a fugitive on the French roads. Having some command of the French tongue, and dwelling much upon his Scottish nationality and the old friendship between Scotland and France, he managed to secure the good offices of a priest, who facilitated his journey to the capital.

In Paris, Mr. Hawthorn had a friend, a fellow antiquarian, to whom he appealed for help. This was willingly given, but it was not easy at the moment to leave France, and Mr. Hawthorn had to spend several months in Paris, where, after his proud fashion, he insisted on supporting himself by teaching. He had to pass as a Scottish Jacobite, a disguise which gave him intense annoyance, for he was a zealous supporter of the Hanoverian Government.

It was April when he found it possible to depart from French soil. A smuggler's sloop landed him by night on the Sussex coast, and he was free once more to assume the character of a law-abiding Scotsman. He had enough money for the journey to the North, but, having acquired frugal habits during his wanderings, he insisted on making that journey in the most inexpensive fashion. Late on the evening of a day in early May, a timber barque from Hull deposited him at the pier at Leith.

He slept the night in a waterside inn, and before dawn next morning he was well on the road for his home. It was a fresh, bright day, very much the same weather as when he had left. He ascended the dean and crossed the strip of rough lawn. As he entered the dining-room the clock was striking seven.

There were two plates of smoking porridge on the table, much too hot to eat.

He strode into the hall. 'Babby!' he cried, 'how often have I told you that the porridge should be dished up earlier?'

But he did not go out into the garden again to wait until it cooled.

The Death Notice

THE announcement on the first page of *The Times*, which Charles Ottery read at Flambard, and every letter of which was printed on his mind, ran thus:

OTTERY. – Suddenly in London on the 9th inst., Captain Charles Ottery, late Scots Fusiliers, of Marlcote, Glos., at the age of 36.

It fitted his case precisely. The regiment was right (the dropping of the 'Royal' before its title was a familiar journalistic omission), Marlcote was his family place, and in June of the following year he would have just passed his thirty-sixth birthday.

I had known Charles since he was a schoolboy, for he was my nephew's friend, and many a half-sovereign I had tipped him in those days. He was the only child of a fine old Crimean veteran, and had gone straight from school into the family regiment, for a succession of Otterys had served in the Royal Scots Fusiliers, though they had not a drop of Scots blood. They came originally, I believe, from Devonshire, but had been settled for a couple of centuries in the Severn valley. Charles was a delightful boy, with old-fashioned manners, for he had been strictly brought up. He always called his father 'sir,' I remember, and rose when he entered the room. He had a rather sullen, freckled face, tawny hair which curled crisply, and pale-blue eyes which could kindle into a dancing madness, or freeze into a curious mature solemnity. What impressed one about him as a boy was the feeling he gave of latent power. He never seemed to put all of himself into anything – there was an impression always of heavy reserves waiting to be called up. He was the average successful schoolboy, not specially brilliant at anything except at court-tennis, but generally liked and greatly respected. No one ever took liberties with Master Charles, for the sheath of pleasant manners was felt to cover a particularly stiff bone.

The War broke out when he had been a soldier for six months, and Charles went to France in September 1914. As his friends expected, he made an admirable regimental officer – one of the plain fighting men who were never sick or sorry during four gruelling years. Being a regular, he had no sensational advancement; he got his company during the Somme, and later had one or two staff jobs, from which he always managed to wangle a speedy return to his battalion. He was happy, because he was young and healthy and competent, and loved his men. After the Armistice he had the better part of a year in Ireland, a miserable time which tried him far more sorely in mind and body than his four years in France. Then his father died, and as soon as the Scots Fusiliers had finished their Irish tour Charles left the service.

He inherited a large and unlucrative landed estate; he was devoted to Marlcote, and he had to find some means of earning money if he wanted to retain it. Through the influence of an uncle he was taken into a London firm of merchant-bankers, and in his quiet resolute way set himself to learn his job. He proved to have a genuine talent for business. His mind was not quick, but it was powerful, and he used to burrow his way like a mole to the bottom of a question. Also there was something about his stability and force of character which made men instinctively trust him, and he earned that reputation for judgment the price of which is above rubies. No one called him clever, but everyone believed him to be wise. In three years he was a junior partner in his firm, and after that his advance was rapid. He became a director of the Bank of England, the youngest man, I believe, except Goschen, who ever entered the Bank Parlour; he sat on more than one Government commission, and he was believed to be often consulted by the Treasury. He figured also in the public eye as an athlete, for he played his favourite court-tennis regularly, and had been twice runner-up for the amateur championship.

Then into his orderly life, like a warm spring wind upon a snowfield, came Pamela Brune. Pamela was my goddaughter, and I had watched with amazement her pass from a plain, solemn child to a leggy girl and then to the prettiest débutante of her year. Almost in a moment, it seemed to me, the lines of her body changed from angularity to grace, the contours of her small face were moulded into exquisiteness, and her thin little neck became a fit setting for her lovely head. She was tall for a woman, nearly as tall as Charles, but so perfectly proportioned that her height did not take the eye; exquisiteness was the dominant impression, and a kind of swift airy vigour. In her colouring she had taken after her father, and I can best describe it as a delicate ivory lit up, as it were, from within, and nobly framed by her dusky hair. Her eyes were grey, with blue lights in them. Beyond doubt a beauty, and of a rare type. The transformation in her manner was not less striking. She had been a shy child, rather silent and reflective, a good companion on a long walk, when she would expound to me her highly original fancies, but apt at most times to escape notice. Now she was so brilliant to look at that such escape was not for her, and she had developed a manner which was at once defiant and defensive. Young men were a little afraid of her, her eyes were so compelling, taking in much and revealing little, and her deep voice had a disquieting candour.

Charles fell headlong in love, and I could see from the start that the affair would not go smoothly. To begin with, she was very young – scarcely nineteen – and was like a bird preening her wings for flight, whereas Charles was thirty-five and fixed solidly on his perch. He was a little set in his ways and cocksure in his opinions, while she had the sceptical and critical innocence of youth. They became friends at once, but their friendship seemed slow to ripen into anything deeper. Pamela had nothing of the flirt in her, and though young men swarmed round her, there was no other suitor to give Charles heart-disease. The trouble was that he got no farther forward. One reason, perhaps, was that he was far too eligible. The girl had a notion that everyone desired the match, and that her parents counted on it, so naturally she revolted. Another thing – she was quicker-witted than Charles, and had a dozen interests to his one, so that his circumscription was apt to show up poorly in contrast. This was bad for him, for it cast him into a kind of irritable despair, and bad for Pamela, since it made her more critical. When he was schoolmasterish, the pupil put him to shame; when his mood was humble, hers was arrogant.

So during the month before the Flambard party the course of true love did not run smooth. The effect of a grand passion on Charles's tough solidity was what might have been looked for. His nature was not elastic, and instead of expanding under heat was in danger of warping. He was so desperately in love that all his foundations were upset. He could not fit his passion into his scheme of life, so his scheme of life went by the board. He was miserably conscious of being in a world which he did not understand, of dealing with imponderable things over which he had no mastery. A hasty word, a cold glance from Pamela, would thrust this man, who had always prided himself upon his balance, into a fever of indecision ...

And just before Whitsuntide they had had something like a quarrel. He had been magisterial and she had been pert – no, 'pert' is not the word – rather disdainful in a silken way, airily detached and infinitely distant. She had not sulked – that would have been far easier for Charles: she had simply set him back firmly among the ranks of her acquaintances. So he had gone to Flambard in a wretched state of mind, and her treatment of him there had been like an acid to his wounds. He found himself in a condition which he had never dreamed of – cut off from the common-sense world which he understood, and condemned to flounder among emotions and problems as evasive as dreams and yet with a terrible potency of torture. Moe was right: Charles Ottery was profoundly unhappy.

HE had entered upon the experiment at Flambard with a vague hope that he might learn something about the future which would ease his mind. What he did learn was that in a year's time he would be dead.

His first reaction was anger. For four years he had faced the daily possibility, even the likelihood, of death. Now, if during those years anyone had prophesied his certain death at a certain time, he would have assaulted the prophet. That kind of thing was a breach of the unwritten rules of the game: one had to pretend to one's self and to the world that one would continue to live: it was the assumption which alone made war endurable. Therefore Charles Ottery's first feeling was wrathful and contemptuous. The Professor was dead; otherwise he would have had something to say to him.

This mood lasted perhaps two days – no longer. Gradually it dawned on his mind that this was a revelation altogether outside the control of the human will. He had believed completely in Moe, and he had seen *The Times* announcement with a blinding clarity which precluded the idea of a mistake. Pamela had shaken him out of his old world, and now he had fallen into a far stranger one, altogether beyond the kindly uses of humanity. He tried to be sceptical, but he had never had much gift for scepticism. Critical in any serious sense he could not be, for he had not the apparatus for criticism. Anger was succeeded by a fear which was almost panic. Charles was a notably brave man, and his courage had been well disciplined and tested. He had always been perfectly willing to run risks, and, if need be, to face death with his eyes open. But this was different – this undefined but certain fate towards which he must walk for the next twelve months. He discovered that he passionately wanted to live. Pamela had dropped out of his thoughts, for she was now utterly beyond him – a doomed man could not be a lover – but his passion for her had enriched and deepened the world for him and therefore increased his love of life.

The first panic passed, and Charles forced himself into a kind of stoicism. Not scepticism, for he could not disbelieve, but a resolution to face up to whatever was in store. He felt hideously lonely, for not

only was he too proud to confide in anyone, but he could think of no
mortal man who had ever been in a like predicament. If he could have
discovered a parallel case, past or present, he would have been
comforted. So since there was no one to whom he could unburden his
soul, he started to keep a diary ... I was not at this time in his
confidence, but I have had the use of that diary in telling this story. In it
he put down notes of his daily doings and of his state of mind, together
with any thoughts that seemed to him cheering or otherwise. It is a
scrappy and often confused record, but very illuminating, for he was
honest with himself.

His first duty was to keep a stout face to the world, and therefore, he
must try to forget *The Times* paragraph in violent preoccupations. He
could not face the society of his fellows, so he went little into the City,
but he strove to crowd his life with intense activities. He practised his
court-tennis for several hours each day, played a good deal of golf, and
took to keeping a six-tonner on Southampton Water and making
week-end expeditions along the coast. From the diary it appeared that
this last pursuit was the best aid to forgetfulness, so long as the weather
was bad. In a difficult wind he had to concentrate all his faculties on
managing the boat, but when there was no such need, he found the
deck of his little yacht too conducive to painful meditation.

Presently he realised that these anodynes were no manner of good.
Each spell of freedom from thought was succeeded by a longer spell of
intense brooding. He had found no philosophy to comfort him, and no
super-induced oblivion lasted long. So he decided that he must seek a
different kind of life. He had an idea that if he went into the wilds he
might draw courage from the primeval Nature which was all
uncertainties and hazards. So in August he set off for Newfoundland
alone, to hunt the migratory caribou.

Purposely he gave himself a rough trip. He went up-country to the
Terra Nova district, and then with two guides penetrated far into the
marshes and barrens of the interior. He limited his equipment to the
bare necessaries, and courted every kind of fatigue. He must have
taken a good many risks in his river journey, for I heard from a man
who followed his tracks for the brief second season in October that his
guides had sworn never again to accompany such a madman. You see,
he knew for certain that nothing could kill him for many months. The
diary, written up at night in his chilly camps, told the story fully. He got
with ease the number of stags permitted by his licence – all of them
good beasts – for, since he did not care a straw whether he killed or not,
he found that he could not miss. But the interesting things were his
thoughts, as they came to him while watching in the dusk by a

half-frozen pond, or lying awake in his sleeping-bag looking at the cold stars.

He had begun to reflect on the implications of death, a subject to which he had never given much heed before. His religion was of the ordinary public-school brand, the fundamentals of Christianity accepted without much comprehension. There was an after-world, of course, about which a man did not greatly trouble himself: the important thing, the purpose of religion, was to have a decent code of conduct in the present one. But now the latter did not mean much to him, since his present life would soon be over ... There were pages of the diary filled with odd amateurish speculations about God and Eternity, and once or twice there was even a kind of prayer. But somewhere in the barrens Charles seems to have decided that he had better let metaphysics alone. What concerned him was how to pass the next eight months without disgracing his manhood. He noted cases of people he had known who, when their death sentence was pronounced by their doctor, had lived out the remainder of their days with a stiff lip, even with cheerfulness.

The conclusion of this part of the diary, written before he sailed for home, seems to have been that all was lost but honour. He was like a man on a sinking ship, and owed it to himself to go down with fortitude. There were no entries during the voyage from St. John's, so the presumption is that this resolve gave him a certain peace.

That peace did not survive his return to England. He went back to the City, where he was badly needed, for the bottom was falling out of business. But he seemed unable to concentrate on his work. The sight of his familiar surroundings, his desk, his clerks, the business talks which assumed the continuity of life, the necessity of making plans which would not mature before the following June, put him into a fever of disquiet. I think that he had perhaps overtired himself in Newfoundland, and was physically rather unstrung; anyhow, on the plea of health, he again began to absent himself from his work. He felt that he must discover an anodyne to thought, or go mad.

The anodyne he tried was the worst conceivable. Charles had never led the life of pleasure, and had no relish for it; so now, when he attempted it, it was like brandy to a teetoller. He belonged to Dillon's, and took to frequenting that club, and playing cards for high stakes. Now, it is a dangerous thing to gamble if you have the mania for it in your blood, but it is more dangerous if your object is to blanket your mind. He won a good deal of money and lost a good deal, and he played with a cold intensity which rather scared his partners ... Also he, who had always been abstemious, took to doing himself too well. I met him one night in St. James's Street, and got the impression that the sober Charles was rather drunk ... Then there was hunting. He had not had time for years to do much of that, but now he kept horses at Birkham, and went out twice a week. He behaved as he had behaved in the Terra Nova rapids, and took wild risks because he believed that nothing could harm him. For a couple of months he rode so hard that he made himself a nuisance in the field ... Then his confidence suddenly deserted him. It occurred to him that any day he might have a smash, and linger bed-ridden till the following June. So he got rid of his hunters and fled from Birkham.

The result of all this was that before Christmas he had begun to get for himself a doubtful name. At first no one believed that this decorous young man could run amok, but nobody's repute is iron-clad, and presently too many people were ready to surmise the worst. City men reported that he rarely showed up at his office, and was useless when he did. Hunting men had tales to tell of strange manners in the field and an insane foolhardiness. My nephew, who was one of his oldest friends, and belonged to Dillon's, would say nothing at first when I asked him about the stories, but in the end he admitted reluctantly that they were true. 'Charles has got mixed up with a poor lot,' he said. 'Drunken swine like L –, and half-witted boys like little E – and fine old-fashioned crooks like B –. He hardly recognises me when we meet in the club, for he knows I don't like his bunch. In the evening he's apt to be tight after ten o'clock.

'God knows what's done it!' said my nephew dismally. 'Looks as if he weren't able to take his corn. Too big a success too soon, you know. Well, he won't be a success long ... I put it down to a virtuous youth. If you don't blow off steam under twenty-five, you're apt to have a blow up later and scald yourself ... No, I don't think it is unrequited affection. I've heard that yarn, but I don't believe it. I saw Lady Pam at a dinner last week, and she had a face like a death's head. She's going the pace a bit herself, but she's not enjoying it. Whoever is behaving badly, it ain't her. My notion is that Charles hasn't given the girl a thought for months. Don't ask me for an explanation. Something has snapped in him, the way a racehorse goes suddenly wrong.'

I confess that at the time I was more anxious about my goddaughter than about Charles. I knew him fairly well and liked him, but Pamela was very near my heart. I could not blame him, for it was she who had hitherto caused the trouble, but now it was very clear that things were not well with her ... She had refused to pay her usual Scots visits, and had gone off with the Junipers to their place on the Riviera. The Juniper girl had only been an acquaintance, but she suddenly blossomed into a bosom friend. Now, the Junipers were not too well regarded by old-fashioned people. Tom and Mollie Nantley hated the business, but they had always made it a rule never to interfere with their daughters, and certainly up to now Pamela had deserved their confidence. It must have been gall and wormwood to them to see the papers full of pictures of the Juniper doings, with Pamela bathing and playing tennis and basking on the sands in the most raffish society … After that she went on a cruise to the Red Sea with some Americans called Baffin. The Nantleys knew very little about the Baffins, so they hoped for the best; but from what I learned afterwards the company on the yacht was pretty mixed – a journalistic peer, two or three financiers, and a selection of amorous and alcoholic youth.

Pamela returned to England before the end of November. The family always stayed on at Wirlesdon till well into the new year, but she insisted on taking up her quarters in London. She acted in several entertainments got up for charity, and became the darling of the illustrated press. I saw her once in December, at a dinner given for a ball, and was glad that Mollie Nantley was not present. The adorable child that I had known had not altogether gone, but it was overlaid with tragic affectations. She had ruined her perfect colouring with cosmetics, and her manner had acquired the shrill vulgarity which was then the fashion. She was as charming to me as ever, but in her air there was a curious defiance. Her face had been made up to look pert, but in repose it was tragic. I realised that it was all a desperate bravado to conceal suffering.

LAMANCHA had a Christmas party at his house in Devonshire, and I went there on the 27th. After tea my hostess took me aside.

'We've made an awful *gaffe*,' she said. 'Charles Ottery is here, and I find to my horror that Pamela Brune is coming to-morrow. I can't very well put her off, but you know that things have not been going well with her and Charles, and their being together may be very painful for both of them.'

I asked if Charles knew that Pamela was coming.

'I told him this morning, but he didn't seem interested. I hoped he would discover that he had an engagement elsewhere, but not a bit of it – he only looked blank and turned away. What on earth has happened to him, Ned? He is rather quarrelsome, when he isn't simply deadly dull, and he has such queer moping moods. There is something on his mind, and I don't believe that it's Pamela.'

'Couldn't you let her know he is here?' I asked.

'I wired to Mollie Nantley, but the only reply I got was about Pamela's train. She is evidently coming with her eyes open.'

Pamela duly arrived during the following afternoon, when we were out shooting Lamancha's hedgerow pheasants. I did not see her till dinner, and I had to go off at dawn next morning to London for an unexpected consultation. But that evening I had a very clear and most disquieting impression of her and Charles. Her manner was shrill and rather silly; she seemed to be acting a part which was utterly unsuited to her kind of beauty and to her character as I had known it. The house-party was not exciting, only pleasant and friendly, and she succeeded in making us all uncomfortable. I did not see her first meeting with Charles, but that evening she never looked at him, nor he at her. He drank rather too much wine at dinner, and afterwards played bezique owlishly in the smoking-room. I had tried to get a word with him, but he shunned me like the plague.

What happened after I left I learned from the diary. Behind the mask he had been deeply miserable, for the sight of the girl had brought back his old happier world. He realised that far down below all his anxieties lay his love for her – that indeed this love was subconsciously the cause of his frantic clutch on life. He had tried stoicism and had failed; he had tried drugging himself by excitement into forgetfulness and had failed not less dismally. Pamela's presence seemed to recall him to his self-respect. He did not notice any change in her – his eyes had been too long looking inward to be very observant: he only knew that the woman who had once lit up his life was now for ever beyond him – worse still, that he had dropped to a level from which he could not look at her without shame. He fell into a mood of bitter abasement, which was far healthier than his previous desperation, for he was thinking now less of the death which was in store for him than of the code of honourable living to which he had been false.

That night he slept scarcely a wink, and next morning he did not show up at breakfast. He told the servant who called him that he was going for a long walk, and slipped out of the house before anybody was down. He felt that he had to be alone to wrestle with his soul.

The diary told something of his misery that day on the high Devon moors. The weather was quiet and tonic with a touch of frost, and he walked blindly over the uplands. Charles was too stiff-backed a fellow to indulge in self-pity, but his type is apt to be a prey to self-contempt. He can have seen nothing of the bright landscape, for he was enveloped in a great darkness – regrets, remorse, a world of wrath with the horror of a deeper shade looming before him. He struggled to regain the captaincy of his soul, but he had no longer the impulse to strive, since he seemed to himself to have already foresworn his standards. There was nothing before him but a dreadful, hopeless passivity, what the Bible calls an 'awful looking-for of judgment.' The hours of spiritual torment and rapid movement wore down his strength, and in the afternoon he found that he was very weary. So he walked slowly homeward, having dulled his bodily and mental senses but won no comfort.

In the dusk, at the head of the grassy rides in the home woods, as the fates ordained it, he met Pamela. She, unhappy also, had fled from the house for a little air and solitude. Both were so full of their own thoughts that they might have passed without recognition had they not encountered each other at a gate. Charles opened it, and held it wide for the stranger to pass, and it was the speaking of his name that enlightened him as to the personality of the stranger.

'Good evening, Captain Ottery,' Pamela said.

He started and stared at her. Something in his appearance held her eyes, for a man does not go through hell without showing it. In those eyes there must have been wonder; there must have been pity too. He saw it, dulled though his senses were, and perhaps he saw also some trace of that suffering which I had noticed in London, for the girl was surprised and had no time to don her mask.

'Pamela!' he cried, and then his strength seemed to go from him, and he leaned heavily on the gate, so that his shoulder touched hers.

She drew back. 'You are ill?'

He recovered himself. 'No, not ill,' he said. He could say no more, for when a man has been wrestling all day with truth he cannot easily lie.

She put a hand on his arm. 'But you look so ill and strange.'

And then some of the old tenderness must have come into her eyes and voice. 'Oh, Charles,' she cried, 'what has happened to us?'

It was the word 'us' that broke him down, for it told him that she too was at odds with life. He had a sudden flash of illumination. He saw that what he had once longed for was true, that her heart was his, and the realisation that not only life but love was lost to him was the last drop in his cup. He stood holding the gate, shaking like a reed, with eyes which, even in the half-light, seemed to be devoured with pain.

'You must have thought me a cad,' he stammered. 'I love you – I loved you beyond the world, but I dared not come near you … I am a dying man … I will soon be dead.'

His strength came back to him. He had a purpose now. He had found the only mortal in whom he could confide – must confide.

As they walked down the ride in the winter gloaming, with the happy lights of the house in the valley beneath them, he told her all, and as he spoke it seemed to him that he was cleansing his soul. She made no comment – did not utter a single word.

At the gate of the terrace gardens he stopped. His manner was normal again, and his voice was quiet, almost matter-of-fact.

'Thank you for listening to me, Pamela,' he said. 'It has been a great comfort to me to tell you this … It is the end for both of us. You see that, don't you? … We must never meet again. Good-bye, my dear.'

He took her hand, and the touch of it shivered his enforced composure. 'I love you … I love you,' he moaned.

She snatched her hand away.

'This is perfect nonsense,' she said. 'I won't …' and then fled down an alley, as she had once fled from me at Flambard.

Charles had some food in his room, and went to bed, where he slept for the first time for weeks. He had been through the extremes of hell, and nothing worse could await him. The thought gave him a miserable peace. He wrote a line to his hostess, and left for London by the early train.

―――――――――

HE was sitting next afternoon in his rooms in Mount Street when a lady was announced, and Pamela marched in on the heels of his servant. The room was in dusk, and it was her voice that revealed her to him.

'Turn on the light, Crocker,' she said briskly, 'and bring tea for two. As quick as possible, please, for I'm famishing.'

I can picture her, for I know Pamela's ways, plucking off her hat and tossing it on to a table, shaking up the cushions on the big sofa, and settling herself in a corner of it – Pamela no longer the affected miss of recent months, but the child of April and an April wind, with the freshness of a spring morning about her.

They had tea, for which the anxious Crocker provided muffins, rejoicing to see once again in the flat people feeding like Christians. Pamela chattered happily, chiefly gossip about Wirlesdon, while Charles pulled himself out of his lethargy and strove to rise to her mood. He even went to his bedroom, changed his collar and brushed his hair. When Crocker had cleared away the tea, she made him light his pipe. 'You know you are never really happy with anything else,' she said; and he obeyed, not having smoked a pipe since Newfoundland.

'Now,' she said at last, when she had poked the fire into a blaze, 'I want you to repeat very carefully all that rubbish you told me yesterday.'

He obeyed – told the story slowly and dispassionately, without the emotion of the previous day. She listened carefully, and wrote down from his dictation the exact words he had read in *The Times*. She knitted her brows over them. 'Pretty accurate, aren't they?' she asked. 'Not much chance of mistaken identity.'

'None,' he said. 'There are very few Otterys in the world, and every detail about me is correct.'

'And you believe in it?'

'I must.'

'I mean to say, you believe that you really saw that thing in *The Times*? You didn't dream it afterwards?'

'I saw it as clearly as I am seeing you.'

'I wondered what tricks that old Professor man was up to at Flambard, but I had no notion it was anything as serious as this. What do you suppose the others saw? Uncle Ned is sure to know – I'll ask him.'

'He saw nothing himself – he told me so. Lady Flambard fainted, and he was looking after her.'

'She saw nothing either, then? I'm sorry, for I can't ask any of the men. I don't know Mr. Tavanger or Mr Mayot or Sir Robert Goodeve, and Reggie Daker is too much of a donkey to count. It would be too delicate a subject to be inquisitive about with strangers … You really are convinced that the Professor had got hold of some method of showing you the future?'

'Convinced beyond any possibility of doubt,' said Charles dismally.

'Good. That settles one thing … Now for the next point. The fact that you saw that stuff is no reason why it should happen. Supposing you had dreamed it, would you have allowed a dream, however vivid, to wreck your life?'

'But, Pamela dear, the case is quite different. Moe showed us what he called "objective reality." A dream would have been my own concern, but this came from outside, quite independent of any effort of mine. It was the result of a scientific experiment.'

'But the science may have been all cock-eyed. Most science is – at any rate, it changes a good deal faster than Paris fashions.'

'You wouldn't have said that if you had been under his influence. He didn't want me to die – he didn't make *The Times* paragraph take that form – he only lifted the curtain an inch so that I could see what had actually happened a year ahead. How can I disbelieve what science brought to me out of space, without any preparation or motive? The whole thing was as mathematical and impersonal as an eclipse of the moon in an almanack.'

'All right! Let's leave it at that. Assume that *The Times* is going to print the paragraph. The answer is that *The Times* is going to be badly diddled. Somebody will make a bloomer.'

Charles shook his head. 'I've tried to think that, but well – you know, that kind of mistake isn't made.'

'Oh, isn't it? The papers announced Dollie's engagement to three different men – exact as you please – names and dates complete.'

'But why should it make a blunder in this one case out of millions? Isn't it more reasonable to think that there is a moral certainty of its being right?'

Pamela was not succeeding with her arguments. They sounded thin to her own ears, in spite of her solid conviction at the back of them. She sat up, an alert, masterful figure, youth girt for command. She had another appeal than logic.

'Charles,' she said solemnly, 'this is a horrible business for you, and you've got to pull yourself together. You must defy it. Make up your mind that you're not going to give it another thought. Get back to your work, and resolve that you don't care a lop-eared damn for Moe or science or anything else. Lose your temper with fate and frighten the blasted hussy.' Tom Nantley had a turn for robust speech in the hunting-field, and his daughter remembered some of it.

Charles shook his head miserably.

'I've tried,' he said, 'but I can't. I simply haven't the manhood ... I know it's the right way, but my mind is poisoned already. I've got a germ in it that fevers me ... Besides, it isn't sense. You can't stop what is to be by saying that it won't be.'

'Yes, you can,' said the girl firmly. 'That's the meaning of Free Will.'

Charles dropped his head into his hands. The sight of Pamela thus restored to him was more than he could bear.

Then she had an inspiration.

'Do you remember the portrait in the dining-room at Wirlesdon of old Sir Somebody-Ap-Something – Mamma's Welsh ancestor? You know the story about him? He was on the side of Henry Tudor, and raised his men to march to Bosworth. But every witch and warlock in Carmarthen got on to their hindlegs and prophesied – said they saw him in a bloody shroud, and heard banshees wailing for him, and how Merlin had said that when the Ap-Something red and gold crossed Severn to join the Tudor green and white it would be the end of the race – all manner of cheery omens. Everybody in the place believed them, including his lady wife, who wept buckets and clung to his knees. What did the old sportsman do? Told all the warlocks to go to the devil, and marched gaily eastward, leaving his wife sewing his shroud and preparing the family vault.'

'What happened?' Charles had lifted his head.

'Happened? He turned the day at Bosworth, set the Tudor on the throne, got the Garter for his services – you see it in the portrait – and about half South Wales. He and his men came merrily home, and he lived till he was ninety-three. There's an example for you!'

Pamela warmed to her argument.

'That sort of thing happened all the time in the old days. Whenever anybody had a down on you he got a local soothsayer to prophesy death and disaster in case you might believe it and lose your nerve. And if you had been having a row with the Church, some priest or bishop had an unpleasant vision about you. What was the result? Timid people took to their beds and died of fright, which was what the soothsayers wanted. Bold men like my ancestor paid not the slightest attention, and nothing happened – except that, when they got a chance, they outed the priest and hanged the soothsayer.'

Charles was listening keenly.

'But the soothsayers were often right,' he objected.

'They were just as often wrong. The point is, that there were men brave enough to defy them – as you are going to do.'

'But the cases aren't the same,' he protested. 'That was ordinary vulgar magic, with a personal grudge behind it. I'm up against the last word in impersonal science.'

'My dear Charles,' she said sweetly, 'you've let your brains go to seed. I never knew you miss a point before. Magic and astrology and that kind of thing were all the science the Middle Ages had, and they believed in them just as firmly as you believe in Moe. The point is that, in spite of their belief, there were people bold enough to defy it – and to win, as you are going to do. A thousand years hence the world may think Moe and Einstein and all those pundits as babyish as we think the old necromancers. Beliefs change, but courage is always the same. Courage is the line for you, my dear.'

At last she had moved him. There was a light in his eyes as he looked at her, perplexed and broken, but still a light.

'You think …' he began, but she broke in …

'I think that you're face to face with a crisis, Charles dear. Fate has played you an ugly trick, but you're man enough to beat it. It's like the thing in the Bible about Jacob wrestling with the angel. You've got to wrestle with it, and if you wrestle hard enough it may bless you.'

Her voice had lost its briskness, and had become soft and wooing.

She jumped up from the sofa and came round behind his chair, as if she did not want him to see her face.

'I refuse to give another thought to the silly thing,' she said. 'We are going to behave as if Moe had never been born.' Her hand was caressing his hair.

'But *you* are not condemned to death,' he said.

'Oh, am I not?' she cried. 'It's frightfully important for me. On June 10th of next year I shall be starting on my honeymoon.'

That fetched him out of his chair.

He gazed blindly at her as she stood with her cheeks flushed and her eyes a little dim. For a full minute he strove for words and none came.

'Have you nothing to say?' she whispered. 'Do you realise, sir, that I am asking you to marry me?'

IT was now that I entered the story. Mollie Nantley came to town and summoned me to a family conclave. She and Tom were in a mood between delight and anxiety.

'You got my wire?' she asked. 'The announcement will be in the papers to-morrow. But they are not to be married till June. Too long to wait – I don't like these long engagements.'

'You are pleased?' I asked.

'Tremendously – in a way. But we don't quite know what to think. They never saw each other for six months, and then it all came with a rush. Pam has been rather odd lately, you know, and Tom and I have been very worried. We saw that she was unhappy, and we thought that it might be about Charles. And Charles's behaviour has been something more than odd – so odd that Tom was in two minds about consenting to the engagement. You know how fond we were of him and how we believed in him, but his conduct before Christmas was rather shattering. You are too busy to hear gossip, but I can assure you that Charles has been the most talked-of man in London. Not pleasant gossip either.'

'But the explanation seems quite simple,' I said. 'Two estranged lovers, both proud and both miserable and therefore rather desperate. Chance brings them together, misunderstandings disappear, and true love comes into its own.'

Mollie bent her brows.

'It's not as simple as that. If that had been the way of things they ought to be riotously happy. But they're not – not in the least. Pam is as white as a sheet, and looks more like a widow than a bride. She's very sweet and good – very different from before Christmas, when she was horribly tiresome – but you never saw such careworn eyes. She has something heavy on her mind ... And as for Charles! He is very good too and goes steadily to the City again, but he's not my notion of the happy lover. Tom and I are at our wits' end. I do wish you would have a talk with Pamela. She won't tell me anything – I really don't dare to ask – but you and she have always been friends, and if there is any trouble you might help her.'

So Pamela came to tea with me, and the first sight of her told me that Mollie was right. In a week or two some alchemy had changed her utterly. Not a trace now of that hard, mirthless glitter which had scared me at the Lamanchas'. Her face was pale, her air quiet and composed, but there was in her eyes what I had seen in Charles Ottery's, an intense, anxious preoccupation.

She told me everything without pressing. She could not tell her parents, she said, for they would not understand, and, if they did, their sympathy would make things worse. But she longed for someone to confide in, and had decided on me.

I saw that it would be foolish to make light of the trouble. Indeed, I had no inclination that way, for I had seen the tortures that Goodeve was undergoing. She told me what she had said to Charles, and the line they were taking. I remember wondering if the man had the grit to go through with it; when I looked at Pamela's clear eyes I had no doubt about the woman.

'He has gone back to his business and has forced himself to slave at it. He is crowding up his days with work. And he is keeping himself in hard training ... You see, he has tried the other dopes and found them no good ... But he has to fight every step of the road. Oh, Uncle Ned, I could howl with misery sometimes when I see him all drawn at the lips and hollow about the eyes. He doesn't sleep well, you see. But he is fighting, and not yielding one inch.'

And then she quoted to me her saying about Jacob wrestling with the angel. 'If we keep on grappling with the brute, it *must* bless us.'

'I have to hold his hand all the time,' she went on. 'That's his hope of salvation. He is feeding on my complete confidence ... Oh no, it's not easy, but it's easier than his job, I've to pretend to be perfectly certain that we'll be married next June 10th, and to be always talking about where we shall go for our honeymoon, and where we shall live in town, and how we shall do up Marlcote.'

She smiled wanly.

'I chatter about hotels and upholsterers and house-agents when I want to be praying ... But I think I understand my part. I have a considerable patch of hell to plough, but it's nothing like as hot as Charles's ... No, you can't help, Uncle Ned, dear. We have to go through with this thing ourselves – we two – nobody else. Charles must never know that I have told you, for if he thought that anyone else knew it would add shyness to his trouble. ... But it's a comfort to me to feel that you know. If anything happens ... if we fail ... I want you to realise that we went down fighting.'

She kissed me and ran away, and I sat thinking a long time in my chair. She was right: no one could help these two through this purgatory. My heart ached for this child not out of her teens who was trying to lift her lover through the Slough of Despond by her sheer courage. I do not think that I have ever in my life so deeply admired a fellow-mortal. Pamela was the very genius of fortitude, courage winged and inspired and divinely lit. ... I told myself that such a spirit could not fail if there was a God in Heaven.

I can only guess at what Charles suffered in the first months of the year. The diary revealed something, but not much, for the entries were scrappy: you see, he was not fighting the battle alone, as he had done in the autumn; he had Pamela for his guide and confessor.

He stuck like a leech to his work, and from all accounts did it well. My nephew said that old Charles had 'taken a pull on himself, but had become a cheerless bird.' People in the City, when I asked about him, were cordial enough. He had been put on a new economic commission at which he was working hard. One man said that his examination of a high Treasury official was one of the most searching things he had ever heard. Our financial affairs at that time were in a considerable mess, and Charles was bending all his powers to straightening them out.

It was much to have got his brain functioning again. But of course it did not mean the recovery of his old interests. He had only one interest – how to keep his head up till June, and one absorbing desire – to be with Pamela. The girl gave him more than the sustenance of her confidence; there were hours when the love of her so filled his mind that it drove out the gnawing pain, and that meant hours of rest. As sleep restores the body, so these spells of an almost happy absorption restored his spirit.

But he had patches of utter blackness, as the diary showed. He held himself firm to his resolution by a constant effort of will. He could not despair when Pamela kept her courage ... But he would waver at moments, and only recover himself out of shame. There were times, too, when he bitterly reproached himself. He had brought an innocent child into his tortured world, and made her share in the tortures.

Another life besides his own would be ruined. Out of such fits of self-contempt he had to be dragged painfully by Pamela's affection. She had to convince him anew that she preferred Tophet in his company to Paradise alone.

In March Pamela told me that she had offered to marry him at once, and that he had refused. He was on his probation, he said, and marriage was to be the reward of victory. Also, if he was to be in the grave on June 10th, he did not want Pamela to be a widow. The girl argued, she told me, that immediate marriage would be an extra defiance to Fate, and a proof of their confidence, but Charles was adamant. I dare say he was right: he had to settle such a question with his own soul.

I met him occasionally during those months. Never in ordinary society: by a right instinct Pamela and he decided that they could not go about together and be congratulated – that would make too heavy demands on their powers of camouflage. But I ran across him several times in the street; and I sat next to him at a luncheon given by the Prime Minister to the American Debt Commission. Knowing the story, I looked for changes in him, and I noted several things which were probably hidden from other people. He had begun to speak rather slowly, as if he had difficulty in finding the correct words. He did not look an interlocutor in the face, but fixed his eyes, while he spoke, steadily on the tablecloth. Also, though his colour was healthy, his skin seemed to be drawn too tight around lips and chin, reminding me of a certain Army Commander during the bad time in '18.

I asked about Pamela.

'Yes, she's in town,' he said. 'The Nantleys have been up since January. She has caught a beastly cold, and I made her promise to stay indoors in this bitter weather.'

Two days later I picked up an evening paper and read a paragraph which sent me post-haste to the telephone. It announced that Lady Pamela Brune was ill with pneumonia, and that anxiety was felt about her condition.

———————

THE diary told the tale of the next three weeks. Charles had to return to his diary, for he had no other confidant. And a stranger story I have never read.

From the first he was certain that Pamela would die. He was quite clear about this, and he had also become assured of his own end. Their love was to be blotted out by the cold hand of death. For a day or two he was in a stupor of utter hopelessness, waiting on fate like a condemned man who hears the gallows being hammered together and sees the clock moving towards the appointed hour.

Some of the entries were clear enough. He thought that Pamela would die at once while he himself must wait until June, and there were distraught queries as to how he could endure the interval. His appointed hour could not be anticipated, and a world without Pamela was a horror which came near to unhinging his mind. His writing tailed away into blots and dashes. In his agony he seemed several times to have driven his pen through the paper ...

Then suddenly the mist cleared. The diary was nothing but jottings and confused reflections, so the sequence of his moods could not be exactly traced, but it was plain that something tremendous had happened ...

It seemed to have come suddenly late at night, for he noted the hour – 1.30 – and that he had been walking the Embankment since eight. Hitherto he had had a dual consciousness, seeing Pamela and himself as sufferers under the same doom, and enduring a double torture. Love and fear for both the girl and himself had brought his mind almost to a delirium, but now there descended upon it a great clarity.

The emotion remained, but now the object was single, for his own death dropped out of the picture. It became suddenly too small a thing to waste a thought on. There were entries like this: 'I have torn up the almanack on which I had been marking off the days till June 10th. ... I have been an accursed coward, God forgive me ... Pamela is dying, and I have been thinking of my own wretched, rotten life.'

He went on steadily with his work, because he thought she would have wished him to, but he never moved far from a telephone. Meanwhile, the poor child was fighting a very desperate battle. I went round to South Audley Street as often as I could, and a white-faced Mollie gave me the last bulletins. There was one night when it seemed certain that Pamela could not see the morning, but morning came and the thread of life still held. She was delirious, talking about Charles mostly, and the mountain inn in the Tyrol where they were going for their honeymoon. Thank God, Charles was not there to listen to that!

He did not go near the house, which I thought was wise, but the diary revealed that he spent the midnight hours striding about Mayfair. He was waiting for her death, waiting for Mollie's summons to look for the last time upon what was so dear ...

He was no longer in torment. Indeed, he was calm now, if you can call that calm which is the uttermost despair. His life was bereft of every shadow of value, every spark of colour, and he was living in a bleak desert, looking with aching eyes and a breaking heart at a beautiful star setting below the sky-line, a star which was the only light in the encroaching gloom to lead him home. That very metaphor was in the diary. He probably got it out of some hymn, and I never in my life knew Charles use a metaphor before.

And then there came another change – it is plain in the diary – but this time it was a wholesale revolution, by which the whole man was moved to a different plane ...

His own predestined death had been put aside as too trivial for a thought, but now suddenly Death itself came to have no meaning. The ancient shadow disappeared in the great brightness of his love.

Every man has some metaphysics and poetry in his soul, but people like Charles lack the gift of expression. The diary had only broken sentences, but they were more poignant than any eloquence. If he had cared about the poets he might have found some one of them to give him apt words; as it was, he could only stumble along among clumsy phrases. But there was no doubt about his meaning. He had discovered for himself the immortality of love. The angel with whom he had grappled had at last blessed him.

He had somehow in his agony climbed to a high place from which he had a wide prospect. He saw all things in a new perspective. Death was only a stumble in the race, a brief halt in an immortal pilgrimage. He and Pamela had won something which could never be taken away ... This man of prose and affairs became a mystic. One side of him went about his daily round, and waited hungrily for telephone calls, but the other was in a quiet country where Pamela's happy spirit moved in eternal vigour and youth. He had no hope in the lesser sense, for that is a mundane thing; but he had won peace, the kind that the world does not give ...

Hope, the lesser hope, was to follow. There came a day when the news from South Audley Street improved, and then there was a quick uprush of vitality in the patient. One morning early in May Mollie telephoned to me that Pamela was out of danger. I went straightaway to the City and found Charles in his office, busy as if nothing had happened.

I remember that he seemed to me almost indecently composed. But when he spoke he no longer kept his eyes down, but looked me straight in the face, and there was something in those eyes of his which made me want to shout. It was more than peace – it was a radiant serenity. Charles had come out of the Valley of the Shadow to the

Delectable Mountains. Nothing in Heaven or earth could harm him now. I had the conviction that if he had been a poet he could have written something that would have solemnised mankind. As it was, he only squeezed my hand.

───

I went down to Wirlesdon for the wedding, which was to be in the village church. Charles had gone for an early morning swim in the lake, and I met him coming up with his hair damp and a towel over his shoulder. I had motored from London and had *The Times* in my hand, but he never glanced at it. Half an hour later I saw him at breakfast, but he had not raided the pile of newspapers on the side table.

It was a gorgeous June morning, and presently I found Pamela in the garden, busy among the midsummer flowers – a taller and paler Pamela, with the wonderful pure complexion of one who has been down into the shades.

'It's all there,' she whispered to me, so that her sister Dollie should not hear. 'Exactly as he saw it ... We shall have a lot of questions to answer to-day ... I showed it to Charles but he scarcely glanced at it. It doesn't interest him. I believe he has forgotten all about it.'

───

'A queer business, wasn't it?' Charles told me in the autumn. 'Oh yes, it was all explained. There was an old boy of my name, a sort of third cousin of my great-grandfather. I had never heard of him. he had been in the Scots Guards, and had retired as a captain about fifty years ago. Well, he died in a London hotel on June 9th. He was a bachelor, and had no near relations, so his servant sent the notice of his death to *The Times*. The man's handwriting was not very clear, and the newspaper people read the age as thirty-six instead of eighty-six ... Also, the old chap always spoke of his regiment as the Scots Fusilier Guards, and the servant, not being well up in military history, confused it with the Scots Fusiliers ... He lived in a villa at Cheltenham, which he had christened Marlcote, after the family place.'

───